Praise for

The WOMAN *at the* FRONT

"An adventurous woman ahead of her time. . . . A fascinating historical novel."   —*New York Times* bestselling author Natasha Lester

"A uniquely female perspective of World War I. . . . A beautiful, touching, romantic women's fiction novel that is sure to delight fans of *Out-
lander* and *Downton Abbey*."

        —*New York Times* bestselling author Lori Nelson Spielman

"An absorbing and immersive portrait of a woman whose courage, determination, and resolve would be exceptional in any age—but forged in
the crucible of the Great War, tested again and again by a society riven
by change, Dr. Eleanor Atherton is a heroine I will not soon forget. . . .
The Woman at the Front is a beautiful book about a terrible war, and the
light it shines on the valor of those at the front lines—the medics, the
stretcher-bearers, and the wounded themselves—is both welcome and
overdue."   —*USA Today* bestselling author Jennifer Robson

"A riveting tale of medicine, courage, and grace under fire during the
Great War. . . . Compulsively readable!"

        —*USA Today* bestselling author Stephanie Marie Thornton

The WOMAN at the FRONT

LECIA CORNWALL

BERKLEY

NEW YORK

BERKLEY
An imprint of Penguin Random House LLC
penguinrandomhouse.com

Copyright © 2021 by Lecia Cotton Cornwall
Readers Guide copyright © 2021 by Lecia Cotton Cornwall
Penguin Random House supports copyright. Copyright fuels creativity, encourages
diverse voices, promotes free speech, and creates a vibrant culture. Thank you for
buying an authorized edition of this book and for complying with copyright
laws by not reproducing, scanning, or distributing any part of it in any form
without permission. You are supporting writers and allowing Penguin
Random House to continue to publish books for every reader.

BERKLEY and the BERKLEY & B colophon are
registered trademarks of Penguin Random House LLC.

Library of Congress Cataloging-in-Publication Data

Names: Cornwall, Lecia, author.
Title: The woman at the front / Lecia Cornwall.
Description: First edition. | New York: Berkley, 2021.
Identifiers: LCCN 2021000504 (print) | LCCN 2021000505 (ebook) |
ISBN 9780593197929 (trade paperback) | ISBN 9780593197936 (ebook)
Subjects: LCSH: Women physicians—Fiction. | World War,
1914–1918—France—Fiction. | Self-actualization (Psychology) in
women—Fiction. | GSAFD: Historical fiction. | Love stories.
Classification: LCC PR9199.4.C673 W66 2021 (print) |
LCC PR9199.4.C673 (ebook) | DDC 813/.6—dc23
LC record available at https://lccn.loc.gov/2021000504
LC ebook record available at https://lccn.loc.gov/2021000505

First Edition: September 2021

Printed in the United States of America
1st Printing

Book design by Elke Sigal

To Matthew Greenwell, who died in war on April 9, 1917,
and to my grandfather Robert Greenwell, who told me his
brother's story and made me promise never to forget.

CHAPTER ONE

Young woman, my advice to you is to go home, sit down, and take up something more useful, such as knitting. If I'd known *E. Atherton* was female, I would not have taken this appointment at all."

That was precisely why Eleanor Atherton had used the initial instead of her full first name. A trick, yes, but she'd already written hundreds of letters, made dozens of attempts to see bureaucrats and official representatives in person, and *Miss* Atherton had been refused every time.

Not this time. Finally, she was sitting before someone who would be forced to listen. The very fact that she was here proved it was not her credentials as a doctor that were lacking. *E. Atherton* was highly qualified indeed, and had been eagerly invited to this interview.

She regarded the man's haughty, irritated, uncomfortable expression. She knew that as a rule female doctors weren't wanted by the military, the War Office, or even the Red Cross, no matter how competent or willing they might be. But the war had dragged on for almost four years, with hundreds of casualties, including doctors. She was certain that if she could just find a way to present herself in person, have the opportunity to speak to someone in a position of authority, then an exception could most certainly be made.

Sir William Foxleigh was the undersecretary to another undersecretary to an assistant director of the War Office. He peered at her over his spectacles with a sharp frown. Her letter of application for overseas medical service sat between them on the polished surface of the mahogany table like a fallen flag. A thick silence followed Sir William's outburst, and he waited—expected, no doubt—for her to rise from her chair and scurry away, suitably chastened.

Even the clock in the corner tsked brisk disapproval, but Eleanor stayed where she was. The oak-paneled office smelled of lemon polish and Sir William's hair pomade, of paper and leather and tobacco, a thoroughly male preserve. There was a vase of flowers in the corner, a pallid bouquet of winter hothouse roses, but they did little to perfume the air, or even add color to the airless room. But then, there was a war on, and it had been endless and dreadful, and all the color, save for black and khaki and gray, had long since been sucked out of the world.

For a brief moment, pinned under Sir William's scornful gaze, Eleanor's starchy determination wilted a little, and a trickle of sweat rolled down her spine beneath her prim navy blue suit. But only for a moment. She was here now, and she'd been trying far too hard for far too long to give in. She'd waited weeks for this appointment, and she simply didn't have time to be cowed by his rudeness or his annoyance at having to deal with an unexpected and unwelcome female doctor.

"I understand that doctors are badly needed in France. I've read of the terrible casualties at Passchendaele and Ypres, and just weeks ago at Cambrai. I've seen those men coming home, maimed and bandaged. There has been a general call for qualified doctors."

Sir William's chin jerked. "For *male* doctors, yes, of course, but not women. What would your husband say—"

"I'm not married."

Sir William scanned her face and figure appraisingly, gauging her age and potential marriageability. "Your father, then—surely he would not want to see you in a war zone, at the front, under fire, dealing with, with . . ." He rolled the air with his hand as he sought the right words. "Well, with unspeakable things."

Eleanor lifted her chin. "My father is also a doctor. He served in the South African war. He has seen all the unspeakable things war leaves in its wake. I grew up on those stories."

Sir William looked more closely at the letter before him. "Dr. John Atherton," he said in surprise. "Why, I know him. We are members of the same gentlemen's club in York."

Eleanor allowed herself to smile, hopeful that now a connection had been made, things would improve. Instead, Sir William removed his glasses altogether and frowned harder. "I've known Dr. Atherton for many years. He has never mentioned the fact that he has a daughter, or that that daughter is a doctor. He's spoken of a son, I believe."

"My twin brother, Edward. He's currently serving in France, at headquarters."

"Does your father know you are here, applying for a medical posting in France? Surely he knows that neither the War Office nor the British Red Cross permit women to serve there."

Eleanor dug her fingernails into her palms. No, her father most definitely had not given her permission to be here. Eleanor felt a twinge of guilt—she'd told her parents she was taking tea with a friend in York today.

"Female nurses are allowed to serve at the front," she countered.

"VADs are encouraged to go to France, and there are female ambulance drivers and clerks, and—"

He held up his hand. "They are not *doctors*. Doctors have specific duties, duties that no woman could undertake. War is not a society picnic or a holiday jaunt, Miss Atherton. Soldiers are rough and crude, mannerless at times. It is to be expected in war." He shifted, his lined face pinkening. "Men have . . . needs. Battle brings out certain . . . animal passions. A medical officer is required to monitor the . . . the most unsavory of ailments. No *lady* would wish to be exposed to such things." He looked at her pointedly, and she held his gaze boldly, unfazed. "Medical officers must oversee sanitation and hygiene, and they go into the frontline trenches to do so, working under fire, where the danger is highest. A great number of good doctors have been killed that way. We do not allow women of any stripe there. And the medical aid posts and Casualty Clearing Stations take in wounded straight from the battlefield, horribly injured, dirty, in pain. It is not the clean, sanitary, clinical environment you no doubt saw at medical school . . ." He referred to her letter again. "At the University of Edinburgh." He read further, underlining her details with a manicured forefinger. "I see you graduated seventh in your class. All women, I assume?"

"There were six women at the beginning, and just two at graduation, but—"

Sir William raised his finger from the page to stab it in her direction like a bayonet. "There, you see? It goes to prove that women are unable to endure the stresses and challenges of a medical career."

"Their withdrawal had more to do with being taunted and bullied mercilessly by their fellow students, and even the professors," Eleanor said. "But it also means I graduated seventh in a class of more than one hundred and thirty *men*."

His triumphant smirk pulled into a tight pinch. He pushed her letter aside, folded his hands together, and leaned forward. "May I ask how old you are, Miss Atherton?"

"I'm twenty-three," she said. "My date of birth is included in my application."

He didn't bother to look. He kept his eyes fixed on her. "Twenty-three. And a virgin, I assume, if you are unmarried?"

Eleanor was taken aback by the intimate question, and he sat back. "You blush. How do you imagine you'd handle the rigors of battle, the sight of male bodies undressed, the sound of men cursing?"

"It would be in a medical context. A wounded *person*, not . . ." Her blush deepened, and her tongue knotted itself, but not out of shyness. It was pure molten desire—not for naked men, but for medicine, and the raw need to serve, the frustration of not being allowed to use her education and skills to *help* those men. She held his eyes. "I would not shirk, Sir William," she said, and knew that was inadequate.

He shifted in his chair. "You *think* you would not, but one never knows until one is tried in battle. There is your future to think of, and the feelings of your father and mother in this matter. As of this moment, there is nothing to prevent you from forgetting this nonsense and seeing sense. My advice is to return home, find a suitable husband, and take your proper place as a wife and mother. Britain needs strong families just as badly as we need fighting men and frontline doctors— *male* doctors." He glanced up at the gilt-framed portrait of King George V that hung over the fireplace. "You would still be doing something vitally important."

"What are my other options?" she asked, ignoring the patriotic speech. "For practicing medicine, I mean, helping with the wounded?"

"Confound it, Miss Atherton, can you not knit?"

"I prefer embroidery, actually," she said. "It has helped me perfect my suturing."

For an instant his brows rose in surprise, then he shut his eyes and rubbed the bridge of his nose. When he looked up at last, his gaze was both baffled and resigned, the suffering look of a man faced with the vexing problem of a willful child—or a difficult woman.

"If you are so set upon this course, I suggest you consider practicing at one of the hospitals here at home that care for women and children." He tried smiling at her, a fond uncle soothing an unruly niece, performing an uncomfortable but necessary role, providing a gentle correction. "*That* would be most suitable, something more genteel, a role that will keep you busy until you marry, eh?"

"Is there anywhere else I might apply?"

The avuncular look faded. "There are hospitals run by women in France—but not under our jurisdiction. They're under the auspices of the *French* Red Cross." He sniffed with disdain. "There's also a convalescent hospital in London staffed by women, and there are female doctors treating refugees in Serbia, but they do not have official support, and there is rampant disease and contagion there. Those women serve at their own risk and expense, and with the understanding that they cannot expect official aid from the king's government."

Eleanor sat forward, hopefully. "Would they—"

He thumped his fist on the table. "Young woman, as your father's friend I *beg* you to go home and stop this nonsense! This is not the kind of life for a well-bred woman." She refused to wilt under his icy glare. She held his gaze boldly until he was the one to sigh and look away. "Do you truly wish to embarrass your parents?"

"I hope to make them proud of me."

She remembered how her mother had cried at the graduation ceremony, sure her daughter had ruined her future with an advanced education and a medical degree. In the eight months since that day, she hadn't stopped looking at Eleanor with a mixture of bafflement and disappointment. It was much like Sir William's terribly pained expression now. Her father had been an army doctor once, and she'd thought—hoped—he'd understand why she wanted this, why she felt *called* to serve as he had. She recalled his flat frown and crisp dismissal the single time that she'd broached the subject.

"I daresay your father would like to continue his career and eventually retire without anything marring his reputation in that community—both the medical one and the social one," Sir William said. "What you do next will reflect upon him, Miss Atherton, and upon your future husband. A good man might think twice before proposing to . . . a woman with such experience."

He pushed her letter across the desk with the tip of one finger and rose from his chair. He took out his watch and glanced at it pointedly.

The interview was over.

There was nothing to do but pick up the letter, fold it, and put it in her pocketbook. Frustration rose, and Eleanor swallowed, tasting bitterness on her tongue. If Sir William knew how far she'd come, all she'd done to become a doctor, he'd not doubt her determination.

She'd dreamed of being a doctor her whole life. She'd watched her father work, and she'd read every medical book in his study. At medical school she'd worked harder than any other student in her class because she wanted to be taken seriously, though excelling had led to jealousy and scorn from her male classmates, not admiration. She'd been bullied, too, like the rest of the women in her class, but she'd endured it, learned to concentrate with all her might on her studies, on the prize of a medical career, and ignore the taunts.

She lifted her eyes to Sir William, a renewed plea on her lips, but he'd already turned away, was crossing the room to open the door for her. She followed, her spine stiff, her expression placid. She'd also learned that at medical school, to not let disappointment or frustration show, no matter how those emotions raged in her breast. It was weakness, and it made one easy prey, a victim—or a casualty. *Find another way.* It had become her motto, her creed, to go around the obstacles in her path.

Find another way.

Sir William paused with his hand on the latch. "Have you considered the possibility of applying to serve as a nurse or a member of the Voluntary Aid Detachment?" he asked. "Much more ladylike pursuits."

Eleanor's simmering frustration came to a boil. She clenched the handle of her pocketbook so tightly that she heard the bamboo crack. A foul curse word—also learned at medical school—rose to the tip of her tongue. She clamped it behind her teeth just in time.

Instead she raised her chin and looked along the length of her nose at the bureaucrat. She was taller by half a head, and he noted that, colored, and subtly rose on his toes.

"I am not a nurse, Sir William, or a volunteer."

She leaned forward, her nose inches from his, her eyes narrowed.

"I am a *doctor.*"

CHAPTER TWO

THORNDALE, YORKSHIRE
FEBRUARY 3, 1918

The errand would take only a few minutes. Eleanor would present herself at the side door of the east wing of Chesscroft Park at precisely 11:00. She would ring the bell and inform the footman, maid, or butler that she had come to see the Countess of Kirkswell's secretary. That efficient gentleman would be summoned, and he would arrive at the door with enough servants to unload the parcels of knitted goods from the doctor's car while he supervised. He would convey his thanks to the ladies of the St. Everilda's Ladies' Knitting Circle on her ladyship's behalf and assure Eleanor that the countess was most grateful for such a steady contribution to the war effort. It would take no more than half an hour.

By 11:30, Eleanor would be on her way back to the doctor's surgery, ready to tackle the list of chores her father had left for her. She would start by taking inventory of drugs and medications on hand. By 1:00, she'd be sitting down to transcribe his case notes into the official patient records. At 3:00, she'd dust and tidy the surgery, and at precisely 3:47, she would leave for the train station to be on time to meet her father when the 4:02 express from York arrived.

She glanced over her shoulder at the bundles of knitted goods in the rear of the car, dozens of pairs of socks and gloves, mufflers and vests for the troops in France.

There may be a shortage of doctors, but never of knitted items.

That was uncharitable of her, Eleanor thought. Not only did the countess support the good works of the villagers by providing the wool, she had opened the entire east wing of her home as a convalescent hospital for wounded officers. After her disappointing interview with Foxleigh two weeks ago, Eleanor had hoped the countess might need another doctor to help with the patients, and knowing Eleanor was at medical school and had graduated, she might consider enlisting Eleanor's help. The request had not come, and her mother insisted that Eleanor must not embarrass her parents by going up to Chesscroft to apply for work like a scullery maid—as if cleaning the surgery at home wasn't just that.

It wasn't as if she knew the countess well enough to request a favor from her. Her ladyship lived a life beyond the touch of most of the villagers. She knew Eleanor by name and by sight, of course, as a member of the community and the doctor's daughter, but aside from an acknowledging nod from the countess and an awkward curtsy from Eleanor upon a chance meeting, they had never spoken directly. Edward was much closer to the noble family, of course, as a dear friend of Lord Louis, the countess's youngest son.

Eleanor bit her lip as she drove, wondering if she might dare to presume on that boyhood friendship to beg an interview with her ladyship and a position at the convalescent hospital. As close as Edward and Louis were, she was an outsider, not one of the Kirskwells' inner circle. Edward had deliberately kept her separate, and her parents had never enjoyed a closer relationship based on their son's connection. It was as if Edward lived two lives.

Another vehicle roared past her in the narrow road, horn honking, throwing in its wake a sudden splatter of thick yellow mud across the front window that landed with a crack so loud it sounded like a clap of thunder or a bomb going off. Eleanor flinched, suddenly blind as muck covered the glass completely, turning day to night. She hit the brakes and felt the car skid.

And still the other vehicle honked frantically as she struggled to control the car. Someone heading to Chesscroft, perhaps. Someone cocky, a city sort, driving too fast, not realizing there was not space for even one car in the narrow lane, never mind two abreast between the high stone walls and thick hedgerows.

She heard the rake and squeal of branches on the roof of the car, and then it came to a stop. There was no crash after all, just a hard bump. For a stunned moment, she sat still, trying to catch her breath and still her pounding heart, holding tight to the steering wheel as the rain drummed on the roof.

"Bloody idiot," she muttered. She squinted at the watch pinned to her lapel. It was 10:36. She'd have to get out and see if there was any damage to the car or if it was stuck in the mud, and she didn't have an umbrella. She'd be late, and she'd arrive at Chesscroft soaked to the skin and muddy.

Worst of all, at precisely 4:04, two minutes after he'd stepped off the train from York and surveyed the damage to the car in stunned silence, her father would skin her alive with a blistering lecture about duty and responsibility and care. He'd remind her that the sight of the doctor's shining, pristine motor pulling up outside a cottage or farmhouse was in itself a source of comfort to the sick and injured. A damaged fender, or even a scratch, would undermine Dr. John Atherton's impeccable professional image, suggest carelessness and undue haste, breed fear and uncertainty in those who must feel the utmost confidence in their doctor's skill and patience. He'd tell her again that he'd only allowed her to learn to drive because her brother was away in France and there were errands to run, deliveries to make, and—

The strident knock on the window beside her startled her. A hand swiped the mud away and the blur of a pale face peered in at her.

"Doc?"

She recognized Charlie Nevins, a farm lad from up in the dales. Sharp words about driving with more care sprang to her lips. She opened the door and held her skirts carefully to one side as she stepped out. Cold rain hit her face, and the icy mud slithered under her feet and instantly soaked the soft leather of her boots. "Charlie? What on earth do you think you're—"

She saw the worry on his face and paused. But it wasn't for her. There was mud on his clothing, and—*blood*.

"What's wrong? Are you hurt?"

He ignored the question and bent to peer into the car. "Is your father with you, El? I need him."

It was serious, then. Her gut tensed.

"He's gone to York today. I dropped him at the station not half an hour ago. What's—"

"Gone?" His eyes met hers, round with despair.

"Where are you hurt?" Eleanor asked again, scanning Charlie's wind-chapped face and rangy body, his raw-knuckled hands, knobby knees, and muddy boots, looking for the source of the blood.

He glanced at the truck, stopped now in the middle of the lane a few yards ahead of the car. "It's not me—it's my da. He slipped on a patch of ice up in the high pasture, cut his leg open on some wire. It took me an hour to get him down. He's in the truck, bleedin' bad. We stopped at the surgery, but your mother told us the doctor was out. When I saw the car, I was hoping he'd be in it." He cast another anxious look at the truck. "Can ye tell me when the doc will be back? Da's in a bad way."

"I can help." She didn't hesitate. She dove into the car for her medical bag.

Charlie shook his head when she emerged and frowned at the black case. "Begging your pardon, but it's your da I need, not you, El."

She blinked the rain out of her eyes and tightened her grip on the handle of her bag. She'd yet to have the chance to use it for anything more significant than delivering liniment for sore joints or syrup for a child's cough, though it had waited, packed and ready, for the whole of the eight months since her graduation from medical school.

"I'm a doctor now as well, Charlie," she said, in case he didn't know that. It felt odd to say that to someone just a few years younger than she was, a village lad who'd been brought into this world by her father, whose older brothers had played cricket on the heath with Edward before they'd all marched off to war, leaving fourteen-year-old Charlie behind to help his father run the farm.

"But it's not a—a *woman's* complaint, or a child." he said. "It's an *emergency.*"

She didn't argue. There wasn't time if it was a true emergency. She strode toward the truck, ignoring the mud and squinting at the cold rain falling into her eyes. Charlie hurried to catch up. "Eleanor, wait—"

"How long ago did it happen? Is the cut deep?"

"Um, I can see the bone," Charlie muttered. "But Da won't want—"

She reached the truck and opened the door. Arthur Nevins lay on the seat, his right leg wrapped in a blood-soaked blanket. His face was white, his lips drawn back in pain. His brow crumpled in confusion when he saw Eleanor. "What the devil—" He looked at his son. "Where's the doctor, lad? I told ye to fetch the doctor."

"He wasn't in the car, Da. It was just Eleanor. The doc's gone to York, but she says she can see to ye."

Arthur Nevins gaped at her, then echoed Charlie. "No offense to ye, lass, but this isn't some female complaint—it's me leg. I need a proper doctor."

She squared her shoulders and pushed the sodden hair out of her eyes. "I *am* a proper doctor, Mr. Nevins." She reached for the edge of the blanket and lifted it. She swallowed hard. The wire had bitten deep into the calf muscles, carved a long, bloody gash. She saw smears of dirt and manure on his skin. *Risk of infection. The wound needs cleaning, possibly cauterizing, and suturing*, her medical brain noted. *Amputation?* She shook off that thought. This wasn't just a patient. She'd known Arthur Nevins all her life. He had four sons. Two were in the army, still alive, and one—Matthew—had been killed at the Somme in '16.

Arthur needed his leg.

"We need to stop the bleeding," she said carefully. "The wound needs cleaning and stitching. Is the bone broken?"

But Arthur flipped the blanket back over the wound. "Leave it be, lass. If I wanted a woman practicing her needlework on me, I'd have had my Muriel sew me up. I need a *doctor!*"

"I'll take him up to the surgery in Ribblesdale," Charlie said.

Eleanor shook her head. "That's ten miles away over rough roads, and we had word last week that Dr. Skerritt was called up. He's gone to France, and his replacement isn't due to arrive for another week. My father is the only doctor—the only *male* doctor—in the district. Charlie, this can't wait. It's very serious. I can—"

"No," Arthur interrupted sharply. He drew the blanket up to his chin like a shy maiden and glared at her over the edge of it.

Charlie stared at her for a moment, rubbing his jaw, assessing her, perhaps, deciding if she could truly help his father or not. "We need to hurry, Charlie."

Charlie took a breath and swiped the wet hair off his forehead, then turned to his father. "Da, see reason. I'm leaving in a fortnight. What will ye do then? Ma can't help with the sheep, and it'll be lambing time soon." He looked at Eleanor. "I turned eighteen last month, and I've been called up. I'm going to France."

Eleanor looked at him in surprise. She hadn't realized that Charlie was old enough, but she saw the stubble along his narrow jaw, the jut of the Adam's apple at his throat. She couldn't imagine him as a soldier. He was tall and skinny, his eyes still wide and blue and innocent. Still, he was full-grown, strong, and able-bodied. She looked at him and knew what his father must be thinking, what his mother feared. Matthew had been eighteen when he left, was killed at nineteen, and now it was Charlie's turn to go.

Worry shimmied up her own spine, but there was another emotion as well, a darker, distinctly selfish one. Charlie was going to France to do his bit while she was stuck in England running errands, forbidden to go. It made her more determined to help Arthur, to do what she was trained for.

"Charlie's right, Mr. Nevins. I'm fully qualified, and you're in a bad way. This is *very* urgent. The wound needs to be seen to at once, cleaned, disinfected, properly cared for. There are germs in the soil, tetanus . . ."

"I ain't got germs!" Arthur said. He turned to his son. "Take me home, lad. Your mother can put a poultice on it for me, and when the doctor's back again, he can see to it."

"No!" It was Eleanor's turn to object. "It will be too late. It could be—" *Fatal.* She stopped herself from voicing her greatest concern aloud. If blood loss didn't kill him, infection would set in. The leg would turn septic, gangrenous. There'd be fever, delirium, and terrible pain. Amputation, too, if it wasn't too late.

She considered her options. The surgery was nearly three miles away, but Chesscroft was less than half a mile up the lane. "We'll take him to the convalescent hospital at Chesscroft," she said to Charlie. "Every minute counts. I'll come with you." She took a wad of clean bandages out of her bag and climbed into the truck.

"What are ye doing?" Arthur demanded, his voice rising an octave as she pressed in next to him and lifted his leg carefully into her lap to elevate it.

"I'm going to put a clean pad on the wound, something to absorb the blood until we get to the hospital."

Charlie slid behind the steering wheel. "The countess's hospital is just for loonies, isn't it? Officers not right in the head?"

"It's a convalescent hospital for all kinds of wounded officers," she said, concentrating on the wound.

"There are real doctors there? Not just nurses?" Arthur asked.

"Yes, Mr. Nevins. *Male* doctors," she said tartly. She pressed the bandage over the wound, and blood immediately soaked the white linen. "Hurry, Charlie. Drive fast."

Minutes later, Charlie flew through the gates of Chesscroft Park at top speed. The truck jumped from the rutted lane to the manicured gravel drive, and Arthur yelped in pain. Eleanor held the bandage in place and glanced out the window, trying to judge how long it would take to reach the east wing. Two minutes, three perhaps, no more than that. She glanced at the black wreaths on the estate's gates, indicating a recent death in the family and a house in mourning. Not a war death this time, but an accident that had claimed the earl's eldest son only three months earlier.

The wadded cloth covering Arthur's leg was soaked in blood, her hands red with it, and she replaced it. She held tight, bracing her shoulder against Arthur's to minimize the jolting as the truck skidded to a stop by the east door. He grunted with pain anyway. "Mind the gears, boy," he muttered weakly.

"Go inside and get help," she said to Charlie. "I'll wait with your father. Tell them it's urgent."

"No offense, lass, but a proper doctor should be a man," Arthur said, staring at her, an older, more weather-beaten version of his youngest son. His mouth was drawn tight with either his conviction or pain, and his eyes were still suspicious.

She changed the cloth again and didn't bother to reply. Her hands were slick with blood. She heard the ticking of her watch, or perhaps it was just the rain on the roof of the truck and the gravel outside. Time was passing, time Arthur Nevins didn't have to spare.

She wondered if Peter Ellersby, one of the doctors here at Chesscroft and a major in the Royal Army Medical Corps, would be on duty today. He'd become a friend of her father's, and he often came to the surgery for supper. He'd be happy to help, she was certain.

"Where the devil is Charlie?" Arthur muttered fretfully.

Eleanor looked up at the pitiless facade of the imposing manor house. The yellow stone glowed against the gray sky, and the crumbling bulk of the original Norman tower peered out from behind it, testament to the fact that there had been Chastaines in this spot since they arrived with William the Conqueror.

How many times had she followed her brother here as a child? Edward and Lord Louis had been playmates as boys, then partners in mischief and misadventure as they got older. They'd climbed and played and swum together, had gone to Cambridge together, and enlisted together, though Louis had eventually joined the air corps, while Edward found a place as an adjutant at headquarters, thanks to his connection to Louis. And now Louis's older brother was dead, and Louis was the new Viscount Somerton and would be the next Earl of Kirkswell.

If he survived the war.

She pushed the grim thought from her mind, concentrated on changing the sodden dressing on Arthur's leg yet again and pressing a fresh wad of linen against the wound, the last one she had. Where *was* Charlie? She couldn't leave Arthur to check.

When the door opened at last, only the countess's secretary stepped out. He stayed under the porch out of the rain and peered at the truck. He pushed his spectacles back up his nose. "Mr. Ross, I need help!" she called. His brow furrowed, but he stayed where he was.

"Yes, Miss Atherton, I understand, but I'm afraid that—"

Charlie shoved past him, his face alight with indignation and worry. "They won't help him!"

"What?" Eleanor said, stunned. "Why?"

"That settles it. Take me home, lad," Arthur said, trying to shift his position on the seat of the truck. He hissed in pain.

"Stay still!" Eleanor commanded.

"They said it's a military hospital, only for officers. They won't take civilians, emergency or no," Charlie said, his voice rough. He looked at Eleanor. "I begged them, pleaded, but the bastards refused to help 'im."

She looked at Mr. Ross, still standing under the porch. He was staring at the blood in horror, his face pinched and pale. Eleanor took Charlie's hand and pressed it against the pad that covered the wound. "Firm pressure," she ordered and got out of the truck. The rain was falling harder now, and she was soaked all over again. Mr. Ross dragged his eyes from the blood and looked at her, taking in her bedraggled condition, the blood on her hands and clothing, and the mud caking her boots.

"This is Mr. Nevins. He's a patient of my father's, but he's away today, and this is an emergency. He needs medical attention at once."

"I can see that, Miss Atherton, but my hands are tied. It's not my decision. I am merely her ladyship's secretary. I write letters, order supplies, I am not . . . Have you brought the consignment of knitted goods by any chance?" he asked hopefully.

Knitted goods—as if a woolen muffler or a vest mattered now, as if they'd stop a bullet on the front or keep a man from bleeding to death here on the doorstep. She ignored the question.

"I need help getting Mr. Nevins inside," she said instead.

He winced. "Another doctor, perhaps, or the village surgery."

Eleanor shook her head firmly. "He won't make it that far. Look at him, Mr. Ross—he's bleeding badly. I cannot treat him here in the rain. Please—I can see to him myself if the other doctors are busy with patients. I just need a place to do it, a sterile room."

"I cannot authorize that!" Mr. Ross said in horror. "I sympathize, of course, but it's quite impossible." Behind him in the half-open doorway, the curious faces of maids and nurses appeared, drawn by the commotion.

"This is a hospital, in't it?" Charlie called.

"Is Dr. Ellersby here?" she asked, breathless now. "He knows my father, he's a friend. May I see him?"

"Major Ellersby is with patients," Ross said. "It was he who said—"

The door was thrust back suddenly, and the maids vanished, and there was Peter Ellersby, wearing a white coat over his bespoke khaki shirt and regimental tie. "What's all this commotion, Ross? We have sick men trying to rest," he snapped. His brows rose in surprise at the sight of her and his eyes traveled from her dripping hair to the blood and mud on her skirt and back again to her face. "Eleanor? What are you doing here? You're soaking wet."

She was so relieved to see him that she almost laughed. What did it matter if she was wet? "Peter, this is Arthur Nevins. He's a patient of my father's. He has a deep laceration on his right calf, and there's risk of shock. He needs immediate—"

Peter's eyes flicked away from her and took in the truck and the two men inside it with a single sweeping glance before he cut her off with a wave of his hand. She stepped back, expecting him to rush forward, but he stayed where he was, next to Mr. Ross, under the shelter of the porch. "This is a military hospital. We cannot treat this man here. If we did, every local farmer would expect—"

"I'm a soldier!" Charlie said quickly. "I've just been called up, and my brothers are all in the army as well. One died at the Somme. The other two are in the thick of it. Can't you just—"

"Impossible," Peter Ellersby sniffed, unmoved. "Surely your father can tend to this," he said, pinning Eleanor with an indignant glare. There was no friendliness in his eyes now, no sympathy or compassion. He kept his hands clasped behind his back and glared down the length of his nose at her. She gaped at him. How could a doctor not be moved to help, to use his skill to save a man who was bleeding to death on his very doorstep?

"My father is in York today," she said through tight lips. "I can do it myself, Peter. I just need to get him inside."

He jerked back as if she'd slapped him. "I am on duty. Refer to me as Major Ellersby, if you please," he snapped, and paused, waiting. Heat rose under her sodden garments. If he expected her to apologize, he'd have a very long wait. "You cannot practice here, on bumpk—farmers. Surely you must see that would be most inappropriate, *Miss* Atherton."

Bumpkins and farmers? She stared at him in stunned silence.

"Look, there's nothing I can do, and I have rounds in ten minutes. Take him back to your father's surgery if you wish, but he cannot come in here."

It was no longer about her pride, or her ability to treat Arthur. It was about saving his leg, and very possibly his life. "Please, Pe—*Major Ellersby*. He won't make it."

"Don't be ridiculous, Eleanor. You know what your father would say. You are overstepping your authority and your experience. He can see this patient tomorrow. Keep the limb elevated. Now go home. I shall see you at supper on Friday evening as usual."

Supper. She shook her head. How many meals had he shared with her family, how many cases had he discussed with her father over brandy and chess? He was a family friend, welcome company, and yet he was looking at her as if she were a stranger—a very irritating stranger.

But she was a grown woman, a doctor, and her father's patient—

her patient—needed her. She gritted her teeth and marched up to him. "He won't make it. He'll die," she hissed. "You can see that, I know you can, even from here. I won't keep you from rounds—I simply need help carrying him inside, a place to wash my hands, some carbolic, a clean examining room, and—"

Peter's jaw clenched. "I said no." He turned away, pushed past the small crowd of curious staff that had gathered again, and was gone. She looked for Mr. Ross, but he, too, had fled, and it was Chesscroft's starchy butler who stood regarding the situation placidly.

Arthur was pale as a lily, shaking badly, in shock. She saw the terrible fear in Charlie's face as his father faded before his eyes.

"What can I do?" he asked her. He swiped a hand across his eyes and left a smear of blood on his cheek. "What can *we* do?"

Eleanor turned to the butler. "Mr. Heseltine, may I speak to her ladyship?"

He scanned her face, his own starchy expression never changing, the stiff dignity of his immaculate posture unrelenting. "Mr. Ross has gone to find her. I heard you speaking to the major. You can do this? Take care of him?"

"Yes," she said firmly. "But not here in the rain, and the surgery is too far away."

"I have my dignity, Jasper Heseltine," Arthur Nevins called. "I won't take charity where I'm not wanted, or let some chit take care of me. No, I say. Charlie, take me home." The effort of the tirade left him gasping. "I won't stay—"

"Heseltine?" They all looked up at the sound of the countess's voice. Her ladyship stood in the doorway, her back ramrod straight, her dark hair perfectly coiffed, though streaked with gray. Her gown was the height of elegance, a day dress or a morning gown, perhaps, though black, for mourning. Lines of grief were etched around her mouth and in the shadows under her eyes, though her face was otherwise immobile as she surveyed the scene on her east doorstep. If she was angry or dismayed, there was no sign of it in her countenance. She radiated authority through her posture, the tilt of her head, the determined set of her chin. She took in everything in a single sweeping glance, then let her eyes go back to flick over the truck, pausing on Charlie and Arthur, and finally on Eleanor. Her brows rose slightly as she noted Eleanor's disheveled state. Eleanor refrained from the urge to tuck back a dripping lock of hair or run a hand over her skirt, now wet and rumpled and soiled with mud and blood. Eleanor dipped a curtsy out of habit, as she'd been taught, but didn't hesitate to speak.

"I have a medical emergency, your ladyship. It cannot wait, and the surgery is too far. I'd like to tend to this man here, before it's too late."

The countess's eyes widened for an instant. "*You* would?"

Eleanor nodded. "I'm fully qualified, a doctor."

"Yes, I know," the countess said. "Or I'd heard."

Behind her Arthur grunted. "Uh-oh, now there'll be trouble. She'll get her comeuppance now," he murmured, and Charlie shushed him.

The countess didn't hesitate, either. She kept her eyes on Eleanor as she addressed her secretary, who had returned to hover behind her. "Mr. Ross, please ask Major Ellersby to come at once. Find some orderlies to carry this man inside." She glanced at Eleanor again. "With Miss Atherton's approval, of course."

Eleanor nodded and turned to direct the men who had appeared as if by magic with a stretcher. They lifted Arthur out of the truck with as much care as possible, but the old farmer roared and swore in pain. The countess didn't turn a hair at the rude language, or the blood.

She turned as Peter arrived behind her. "My lady, I'm sorry you were disturbed," he said, his tone deferential now. He frowned as they carried Arthur toward the door and stepped in front of the stretcher, forcing it to stop. "I thought I'd seen to this matter. All this will be cleared away at once, of course. These are local villagers. They're just leaving."

"Leaving? Even I can see that this man is in no condition to leave." The countess looked at Eleanor. "Miss Atherton says he needs immediate care. Is that correct, Miss Atherton?"

Eleanor avoided Peter's eyes, but felt his glare burn into her forehead like sun through glass. "Yes, your ladyship," she said firmly.

"I overheard you saying you've given three sons to the cause," the countess said to Arthur. "And now you're going over as well, young man," she added to Charlie. "I have a son over there myself."

"We know it well, your ladyship," Charlie said. "We're all praying for Lord Louis's safe return. We were grieved to hear of Lord Cyril's passing."

The countess lowered her gaze, but not before Eleanor saw the sharp glitter of tears in her eyes. They were gone when she looked at Peter. "Take this man inside at once, Major. Give him whatever treatment is required—the very best care."

"But, your ladyship—" Peter began, drawing up to attention, looking affronted.

The countess drew herself up as well. "A man who has given so many sons to the cause deserves our respect, Major. Do you not agree? This is a hospital, is it not?"

"For officers, for heroes," Peter murmured.

"Then make room for one more hero," the countess said. She turned to Eleanor. "I'm certain the major can see to this quite competently from here. Would you join me for a few minutes, Eleanor?"

It was on the tip of Eleanor's tongue to object, to insist that Arthur was her patient, that she could perform the necessary medical care, but the countess's brows rose at her hesitation, and there was nothing to do but to politely murmur her thanks and acceptance.

Arthur would receive the treatment he needed, and wasn't that what truly mattered? It was a victory. Except for the small niggle of defeat in her own breast at yet another missed opportunity to practice medicine, to prove her skills equal to any emergency. Perhaps the countess's invitation meant trouble, a scolding for interfering, for daring to imagine herself a capable physician.

She glanced again at the Nevinses as she entered the house, but they were on their way down the hall, following Major Ellersby's indignant figure, and she was on her own.

CHAPTER THREE

S ervants took Eleanor's wet coat away to dry it by a fire. She removed her boots as well and donned a pair of the felt slippers the
servants wore over their shoes when they worked so their hard-soled
footwear would make no sound and leave no marks on the polished
floors.

The countess led the way through a door covered with green
baize. Unlike the stripped-down medical wing, here the ancient oak
floors glowed with polish, and glorious paintings hung on damask
walls. The busts of past earls stared down at her from niches in the
wall, and Eleanor recognized the bronze countenance of the current
earl, his unsmiling face stamped with an expression of distant dignity
and noble suffering. As a doctor, she wondered if his lordship's teeth
troubled him, or his digestion. Perhaps his wild youngest son was the
cause of his worries. No doubt with Louis at war and his eldest son so

recently dead and buried, the lines on the earl's face were now deeper still.

The countess opened a door to an elegant sitting room. A portrait of Louis Chastaine, painted perhaps seven or eight years earlier, when he was about sixteen, hung above the fireplace. Eleanor's heart skipped. She remembered him then, sharing adventures and getting up to trouble with Edward on half-term holidays and long summer afternoons. Louis's rascal's grin was still the same—or at least the same as the last time she saw him, on his way to war with Edward nearly four years ago. The artist had done well—Louis's painted gaze was full of all the dash and daring it held in life.

As a girl, she'd had a crush on Louis Chastaine, and the kicking of her heart now told her she hadn't grown out of it, that she was just as smitten as she'd been the first time she saw him with Edward. Her brother had thrown mud on her frock and pulled her hair, but when Edward had run away laughing, Louis had surreptitiously given her his handkerchief to dry her tears before he followed his friend. She'd loved him from that moment on, had slept with that handkerchief under her pillow for weeks until the maid found it and threw it away. She tried to picture him now, to imagine the battlefield and Louis's place on it—or above it, rather, since he was a pilot.

"That's my favorite portrait of him," the countess said. Eleanor realized she'd stopped in the middle of the floor to stare at the painting, and her ladyship stood beside her, holding one elegant hand to her cheek as she, too, regarded her son's image. "There are other portraits of him, even several photographs from before he left for war, and some taken in France, but this one . . ." the countess began, but her voice faded. Eleanor glanced at her, but she turned away, settled herself on one of the antique settees that flanked the fireplace under the portrait. "Please sit down." She indicated the seat opposite her own, and Eleanor silently perched on the edge.

"You're all grown up, aren't you?" her ladyship said. "I remember you as Edward's little sister, in pigtails and pinafores." Once again her bland gaze flicked over the mud on Eleanor's skirt and the smears of blood on her blouse. Her hair was wet, and it would twist itself into frizz as it dried, turning her into Medusa before her ladyship's wondering eyes. She hoped her face was clean, at least. She nodded politely, did her best to look professional and brave, the doctor's daughter, and a doctor in her own right.

"I don't know why Edward didn't bring you with him when he came to visit Louis. I daresay he was here as often as he was at home."

"A sister isn't much wanted on the adventures of two boys," Eleanor said quietly. She had been very firmly warned away, in fact, threatened with snakes in her bed and sharp pinches and Papa's bitterest and most poisonous medicine in her milk if she followed her brother to Chesscroft.

Her ladyship tilted her head. "I daresay they'd not leave you out now."

Eleanor felt herself blushing at the compliment.

"I heard that you were at university, studying medicine."

"Yes, your ladyship. I graduated last spring."

"So you really could have treated that poor man?"

Eleanor looked at her in surprise. "Yes, of course. I'm a fully qualified physician."

The countess's brows rose, and she smiled faintly. "Just like your father, while your brother chose a different path altogether. Laws at Cambridge, though I believe he once had expectations of attending medical school, did he not?"

Eleanor studied her hands. "Y-yes." Heat rose between her shoulder blades despite the dampness of her clothes. "He . . ." She swallowed, stumbling over the explanation, the excuse. "He did not—that is, he decided to attend Cambridge instead." The real reason he had made that decision was a private family matter. She felt her cheeks heat under the countess's curious eyes. Thanks to Louis's friendship,

Edward had landed a plum posting at British headquarters, and his future was bright indeed, his star on the rise. He seemed content, even if her father had been disappointed—no, *furious*—when his son had failed the medical school admission exams and his daughter had passed. It had been a surprise to everyone, but to no one more than Eleanor. She still could not understand how it had happened. She'd been with him on the day of the exam, had seen his cocky self-assurance. She remembered how she'd frozen with nerves when the test began, even though she'd studied hard, had been prepared . . . Edward had been uncharacteristically kind to her on the train home as she struggled to contain the certainty that she'd failed. She had always refused to cry in front of him, to show him any weakness he might use to mock her. Instead he'd handed her his handkerchief without a word and sat back to read the newspaper with one leg propped on his knee, humming a popular little dance hall ditty and saying nothing at all.

"I hope you don't mind that I asked Major Ellersby to see to your patient," the countess said, changing the subject.

"I didn't come to interfere," Eleanor said. "I was nearby, you see, on my way here. The ladies' knitting circle has completed another consignment of socks and mufflers for the troops, and—"

Her ladyship smiled faintly. "Oh, I haven't brought you here to rebuke you, Eleanor. On the contrary." She hesitated. "Please thank the ladies of the knitting circle. I shall write a note when—" She drew a sharp breath and paused again, seemingly gathering herself before beginning again. "When I saw you today, I was hoping . . . it seems . . . It seems I have need of some *discreet* medical services."

A jolt of surprise coursed through Eleanor. "Are you ill, my lady?"

"No, no. Not at all. It's Louis—"

"Oh, no!" The outburst was not mannerly, but it was out before Eleanor could stop it. She braced herself. Was Louis dead, killed in action? Did Edward know? Perhaps the countess wanted medication to help her sleep, to soothe her fears, to keep the ghosts of her dead sons at bay, two of them now, so close together—

"Oh, he's not dead! I didn't mean to alarm you. He's only wounded, or so I'm told." The countess put a hand to her brow. "I'm not explaining this well. Perhaps I should start at the beginning. I received a letter from a friend in France—Colonel Sir Hugo Ferris—nearly ten days ago. He wrote to tell me that Louis had been wounded. He said Louis's plane was shot at, and those terrible contraptions are so fragile. It caught fire, but he managed to land it, narrowly missing a platoon of French soldiers. Louis broke his leg rather badly, and Sir Hugo said it was a miracle he survived at all, that Louis might easily have burned to death, and only his extraordinary skill as a pilot had saved him. Perhaps it was luck, too. Louis has always been lucky." She blinked rapidly, as if staving off tears, and her hands tightened to fists, the knuckles white against her dark skirt. She glanced up at the portrait again before she continued. "But luck runs out," she murmured. She tilted her chin up. "Sir Hugo says I must be proud of Louis, that my son is a hero, but I'm not. I suppose Sir Hugo meant me to be comforted by his letter. In truth he only wrote because he thought it was *good* news—the French have awarded Louis a medal for gallantry. Louis, of course, would never think to tell me himself." She shook her head. "But it's not good news. I can only think of what *might* have happened to my son—my only surviving son." The countess drooped a little, as if the steel in her spine was buckling under the terrible strain.

Eleanor didn't know what to say. Fear for Louis dried her throat. Over the ragged edges of dismay, she went over the medical responses in her mind. "Was his leg—" She hesitated over the word *amputated*. "Did they . . . Are his injuries very serious?"

The countess made a helpless gesture. "I don't know. Louis hasn't written to me, nor has he replied to the letter I wrote to him. My husband is in London, very busy at the War Office. He doesn't worry as I do. He believes that if there were truly serious news, then he'd be the first to know. The fact that he has not received official word means all is well. He says I shouldn't interfere or coddle Louis." She raised her chin. "I wished to know everything, so I made further enquiries. Apparently, Louis was fortunate enough to land quite near a medical aid post. The medical officer saw to him at once and sent him on to a Casualty Clearing Station within the hour. It was sheer chance that Sir Hugo was visiting a wounded adjutant there. If he hadn't seen Louis arrive, I fear I'd know nothing at all about any of this. Louis is— distant. Even now. *Especially* now. I asked him to come home when his brother died last fall, but he merely sent his condolences and said that he simply could not take leave, even to come home for the funeral. They weren't close. Cyril was raised to be the next Earl of Kirkswell, while Louis was perhaps allowed too much freedom to do as he pleased. I believe he chose to become a pilot because it was the most shocking thing he could do, the most dangerous. If he dies . . ." The countess looked up, her eyes dark with determination, not grief. "I cannot let that happen. I have only one son left, and I won't give him up. I want him home, alive. I know he will refuse if I ask him to come, and his father would never order him back, even now. Yet his return is imperative. He has responsibilities to his family, to his title, and that must outweigh other concerns." She met Eleanor's eyes. "I suppose you think that's selfish."

Eleanor thought of all the local men who'd fought and died, leaving their mothers mourning and their fathers without sons to carry on farms or smithies or shops after them.

"What treatment has Lord Louis had?" Eleanor asked.

"A surgeon at the Casualty Clearing Station set Louis's leg. In other circumstances, he would have been sent back to a base hospital at once, or home, but he cannot be moved until the bone sets, and there's still some danger that he might . . ." She looked down at her ruined handkerchief and set it aside. "Louis must remain right where he is for some time yet. And the burns—" She paused. "There's a pilot here at Chesscroft recovering from burns. He is terribly disfigured, will never be the same. When I look at him, I imagine Louis like that and fear the worst."

Eleanor knew the platitudes doctors used, the kind words meant to ease the suffering of a loved one, to prepare them when there was a possibility of a bad outcome. Louis was a hero, and England was grateful for every mother's sacrifice, honored every fallen warrior, medical care at the front was excellent, he hadn't suffered—or wouldn't. She struggled for something to say, something real and comforting, but she sat mute, unable to speak, as if the countess's fear were contagious.

The door opened, and the butler glided in with the tea tray. The countess composed herself. "Ah, thank you, Heseltine. Any word on our—Miss Atherton's—patient?"

"He's being cared for now, your ladyship," Heseltine said blandly. "The wound is quite serious. Another hour and it might have proven more serious still." He glanced at Eleanor, acknowledging her with a brief and sympathetic smile, though his starchy demeanor offered no entry for her questions. He was on duty and would not be distracted.

"Thank you, Heseltine. I'll pour the tea. Keep me apprised of his condition." Heseltine bowed crisply and departed.

The countess turned her attention to the tea, continuing their conversation as if the interruption had never happened. "I want Louis here at home, where he can receive the best possible medical care. I think he would recover better in familiar surroundings. And if the worst should happen . . . Sugar? Milk?"

"Um, plain, please," Eleanor said, and took the cup.

"I'd like you to go to France and bring him home."

"Me?" Eleanor was so surprised she nearly dropped her teacup. She set it carefully down on the table. Was Louis as far gone as that? She imagined the carved stones in the family crypt that bore the names of eight generations of Chastaines. The inscription on the most recently carved slab was still fresh, the grief still raw. "Is he— Does he *wish* to come home?"

The countess's gaze hardened. "It isn't about what he wants anymore. Louis is the last of his line. And even if they are the best in the world, with all the right intentions and the finest training, I can only imagine how busy the doctors are at the front, how easily little things might be overlooked, how standards of care might be neglected because there are simply too many, too much. No, Louis has done his bit, proven his courage, been wounded, and earned a medal. It's time for him to come home. I know other people cannot do this for their sons, but *I* can. If that's arrogant, then it's the privilege of my wealth and class." She scanned Eleanor's face for censure, but Eleanor kept her countenance flat.

"You're wondering why I've asked you to go."

"Yes," Eleanor admitted.

The countess's gaze turned thoughtful, and Eleanor had the sense that once again she was being examined, assessed. She held the countess's eyes and waited for both verdict and explanation. The countess looked away and sipped her tea. Eleanor could hear the clock ticking in the silence. "I was impressed with what I saw today. You handled the situation with confidence. You were ready to wage war on that man's behalf, so to speak. You didn't mind about blood on your skirt, or the mud, or the rain, or even the major's refusal. The patient was your primary concern."

"I've known the Nevinses all my life. They are my father's patients," Eleanor murmured.

"But they are not *your* patients, are they?"

Eleanor looked at her tea and didn't reply.

"I assume it's because of your youth and your sex that your skills are not being used to their full potential here in Thorndale." The countess sipped her tea. "I did speak to your father some months ago when one of my doctors was sent to France—there's a dreadful shortage of doctors over there. I asked him if he might spare you to assist here at the convalescent hospital. He refused on your behalf and asked me not to approach you directly."

Eleanor gaped at her. "You wanted me to . . ." She stopped. Her belly curled, and bitterness filled her mouth. She picked up her cup and forced a sip of tea past her tight lips. "I—I didn't know. My father didn't tell me. I would have—"

"He declined on your behalf and asked me not to take the matter any further. Major Ellersby also felt it would be inappropriate."

It was a day for bombshells and surprises, it seemed. First Arthur's injury, then hearing of Louis's. But it was her father's high-handed decision on her behalf that truly infuriated her, a decision made without even telling her. The teacup shook in her hand, rattling against the saucer.

She looked up to find the countess regarding her with interest. "You are the sister of one of Louis's dearest friends. Surely it would be a comfort to him to see someone he knows, don't you think? The fact that you are a doctor, and a very determined one, would be of comfort to me. Your father has been the practicing physician here for many years. He knows this village, this district. He knows the patients, and their illnesses, and even the *potential* types of sickness or injury they're likely to suffer. I daresay he could manage without you for a short while, could he not? A few weeks at most."

Of course he could manage. He already did and had always done so. She was an unwelcome distraction, an embarrassment, even. But to accept the countess's commission and go to France? He'd never allow it.

But this time she could answer for herself. Still, that answer stuck on her tongue like treacle.

"I have many powerful friends who could assist your career, Dr. Atherton," the countess continued. "The countess of Dillby is seeking a new physician, since hers was called overseas. She'd gladly accept a woman. So would Lady Bradford, and— Well, there are many important women of my acquaintance who would be pleased to have your services, and I could certainly recommend you to others if you wish it. Do you?"

Suddenly everything rushed toward her like a strong wind—all the desire, and longing, the years of hard work. This was the chance she'd hoped for at last, and this time it was for her to decide whether to accept or to decline the countess's request. Was she brave enough, bold enough to stand against her parents for this? Did she want it enough?

Yes, she wanted this. Very much.

She hadn't realized she'd spoken aloud until the countess gave her a genuine smile. "Excellent. I am sure Louis could not be in better hands. I'll have my secretary make arrangements at once. Can you be ready to leave tomorrow?"

Tomorrow. Eleanor felt the sharp edge of panic. She thought again of her father's stern and certain disapproval. Her mother would faint, and cry, not because of any danger her daughter might face, but because of the scandal this might cause, the gossip, the terrible pity of having a bold daughter, a thankless, ungrateful girl who refused to accept her proper place. "I must speak to my parents." The familiar dutiful words tripped off her tongue.

The countess frowned. "I was hoping for an answer now. You are my best hope, perhaps my only hope, of bringing him home." The words were clipped, impatient now. "He would never come home if I went, or even his father, but you are . . ." She looked at Eleanor's hair, her face, the lace collar of her blouse, her trim figure. "He'd not say no to you."

Ah. Something clicked in her chest, deflated. No doubt the countess knew her son couldn't resist a pretty face, a coquettish smile, a well-turned ankle. She was meant as bait, something feminine and soft to dangle before Louis, a siren to lure him home. Surely she was the least siren-like woman in all England, and didn't her ladyship know that Louis preferred bouncy, bubbly, blond beauties? Edward had told her that once, just to be cruel, when he realized his twin sister had a crush on his friend. He made it clear that Louis didn't care for skinny redheads, or freckles, or women who were too clever for their own good. "You'll be a spinster, as ugly and speckled as a spaniel," Edward predicted.

"We all find ourselves doing things in war that we would otherwise never have to—making sacrifices, taking on roles and challenges we never imagined ourselves capable of before," the countess said. "We must be courageous now more than ever before." She rose to her feet. "Thank you for coming, Dr. Atherton. I will look for a note from you tomorrow."

Dr. Atherton. Not "Miss Atherton" or "Eleanor"—*Doctor*. Eleanor got up, took the countess's proffered hand, and shook it, her mind reeling.

She glanced up again at Louis's portrait, at that wicked, infectious grin. *A dare*, he promised. *An adventure.* This was her chance to prove herself, to truly be a doctor. Would she refuse now, backing down from all she desired? Louis's blue gaze demanded an answer.

She kept her eyes on the portrait as she spoke. "No. I don't need time to think. I'll go."

She looked at the countess and saw triumph bloom in her eyes before she schooled her features into a gracious aristocratic smile.

"Thank you, Dr. Atherton. I shall make the arrangements at once."

Eleanor dipped a curtsy, opened the door, and went through it.

She'd made the right choice, of course. She wouldn't fail. She'd prove she was a capable doctor. She'd bring a hero home from war, deliver him safely back to a grateful mother and a proud nation.

She'd make her parents understand that she was meant to do this, make them proud of her at last.

And Edward, too.

CHAPTER FOUR

Eleanor stopped to check on Arthur, but a nurse crisply informed her that he was being taken care of and she need not worry herself. She summoned Charlie instead.

"Da's doing fine. The doctor says he'll keep his leg, but he's to stay here overnight. He needs to be watched, and they don't want to move him, just in case. There's still a chance of bleeding and . . . and other things." He scratched his head. "I'm sure the doc knows what he's doing. Thank you for all ye did for him today. He can be stubborn about things. Come on, I'll give you a ride back to your father's car, make sure it's running."

She followed him out and climbed into the truck. "I'm going to France myself," she said, trying out the words, the truth and reality of it. She felt her chest tighten, with both apprehension and anticipation. *She was going to France!*

Charlie glanced at her, his mouth round with surprise. "You?"

Her chin rose in imitation of the countess's haughty gesture. "Yes, me. Lord Louis was wounded. Her ladyship wants me take over his medical care and bring him home."

"Bring him home," Charlie repeated flatly and started the engine. "Lucky lad. No one offered to bring Matthew home when he was wounded. Took him a week to die, or so we heard."

"Are you afraid, Charlie?" she asked.

He kept his eyes on the road, considering for a moment, before he replied. "I've read Fred and Will's letters, talked to the lads in the pub who've come home hurt. I know what to expect." He glanced at her. "I can't very well tell you I'm afraid, now can I, if you're going over there, too. But you've had letters from your own brother. Surely you already know what it's like."

Headquarters was well behind the front lines, and Edward enjoyed the exalted company of senior commanders and titled visitors. His letters were filled with descriptions of dinners and parties given for dukes and duchesses, even the Prince of Wales. The worst hardship Edward reported was the way the mud stuck to his polished boots and the difficulty in getting the London papers on a timely basis. Perhaps her brother was simply being cheery, sparing their mother the burden of worrying about him, while understanding that as a doctor and a former soldier himself, their father would read between the lines and know the truth.

"I'll be in the same regiment as Fred," Charlie said proudly. "He'll show me the ropes quick enough. It's Da I worry about here at home, managing the farm alone. He'll have a time of it without me. The young shepherds are all in the army and there's only the old gaffers to help now, and they can't get up the high fells like they used to. And Ma will fret, but it can't be helped." He squared his shoulders. "Can't last much longer now, can it? It's been nearly four years, and everyone's said all along that it will be done by summer or by fall or by Christmas. They've got to be right eventually, don't they?"

They reached the place where the doctor's motor sat askew in the lane with the front bumper pressed against the stone wall. Charlie pulled to a stop and whistled. "Not too bad. Just a bit of a crumple."

"My father won't be happy," she said. It was an understatement, but the car would be the least of it.

"You can tell him that you did a good deed today, that you saved my father's life," Charlie said with a faint smile. He shook his head. "I'd never have believed it, Eleanor. You were such a quiet lass, always reading books and thinking, and now— You really are a doctor, aren't you?" He sobered. "If I'm ever sick, and you come instead of your father, I'll let you treat me."

It was a small victory, but a victory nonetheless. "Thank you, Charlie. I'll remember that, when you're home, safe and sound, and the war is over. You will be careful, won't you?"

"As careful as a nervous ewe in a lightning storm," he quipped and grinned. "Don't you worry about me. Ma will do enough of that for everyone."

But she did worry. She worried about Charlie, and Arthur, and even Edward. And Louis, too, since his famous luck had run out, and there was still a possibility that he might . . . No. She wouldn't let that happen. War was a terrible thing, but she had an opportunity now, a chance to bring one man safely home.

And once she'd done that, the future would be bright indeed.

CHAPTER FIVE

Her mother was in the sitting room when Eleanor got home. Grace Atherton's knitting needles clicked as she worked on yet another sock or mitten for the troops. Eleanor looked around the warm and homely room. It was the same as always, a familiar tableau that never changed. Nothing was out of place or missing, yet everything had altered since she was here this morning—and even more would change before the shadows of the winter evening crept in for the night and spread themselves across the worn rug.

"You've been out for quite a while, Eleanor," Grace Atherton said, glancing up with a hopeful smile. "Did you drop off the knitting? Were they pleased to get it?"

Eleanor hesitated before replying. She'd forgotten the bundle in the back of the car until she returned to the vehicle. She'd had to make a second trip, to slip back to the east door and deliver it. It *was* the errand she'd set out on, an important one to her mother and to the rest of the knitting circle, representing their contribution to the war effort. Eleanor marveled again that the events of the day, starting with that simple delivery, had led her to a chance to make an important contribution of her own. "I—" she began, but her mother barreled on without waiting for an answer.

"Dare I hope you're late because you met Peter while you were at Chesscroft? What did you talk about?" She looked back at her knitting. "No, don't tell me yet—I must finish this row before I lose count. If I get this mitten done today, that will make nine this week. The tea is still hot if you want a cup."

"Four and a half pairs. That will put you near the top of the board, won't it?" Eleanor said, warming her hands at the fire. The St. Everilda's Ladies' Knitting Circle kept track of each member's weekly contribution of completed items.

Her mother sniffed. "Lydia Pickersgill has already finished six pairs of socks and two mufflers this week, but what else has she to do with her time?"

"How is Lydia's gout?" The widow rarely left her cottage, citing her ailment as making it impossible for her to walk. In truth, she had four sons away at war, and without her boys to cook and clean for, and with fear for their safety gnawing at her day and night, what else had she to do but knit and suffer?

"She says the wet weather has her feeling particularly poorly." She peered at Eleanor. "You might pick up your own knitting needles, Eleanor. Even the queen and the Princess Royal are knitting for the soldiers. It's been a hard winter already, and they're predicting more cold days ahead. The need for warm socks is crucial, and the feet you save might well be your own brother's."

She sounded like a propaganda poster.

Eleanor studied her mother's face, noted the lines of middle age made deeper by the firelight. She was squinting at her knitting, and it was on the tip of Eleanor's tongue to remind her she'd only make her eyes worse or give herself a headache, but Grace Atherton was too proud to admit she needed glasses.

"I was invited to tea by the countess today," she said instead.

The click of the needles stopped, and for a moment there was stunned silence. "Tea? For delivering a load of knitting?" She sniffed. "If her ladyship wishes to offer her thanks to the knitting circle, there are others she could invite to tea. I do hope she's not trying to involve you in those dreadful suffrage activities she espouses. I cannot approve of such foolishness. A woman's place is in the home. She serves best as helpmeet and guide that way, not by involving herself in politics. Instead of serving tea, the countess would do better to join the knitting circle and lend a hand."

"She donates the wool, Mama, and she arranges for shipment of the finished goods to France at her own expense. She's given her home as a convalescent hospital, and chairs the local Volunteer Reserve, and the earl works at the War Office."

"Well, I suppose that's just fine for grand folk like them, but there's always more work to do. There's nothing unimportant about knitting and rolling bandages, Eleanor. *Why* did she invite you in to tea?" She looked up, a new idea making her eyes sparkle. "Was it Peter's doing, by chance?"

Not at all, she thought. But then, if he hadn't refused to treat Arthur, causing the countess to be summoned, she wouldn't have been invited to tea, so perhaps Peter Ellersby had everything to do with it after all.

"She wished to tell me that Lord Louis has been wounded—"

Her mother dropped her knitting and clapped her hand to her chest "What? Is he dead, maimed? Was it that dreadful gas? Lydia's middle son was gassed, and blinded for nearly a week. Was Edward with him?"

"No. I'm sure we'd hear directly if Edward were wounded. Louis is alive, but he broke his leg while landing his plane under enemy fire and suffered burns. He's in hospital in France."

Her mother exhaled in relief. "I would not wish her ladyship the terrible grief of losing a son, of course—not so soon after Lord Cyril's death—but I don't see why she'd bother *you* about a broken leg."

Eleanor clasped her hands together tightly. "She—the countess—wants me to go to France and bring him home."

Her mother barked a laugh. "Who? Louis? Very funny. Why on earth would she want *you* to go to France? Has he forgotten the way home? Is it the chauffeur's day off?"

Eleanor felt her shoulders tense. "She asked because I'm a doctor. Louis will need medical care on the journey."

Grace Atherton's smile fell and her brows rose in surprise, as if she'd forgotten her daughter was a doctor. "And she asked me because I'm a family friend, of course," Eleanor added quickly to soften the news.

"You? Lord Louis is Edward's friend, never yours. We owe the countess nothing. The Kirkswells are not even your father's patients. They bring in their fancy London doctor when they've a need, as if your father's not good enough for them, and you—" Her face was red, and Eleanor could see the pulse pounding in her throat.

"Mama?" Eleanor rose to fetch the smelling salts from the box on the shelf.

"You can't go to France!" her mother managed.

Eleanor gritted her teeth and forced a smile, clutched the tiny vial tight in her fist. "Of course I can."

"What about Peter? He's coming to *supper*!" She looked mournfully at her daughter. "He wished it to be a surprise, but I might as well tell you that Peter has spoken to your father. He intends to propose on Friday evening, and then you'll have your wedding to plan, and Peter will not allow you to go haring off to France. Her ladyship will have to find someone else."

Eleanor gaped at her mother. "Propose? Peter Ellersby? To me?"

"Of course you. Surely it isn't a complete shock. He's been attentive and charming for months. For heaven's sake, Eleanor, can you not recognize a courtship when it's right in front of you?"

A courtship. Was that what it was? Her parents had offered much more encouragement than she had. It was Mama who invited him to supper and sang his praises, and her father was the one he conversed with, played chess with. Of course, Peter did sometimes walk her to church on Sundays if he wasn't on duty, or amused her with silly, meaningless compliments on her dress or her hair. She'd once hoped he'd be a kindred spirit, someone to discuss interesting medical cases with, or the latest advances brought about by the war for managing pain, or infection, or shell shock, but he changed the subject whenever she brought up medicine. He said it wasn't a suitable topic for a summer day, or an autumn evening, or a pretty woman. Even if that woman was a doctor. Instead they spoke of the weather, or of how terribly difficult it was to get properly tailored uniforms in York these days.

Well.

She supposed she should feel *something* other than utter astonishment—flattered by his attention at least, his *courtship*, but all she could think of was his stiff indignation this morning, his haughty refusal to treat Arthur Nevins.

She could only imagine what he thought of *her* behavior today. "I don't think—that is, *if* that, um, *occurs*, I *may not* say yes," she said to be diplomatic, to soften the blow.

He mother flinched in horror anyway. "Not say yes? Don't be silly. Of course you'll say yes. Peter Ellersby is a fine man, a doctor like your father, and a major in the RAMC. There's a baron in his family tree. You'll not get a better offer at your age, and you'll be an old maid if you refuse him, or you'll have to settle for a far less advantageous match. After the war there will be even fewer men to choose from. It's a terrible thing to say, but it's true enough. Your father approves of Peter, and that alone should be good enough for you, Eleanor. I only wish to see you happy and fulfilled as a woman. Why can't you settle down? This is why I was reluctant to see you go to university. I feared then that you'd become the kind of woman no man would ever want, overeducated and stubborn, and I can see I was right." She shook her head fervently and closed her eyes. "Nothing good comes of being too clever."

"I graduated seventh in my class, Mama," Eleanor said, feeling her belly tense at the old familiar argument. "That means I am a better doctor than more than one hundred and thirty others, all men save one."

Two hot spots of mortified color appeared in her mother's cheeks. "A woman is *never* better than a man, Eleanor. Peter is a fine doctor, and after the war he'll rise. Imagine being the wife of a doctor who treats the cream of the aristocracy, an esteemed Harley Street physician."

It never occurred to her mother that Eleanor could become an esteemed physician in her own right.

She raised her chin. "I told the countess I would go. It is a medical matter that cannot wait," Eleanor said, bringing her mother back to the matter at hand. "She wants me to leave at once—tomorrow, in fact."

Her mother shot to her feet, and the ball of wool in her lap tumbled across the carpet, unraveling in an endless gray exclamation point. "Tomorrow! Don't be impertinent. Your father will never allow it."

Eleanor kept her spine stiff. "I'll only be gone for a week or two, and it is a tremendous honor to be asked by the countess herself. And Louis—Viscount Somerton—is a hero. Think of what the knitting circle will say," Eleanor suggested brightly, trying to soothe her mother. She crossed to take her arm and ease her back into the chair, but her mother shook her off.

"I'm thinking of what *your father* will say—and Peter." She glanced at the clock. "Oh, where is your father? The train from York must be late."

Eleanor glanced at the clock. "His train isn't due yet. I'll fetch him from the station later."

Her mother sniffed. "Why can't a servant go and fetch him, or the earl? Lord Louis, I mean."

Eleanor folded her hands patiently. "The countess wants this done with the utmost discretion, by a doctor. She fears that the journey might cause complications, might—well, it might make his recovery longer and more difficult without the proper care. There is still a chance that he might . . ." She couldn't say it out loud.

"But you're a woman, a *young* woman, gently raised."

"There are plenty of women serving in France—as nurses, or ambulance drivers, or couriers."

"But not as *doctors*, Eleanor! Female doctors are not allowed by the War Office or the Red Cross. I insisted that your father check into it, just in case you could be called up. I know they don't need or want female doctors. Women might temporarily act as locums at home, freeing a man to serve. You are assisting your father. That is quite enough. More than enough, I think."

Frustration rose. "But I'm *not* assisting! Father will not let me handle even the most basic cases!"

Mama's nose shot skyward. "Of course not. What would people think? You were raised to be respectable, to take your proper place in society as a wife and mother!"

Eleanor shut her eyes. "But I'm a doctor, Mama."

"Then you intend to defy your father?"

"Apparently she already has."

Eleanor turned to find her father standing in the doorway, still wearing his coat. He set his medical bag on the chest beside the door.

His eyes remained on Eleanor even though her mother hurried across the room to take his hat and coat.

"I took an earlier train back. I met Francis Ross at the station when I arrived. He told me that you spoke with her ladyship today. He was at the station making arrangements for your trip tomorrow." He raised his brows expectantly, his expression bland and haughty. It was the look he used for difficult patients—or his impossible daughter. She hated that look. It tied her tongue for a moment, but he offered no further comment and simply stood stiffly in the doorway and waited for Eleanor to explain herself.

Eleanor felt eight years old again. "I-I didn't know myself until an hour or so ago. The countess asked me just this morning."

"John, tell her she cannot go to France. Forbid it! She won't listen to me or see reason," her mother said.

The doctor glanced at his wife. "It's gone beyond that. Saying no at this point would make us look petty and rather foolish. Was that your intention, Eleanor, to leave me no choice in the matter?"

"No choice? What do you mean?" Mama warbled in horror.

"This is *my* choice, Papa," Eleanor said, but he ignored her.

"We cannot refuse to aid the earl's son, a war hero, a neighbor, when her ladyship has asked personally."

Her mother blinked back agitated tears. "Then perhaps we could leave the matter to Peter—he surely won't allow his wife-to-be to go off on such a dangerous, foolish journey!"

"It is my understanding that Peter has not even spoken to Eleanor yet. Am I wrong, Eleanor? Has he proposed to you?"

She shook her head.

Her mother made a small sound of breathless horror. "But he will!" Her shaking hand crept to her flushed cheek, and her chest heaved. "Oh, this is a *disaster.*"

Eleanor caught her mother's hand. "Come and sit down, Mama. Do you need the smelling salts, a bit of brandy?"

Grace pulled away, slumped into the chair, and twisted her hands together in anxious knots. "What are we to do? What are we to do?"

"Eleanor has made her own decision. There is nothing to do," her father said impatiently.

She searched his face for a morsel of understanding, or love. No. Not there. There was nothing there but icy resolve. She forced a smile, trying to move past the terrible tension. "I'll bring Louis back safely."

"War is not a game, Eleanor."

She stared at him, her mouth dry, needing more, wanting his blessing, even now. She held her father's gaze, pleaded silently.

"You'd better go and pack," he said, turning away.

"Wait—what about Peter?" Mama asked, her tone hopeful with a new idea. "Perhaps the countess could be convinced to send Peter instead."

"No!" The word escaped before Eleanor could stop it.

Papa frowned. "He's on duty, Grace, overseeing the medical care of the convalescents. He's needed here, and his work is important."

Mama's face crumpled. "This is mortifying! How will I hold my head up in the village?"

"Go upstairs and rest," Papa said impatiently.

Her mother stiffened at her husband's crisp command, but obeyed at once, her knitting forgotten.

Her father picked up the paper pattern she'd dropped. "'Men's mittens, size eight, half thumb,'" he read aloud. "I trust everything was quiet here today?" he asked without looking at Eleanor.

"Arthur Nevins cut his leg. I saw him on the way to Chesscroft. He was in a bad way, and—"

"I'll check on him tomorrow," he cut in, not asking for details.

"I was concerned about the bleeding, and infection. The laceration was deep and dirty, and there was significant blood loss and shock." Still her father didn't reply. "Charlie's been called up. He's worried Arthur may have trouble seeing to things on the farm, and—"

Her father set the knitting pattern down on the table. He walked past her and went down the hall to the surgery and closed the door behind him.

For a moment she stayed where she was, staring after him.

She knocked on the door of the surgery.

"Yes?"

He was seated at his desk, looking at the list he'd left her, the chores that remained undone. "You raised us to love medicine. You showed Edward and me how the body works, how it fails, and how a doctor can restore it again. You told us stories of interesting cases, taught us the science and mystery and magic of all of it. How could I want to be anything else, anything less than a doctor? Why did you allow me to go to medical school if you didn't want me to practice?"

He set the list down and clasped his hands before him. He looked at her coldly. "It was never about you, Eleanor. I expected Edward would be the one to go to medical school, not you. My son, not my daughter. You were raised with an appreciation of a doctor's job because I expected you to *marry* a doctor, to support *his* ambitions."

She shut her eyes, gripped the back of the chair. "Then why did you let me go to medical school?"

"I allowed you to write the admission exam for your brother's sake, to spur him to do better, work harder, and not let himself be outdone by a girl." He lowered his eyes to the list. "When he fai—*did not pass*—I thought to teach Edward another lesson by letting you go in his place. I expected his pride would force him to sit the exam again, do better. I doubted you'd last a month at university. I *expected* you'd fail, come home in tears, and give up the foolish notion of practicing medicine. When you did not, I let you continue, to see just how far you'd go before you failed. It was meant to be a lesson in humility, to teach you your place."

She'd simply been the means to an end, a tool to shame Edward. It appeared to be her function in life as far as her father was concerned, her only use. But Edward had balked, while she had taken the bit in her teeth. She gritted them now.

"But I didn't fail. I am a doctor. It's too late to tell me no, to expect me to be less than I am. Aren't you at least a little bit proud of me?"

He frowned at her, and she recognized the familiar signs of his annoyance. "You could still fail, Eleanor. You made it through medical school. I was—surprised—and yet I thought, quite correctly, I believe, that such an education would make you suitable for life as a doctor's *wife*, a helpmeet." He shook his head. "I have never wished or expected you to practice as a doctor in your own right. In my opinion no woman is fit for that. I am still hopeful that you'll see sense. It's not a life for a woman." She held his gaze. She knew there were tears glittering in her eyes, but she refused to let them fall. It was too late for that, too. He looked away first, turning his attention back to the list, dismissing her. "You'd better go and pack."

"Will you forgive me if I go? Will Mama?"

He picked up his pen. "Close the door on your way out."

CHAPTER SIX

W hat did one wear to a war zone?

Edward sent pictures of debutantes and duchesses visiting HQ in stylish dresses and pearls. The women who worked as clerks and messengers or ambulance drivers wore prim military-style uniforms, and nurses and members of the Voluntary Aid Detachment wore saintly, nunlike attire.

But Eleanor was none of those. She was a civilian and a doctor.

She chose sober, professional, dark-colored clothing that would not show mud or blood. She packed warm woolen stockings, sensible boots, and the heavy, porridge-colored cardigan she had worn on damp, chilly student days in Edinburgh. When she was done, virtually everything in her case was black, navy, or gray.

She opened the writing desk, looking for the leather folder she used for stationery, pens, and pencils. She'd need to keep records of

Louis's condition, which she would turn over to the doctor his mother chose for him here in England—his lordship's Harley Street man, most likely, the very best. She fully intended to impress him.

She looked at the stack of correspondence that filled one of the cubbies of her desk. There were several letters from a medical school friend, a woman who'd left the bullying and challenges of their university classes to marry a doctor. They lived in London now. "You can hear the guns all the way from France," she'd written to Eleanor. "When there's a barrage, the sound wakes me in the night, like distant thunder, but deadly and unending. I think of the men facing the bombardment and how terrible it must be there, for it is bad enough seeing the conditions of the poor wretches who've returned to England. They cannot even bear to be looked at. Even if I'd become a doctor, I would not be allowed to do anything for them. At least as a volunteer I can offer them tea, a welcome home, small comforts." But Eleanor was a doctor. She'd braved the bullying and the hardships and made it through. This was her chance to do more than offer tea and a smile. This was her chance to ease pain, to heal, to help. Even if it was just Louis, just one man.

The other mail in the cubby was mostly postcards and letters from Edward, addressed to her mother, read and passed on to her, though they contained no message for her. She opened one envelope and took out a photograph of her brother looking smart in his uniform, standing next to Field Marshal Sir Douglas Haig. She studied Edward's smiling face. Was he in danger? She'd know, wouldn't she, since they were twins? But they'd never been particularly close. They'd been too competitive. Edward had been the apple of her mother's eye and her father's legacy for the future. Eleanor was simply a girl, an extra child, and of little importance beyond her ability to goad Edward to do better, to work harder so she would not outdo him. And oh, how hard she'd tried to claim just a scrap of her parents' love and admiration! In the end, he'd grown bored of their expectations, their fierce pride, and he'd scarpered, taken up with Louis Chastaine, joined a social circle where his parents—and Eleanor—could not follow.

They hadn't really spoken since the day they'd traveled together to write the medical school exam at Edinburgh, their father's alma mater, and one of the oldest and best medical schools in Britain. Edward ignored the prestige of it. He'd gone with bad grace, frowning, getting on the train and slumping in his seat, ignoring Eleanor entirely. He wanted it over with, had plans with Louis that evening—if he made it back in time. Sitting the entrance exam was everything to Eleanor, but to Edward it was an interruption of his gay and carefree life. She couldn't understand how he could feel that way—he'd been raised for this day, with the expectation that he would write the exam, study hard, graduate, and join his father's practice. She noted the sharp-edged resentment in the set of his jaw as he stared out the window of the train.

He'd glanced at the textbook in her lap with disdain. "Don't you think you've studied enough?" he asked. She'd looked up at him, saw the anger behind his insouciant air. It made her angry as well. She'd worked hard for months—years—with far less encouragement or assistance than he had received. She'd studied while he went to dances and parties with Louis, flirted with girls, and came home drunk. Her father had hired a tutor, bought textbooks, insisted his son study. She'd had none of those advantages. And yet now, he mocked her. "And you could have studied harder. Do you want to fail?" She'd braced herself for one of his jibes, something about being unfeminine or a bookish bluestocking, or a foolish girl who secretly wished she'd been born a man, but he simply regarded her, his gaze flicking over the book in her lap. He looked up at her, studied her face for a long moment, and she held his gaze and waited for it. Instead, he reached toward her. She flinched, but he merely tucked back a wisp of hair that had fallen from her prim coiffure. She pulled away, raised her chin, and scowled at him, still sure the unexpected kindness would turn into something unpleasant. Instead, he'd tilted his head and smiled at her, giving her the dazzling white, charming, devilish grin that he'd learned from Louis. She blinked at him. "Buck up, old thing. You'll do fine."

"And you?" she asked him.

His gaze slid toward the window, the smile fading to a smirk. "Oh, I daresay I'll be fine as well." He held out his hand, palm down. "See, steady as a rock."

She'd wished she could say the same. She'd wondered later, still wondered, if that unexpected moment with her brother had galvanized her in some way, stiffened her determination. She remembered how she'd envied his confidence that day, the easy way he'd strolled into the university building, whistling a bright little tune as if he hadn't a care in the world.

They'd walked into a room filled with men. Their eyes had turned hard or sharp or hostile as they looked at Eleanor, the only woman in the room. The haughty proctor had made her sit at the back of the room, where she wouldn't disturb "the serious students," and warned her not to faint. For the first time in her life she'd questioned if she could truly do this, if she had the strength and the courage to become a doctor. She knew she was smart enough. But she'd been nervous when the exam started, and the answers wouldn't come. She barely recalled her own name that day. By the end of the allotted time, she'd been so sure she'd failed. But Edward was waiting for her by the desk as the men handed in their completed exam booklets one by one, still jaunty and calm. He'd watched her come toward him, taken her elbow, and led her to the door. He'd been so damnably, hatefully jaunty on the trip home, while she blinked back tears of defeat and frustration. He'd handed her his handkerchief, patting her hand as he pressed it into her palm. "Don't fuss, Eleanor. People are looking," he'd murmured. He'd gotten off the train in York to meet Louis and left her to finish the journey alone. Her parents had been at the station, their smiles fading as she got off the train without Edward. They did not ask about the exam, and for once she was glad of their lack of interest in anything to do with her. Her stomach was churning, and she couldn't have answered even if they had chosen to inquire.

She'd waited for the results to arrive in the mail, dreading the day. At last her father called them into his study, and they stood before his desk, staring at the two envelopes that lay on the blotter before him. There was no question that he'd be the first to open them and read the results. Eleanor waited, her teeth gritted. Her father would grin, clap Edward on the back, and tell him how proud he was. Then he'd scan her letter, his expression bland, and hand it to her to read for herself that she'd failed. He'd turn to Edward and proudly invite his son to join him on his rounds to visit patients. But that's not how it went at all. Her father had opened her letter first. She saw surprise flick over his face. He set the letter down without comment and opened the other one. His face reddened as he scanned the words. He read them again, and his brow furrowed. The clock ticked in the silence. At last he set one letter down silently. He stood and held the other one out. She heard Edward sigh, saw him reach for it. "No," their father said crisply. He kept his eyes on Edward as he handed the letter to Eleanor. "Leave us," he told her sharply. "And shut the door behind you." She closed the door and held the single printed page up to her face. She took note of the university crest, the weight of the vellum paper in her hand. She read the words twice, sure she hadn't understood them correctly the first time. *Dear Miss E. Atherton, It is with pleasure that I hereby announce . . .*

For the first time in her life, she heard John Atherton yelling. At supper he announced to their mother that Eleanor had passed the entrance exam and Edward had not. Grace had been stunned, dismayed, had burst into tears. No one had spoken a word to Eleanor or offered congratulations. Edward had not even glanced at her. He'd concentrated on eating, had gone out as soon as the meal was over. A week later he announced he intended to go to Cambridge and study laws, not medicine. Mama had cried and taken to her bed as if it were a terrible tragedy. Her father had said nothing at all, had been silently, coldly furious. He allowed Eleanor to make arrangements to go to school over her mother's objections. Edward had packed his bags for Cambridge, planning on rooming with Louis. She drove him to the station, where she found Louis already waiting.

"Good luck at school, old girl" was all Edward said as he got out of the car, his eyes on the train and on the pretty young lass with Louis. Edward walked away without another word. Only Louis waved to her with a wink and a grin before he bent to kiss the girl goodbye.

A year later, the war began, Edward joined up with Louis and left for France, and she hadn't seen him since, except in the photographs he sent home. Mama had something to brag about to the knitting circle, crowing about the exalted company Lieutenant Atherton was keeping and how handsome he looked in uniform. Papa read Edward's letters and said nothing at all, but a framed portrait of Edward, standing next to Field Marshal Haig and the Prince of Wales, appeared in his surgery one day.

Her brother had scrawled a postcard to her for her graduation. *Congratulations. Best, E.* was all it said.

She stared at the postcard in her hand, now months old, and wondered how it would go if she saw Edward in France. Would he be glad to see her? Louis was more a sibling to Edward than she was. Her brother felt shamed by his own family, and he believed his friendship with Louis made him part of the class he should have been born into. He'd told her that once, when he was drunk and dismal—that he detested their parents, their foolish middle-class pride, their poky Yorkshire village life. "They think they're so important, better than everyone else in the bloody village, the good doctor and his wife. They lord over everyone, so smug and superior. They're small people, same as the farmers and shopkeepers and the rest of the people they serve. Money is what makes the difference. Money, education, and connections—connections most of all. That's how men rise out of the mud of a place like Thorndale. Papa will always have the mud of this place under his fingernails, no matter how hard he scrubs them and pretends he's different."

"Connections like Louis?" Eleanor asked.

"Yes, to start with." He'd puffed out his chest. "I'm accepted at Chesscroft."

"You're still an Atherton."

He'd narrowed his eyes. "For now, until I can make my name count, and I will—just watch me."

That conversation had happened a few days before the earl had given a weekend party for his sons' highborn friends and Edward had been pointedly left off the guest list, though Louis had tried to include him. For the first time Edward had truly understood that the difference between the Athertons and the Chastaines had less to do with fortune and everything to do with blood and breeding. Edward was as humble as the rest of his family, it seemed. A few weeks later the twins had gone to Edinburgh to write their entrance exams, and the world had changed, turned upside down, gone to war. Edward was a soldier, and she was a doctor.

A doctor on her way to France.

Eleanor stared at herself in the mirror. Her skin was so winter pale it was almost white against the freshly washed russet leaves of her hair, which hung long and loose over her shoulders, making her look innocent and young, a novice about to take holy orders, a girl about to take her first steps into independent womanhood.

She clenched her fist, pressed it against the ache and burn that lay under the armor of her ribs, armor that had protected her tender heart against all the blows of insult and rejection. Her heart was filled not just with blood but also with potential, pride, and determination. It was her destiny to be a doctor. She was Joan of Arc, she was Marie Curie, she was Aspasia, and she finally had the opportunity she'd longed for, and she would not fail now. It was her destiny.

But destiny offered no guarantees of success. There was the possibility that she might be killed. It was war, and men died every day. The enemy, the bombs and bullets and bayonets, would not make exceptions for a woman.

She thought of the photographs she'd seen of the front, of wounded men, crosses and corpses, heartbreaking devastation. But there were other pictures, too, of living men, hollow-eyed and battle-weary, yet still with dignity and pride in their eyes. They'd been bloodied, but remained determined.

"I will bring him home," she whispered to her reflection. Home to the bosom of his family, the next heir, the hero. Then she'd establish a practice of her own with the countess's grateful support. She'd impress her father at long last and show her mother that a woman could be smart, successful, and admired. She'd marry if and when she chose, have her pick of husbands, and break the hearts of the countless suitors she did not take.

She laughed and gave a theatrical toss of her head, her hair swinging around her like a red cloak, waist-length and glossy in the lamplight. It was her best feature, her vanity, and her beauty. She picked up her brush, counted the long strokes, plying the boar's hair bristles until the silken locks crackled, then she braided it into a thick, gleaming rope, a red line the world dared not cross without her permission.

She added a set of tortoiseshell hair combs to her luggage, and bright pink ribbons that glowed like venal sin among the sober garments.

Then she closed the lid, buckled the straps, and carried the case across the room, her feet bare, her nightgown swirling against her legs with every stride, and set it by the door.

"I'm ready," she said to the room where she'd slept since childhood, her nursery, sickroom, schoolroom, and haven. She'd left it to attend university, and she had found the room smaller than she remembered when she returned, like an outgrown shoe.

She wondered if it would feel smaller still when she came home from war.

CHAPTER SEVEN

The next morning, Eleanor set her tidy and sensible brown leather case by the door and went into the sitting room. Her mother was perched on a straight-backed chair by the window with her knitting needles idle in her lap.

"Is Papa in the surgery?" Eleanor asked.

"He's out. He had patients to see." Her mother added nothing to the bare-bones statement, no personal message, no farewell from her father. "It looks like rain. Have you packed an umbrella?" She ran her eyes over her daughter. "That hat, Eleanor, really."

Eleanor touched the brim of the simple woolen cloche. "It's practical."

Grace Atherton sighed. "I suppose that's what matters." She looked at the skein of dark gray wool in her hands, a color that very nearly matched Eleanor's hat, and sighed. "No one wears color anymore. Women dress for practicality or mourning. Hopefully it will be over soon and things will return to normal—yet how long have we been saying that now? I've spent three terrible years worrying about your brother, and now you . . ." She turned away. "It's not safe, not a place for a decent woman. People will question your upbringing and blame me, though it's not my fault. And if you're injured—" She paused. "Men are pitied when they come home maimed, scarred, missing limbs, their wits gone. For a woman, it would be better if you didn't come home at all."

Eleanor's mouth dried. "Mama," she said softly, but her mother's face had turned to stone.

"That's why your father went out. He can't bear to see you doing something so foolish. It isn't too late. You can still change your mind, stay, marry Peter." But Eleanor kept her face impassive, and Grace Atherton fell silent.

The rumble of a motor sounded, and her mother twitched the curtain aside and peered out the window. "It's her ladyship's car. Her secretary is getting out."

Eleanor crossed to kiss her mother's stiff cheek. "Tell Papa good-bye for me."

Her mother caught her wrist. "What about Peter? Have you no message for him?"

Eleanor hesitated a moment, then shook her head. That would surely be message enough. Her mother's grip tightened slightly. "Elea-nor," she whispered, filling the word with loss. "How I wish things could have been different. Now it's too late."

It was unexpected, this show of maternal emotion. All her life Eleanor had looked for it, hoped for it, and now there was no time left. "I'll be home in a fortnight, Mama," she promised. And then what would happen? Her mother would not be any happier with her if—when—she became a doctor with the countess's support. Nothing would change. She'd still be a disappointment in her mother's eyes.

Her mother knew it, too—her hands went slack on Eleanor's sleeve and dropped away, falling back to her lap like two dead doves.

There was no more to say, and no time. There was a knock at the door, and Eleanor went to open it. Francis Ross stood in the doorway, impeccably dressed. He touched the brim of his hat without smiling. He indicated her case to the chauffeur behind him with the point of a gloved finger, and the driver nodded to her as he stepped forward to take her luggage, turning smartly to carry it to the shining automobile at the end of the walk. "Shall we?" Mr. Ross swept a hand toward the car, and Eleanor nodded and drew on her black kid gloves. She preceded the secretary to the car and waited while the chauffeur opened the door for her. Eleanor got in and settled herself on the leather seat, and the secretary rounded the car and got in next to her.

She looked up at the house. Her mother stood at the window. Eleanor waved, but the curtain fell shut.

They drove the short distance to the station in formal silence. The chauffeur handed her out. "Thank ye, miss," he said briefly, glancing at Francis Ross to make sure he wasn't observing. He gave her a smile. "We're all fretting about the young viscount, especially now, after Lord Cyril's death. Bring 'im back safe, eh?" When Ross got out of the car, the chauffeur stiffened to attention, his face falling back into placid lines.

"Are you ready, Dr. Atherton?" Francis Ross asked. He escorted her to the platform. She watched people taking their leave of loved ones before they boarded. Other than the stiff secretary, there was no one here to see her off.

He handed her a leather folder. "These are the necessary letters and warrants from her ladyship, and your itinerary through to Calais. From there, you'll take the train to Arras, and ask for further directions at the station there. Viscount Somerton is at the number forty-six Casualty Clearing Station at Sainte-Croix. I believe he still uses the family name, rather than his title, and is listed there as Lieutenant Chastaine."

She took the folder. "I see. Thank you."

He tipped his hat again. "Have a good journey, Miss Atherton," he said, and left her. She boarded the train, found the right compartment, and took her seat, her heart thumping in her breast, her hands clasped tight together on her lap. The whistle blew and the train lurched forward, leaving the platform and the little crowd of well-wishers behind, nosing along the track, gliding into the open countryside in a cloud of noise and black smoke.

As the train pulled away from Thorndale, she saw her father's car parked on the road. He stood beside the dented bumper, watching the train depart.

Eleanor put her gloved palm against the glass and wondered if he'd see it.

If he did, he gave no sign.

CHAPTER EIGHT

CALAIS

A dozen times, she read the itinerary her ladyship's secretary had prepared. Thorndale to Leeds, Leeds to London, London to Folkestone, Folkestone to Calais, then on to Arras, where she'd have to inquire about transportation to take her the last few miles of the journey to the Casualty Clearing Station at Sainte-Croix. The whole trip would take three days, possibly longer if there were delays crossing the Channel—or on the rail lines in France, with troops moving up, or ammunition trains rushing more bombs and bullets to the front, or wounded being carried back to hospitals in the rear. Even in England there was danger, the chance of a surprise enemy attack or a zeppelin raid. German U-boats lurked in the Channel, waiting to pick off British ships as they butted back and forth across the narrow waterway.

There was always the chance she might not reach France at all, that she could become one more casualty of the endless war.

She scanned the Yorkshire countryside as the train rushed south, memorizing it just in case. The familiar landscape of hilly fields bordered by ancient stone walls and filled with flocks of winter-weary sheep gave way to gray cities that huddled under shrouds of smoke as factories chuffed and coughed under the endless strain of making materials for the war. Boxes and crates marked MUNITIONS stood in towering stacks at the stations, ready for shipment to the front lines. So many bombs and bullets. There was no need to ponder the harm they could do to human flesh—the evidence was all around her. At every station new-minted recruits stepped aside to make way for columns of hollow-eyed soldiers hobbling on crutches, or pushed by VADs in wheeled chairs, or carried off the trains on stretchers, bandaged and broken. Mothers shuddered and pulled their children away.

Eleanor looked at the recruits and thought of Charlie Nevins. Like him, they seemed far too young to be going to war. They were pink-cheeked and fresh scrubbed, their eyes soft and wide, their new uniforms clean and stiff over thin shoulders squared under the weight of patriotism, pride, and expectation. Entire families stood in their own little battalions around "our boy," holding him, touching him, protecting him for as long as they could. Mothers sobbed as the trains pulled in and the lads boarded.

The ones who'd already been to war watched the tender farewells, gray-skinned and grim, their eyes hard as flint. Their uniforms were worked in, the khaki wool rough and rumpled, the cuffs frayed. They carried themselves with terrible weariness or a fierce facade of prickly pride that made them look as if they'd be blown apart now by a kind smile or a mother's kiss. They stared at the green lads from behind cigarettes gripped tight between grimy fingers and looked away when the women cried. Eleanor shivered at the sight of them.

Surely being in France, seeing wounded men, battlefields, a hospital so close to the front lines, would change her as well, harden her or break her. She wouldn't know until she got there, stood in the places where the hollow men had been, saw what they'd seen. A frisson of nausea made her swallow.

Handkerchiefs fluttered as the train departed again, white against black smoke, khaki uniforms, and the gray sky.

Did hope have a color? Did love, or joy? Those things seemed in short supply, like rationed butter. So were courtesy and manners. At every slight, every late train or jostled woman on a crowded platform, the cry was always the same, a chant, an excuse, or a blessing. "There's a war on!" The precise meaning was determined by the tone, whether it was yelled in anger or frustration, whispered in sorrow, or sung with hubris or as a dark jest. The phrase had taken the place of *Please* or *Thank you* or *Excuse me*.

On the train, as their mothers disappeared in the distance, the young soldiers' smiles turned manly and knowing and their faces hardened. They squinted, took the measure of the lads around them as they bummed cigarettes or matches to light them, and coughed at the first drag. They slouched in their seats, feigned sleep, and pretended they weren't afraid.

It was late afternoon when Eleanor's train arrived at Folkestone, her last stop in England. Bellowing sergeants rounded up their men, restless and stiff after hours on the train, and marched them away to wait for the boats. Civilian passengers bound for France were hustled into a crowded waiting room that smelled of sweat, tobacco, and fish pies.

And then they waited.

Ships traveled across the Channel at night to avoid German U-boats. Eleanor read the posters while she sat for interminable hours, memorizing the instructions in case there was a need to abandon ship. Many ships had already been torpedoed.

She must have drowsed. A porter shook her awake. It was dark, and the ship was waiting.

Eleanor had never sailed before—she'd never done any of the things she was doing lately. She stared out at the dark waters, along with the watchers with their heavy binoculars looking for signs of enemy submarines in the black water, and wondered if this would be her last voyage as well as her first. She stood with the soldiers who crowded the rails, looking back at the twilit coast of England as it retreated into the mist. She wondered how many of these eager young men would come home again, and how many were crossing the sea forever. They traveled in a slow zigzag pattern toward the dark coast of France.

She was almost limp with relief when they reached Calais and the boat eased its way into port, sidling carefully past hospital ships lit with the red and green lights to identify them as medical vessels. They'd sail as soon as they were full, taking the wounded home to England, perhaps for good, their war over—if the U-boats allowed them to slip past.

It took an hour for the soldiers to disembark, form ranks, and march away. When Eleanor left the boat with the other civilians it was long past dark.

In French, Eleanor asked a harried female porter for directions to the train station. "There are no taxis. You must walk." The porter offered directions in rapid French, and Eleanor followed her points and hand gestures and left the station, hauling her case and her medical bag with one hand, holding on to her hat with the other. The streets were busy, even in the dark. Perhaps especially in the dark. The blackout was nearly total, and with so little light to see by, the men were bolder here. They called out to her as she rushed past, in French and in every conceivable English dialect, including the colonial accents of Canada, New Zealand, and Australia. It didn't matter what she looked like, just that her silhouette was female.

Her cheeks heated at the crude suggestions they made. Her stomach rumbled for something to eat, but she didn't dare stop. She reached the train station and tumbled up to a ticket booth. "Arras?" she asked, all but breathless.

The ticket seller regarded her without interest. "*Là-bas*," he said blandly, pointing toward a crowded platform filled with soldiers.

"Is there—" She swallowed, remembering the soldier's rude calls on the street. "Is there a waiting room for ladies? A place for tea, or coffee?"

He regarded her over his cracked spectacles. "Zer eez a whar on," he said, as if it explained everything. "You will have to wait on ze platform."

"And the train? What time does it depart?"

He shrugged. "It must come in before it can go out. It has not arrived. Priority is given to trains transporting troops and supplies, then to hospital trains. Sometimes there is damage to the tracks, or other delays. *Zer eez a whar on*."

"As you've said," she replied, snappish with hunger and fatigue.

"Just so," he agreed dully. He turned away to shuffle papers, his black-clad back a clear dismissal.

Outside, the platform was blue-gray with cigarette smoke. Soldiers lounged on couches made by piling their packs together. Their rifles, new, clean, and gleaming, were standing upright in tidy triangles like bundles of mown hay.

Eleanor looked down the tracks for the train, but beyond the station there was nothing save the dark and empty winter landscape. She found a spot by the pillar and sat primly on her suitcase, balancing her doctor's bag on her knees, and did her best to be as invisible as possible.

She listened as the recruits chattered and laughed. "I promised my da I'd kill a hundred Huns," one said. "My brother's only killed forty. He's with the 166th, the Liverpool Scottish. Been here since Third Ypres, last summer." He pronounced the name of the town as "Wipers."

"You should've signed up as a gunner," one of his mates suggested.

"Those blokes can kill a hundred men with just one shell. You'd be done in no time."

The original lad grinned. "Aye, but we're the brave ones, eh? Getting up close, looking 'em in the eye. We're trained killing machines. Bayonets, Mills bombs, machine guns, rifles—I'd use my bare hands if I had to. Won't take me long to do a hundred. I intend to go home covered with medals, carried on the shoulders of a dozen cheering sergeants, just so I can give them orders for a change."

"Got a girl at home?" someone asked.

"I got a sister," one of the lads said.

"Pretty?" another asked.

"Aye—she looks just like me."

There was a general groan of horror, followed by jokes about how the unfortunate lass would never find herself a sweetheart with a face like that. Several of the lads offered to write to her anyway with indecent proposals that made Eleanor blush. Even the poor lass's brother was laughing. Did Edward joke about her that way with friends—or worse, with Louis? Though they were twins, she looked nothing like her brother—he was fair-haired, and his charming grin and handsome face broke hearts. His eyes were so blue they made women sigh. Hers were plain hazel—*A color that puts one in mind of a swamp*, he'd teased her once. He told her she was too serious, her smile too infrequent. She had no experience with romance, no idea how to flirt or play the coquette to attract male interest. Edward had assured her that it didn't matter a whit, since she was not the kind of girl any man would find appealing, even in the dark, even if he was *desperate*. He predicted she'd end up an old maid.

She'd heard the same from her male classmates, about how being clever never kept any woman warm at night. The one who'd come up with that witticism was far less clever than she was, but still the quip had stung her feminine heart, stuck there like a dart. If she wasn't pretty or womanly, or appealing, didn't it make sense to try even harder to prove her worth as a doctor?

She wondered why on earth Peter Ellersby had wanted to marry her.

Her ears pricked as the young soldiers quieted and their comments dropped to whispers, their laughter to rough sniggers. When she glanced at them, she found them grinning at her, their eyes roaming over her prim suit and dull hat.

"Skooz-eh me, mam'zelle—parlay voo?" one called out, and the others laughed. Hot blood rose in her cheeks. She held her tongue between her teeth, turned her eyes forward, and stared at the far wall.

"She doesn't understand. You need proper French lessons," one of the others suggested. "And I don't mean talking. My brother says that's the thing to ask for. You say, 'Do you teach French, mam'zelle?' and for a few francs, she'll take you upstairs and—"

A train whistle screeched like an incensed maiden aunt, and Eleanor shot to her feet. The soldiers rose as well as a train chuffed into the station at last. She saw the red cross painted on the front.

"Wounded!" a sergeant called. "Get back, lads, and give 'em room."

CHAPTER NINE

The recruits were silent as the train arrived, their grins gone, their eyes wide.

Eleanor held her breath as the doors opened. The terrible smell of blood and wounds and sweat overwhelmed the fog of cigarette smoke and hot metal.

There was another smell as well, one Eleanor didn't know. "Gas," the sergeant in charge of the recruits said, glancing at her. "Poor blighters. It sticks to their clothes. You'd best keep back, miss. Cover your nose with your hankie, turn away, and don't look."

But she did look. The walking wounded got off the train first, helping one another, or assisted by orderlies and nurses. The recruits stared.

Then came the stretcher cases, carried off the train with as much care as possible. She saw men swathed in bandages that covered their faces or the stumps of missing limbs or wrapped their battered bodies.

Their eyes were dull and dead as they looked dispassionately at the new men, took in the clean, whole bodies, the bright collar badges, the cigarettes, the shiny new boots.

The orderlies laid the stretchers down in rows along the platform and went back for more.

"Anyone got a fag?" one of the stretcher cases croaked to the recruits. The effort made him cough. Eleanor noted the bandages around his torso, arms, and neck. He had cuts and bruises on his face and head as well. Burns had singed his hair down to the scalp in places, and the skin shone raw and red.

One of the lads stepped toward him. "I do, mate," he said. He bent to put a cigarette between the patient's cracked lips and searched his pockets for a match.

The man on the ground was breathing shallowly, and Eleanor could hear the air rattling in his lungs.

"Don't!" Eleanor hurried forward. "He can't. He's got a chest wound." The soldiers frowned at her, and the wounded man regarded her with dull surprise, then fury.

"Not another bloody nursing sister who won't let a man smoke in peace," the patient rasped, glaring at her balefully. "Why aren't you in uniform, sister? New here?"

"I'm not a nurse. I'm a doctor," Eleanor said. She crouched down next to the stretcher, moved to check the dressing. It needed changing. She could smell the old blood. She looked for help, but everyone was busy. More stretchers poured off the train. The row reached almost to the end of the platform now.

She heard the mutters of surprise around her. "A doctor? Her?"

She reached to look under the bandage, but the patient pushed her away. "Get off! What the devil do you want with me? I only want a cigarette. The damned medical officers are bad enough without some bloody woman poking at me. No more pills or shots! I've had my fill. Let me die in peace!"

Eleanor's hands froze. She saw fear and fierce pride in the man's eyes.

"How'd it happen, mate?" one of the recruits asked, jostling Eleanor aside to light the cigarette anyway. The patient took a long drag and glared defiantly at Eleanor. She winced as he puffed blue smoke into the air and coughed. When he could speak, he turned his eyes to his audience, regarding each face.

"Ypres Salient. Whizbang came over the top. We were frying sausages for breakfast, me and three other chaps. They were almost ready, nice and golden brown, when—" He took another puff, then coughed, grimacing at the pain. Eleanor grimaced as well. "My mates were killed instantly," he said when he could speak again, his voice a harsh gasp. "The back of Stokes's head was gone. Partridge lost most of his face. Kelso . . . well, he simply vanished—except for one foot, still in his boot, left behind, right where he'd been sitting a minute before." He met their eyes boldly, his expression cold, distant. "Worst of all, the goddamned sausages were blown to kingdom come."

For a moment, there was silence. Eleanor swallowed, watching the sharp intake of skin and sinew in the wounded man's cheeks and neck as he struggled to draw air into his lungs. Every breath crackled and gurgled, was obvious agony.

"'S'truth! That's not funny, mate," someone muttered.

The patient looked at them all. "Isn't it? Three men dead, one only half-dead?" Still no one laughed, and the man shut his eyes. "You'll see. You'll understand soon enough. Half of you will be dead this time next week." He began to cough again, his face white with pain.

Eleanor moved in as the others drew back. She slipped an arm behind him and raised his head to ease his breathing. She took the cigarette and tossed it away. The cough racked his body, and he met her gaze. Fear replaced the coldness in his eyes as he fought for breath. He clutched her hand fiercely.

Someone tugged on her arm. "Here now, that will do. Let him be."

Eleanor ignored the gruff command. "He's choking. He needs a fresh dressing—"

"I just wanted a fag, in case it's my last." The patient gasped. "Just one last fag . . ."

The hand on her arm tightened, dug in, pulled her sharply away from the patient. "Ye shouldn't have given him a bloody cigarette, ye fool," said someone with a thick Scottish brogue. "He's a gas case. It'll kill him."

He meant *her*, thought she'd given the soldier the fag. She shook him off and turned. "I did no such thing. He's—" She met a pair of eyes as gray and cold and forbidding as the North Sea, and the rest of the rebuke died on her lips. The chill took her breath away, made her shiver, and she stared, her gaze locked with his, unable to look away.

"She says she's a doctor," someone told him, and she watched dark brows rise and disappear under his cap.

"A doctor?" His gaze roamed over her. She held her breath and waited. Waited for what? A scolding, laughter? He offered neither. He was silent. She read curiosity in his eyes, and deep exhaustion, and a guarded flatness that made her want to look inside him, to know what he'd seen, what he knew. Or perhaps she didn't. She sensed he was assessing her as well, reading her, dissecting her, gauging her reason for being here, her honesty. No one had ever looked at her that way, so deeply, as if knowing everything about her was the most important thing in the world. Her heart thumped against her ribs in surprise.

He looked away when the soldier began to cough. He turned his back to her and gave his attention to the patient. She studied his profile, still breathless, saw a well-shaped jaw, high cheekbones, long lashes. There were deep lines around his mouth, and his skin was gray with fatigue. He needed rest, and certainly a bath, but he moved with easy grace, his movements sure, even crouched on the platform in mud-caked boots that must have weighed a ton and a filthy, ragged greatcoat that enveloped and hid his body. She could see only that he was long limbed and tall. She noted the bony wrists and long fingers as he flicked the paper tag tied to the man's tunic and read it. "Private McKie."

"Aye, Sergeant," the man grated.

"A Scot?"

"Aye—from Clydebank."

"Near to Glasgow. Did ye work at the shipyard there?" Eleanor noted that as the sergeant was talking, his brogue grew as rich as warm whisky, the tone just as soothing, and as he spoke, he fixed the dressing, adding a fresh pad of clean gauze he'd gotten from—somewhere. She looked around, but he had no medical bag, no kit. McKie's eyes brightened, and his breathing grew a little easier. The big Scot kept on talking to his countryman, his hands moving, checking, adjusting. He prattled on in a Scots-English patois about ships, a particular pub on Sauchiehall Street, and a married cousin who lived in Paisley. Eleanor listened, familiar with the speech because of her time in Edinburgh. McKie listened, too, his face softening as the sound of a voice from home took him away from pain to happier thoughts for a moment.

It was like magic.

When a pair of uniformed orderlies with Red Cross armbands came to collect the stretcher, the sergeant glanced up at them and nodded before turning to McKie again.

"There now, laddie, all ready to go. Ye'll be in Scotland afore ye know it. Have a wee dram for me when ye get home, aye?"

"Aye," McKie sighed. "Goodbye, Sergeant."

The sergeant rose to his feet as the bearers lifted the stretcher. He towered over Eleanor, tall and broad shouldered. He looked at her again, as if he was surprised to see her still there. His eyes moved over her once more, top to toe. This time he regarded her with a purely male interest that heated her skin despite the cold.

Then he turned on his heel and marched down the platform without a word. She stared after him, breathless, feeling as if she'd been struck by lightning.

She saw a red cross brassard on the sleeve of his greatcoat, so dirty it was nearly invisible. Was he a doctor? In a few brief moments he'd offered comfort, care, and reassurance, here, surrounded by so much suffering and pain. It seemed miraculous. She realized her hand had tightened on the side of her skirt so she could pick it up, run after him, reach him before he disappeared, but others stepped between them, oblivious and busy, unaware of her or him.

She let the wool drop, smoothed her hand over it, and watched as he paused to take one end of another stretcher, helped carry another patient away, and disappeared through the doors at the end of the platform.

"Arras," a laconic voice called in French. "The train for Arras is next. Please board at once."

CHAPTER TEN

Eleanor stood back as the hospital train pulled away and another chuffed into the station behind it, and the noise and bustle renewed itself as the station filled with a rush of passengers, both military and civilian. Sergeants yelled orders, men called to one another, and bodies pressed toward the open doors of the carriages. Eleanor found a conductor and caught his sleeve. "*Pardon*, is this the right train? I need to get to Sainte-Croix, to the Casualty Clearing Station there."

"*Oui, mademoiselle*, the train goes to Arras. From there—" He shrugged and turned away. She filled in the blank for herself.

There is a war on . . .

A group of young women passed her, and she recognized the smart uniforms of the Voluntary Aid Detachment they proudly wore. One of them paused in her rush for the train, obviously having overheard Eleanor's exchange with the conductor. "You're not by chance going to 46/CCS, are you?" she asked. "Casualty Clearing Station forty-six?"

Eleanor looked at her with relief. "Yes, I—"

The young woman smiled, her eyes widening with delighted surprise. "I say, you're not Colonel Bellford's wife, are you? Have you come to surprise him? He's a canny one! Hasn't said a word to anyone about it, but he did mention to one of the docs that he has an anniversary coming up. I bet that's why you're here. Am I right?"

"No," Eleanor said, confused. "I'm not—I'm not married." The young woman was pretty, her hair neatly cut fashionably short and curled, the white cap and veil that was part of her uniform left off for the moment. She wore the plain blue VAD dress with a white collar and cuffs under a dark blue cape, but her garments were tailored, cut to fit her perfectly. She had the accent and forthright manners of the upper class, Louis's class. There were many examples of the determined sort of titled ladies who volunteered to do their bit at home or overseas, to use their spare time and money—or their family's money—to help the cause. Perhaps this woman was one of those, the daughter of an earl or the granddaughter of a duke.

Her haughty smile faded to bafflement, and she flicked an assessing glance over Eleanor's clothing. "Not Mrs. Bellford? You're not a new VAD or a nursing sister, are you? You shouldn't be out of uniform. It's not safe or proper. Matron Connolly is a stickler, and she'll skin you alive for traveling in civvies, even that terribly dull and respectable suit."

Her sensible, practical, professional suit. Eleanor suddenly felt dreadfully frumpy. "Actually, I'm a doctor. It's been hours since I had a chance to rest, or—"

"A *doctor*? You?" The VAD's friendly manner iced over, her pert nose shot skyward, and she glared at Eleanor down the narrow length of it. "I suppose you're one of those do-gooders who's come to show all the male medical officers how it's *supposed* to be done, are you?" She was shouting, and people were turning to stare.

"I— No, of course not. Please excuse me," Eleanor said. She tried to step back, but hit the wall of rushing bodies behind her. She glanced about for a dignified exit. She should be used to this by now, being scorned for being a doctor and a woman, but she'd been grateful for the VAD's friendly words, her offer of assistance, the momentary sense of comradeship. She reached into her pocket for her ticket as she moved toward the first-class carriage.

The young woman stepped in front of her. "No, you don't— You can't ride in here." Her tone grew plummier still, dripping with aristocratic disdain. "These carriages are for officers and female *military* personnel and volunteers only. *Civilians* must travel in third class—if there's room. If not, you'll have to take the next train, or the one after that. So busy today."

"But I have a ticket for first class!" Eleanor exclaimed.

"So? There's a war on!" the VAD said as she swished away. She nimbly climbed the steps into the first-class carriage, not an easy thing to do with her nose so high in the air. Other uniformed nurses and a few officers followed, passing Eleanor without a single glance, though some of them must have heard the exchange.

Eleanor gritted her teeth. She couldn't wait for another train. She wanted sleep, and food, and a bath. Louis was waiting for her, in pain, possibly even— No. She wouldn't think of that. She'd agreed to come here, to get him home. Turning back or failing were not options. She could do this, would see it through, would prove to her parents, and the countess, and even the haughty VAD, that she could do this.

She picked up her case and hurried along the length of the train before it left without her, looking for space. Every car was full. As the whistle blew again, she jumped into an open door in the last third-class carriage.

And wished she hadn't.

A sea of male faces stared back at her. Her stomach tensed as she realized she was the only woman, and the only civilian, in the carriage. Every seat was crowded with soldiers. She tightened her grip on her medical bag, and the conductor took charge of her suitcase and stowed it among the military packs. She began to walk along the length of the carriage, looking for an empty seat. Whispers and whistles followed her. Her knees trembled, and she closed her ears to lewd suggestions. "You can sit on my lap, mam'zelle" and "Nice cozy space here" or "Over 'ere—we'll keep you warm, luv."

Embarrassment heated her cheeks and anxiety closed her throat. She gripped the handle of her bag tighter. She forced herself to look at the soldiers, meet their eyes, let them see how unaffected she was, how brave.

How out of place.

It reminded her of the day she'd walked into the exam room in Edinburgh and met a hundred pairs of male eyes full of curiosity or affrontery, mockery, or surprise, or just plain male interest in an unfamiliar female who had arrived unexpectedly and was decidedly out of place.

"Here, miss," said a blond soldier, rising from his seat. His smile was kind and respectful, a Yorkshire kind of smile, open and honest. It made her pause before him. He grinned. "Come on, lads, shift over and make space," he said to his companions, and they moved at once, opened up a small square of space for her.

Eleanor slid onto the seat, her back stiff, her eyes fixed on the door at the far end of the carriage. The blond soldier slung his arm across the top of the seat behind her and slid closer until his thigh touched hers. "There, now. This is fine and dandy, ain't it?" His voice was different now, a slow drawl, a cad's tone. She pulled away, sent him a look of warning, narrowing her eyes and pinching her lips to prim censure, the way she looked at Edward when he teased her, but it simply made the soldier laugh. It never worked with Edward, either. In fact, it made him meaner, more determined to make her cry, or shout, or flee. She couldn't do any of those things here. Someone was looming over her shoulder, and another man leaned in from the opposite side, and she realized she was trapped. She fixed her gaze on the medical bag on her lap, her only barrier. She imagined opening it, reaching inside for a scalpel. She'd leap up onto the seat like a pirate, brandish it, and warn them all back. But she wasn't a pirate. She was a respectable woman, a dignified, fully trained doctor. She schooled her features to placid indifference and ignored them.

The man behind her laughed, so close that she could feel his warm breath on her ear, smell stale tobacco when he spoke. "They said war would be hard and lonely, that we'd not see a pretty face for the duration, lads. If they lied about that, what else did they lie about?" He made a kissing sound beside her ear, and Eleanor flinched, then righted herself, her chin still high. "Perhaps it won't be so bad after all," he said cheerily. The others laughed, their eyes bright, smiles wide.

"Cat got your tongue, love?" The blond soldier leaned nearer and put his hand under her chin, trying to pry open her mouth to look. She swatted his hand away. He only laughed. "Are you French? No English, is that it?"

The men around her crowed with delight. "Parlee-voo?" someone yelled at her. "Couchee?"

Eleanor thought of Private McKie, of all he'd seen, of the old man's gaze peering out of his young and battered face. *You'll see. You'll understand soon enough. Half of you will be dead this time next week.* She swallowed the tight edge of fear, considered that instead.

"I'm English," she said tightly.

The blond tilted his head and grinned, looking her over again. "English, eh? What's an Englishwoman doing here, then?"

"I've heard they send performers from the music halls to entertain the lads at the front. Are you famous, ducks? Do you know Gertie Gitana? I saw her at the Palace. Sing 'Nellie Dean' for us?" the man behind her said.

"No—" she began, but a hopeful cheer drowned her objection.

"Sing 'Tipperary,' or 'Lili Marlene,' or 'Take Me Back to Dear Old Blighty,'" they screamed at her. They crowded closer, took up all the air and every inch of space and pressed in on her. She smelled sweat and fried onions and wool as well as tobacco now.

"Wait, lads, maybe she's not a singer after all. What's in that black case of yours? Is it some kind of musical instrument?" the blond man asked. Now he reminded her of Edward at his worst, his teasing turned to torment, cruel-witted and determined to make her cry.

The soldier reached for her bag, and she held tight. "Don't—it's medical supplies!" She was beginning to feel breathless, claustrophobic, and overwhelmed instead of determined and brave.

The blond frowned. "Medical supplies? Are you a nurse, then?" His blue eyes narrowed. "How come you're not dressed like one?"

"I'm not—" she began, but someone caught a strand of her hair and wound it around his finger, tugging it playfully. She pulled away, and it hurt, but he held on to the errant lock. When she turned to frown at him, he grinned at her. "Will ye give me a sponge bath if I end up on your ward, Sister?"

She gave him a sharp glare. "I'm not a nurse. I'm a doctor!"

Stunned silence fell. Teasing smiles faded like sugar in the rain.

The man who held her hair yanked it. "You? A doctor? Are they sending bloody women to cut us open, to chop off our arms and legs? I've heard the stories—the cures are worse than the bloody wounds, and the damned doctors kill us faster than the bloody Huns." He slapped his forehead. "Let me guess—they're saving the real doctors for the bloody officers and sending us coldhearted, vicious spinsters." He pulled her hair again, hard this time, and she winced at the pain.

"I'm not—" she protested again, but the laughter had turned to snarls and growls and felt dangerous.

"If you want to practice your needlework, go home and stitch a sampler. You shouldn't be here, torturing good men!"

Grumbles of agreement filled the space. She heard whispered insults, barbaric suggestions about cutting *her* legs off. She was trapped, unable to move, couldn't get up. The blond soldier pushed his face close to hers, hard and cold and mean now, all the flirtatious teasing gone from his eyes. "Seems to me that you don't know your place."

He ran his eyes over her again, and his gaze fell on the black bag in her lap. "Let's see what you've got in here."

Eleanor held tight, but he tore the case out of her grip. She struggled to rise to her feet, to reach for her property, but someone gripped her shoulder, holding her back. "Return that at once, if you please," she ordered sharply. Showing fear or tears would only make the teasing worse. The male students at medical school had taught her that.

She looked at the fierce faces around her, smelled the sweat rising from male bodies, felt tobacco-scented breath on her cheeks. This was still just teasing, wasn't it? She looked around for a friendly face, but didn't find one. Hands gripped her shoulders, held her back as they tossed the bag from hand to hand, laughing at her, mocking her. *Sawbones, spinster, pill pusher . . .*

She was tired and hungry. She was overwhelmed, annoyed, and trying desperately not to be afraid. Anger bloomed in her breast, fierce and hot. With a curse—she'd learned that from Edward as well, or perhaps Louis—she gritted her teeth as she bunched her fist and swung at the man who held her.

She hit him square in the eye. He reeled back with a surprised cry. "Doctor? She's more a prizefighter!" he wailed, and the others laughed like jackals scenting prey.

Eleanor realized she'd made a grave mistake. The soldier's eye was swelling. Hitting him hadn't helped—it had made things worse. The faces around her changed, grew sharper and more dangerous, all pretense of harmless fun abandoned. Her hot anger turned to cold sweat. The rude comments and suggestions grew louder, more obscene. They touched her, plucked at her hair and her clothes, and kept on throwing her bag.

She spun, moved sideways, tried to find a safe spot to stand, but the pinches and pokes came from every direction. They were taller than she was, broader and stronger. Fear made her sweat, closed her throat with panic.

A hard pinch on her bottom made her gasp, and she bunched her fists again, lashed out at the grinning faces, but now they were smart enough to stay out of reach, fending off her blows, laughing at her.

She thought she'd grown immune to rude comments at medical school, had learned to stare down bullies who imagined a woman was easy prey. The crude, cruel jokes she'd endured from male students had hardened her and had made her realize that showing hurt feelings wouldn't stop them. It made the teasing worse. And Edward had teased her, had known what to say to hurt most. She'd learned to face them all, her expression flat and impassive, stare them down until they grew bored and went away. But these men weren't going to go away. There was nowhere to go. She wondered how long it would take to reach Arras. She straightened her spine, tilted her chin up.

"I want my property back," she said in clipped tones, looking around, fixing every man in view with a determined glare. "Now!" she insisted when no one moved to obey.

The blond soldier caught the bag. He gave her a slow, cheeky grin and held the bag above his head. She'd have to jump to reach it. "You'll have to pay a forfeit for it. I want a kiss for luck. In fact, you can give us all a kiss," he said, and a cheer went up. He puckered his lips, leaned closer. Hands shoved her forward, pinning her arms at her sides. She dug in her heels and turned her head away, but they only pushed harder. "Stop," Eleanor gasped, as frightened as she was angry now.

They called out obscene encouragement as the blond man's lips came relentlessly closer. She shut her eyes and struggled to free her arms, wondering if she could kick him without falling. If she fell to the floor, they'd never let her up, they'd—

She was in trouble.

CHAPTER ELEVEN

L et her go."

The three words cut through the boisterous laughter like a bayonet. The men around Eleanor froze and stared at someone standing behind her. The blond's pucker turned to a gape of surprise. The hands on her fell away, and the space around her opened and she could breathe again. The raucous soldiers stepped back and fell silent.

She turned to look at her rescuer. It was the grim-faced Scottish sergeant from the platform. He stood behind her, taller than most of the recruits, his eyes cold as he glared at them.

"You—" He pointed at the blond. "Give her back her bag. The rest of you go and find places to sit or stand at the other end of this carriage. Make it quick, or I'll have ye all on report." He sounded like a headmaster addressing unruly schoolboys.

The blond looked at his boots as he handed the bag back to her. "We were just having a bit of fun, Sergeant. No harm done."

Eleanor hugged her medical bag tight against her chest, her hands shaking, her heart pounding. She kept her eyes on the sergeant. His cap shaded the glittering ice of his eyes, making him even more menacing. His frown deepened.

"Fun? Is that what ye call it? Were ye raised without manners, Private? Is that how ye treat women wherever it is you're from?"

The blond blushed to the roots of his hair, his eyes downcast. "Manchester," he mumbled. He shifted, and looked up at the Scot. "It's just that—she says she's a *doctor.*"

The sergeant's expression didn't change. He hadn't even glanced at her yet, but suddenly she felt safe. She'd seen him care for the wounded soldier on the platform, watched him perform magic. "What of it? If a shell hits ye, ye'll be glad of a doctor, any doctor, to save ye. Now go on, go find a space at the other end of the carriage."

The man looked at the Red Cross brassard on the sergeant's sleeve, dirty and worn, tattered and stained with grime. His jaw dropped for a moment, then flapped, as if he intended to ask a question. "Go," the sergeant growled, cutting him off before he could speak, and the private turned and marched down the car to join his fellows.

Only then did Eleanor turn to him. "Thank you," she said, straightening herself, clutching her bag. She had to tip her head back to meet his eyes. He tipped his down to look at her, the brim of his cap casting his eyes into shadow. The corners of his mouth were flat and hard, his jaw tight with disapproval or anger. She felt her skin flush. She knew she was a mess, her hat askew, her clothing rumpled. He was staring. Was her face dirty? She resisted the urge to smooth a hand over her cheek to check. She probably couldn't have looked less like a doctor if she tried. But she was a doctor, even if the altercation had left her worse for wear, and she surely couldn't look as bad as he did. She lowered her gaze, letting it run over the length of his body. He had the powerful, long-legged build of a Highlander, the quiet, canny strength of one, sure of himself and proud. She'd learned to identify Highland men in Edinburgh by those characteristics alone, even before they spoke. He might not be wearing a kilt, but his origins were as distinctive as the rugged land that bred him, hard and spare and cold. But there was beauty in the harsh Highland landscape, a kind of magic, and this man certainly had all of that. He stood stiffly before her, silent now, his hands in his pockets, looking as if only his tattered greatcoat held his long limbs upright, like a carapace, or a splint. His eyes were sharp with disapproval still, but now it was all for her, not the recruits. It put her on her guard, and she raised her chin. "I could have managed."

His face softened slightly. One eyebrow rose into the shadow of his cap, and his lips rippled before he schooled them back into a stern line. "Aye, but it was the men I was worried about. What do ye weigh in at? Seven stone or so?" The flicker of amusement in his expression faded as quickly as it had come. "Sit down," he said, indicating an empty seat with a jerk of his head—there were quite a number of empty ones now, thanks to him. She slid across the wooden bench until she was pressed against the window. He folded his big body onto the seat opposite hers, angling his knees to form a barrier across the aisle, making a safe space for her. He cast one more scowl at the men who were watching him, chastened and solemn.

"Ye shouldn't be here," he said.

"There was no room in the other carriages."

He frowned again. "I meant in France. Ye shouldn't be in France, or on this train at all, heading toward the front."

"Because I'm a doctor?" she demanded. "I have a legitimate reason for being here."

He folded his arms. "Have ye, now? I ken you're a doctor. I heard ye say so on the platform, and to the lads here, but you're not wearing a uniform, and I doubt very much you've got a commission or permission to serve." He rubbed his face with his hand. "Husband or brother?"

"What?"

"I'm guessing you've come to visit someone. Someone wounded, no doubt. So is it your husband or your brother?"

She tightened her hands on the handle of her bag. "Neither. He's—" She pursed her lips. Louis wasn't a friend, either, really, not of hers, anyway. "He's in hospital at Sainte-Croix."

"Not a hospital—a Casualty Clearing Station. Number forty-six."

She felt hope rise. "Do you know it?"

He glanced out the window, though the landscape was invisible, dawn still an hour or two away. The sky was cloudy, more gray than black, even now. There would be no glorious sunrise, it seemed, just a lighter gradient of gray to mark the coming of the day. She could see his reflection and her own in the glass as he scanned the bare fields.

"Aye, I know it." He looked back at her. "They don't get a lot of visitors. The officer in charge doesn't encourage it. Do they know to expect ye?"

"Um, no." At least, the itinerary her ladyship's secretary had prepared made no mention of whether they knew she was coming or not.

"Then how will ye get there? It's four miles from the station at Arras. The chaplain usually comes if he knows to expect someone, but not otherwise."

"I expected there'd be a cab."

He looked at her as if she were a helpless kitten stuck up a tree. "A cab," he drawled. "No. There are no cabs. Not even a farmer's cart. There's a war on."

She gritted her teeth. "Yes, I know. I can walk if I have to. I'm used to that. Four miles isn't so far."

He glanced at her feet. "It's too far in those fancy wee boots, and too dangerous for a civilian. Ye need someone who's going that way to take ye."

She bit her lip. "And you—are you going that way?"

"As it happens, I am." He was silent for a moment.

"Then will ye—will *you* take me?" For an instant she had fallen into the familiar Scottish brogue, unintentionally mimicking him. His lips quirked as he noticed, and she wondered if it was that or the double meaning of *take me* that amused him. She cast about for something else to say, a way to change the subject, to hide her mistake. "Are you—" She looked him over, took in his ragged uniform again, his scuffed boots, the Red Cross brassard. "Are you a doctor?"

He grinned again, and this time it pleated the corners of his eyes and mouth for a second with genuine amusement. "Nay, I'm a stretcher bearer. We fetch and carry for the doctors. We go out into No Man's Land and find the wounded, administer first aid, and carry them back to the medical officers at the aid posts. From there, they end up at Casualty Clearing Stations like number forty-six."

He held out his hands. They were big and dark and long fingered, the knuckles and wrist bones raw and knobby. They were also blistered and scratched, covered with small scabs and scars. Dirt had been ground into the lines in his skin, like the hands of Yorkshire sheep farmers or of coal miners. "Ye can tell a bearer by his hands. The wooden handles of the stretcher leave blisters. Bullets split the wood, and the splinters go deep into your flesh, or the wet makes the wood crack and swell, and it pinches your skin." He pointed to a jagged scar along the outside of his thumb. "A soldier bit me once, mad with pain."

She looked at the injury, saw the teeth marks, and winced. "Where I come from the farmers use lanolin on their skin," she said.

"And where's that?"

"West Yorkshire." She saw no recognition in his eyes, unlike when he'd spoken to Private McKie at the station. "You were—kind—to Private McKie, the soldier at the station."

He looked out the window again. "Part of my training. Keep them calm, don't let them panic. Talk to them, soothe them. They rest easier that way, don't think about—" He stopped.

"What, death? Will he die?" Eleanor asked in horror.

He shrugged. "According to the tag on his tunic, he has shrapnel buried in his hip and thigh. There's splinters of bone from the soldier beside him in his jaw, and before the bearers got to him, there was a gas attack."

"Poor man."

He raised his brows. "Poor man? He's one of the lucky ones. That's a Blighty, the kind of wound that gets ye sent home and out of the fighting for good. There's a chance he'll survive, even with all that. I've seen men hurt worse who made it." He was silent for a moment. "If he does live, he'll remember the way it felt the very moment when that shell landed, the way everything looked and felt and smelled. He'll never forget, and he'll feel it all over again whenever it rains or snows, and in the middle of the night. His loved ones will cry over the scars, flinch at the sight of him, recoil at his touch. The only ones who'll understand will be men who've been here, those who can share the memories and their own wounds." He fell silent for a moment, his eyes on the invisible world beyond the window again. "Still, some men, many men, pray for such wounds. I can't tell ye how many times I've found a wounded lad on the field, and that's the first thing he'll ask me—'Is it a Blighty?' His leg might be gone, or his guts spilling from his belly, but that's what he'll ask."

"What do you say?" she asked.

He fixed his gaze on her. "I lie. I tell them they'll be home before they know it. I suppose that's true enough, in a way, if you're of a religious mind."

"Are you of a religious mind?"

He looked at her as if she were daft, his eyes widening—gray eyes, still cold as the sea, or some Scottish loch, perhaps. "Here? No. I was raised in the kirk, and to believe in God, o' course, and I suppose I'll go back to it on Sundays when I'm home again. *If* I make it home again."

Eleanor stared at him, her belly cleaving tight against her spine now. He sounded resigned, bone-weary.

She frowned, and he caught her look, held it. "Have I shocked ye? That's why ye shouldn't be here. You'll see things you'll never forget, things ye can't fix, doctor or no', and they'll give ye nightmares."

"You can't fix them, either, but you try."

"Aye."

"Why?"

He scanned her face. "Ye want to know why I'm a bearer?" She nodded, and he flashed a quick, humorless grin. Even that made him look younger, handsomer, quintessentially Scottish. Her heart pitched sideways in her chest a little. She waited for him to speak. He sat back and folded his arms over his chest.

"All right, then. For one thing, I'm six-foot-five, and strong enough to lift a heifer. They choose the biggest, brawniest men. Carrying a wounded man who's soaked to the skin with mud and water is hard work, and if they're unconscious, they weigh even more—deadweight. I was chosen for the job, plucked out of the infantry, trained to find wounded men on the battlefield, to stop bleeding, give morphine, bandage wounds under fire, and get them back to where a medical officer can do more."

She felt breathless looking at him, this big Scot with scarred hands and guarded eyes. Who, she wondered, when this war was over, would soothe him, fix *his* nightmares? He probably had a pretty Highland lass at home, a wee wife in a neat little cottage waiting for him, watching a long, dusty road that skirted high hills and deep lochs, hoping to catch sight of him marching home to her, mad with joy, her wee house, her arms, her bed, full of him again at last.

"What's wrong with him?" the sergeant asked, shaking her out of her reverie.

"Who?"

"The lad you're going to visit."

"Broken leg—his femur. He's a pilot."

He winced. "Those lads take daft chances. And what can you do for him?"

"I've come to take him home."

She saw his jaw tighten. "Lucky chap." He looked hollow for an instant, hopeless. She did what he'd done with McKie, and began to talk.

"I'm Eleanor Atherton."

He hesitated. "Fraser MacLeod," he said at last.

"And where are you from, Sergeant MacLeod?"

"I doubt ye'd know the place. Have ye been to Scotland?"

"I was at medical school in Edinburgh."

"I mean the Highlands."

She tilted her head. She had, but she wanted to see them through his eyes the way he'd made McKie see Glasgow. "Tell me about them."

He shut his eyes. "The air is so clear and cold ye can hear a blade of grass bend in the wind a mile away. It smells of heather and pine and peat, clean. There's no blood or rot or gun grease—unless of course there's a hunt. It's fine territory for game—grouse, red deer . . ." She watched the fine blue veins in his closed eyelids, the shift of his eyes beneath them as he scanned the scene in his mind. The furrow between his brows eased. Perhaps he'd sleep. It would do him good. He was haggard, and his skin was gray with the need for it.

"Where was your home? What's it called?" she asked.

"Glen Carraig, MacLeod territory. My kin have lived there for four hundred years."

Eleanor had no idea where the Athertons were four hundred years ago. "Do you come from a large family?"

"Five sisters and two brothers—both too young to fight in this war, thanks be."

"No wife?" she asked.

He opened his eyes, looked at her, his gaze sharp and curious, gauging her reason for asking. She felt her cheeks grow hot, and she quickly babbled on.

"I can't imagine growing up in such a large family," Eleanor said. "I have just one brother."

"Is he the pilot you're going to see?"

She realized that she'd been staring into his eyes, listening to every word, and she'd forgotten about Louis, and the war, and the whole rest of the world. "No. Edward—my brother—is stationed at general headquarters."

"Then the pilot is your sweetheart?" he asked, bolder than she was.

She blushed in earnest now. "No. He's a friend—well, he's a friend of my brother's, at least. A viscount."

"Ah, rich, titled, and brave as the devil. And lucky." He looked at his hands again. "If there aren't any delays, we'll be in Arras in few hours," he said. "We have priority on the tracks, since we're bringing up troops. They make hospital trains wait, but fresh soldiers and munitions are important." He said it bitterly.

"Do you work at . . ." She paused, uncertain of the correct words. "Are you posted to the Casualty Clearing Station?"

"I'm at the front, where I'm needed," he said with stiff pride.

"I see." She was suddenly tired. Perhaps it was the movement of the train, or the stress of the journey. She stifled a yawn.

"Ye can sleep if ye like. Ye should." He glanced down the train, where the recruits were sleeping or talking or playing cards. "Ye'll come to no harm. They're likely all good lads, but it's probably their first time away from home—" He shrugged. "No excuse, of course, but . . ." He stopped again, and she saw the hollows around his eyes deepen, and his jaw tightened. She realized that Sergeant MacLeod knew what those lads were going into, what would happen to some of them, or all of them. They were just boys, young men. She felt sorrow fill her chest. She drew in a sharp breath, sympathetic now, afraid for them. He straightened as he turned back to her, the shadow gone from his eyes, or at least hidden.

"You'll learn to take sleep where ye can get it if you're here for any length of time," he said. "And there might be a long wait when we get to Arras station before anyone can come for ye if they're busy at the CCS."

"Will they come?" she asked.

"Aye. There will be wounded to send on, men being sent back to general hospitals or home to England—and there's supplies on the train for them. They'll come to collect those."

"Wounded?" she asked, her hands tightening in her lap.

"There's a war on. There's always wounded," he said bitterly. "Now if ye don't mind, I intend to get some sleep while I can. Not to worry—after so long here in France I'm a light enough sleeper that I'll hear if there's anything amiss." He pulled his cap low over his eyes, crossed his arms over his chest, and was still.

Eleanor stared at the lower half of his face. He had a strong, stubborn chin, dimpled and glistening with dark stubble. His mouth was firm and kind, the lines around it deep furrows carved by exhaustion and hard work. His nose was large and well shaped, and his cheekbones—

"I canna sleep if you're staring at me," he said without opening his eyes, and she felt her breath catch.

"I wasn't staring!"

He raised his cap and lifted one eyebrow. "Aye, ye were. I don't mind. But if ye don't go to sleep yourself, I can't stare at *you*."

The gruff, unexpected flirtation sent warmth cascading through her. She looked away, out the window, unsure how to reply.

He leaned back again, and the train rumbled on. At the end of the carriage the men started singing "It's a Long Way to Tipperary," low pitched and slow, a lament instead of a celebration. Perhaps they were afraid after all. She glanced at Sergeant MacLeod again, but his head had lolled sideways and he slept.

She'd never sleep, couldn't, in such a strange place. She stared out the window instead, at Sergeant Fraser's reflection and her own, and wondered what time it was. It was somewhere in the middle of the night, with hours to go until dawn. It felt oddly intimate, sitting here with a sleeping stranger, a man who'd rescued her. Perhaps she'd keep watch on him.

But the motion of the train relaxed her, and her eyelids grew heavy, and she gave in and let her eyes drift shut at last.

CHAPTER TWELVE

Fraser stared down at the young woman sitting across from him. She was still fast asleep, snoring lightly, her hat askew, though the train had been in the station for ten minutes. She'd been oblivious to the clatter of the recruits disembarking. A long lock of hair snaked out from under her hat and across her shoulder, as red as the absent sunrise. She had a dash of freckles across her nose, and she looked too young to be a doctor, too soft.

"Miss Atherton. *Doctor.*" He said it again, but she didn't move.

She stirred when he touched her shoulder gently, carefully, so he wouldn't startle her. It was like reaching for a fledgling in a nest, rescuing it after the hunters had taken its mother, tucking it away in his coat for safety. That wee memory of home, that other life he tried so hard not to think about here, made his breath catch, and he pulled his hand back. He'd dreamed of the glen and the hills, the scrubbed sky so vividly blue it almost hurt to look at it. She'd done that—made him see things he'd pushed from his mind, things that were too painful to think of here, and brought only longing and regret. Not this time. He'd rested, and dreamed, and woken . . . happy. At least until he came back to the war, and to duty, death, and danger. But Eleanor Atherton, sweetly fast asleep across from him, made him hopeful, more sure than he had been that good things really did still exist in the world— like pretty lasses and innocence and the smell of heather on the wind.

She opened her eyes and peered up at him, as wide-eyed and innocent as a wee bird, too. For an instant she blinked, no doubt disoriented, wondering where she was. *Och*, her eyes were the same hazel-green as the hills above Glen Carraig. He'd all but forgotten the pleasure of that sight, but the old reaction to them, joy, excitement, delight, came back to him like a gut punch. Perhaps it was just that it had been months—years—since he'd last seen any woman other than a nursing sister or a VAD. He hadn't been tempted to stare at any of them the way he was staring at Eleanor Atherton now. Maybe it was the fact that she was a civilian, in civilian clothing. He glanced at her again. No—her dark blue suit was severe and could never be accused of inspiring admiration or lust. The white lace that edged her collar was pretty, though, like froth on the sea, and the slender white column of her neck rose out of it gracefully.

She blushed slightly when she realized where she was, and that was decidedly the prettiest thing he'd seen in a very long while. She was—or so a more sentimental man might say—a delicate English rose, the essence of womanhood, exactly what they were fighting for. He remembered how she'd fought the soldiers who'd threatened her. She'd blackened one man's eye. Hardly a delicate flower, then—more akin to a Scotswoman, a hardier breed than an English rose, in his opinion. She was also a doctor, which meant she was smart, capable, and strong-minded. He tried to picture her with a scalpel in her hand, bending over a septic belly wound. That would be the true measure of her, he thought—if she could do that and still be capable of blushing, still regard the world with those guileless eyes, then she'd truly be the kind of woman worth fighting this war for.

She went from soft and sleepy to full alert in an instant, her spine straightening, her shoulders unfurling, her eyes wide and clear.

"Sergeant MacLeod," she said. She remembered his name. The sound of it on her lips was gratifying, another brief moment of pleasure.

She preened, straightening her hat, shoving that loose tendril of hair under the felt brim. She stopped suddenly, her hand in midair, her head tilted, on alert. She flinched and turned to look at him, her eyes wide again. "Good heavens! What's that noise?"

It took him a moment to understand that she meant the artillery, the vibration in the earth, the hum in the air, the constant thump and boom. He'd been here for nearly two years, and he'd grown used to it. He automatically gauged the location of the guns, the level of fire, and how far away it might be. Rapid fire meant there'd be an advance somewhere along the line. Both sides liked to set up just before dawn and bombard the enemy trenches, softening them up for a raid at first light. There'd be wounded, first from the shelling, then from gas, then from hand-to-hand fighting . . . But this bombardment was halfhearted, slow, which meant that things were almost quiet for the moment—or as quiet as they got in war. The guns Eleanor Atherton heard were somewhere beyond Vimy Ridge, far away. It was safe enough here.

The familiar alertness left him, the instinct to listen for the faint cries of men in pain, for the whistle of incoming bombs and the menacing whiz and thock of bullets, and he relaxed.

"It's the artillery. There's naught to fear. It's miles away," he told her.

She looked out the window, scanning the winter landscape, the trees, the ground, the huddled buildings of Arras, all as dull graybrown as a sparrow's breast in the dawn light.

"Is it ours or theirs?"

"Both," he said. "We're at Arras now, closer to the front lines."

"Which way is it?"

He raised an eyebrow "To the east."

She blushed slightly. "Oh. Yes, of course it is. Is Sainte-Croix . . ."

"Southeast toward Bapaume, behind our lines," he said. *For now.*

He moved aside to let her rise. Standing, she barely reached his chin. He gestured toward the door and let her precede him. She moved with purposeful strides, clutching her black medical bag like a talisman against harm, her chin high. The confidence was feigned, he thought, noting the tension in her shoulders.

Outside, the recruits were already lined up on the platform, a seasoned sergeant and a tired-looking lieutenant on hand to meet them. The sergeant was bellowing orders—they were going to march to a rest camp, then they'd drill, and later they'd get orders and postings. Fraser scanned their faces. Some looked eager, some worried, and some were flat-faced with fear, trying not to let it show, keeping their eyes forward, but blinking every time the earth shuddered under the force of the distant guns. If they were afraid now, they'd be terrified by what was to come. He didn't envy them those first bitter days in an icy, stinking, mud-filled trench. For others, the ones with brothers or cousins in the ranks who wrote home, they'd understand at least a little of what to expect, know to keep their chins up and their heads down.

"Stick close to me like you was on your muvver's leading strings," the sergeant yelled. "Stay on the track, put your feet where I do. You're not in England now. Don't step out of line for anything. For'ad 'arch!" He set off at a brisk pace, and the lads followed, disappearing down the road into the gray mist of dawn.

Behind him, Eleanor Atherton walked across the wooden platform, toward the pile of bags, parcels, and crates being unloaded from the train, her boots a prim staccato compared to the rumble of the soldiers marching away down the road.

Fraser looked for the ambulance from 46/CCS, bringing wounded for evacuation and coming to collect mail and supplies, but the rutted track and sidings were empty. It could be hours before anyone came. He'd walk if he were alone, but there was Eleanor Atherton to consider. And the road was rough, and not safe. If the artillery lads decided to lob a shell or two this way, or there was an offensive, there'd be danger. He'd have a hysterical female on his hands. He had smelling salts in his greatcoat, among the other essentials he carried. He looked over to find her struggling to pull a black suitcase with an umbrella strapped to it out of the jumbled pile.

As if an umbrella would do her any good against the kinds of things that fell from the sky here. A laugh gathered in his chest, a rare feeling. He crossed and picked up the case for her. She turned and looked up at him, and again he felt the shock of those eyes, wide, soft-lashed, and feminine. His hand tightened on the wee handle of her bag.

"Ye can leave it here. It won't come to any harm. There's no sign of anyone coming yet, so we may as well go inside where it's warmer, make ourselves comfortable for the time being. We might have a long wait." She looked dubiously at the dark station, the windows blackened to hide the light from the enemy. It looked gloomy and deserted.

"What time is it?" she asked.

He looked at the sky. "Near to five o'clock, I think," he said. He took her arm, guiding her toward the door. He was used to the dark, could spot a twitching hand or a pale face in the pitch-blackness of a shell hole. Bearer teams often went out at night when there were wounded to bring in.

He opened the door of the black-curtained waiting room for her and followed her inside. A sleepy stationmaster regarded them from his ticket booth in the corner, where he huddled in the light of a shuttered lantern. "*Bonjour*," he said, barely glancing at Fraser before turning to the woman with him. His eyes roamed over her with interest, and Fraser stepped in front of her.

"Sit down," Fraser said to her. "Tea *pour la dame*?" he asked the stationmaster in his terrible Scots-accented French. He dug in his pocket and dropped a few sous on the counter. The Frenchman snatched up the coins and shuffled away to set a battered kettle on top of the wee stove in the back of his cubby. He peered into a pair of chipped cups and wiped them on his sleeve. Fraser hoped the lass wasn't picky. He glanced back at her.

She was perched on the very edge of the bench, doing her utmost to look brave and unfazed by the grubby little waiting room, but there was a bloodstain under the bench opposite hers, and she was staring at it. No doubt it was left behind by the last consignment of wounded to pass through. She was still flinching every time a distant gun fired, not used to that yet. She looked like she was holding herself together through sheer stubbornness, though she was no doubt tired, hungry, and bewildered.

He set the steaming cups of tea on the bench. "There'll be a hot meal at the CCS. Until then, we'll have to make do." She was pale as milk, and he reached for the flask in his coat. "Here," he said. She drew off her gloves, took the flask and sipped, then coughed.

"That's whisky!"

"What else would it be?"

She wiped a drop from her lower lip with her fingertip. "I was expecting water."

"Are ye teetotal, then?"

She blushed. "No. I mean, I don't imbibe heavily or often, but I'm not—" She stopped talking. "I like whisky." Her voice dropped to a whisper. "I actually prefer it to sherry."

Either the confession or the drink put a spot of color in her cheeks. "Is that a secret?" he asked.

She studied her hands. They were long and neat fingered, the nails cut short and square. "No, it's not a secret. It's—well, I learned to like whisky when I was at school in Scotland. My mother believes women—ladies—should only drink sherry, and then only—" She bit her lip and broke off. "Have you been to Edinburgh?"

"Aye," he said. "There's a wee pub near the university. It's got a lion over the door. Do ye know it?"

She smiled. "Yes, of course—the Glen Lyon."

"The very one," he said. "Good place for ale. Brewed with heather."

She laughed. "Yes, that's it." He grinned at her, and her eyes narrowed. "That's almost word for word what you said to Private McKie!"

Fraser gave her an apologetic grin. "Aye, but there's a pub like that everywhere."

She considered that. "True enough," she said. She picked up her teacup. She wrapped her palms around it and put her face over the steaming liquid.

"I warn ye, the French canna make proper tea," he said.

"It's hot at least." She sipped and made a face, then swallowed with effort.

"Do ye want some whisky in it after all?"

She looked at him primly. "No thank you."

"Another of your mother's rules?"

"One of my own. Medicinal purposes only."

He put the flask away. "You'll not get whisky here, unless your titled pilot has some—usually it's officers only. Everyone else makes do with rum rations for medicinal purposes. For fun, there's only the rotgut wine the French overcharge the enlisted chaps for at the estaminets."

He took a sip of his own tea. It was thin and pale, the tea leaves limp and flavorless, on their second or possibly third go. She sipped again and grimaced, and he wondered if she'd reconsider his offer of whisky now. She murmured something under her breath that sounded suspiciously like "There's a war on."

"I prefer coffee myself," he said. "Though I haven't had any of that in a very long while," he admitted.

"Is that what you miss about your home?" she asked.

He thought of all the faces and places and scents and sounds of home that he missed. He'd shut them from his mind, had stopped thinking about them with longing or loss or anything else. That way lay madness, the desire for what he'd once taken for granted, couldn't have now, and might never have again. There was a bitterness in his mouth that had nothing to do with the tea. He sipped again, silently damning her for being pretty, for making him remember what it felt like to be a man, charming and handsome around women. Now he was angry, battered, scarred, and hopeless. Her presence reminded him of that, too. He couldn't remember the last time he'd felt clean and whole, had slept deeply, or had walked without looking over his shoulder watching for danger and listening for the desperate cries of the wounded.

She was gazing at him with her soft eyes, trusting and clean, pure, waiting for an answer to her question, unaware of the hornet's nest she'd poked with it. He felt anger flare in his breast, frustration at the madness of all of it, the war, her presence here, even the *mallaichte* tea.

She didn't belong here, not for any reason. It would destroy her, too, make it impossible for her to go home again, pick up the threads of an ordinary, once-familiar life. He opened his mouth to tell her so, to insist she go back where she'd come from, but the hinges of the door interrupted with a whining cry.

The Reverend Captain Hanniford Strong, the chaplain assigned to 46/CCS, came in. He was leading a shaking soldier with a bandage over one eye. Fraser rose at once, ready to go out and assist with the stretcher cases, but the chaplain caught sight of him and gave him a cheery smile. The chaplain was always cheery. "Sergeant MacLeod! Nice to see you back. Was your trip successful? Did our patient reach the base hospital safely?"

Fraser had agreed to accompany an amputation case who needed monitoring to the base hospital in Calais, and to fetch the mail and supplies for the CCS, since he was going that way. An orderly or a nurse could have done it, but Fraser had been on the line for thirty-two straight days, and Chaplain Strong had arranged for him to escort the patient for a change of scene and a chance to rest, if only for twenty-four hours.

Eleanor Atherton certainly was a change of scene.

"He was alive and improving when I left him. No further bleeding," he told the chaplain.

"Praise the Lord for that."

"Do you need help unloading?" Fraser asked, but the chaplain shook his head and pointed to the cup in Fraser's hand. "Finish that while it's still warm. There's just walking wounded this morning, and Private Gibbons and I can manage. There's no need to stir yourself yet."

Eleanor shifted, and Strong glanced at her, noticing her for the first time, then looked again.

She wasn't looking at him. She'd risen to her feet as Private Gibbons led the walking wounded into the waiting room. Her eyes flitted over each man, and Fraser suspected she was assessing their wounds with a professional eye. There was a lad with an eye injury, a man with his arm in a sling, one with a bandaged jaw, another with his hand clasped over one bloody ear. "*Bonjour, madame*," the chaplain said.

"This is . . ." Fraser hesitated, unsure of how to introduce her. "This is *Miss* Atherton, from England. She's on her way to see a patient at forty-six. Miss Atherton, this is Chaplain Strong."

The chaplain's smile barely faltered, though Strong knew the kind of welcome an unexpected female visitor was likely to get at the CCS. "Good morning, Miss Atherton. It's a pleasure to meet you. And who is the patient you're visiting?"

"Lieutenant Lord Somerton," she replied.

The chaplain tilted his head in confusion. "Lieutenant Lord Somerton, you say? At 46/CCS?"

She frowned quickly. "No—it's Chastaine. Lieutenant Louis Chastaine," she said. "He uses his family name instead of his title, I understand. It's only a few months since his older brother died."

The chaplain's brows rose with recognition of that name. He flicked a quick glance over her. "Yes, of course—the flier with the broken leg. I'm sorry to hear of his loss—was it in combat?"

"An accident at home." She didn't add any details.

"I see," the chaplain said. "Lieutenant Chastaine is indeed at forty-six. The surgeon who set his leg felt that travel over the rough roads would make the injuries worse and cause complications that could leave him permanently lamed, or worse." He gave her a kindly smile. "The doctors will explain it all to you, of course, and they can allay your fears and answer any questions better than I, but I can assure you he's under the best possible care with Colonel Bellford and Captain Blair, both fine surgeons." He grinned. "Your lieutenant has had quite a number of important visitors, though none so pretty. A French general came and pinned a medal to his pajamas, right there in his bed on the ward, and kissed him on both cheeks. He had a band with him, but Matron Connolly wouldn't let them inside. They stood outside the tent and played a rather stirring march. Your young man is very humble in the face of all the fuss. I daresay he'll be glad to see a friendly face. Are you his . . . ?"

Fraser crossed his arms. "She's a doctor."

"*A doctor?*" Reverend Strong's smile slipped a little, and he regarded her more closely. "Oh. Do you—are you . . ." He paused and shut his eyes for a moment, and Fraser wondered if he was sending up a wee prayer. She'd need it. The chaplain's eyes opened again. "Is Colonel Bellford expecting you?"

Eleanor reached for her medical bag. Was she ever without it?

"I have a letter here from the Countess of Kirkswell. She's Louis's—Lieutenant Chastaine's—mother. She asked me to escort her son home just as soon as it's safe for him to travel." She took a small leather folder out of the bag and extracted a letter, which she held out to the chaplain.

He stepped back from it at once. "Oh, it's naught to do with me. It's the colonel who'll want to see your letter. I'm just—" He slid his eyes to Fraser, looking for help. Fraser simply regarded him. "I'm just the messenger, one might say, or is that you, Sergeant MacLeod?"

"I merely promised her a ride to 46/CCS," Fraser said.

"Oh," Reverend Strong said again, and took a deep breath. "Well then. If you'll wait inside where it's warm for a few minutes more, I'll get the sergeant to help us load the supplies after all. Finish your, um, tea, and we'll come and get you when we're ready to go."

Fraser set his own cup down, glad for an excuse not to have to finish it, and followed the chaplain outside.

Outside, Reverend Strong paused and looked up at the bruise-gray sky. "Colonel Bellford is not going to like this," he murmured, and Fraser wondered if he was addressing the comment to him or to God.

"He'll hate it," Fraser agreed.

"He doesn't like surprises."

"I ken it," Fraser said.

"And you know how he feels about female visitors, Sergeant. He barely suffers female nurses. He says a pretty face does more harm than good to the sick and wounded." He pointed back at the station. "In case you didn't notice, Sergeant, that young woman is *very* pretty."

"I noticed."

"And she's a *doctor*!" He said it as if Eleanor Atherton were the devil incarnate.

Fraser rubbed his mouth to hide a smile. "Aye, she'll set the cat among the pigeons, but it's hardly her fault, and I couldn't very well leave her where she was. How long could it take to pack up a viscount and send him on his way? Perhaps his batman or his valet could help." He was being sarcastic, and it earned him a sharp look from the chaplain.

"The lieutenant is some weeks away from being ready to travel. He has no servants, and I didn't even know he had a title. What I do know is that he's got friends in high places—generals and staff officers come to visit him, or they send him lavish gifts. And he's a handful. He flirts with the VADs and nurses, and he starts arguments with the other officers on his ward simply because he's bored and it amuses him to do so. It's all anyone can do to keep him in bed for his own good. I spent three hours sitting with him yesterday, reading to him, just to keep him still."

"Then perhaps Miss Atherton is just the distraction he needs."

The chaplain sighed. "Only the Lord Himself knows what devilment Lieutenant Chastaine will make out of her presence." He looked skyward again. "Did she have to be a *doctor*? Colonel Bellford is not only an eminent surgeon, he's a career army officer, and as such, he's a stickler for rules, propriety, protocol, and military efficiency." He leaned closer to Fraser. "I believe he likes the idea of having such an important patient in his charge," he whispered. "D'you see what this means, Sergeant MacLeod? The colonel will send that poor lass packing the minute she arrives. She'll be terrified."

Fraser considered the soldier with the black eye and swiped a hand over his own eye. "It will certainly be interesting to see how she'll manage."

"Perhaps we could just . . ." Strong let the rest of the suggestion make itself.

Fraser frowned. "You're not saying that we should leave her here at the station, are ye? From what I've seen, she's a determined wee lass. I have a feeling she'd walk to forty-six by herself if she had to."

"I wasn't suggesting we *abandon* her, Sergeant!" the chaplain amended quickly. "I simply thought . . . perhaps we could warn her, and perhaps she'd decide on her own to go back . . . Well, I suppose not." He pressed his palms together and propped them against his nose. "Perhaps it's not necessary to tell Colonel Bellford she's a doctor," he said after a moment's consideration. "Not a lie, per se, but an omission for caution's sake—and caution is always the best course."

Private Gibbons came to stand before them, tugging on his ear, his usual bland, patient smile in place. "Should I begin loading the boxes, Reverend? It's going to be light soon."

"Morning, Tom," Fraser greeted him, and the lad's grin widened. Gibbons's father, uncertain of what to do with his simple-minded but good-hearted son, had put him in the army, hoping he'd learn skills and find a career. Reverend Strong had taken Tom under his wing, and the lad helped where he could at the CCS, doing every job with gentle grace. The fact that he topped six foot in height and was as strong as two men together made him useful indeed.

"Hello, Sergeant. Not morning yet, but almost, though," Gibbons said, squinting at the sky. There was no sunrise, and the day would unfold in continually lighter shades, from the gray of gunmetal to the depressing beige of dirty fog. Still, it was safer to travel when the half-light made it harder for snipers to see and the artillery had more important targets to focus on.

"My, yes, it is getting late, isn't it?" the chaplain said, glancing at his watch. "Let's get to loading these supplies." He sent Fraser a sideways look. "We'll have to leave enough space in the back for the sergeant and one other passenger," he said to Tom Gibbons.

"The lady over there?" Gibbons asked, and Fraser turned to see Eleanor Atherton standing on the platform beside the pile of supplies, her medical bag in her hand, her suitcase at her feet.

"Yes," the chaplain said, sighing.

"The colonel doesn't like it when ladies come a-visiting," Gibbons said.

Strong shot one more pointed look at Fraser. "No, he doesn't, but it can't be helped. Come on, Tom, we'd best make haste."

Fraser and Gibbons carried the boxes to the ambulance and passed them up to the chaplain. "As I recall, the colonel has a way of turning near to purple when someone crosses him," Fraser said.

Reverend Strong chuckled. "That he does. If he's merely angry, he yells. If he's furious, he speaks quite calmly, but it's that particular shade of purple that gives the depth of his fury away."

"He'll be purple when he meets this lass," Gibbons said.

"I fear he'll have her in tears."

"Perhaps, but she seems more than capable of—" Fraser paused. He had no idea what Eleanor Atherton was able to endure. He'd seen her face down unruly soldiers, bad tea, and the sound of the artillery. Still, everyone had a breaking point. "Will ye keep an eye on her while she's at forty-six, Reverend?"

"Of course," the chaplain agreed. "If she simply expects courtesy. If she wants coddling and pampering and three-minute eggs served to her with buttered toast points, then she shouldn't have come here, now, should she? No matter who protects her, she's going to see and hear things that will shock her. I can't help but remember one of the chaps on the ward, a lieutenant. Shrapnel had taken half his jaw. His young fiancée came all the way from England to visit him. She started to scream when she saw him. The nurses had to drag her out. She refused to see him again. The poor man found a gun and shot himself the next day. Colonel Bellford sedated the young woman and sent her back to England. Her reaction made other men fear how their own wives and mothers might react to their wounds. Miss Atherton looks—delicate. Is she delicate, do you think?"

"She's a doctor. There was a hospital train unloading at Calais— gas cases, shrapnel, amputations. There was a lad who couldn't breathe, a stretcher case. He'd been gassed, wounded everywhere. She tried to help him."

"Did she?" He heard the surprise in the chaplain's voice.

"Aye, and she made it this far. Is the flier she's come to see bad off?"

"Meaning will she scream when she sees him, cause him to shoot himself? No. If a lass swoons at *his* feet it won't be because he's ugly. He's a lucky man. His plane went down in flames, and he stayed with it until it crashed. His leg is broken, and he has burns on one arm, but the rest of him is sound enough." He nodded in Eleanor's direction. "And now I see he's luckier still."

A small kernel of jealousy formed in Fraser's chest, and he rubbed at the spot, frowning.

Gibbons shifted a crate in the back of the ambulance, and Fraser handed up another one.

"You needn't worry about her, Sergeant. You've been chivalrous in escorting her here. I'll keep an eye on her once you've gone back to the front," the chaplain promised.

"I'm not worried," Fraser said. Of course he wasn't. He had duties to attend to, wounded to bring in. They'd take his full attention, and he'd forget all about Eleanor Atherton in a day or two, if not sooner.

He looked at the prim figure on the platform, holding her collar close to her throat against the cold wind, but giving no sign of discomfort aside from that. Somewhere off to the east, beyond the CCS, a shell exploded, and she flinched. He wanted to go to her, reassure her. He felt a surge of irritation. He didn't have time for this. If he let her get stuck in his head, he'd think of how life was before the war, remember home and manners and dances with pretty lasses. He'd go mad. He'd grown a thick skin over his emotions. Chastaine was lucky, wasn't he? Fraser was considered lucky, too—he'd survived here for nearly two years when most bearers didn't live more than a few weeks. He had that in common with her flier—those lads died just as fast as stretcher bearers.

He concentrated on lifting the next box and passing it up to Strong, ignoring the blisters on his hands, the exhaustion he felt. When the next shell hit, nearer and louder, he willed himself not to glance at her.

It was her own fault for coming, and if she saw things that shocked her, got herself in harm's way, it was naught to do with him. They finished loading, and he crossed to fetch her.

"Is there a problem?" Eleanor asked Fraser. He followed her gaze to Strong's unhappy face.

"No. It takes a great deal to ruffle the chaplain's feathers," he said, picking up her case and striding toward the truck, leaving her to follow him.

"I'm used to ruffled feathers, Sergeant," she said.

"Aye? Then ye should know that the commandant of 46/CCS dislikes visitors in general, but most of all he hates the distraught wives and mothers and sisters of his patients. He has no time for outbursts of grief, hand-wringing, sobbing, fainting, or sighing. In Colonel Bellford's opinion, women in a military setting do more harm than good. Coddling and petting a wounded fighting man, treating him like a sick child, only makes him weaker, encourages self-pity and despair. Healing takes longer. And when other men see family visiting the lucky ones, the colonel fears they'll fall into depression and homesickness. In his opinion, women should be banned, kept in England."

She sniffed, and he sensed her stiffening with indignation. "But there are female nurses, surely."

"Aye. He tolerates those because he must. But you're not a nurse, or even a visiting mother or sister. You're a doctor, sent to check up on him, to take over one of his patients. He'll definitely see that as meddling."

"Oh," she said. She frowned, but she didn't look cowed or afraid.

"The colonel has the authority to send ye home," he reminded her. "You're not in England now."

"Theresawaron," she muttered.

"What?"

"There's. A. War. On. I've heard that so often that I think I'll embroider it on a sampler when I get home. It appears to mean that rules, manners, and courtesy don't apply, or that they've been suspended for the duration," she said. "I am here only to assist Louis, to help him get home safely. Surely the colonel wants that as well, not just for Louis but for all the patients in his care."

"I didn't say he wasn't a good doctor. He is that, and a fine surgeon," Fraser said, picking up another box. "He's just a stern commander. Are ye sure ye want to get on that truck? The train is still here. Ye can still get on board and go back."

"Thank you for the warning, but I am here now, and I have a job to do," she said, drawing her chin to a stubborn point.

"Just so ye know I did warn ye," he said, and led the way toward the ambulance. He didn't offer his arm or take her elbow. He let her navigate the broken, stony ground herself.

When they reached the truck she began to walk toward the front, and he stopped her. "We ride in the back. The chaplain drives, and Gibbons watches the road for him."

He put his hands around her waist and lifted her up into the back, aware of the slimness of her waist under her bulky clothing, the firm grip of her hand in his, the lithe way she moved. And suddenly it mattered a great deal that she was here, that Bellford would be displeased, that she would see things that would shock her, perhaps find herself in harm's way. He let her go, frowned, and shook off the maudlin, misplaced emotion. It was her own fault for coming, and naught to do with him.

CHAPTER THIRTEEN

W hen Fraser had followed the chaplain outside, Eleanor had
stayed inside and tried to help with the wounded. They took
the bench she'd vacated, and one man was holding his head and rocking, muttering under his breath. He was shaking with fear, or perhaps pain.

"Are you in pain?" she asked him. An orderly stepped in front
of her.

"Oy. This isn't a circus. These lads have been through enough
without folk staring at them. You'll set him off again."

"What's wrong with him?"

"Nervous. That's the diagnosis," the corporal muttered. "He needs
a long rest somewhere quiet. Doesn't like anyone looking at him."

She'd heard her father and Peter talking about nervous cases, also
called shell shock or neurasthenia. Some doctors thought those patients were cowards and malingerers. Some sufferers had been shot

earlier in the war for dereliction of duty. Other physicians saw it as a mental condition—nervous exhaustion, terror, stress. She looked at the poor soldier again. He put his hands up to his ears and keened.

"Please, miss, for the love of Christ, go away afore he starts to scream," one of the other soldiers pleaded. "He saw a woman—a civilian—blown to bits on the road with her little girl. He can't bear to look at women now. Even seeing nurses gives him fits."

Eleanor backed away, then went outside. Fraser was helping the chaplain load the back of the ambulance with boxes and crates. The chaplain was still looking at her doubtfully. She gritted her teeth so they wouldn't chatter in the icy wind and be mistaken for fear. It was a fearful place—the air smelled strange, metallic and smoky, and the very air shook with the constant roar and vibration of the guns. She searched the sky for bombs as she got into the back of the ambulance, but saw nothing. Sergeant MacLeod had said they were far away, to the east, that it was safe here. She certainly didn't feel safe. Shouldn't it be morning by now? Was the sky here always this sickly yellow-gray color? Off in the distance, another gun exploded, making her flinch again.

Sergeant MacLeod got in beside her. She wanted his company, the reassurance of him, the familiarity, though she'd known him for mere hours. He made her feel safe, protected. Perhaps it was his height, his uniform. "All right?" he asked, and even the sound of his voice was comforting in this terrifying place. She resisted the urge to move closer to him.

"All right," she agreed. She shifted over on one of the long shelves—which she knew usually held stretchers or wounded men—to accommodate him, but he shifted as well, sat close to her.

"Hold on tight to the straps," Fraser said. "I'll sit next to ye to keep you from tumbling out if we have to make any sudden stops or swerves, but mind if the boxes shift."

"Ready to go, Miss Atherton?" the reverend asked from the front seat. A tall lad stood behind him, smiling shyly. "This is Private Gibbons, Miss Atherton. She's a doctor, Tom, here to visit one of the wounded officers at 46/CCS. She's not here to serve, lad—though we all serve as best we can, of course."

"That's good," Gibbons said. "Because the colonel says lady doctors are as much use as two-legged mules and—"

The chaplain gripped the young man's shoulder. "We know what the colonel says," the chaplain said gently.

Another shell landed somewhere close enough to make the truck rattle, and Eleanor gasped.

The chaplain patted her arm. "Not to worry, Miss Atherton. The guns are a good way off this morning. And we've got Sergeant MacLeod with us. Did you know he's considered lucky? He's been here since '16 and never even been wounded, which is nothing short of a miracle. There are soldiers who watch for him when they're hit or one of their chums is wounded. They think he has a charmed life, and they believe they'll survive anything if they see Sergeant MacLeod coming for them. Forgive me, Sergeant, but I prefer to put it down to the fact that God knows we need good men like Fraser MacLeod down here, and with him beside us, and the good Lord upstairs, we'll be just fine." He started the engine. "Ready, Tom?"

The lad held up a pair of binoculars. "Aye, Reverend." He leaned out the window.

"Hold tight, Miss Atherton," the reverend said, and he swung the vehicle out onto the road.

The ambulance moved forward, lurching over the rutted track, and she clung to the strap and wondered how wounded men endured such a jolting.

"Left!" she heard Private Gibbons call out, and the vehicle swerved. Sergeant Fraser's body moved with the call like a man on horseback, fluid and easy. She bumped into his shoulder and straightened herself at once.

"What's wrong with the road?" she asked him.

He shrugged. "Winter rains, too many boots marching over it, and shells lobbed from miles away, aimed at the rail lines or the station to disrupt transportation and unnerve and inconvenience folk. It's safer to travel in the dark, but there's always new damage to watch for. It wouldn't do to break an axle or puncture a tire—or to attract a sniper."

Eleanor felt the skin between her shoulders tingle, as if her back were in the crosshairs of some unseen gun.

"Relax, Miss Atherton. The guns are pointing the other way at the moment, and they're a dozen miles from here."

"Only a dozen miles?" she asked.

"Aye, for now. We usually know when there's a battle planned— our side or theirs moves up men and supplies, and the senior officers drive back and forth in fancy cars with observers and advisers, and they put the medical staff on alert, even if they won't say exactly when things will start. Things have been quiet for the past week or two, and we haven't heard of anything being planned, so there's naught for ye to fear, especially if you're not going to be here very long."

"I'm not afraid," she said.

He raised one eyebrow. "If this doesn't scare ye, what does?"

She drew herself up, stiff and prickly. "I'm not a hothouse rose, Sergeant." She lowered her eyes, hiding the lie. She *felt* like a hothouse rose, out of place amid the mud and men and the harsh sound of the guns. The sight of the neurasthenic lad had shocked her, even though she'd seen wounds and blood before, and she was a grown woman of nearly twenty-four. She was a doctor, and she couldn't help him. She hoped someone could.

"Are *you* afraid?" she asked. "Not now, but—in battle, I mean."

He hesitated for a moment. "I've made my peace with things. If it's my time to go, nothing will change that." She wished she could see his expression better, but it was too dark inside the vehicle, even with the tarp at the back open to let in air and what little light there was. "I only hope I won't end up like some of the poor blighters we carry in with their faces half gone, or their limbs shot away, or their minds destroyed."

She swallowed, but said nothing. She'd seen such men on the streets of Edinburgh and York, disfigured and maimed, forced to endure the stares of the horrified and the curious.

"Left!" Gibbons called. This time she braced herself.

"When ye get to the CCS, promise me something," Sergeant MacLeod said.

"What?"

"Stay inside. Don't go wandering in the wood, or away from the tents. It isn't safe."

She stiffened again. "I am perfectly capable of taking care of myself," she said.

"At home perhaps ye are, in your own Yorkshire village, where you're known and there's no real danger," he said as if he'd read her thoughts. "But here you're a civilian, and a woman. Either side might take ye for a spy. And men—men change in war. They're here to kill. No one will know or care that you're a doctor, or an Englishwoman, or just visiting." His voice was gruff and hard.

She felt a lump in her throat and swallowed.

"Chaplain Strong will see ye back to the train when you're ready to go. Your wounded flier will need an ambulance anyway."

"Not you?"

"No. I'll be on duty," he said sharply.

"Of course. I hadn't thought." She'd probably never see him again once they reached the CCS. She felt the fact like the loss of a friend. She didn't want to lose his company. He'd been kind. He made her feel safe. He hadn't looked at her with surprise or distaste because she was a doctor. He made her feel . . . feminine, perhaps. The way he looked at her made her breath catch, and she liked it.

"I was only in Calais because I was tasked with escorting a wounded man who needed someone to watch him. It wasn't leave, or a lark," he said raggedly.

"No, of course not," she said.

"Right! Right!" Gibbons yelled, and the ambulance lurched over a deep rut.

She looked out the back of the vehicle. Deep puddles shone like pools of polished metal in the pale glimmer of dawn. There was fog over the fields, a veil drawn down to hide whatever it was that lurked in the distance, but close to the road, they sidled past the ghostly silhouettes of broken fences and blighted trees, and shattered carts and ruined vehicles lay by the side of the track. They drove by roofless houses, damaged beyond repair. She'd seen photographs of such sights in newspapers and magazines, but here, before her eyes, it was far worse, the smell, the sounds, the stark sorrow and destruction almost overwhelming. The enemy was just twelve miles away. Her father drove to see patients twelve miles from Thorndale. It was considered close by, in the neighborhood.

There's a war on, she thought. It had another meaning here, a deadly one, a warning.

They turned off the road, and the vehicle tiptoed awkwardly over more ruts before it pulled up in front of a gathering of tents and makeshift buildings that stood around a stone farmhouse. She saw signposts pointing toward RECEPTION, TRIAGE, CMO, and SUPPLY. Below those, waggish handwritten signs indicated the way to Piccadilly, and Tipperary, and Buckingham Palace.

Sergeant MacLeod climbed down and turned to reach for her, setting his big hands on her waist once again and lifting her with ease. She put her hands on his shoulders and held his gaze as he swung her to the ground. For an instant his face was close to hers, and a shock raced through her, a desire to hover there, in space, in his arms, but he set her down at once and stepped back, though his eyes stayed on hers. "As I thought. Seven stone even," he murmured.

He looked away, scanning the collection of white bell tents, small huts, and the wooden walkways that ran between them like sutures, and she followed his gaze. She noted the orderlies, the few wounded she could see, and the nurses hurrying by. His stance relaxed, the tension in his body easing. She felt it, just by standing beside him.

"Is it quiet, then?" she asked.

He nodded. "Aye, but there could be wounded arriving any minute. Dawn is a favorite time for attack." He scanned her face again. "I have to get back," he said, almost an apology instead of a farewell. "And ye best get to your flier."

She'd forgotten Louis even existed. "Oh. Yes, I suppose so," she murmured.

He caught the arm of a passing orderly. "This is Miss Atherton. She's here to see a patient named Chastaine, an officer, Flying Corps."

The man looked her over boldly, then grinned. "The lieutenant gets a lot of visitors. You could just follow the well-worn path, of course, but I'll take you to him. You'll need to see the sister in charge before going in, just so everyone's decent and proper and no one gets an unexpected surprise, if you know what I mean." He gave her a jaunty wink.

"That'll do, Corporal," Fraser said gruffly.

The orderly's flirtatious gaze dropped at once, and his smile faded as he came to attention. "Aye, Sergeant. If you'll come this way, miss."

Eleanor looked at Fraser MacLeod expectantly, but he took a step backward.

"I've got to go. I'm due back to my unit." For a moment he let his eyes travel over her, his expression thoughtful, as if he was memorizing her. "Stay inside," he reminded her, and then he turned and left her, striding away along the duckboards, pulling up the collar of his greatcoat against the wind, and she watched him go, holding her breath, hoping he'd turn, look back at her, but he didn't. He rounded the corner of a tent and disappeared.

"If you'll come this way?" the corporal said again.

"I didn't get to thank him," Eleanor said.

"He'd likely say he was just doing his duty. Sergeant MacLeod is a good man. Now let's get you inside and out of this wind."

CHAPTER FOURTEEN

Captain David Blair, RAMC surgeon, sat on the bench outside the triage tent, letting the cold morning wind scrub the smell of the operating theater out of his hair and off his skin. He held his pipe between his teeth, unlit. He was too tired to go fill it and find a match to light it.

Four hours to pick shrapnel out of a man's chest, arms, and jaw. Three hours before that to remove a kidney with a bullet lodged in it. He'd been quick and precise, but the patient had died anyway. He hated losing patients, though it was hardly a rare occurrence. No matter how skillful the surgeon, how deft his hands, how quick and careful, the war was quicker, and the waste of limb and life was tragic and constant. David Blair, score of one, the war—hundreds. Thousands. Tens of thousands. The lad he'd lost today had been fresh from England, on the line for just two days. He'd looked to be about fourteen, though his papers swore he was nineteen.

Perhaps it was another trick of this war, making him feel so old and tired that everyone else looked too young to his eyes. He aged years every single bloody day. He looked at his unlit pipe dolefully. He was out of the good tobacco, and he wanted food and sleep and a bath that would clean away the blood and the iodine that had soaked through his operating gown to his skin—a proper bath, in a full-size tub, with unlimited hot water, and fragrant soap that didn't contain the faintest hint of carbolic. He frowned, knowing he'd have to settle for a few inches of lukewarm water in a chipped basin. He rubbed his hand over his face, trying to recall the last time he'd been well rested and clean. He wanted a drink, too, but he was on duty for another twenty-four hours. This time tomorrow he could drink himself blotto and sleep for sixteen hours after that. Then he'd be back at it, doing the impossible task of putting the next mangled lad back together if he could. *David Blair, score two . . .*

He'd been here since '17, nearly eight months. Fool that he was, he'd been *glad* to come, because he hated the junior position in the London hospital that saw him doing nothing more than sterilizing instruments and lancing boils. He'd thought the war would be his chance to perform real surgery, to save lives and do proper honor to the Hippocratic oath by healing broken bodies and holding death at bay.

He never knew what happened to the ones who survived surgery. Once they left his table and were stabilized, they were sent up the line for further care as quickly as possible, no longer his concern.

He stared into the black mouth of the pipe again like an anxious addict. It really was a filthy habit, and he'd promised his mother he'd give it up, but it was one of the few comforts in this place—when he could get tobacco, of course. His brother, Patrick, serving with the Canadians, seemed to have an unlimited supply, and better stuff than the British got. He was happy to share it with David, and they made it an excuse to see each other as often as they could here in France.

He listened to the guns, noted the volume of artillery and the direction, and hoped Pat was out of it for the moment. Bellford would inform them if there was a push on and they could expect heavy casualties. Then getting drunk would have to be postponed. The colonel hadn't said a word this morning, though, and the guns thumped away in the distance, drumming up new business for medical officers and surgeons and the ambulance corps, but without a concerted effort. It was just each side sending their regards to the lads across No Man's Land. With luck, it would be a relatively quiet day.

David leaned back against the post behind him. It was a cold morning, gray and overcast, but it was the first time he'd seen daylight in three days, and he didn't care about the weather. He should go inside, catch up on writing letters to the families of the fallen he'd operated on or pronounced dead. He'd promised Reverend Strong he'd get to it as soon as he had a minute, since the good padre believed such missives offered comfort and closure to grieving widows, mothers, and fatherless children. They always wrote that their lad had died bravely, without pain, lucid and noble to the last, and that his final thoughts and words were for those he loved. It usually wasn't true. They died in screaming agony, or silently, their eyes blank. So much for the fine dream of being a surgeon who saved lives. Instead, the war had made him a liar and a butcher, patching broken bodies together as fast as he could, fearing—knowing—it was never enough. What was he against the destructive force of bullets, or gas, or a two-hundred-pound shell? He didn't feel like a hero, a trained surgeon who spent his days saving lives and fixing the world's ills—he felt like a cog in a ghastly machine. The war blighted everything it touched—a man's body, his mind, his soul.

Maybe he'd write to Patrick instead, ask him to send more tobacco. Lucky Canadians—according to Pat, there was plenty of everything a man could want in Canada—it was a land of plenty and opportunity, and of clean, wide-open spaces. His brother had left England six years ago, bought a ranch in the foothills of Alberta in the west, and spent his days raising cattle and horses. Before the war, Patrick had been breeding horses and looking for oil on his land, like most of his neighbors. "Neighbors," they called them—it always made David laugh, since Pat's nearest ones were a three-hour ride away, through green rolling hills, over high rivers fringed with cottonwood trees, under skies so blue in the summer that it dazzled a man's eyes to look at them. Or so Patrick told him. David had never been to Canada.

His brother had asked him time and time again to come out and join him, but there'd been medical school, and his first hospital posting, and his dying mother to care for. He was tempted now, though. Perhaps he'd go after the war—if he lived, of course. No one made long-term plans anymore. *Nothing past tomorrow* was the new motto. He'd told Pat he'd think about it, and some days, most days, it was all he thought about.

"Good morning, Dr. Blair. Have you had a few minutes to write those letters?" Reverend Strong asked, passing by, his arms laden with supplies.

David opened his eyes, and Hanniford Strong smiled at him, a tireless, efficient, endlessly busy man with true faith shining in his kind eyes, a certainty of heaven that made him willing to do even the very worst tasks. No matter how bad things got, the chaplain's smile never dimmed. David wished he had that kind of faith, that strength. The chaplain surely did more good than he did. In fact, he was certain of it, and felt shamed. He sat up straight, like a lad in Sunday school.

"I've been in surgery. I'll do some now," he mumbled.

The chaplain smiled. "I'll just put these supplies away and see the colonel, then perhaps you and I can have a cup of tea and a bite of breakfast and tackle them together."

David nodded. It really was impossible to say no.

He rose to his feet. Perhaps he should offer to help unload the supplies, but the chaplain had the faithful Private Gibbons to help. He saw

Gibbons now, wheeling a laden cart away from the ambulance, which for now held nothing more menacing than crates and bundles.

Then he saw the rangy and ragged form of Sergeant Fraser Mac-Leod leap out of the back—now there was another good man, nearly as good as the chaplain. The stretcher bearer's heroic deeds seemed just as endless, his determination to save others almost as saintly.

Then MacLeod reached for something in the back of the vehicle, and it turned out to be *someone*—a woman. MacLeod swung her to earth in a graceful arc, and she caught her hat as she landed and held it against the wind. She was clad in one of those dreadfully boxy suits women favored, half military, half sober mourning wear. There wasn't a single feminine detail about women these days, nothing to tempt or entice a man away from his duty, distract him with thoughts of sex. She half turned, and David grimaced. Gack—the damned getup was even worse than the terrible habit-like uniforms the VADs wore. Then she lifted her chin and he saw her face, nothing more than a distant impression of wide eyes and a prim mouth. She had lace at her collar, and long tendrils of red hair crept out from under her ugly hat. He wondered who she was, why she'd come to 46/CCS. Possibly a visitor, or perhaps she was a do-gooder from some committee or other sent to bring comfort and cheer, or order, or better morals to the troops. She was probably traveling with crates full of badly knitted mittens and mufflers to hand out to the men.

But he doubted MacLeod would be so solicitous if that was the case. Like most soldiers who'd seen the worst of this war, he had no patience for the uninformed and clumsy interference of do-gooders who scurried back across the Channel as soon as their curiosity was satisfied.

David watched as she followed the sergeant over to an orderly, who grinned at her besottedly until the sergeant barked at him and he twitched to attention. Pretty, then? A pretty face would be a tonic indeed, a pleasant change from the grim-faced matron.

"Who's that?" he asked Tom Gibbons as he passed.

"Who?" The young man gave David his usual guileless smile.

"The woman you brought, Tom, the one who just got out of the ambulance you were in."

"Oh. That's Miss Atherton. She's a doctor," Gibbons said, and continued on.

David stared after him for a moment in surprise, then hurried to catch up to the private. "A doctor? She's not—she's not here to replace Carrington, is she?" Geoffrey Carrington, captain and surgeon, had died when a shell hit the ambulance he was in. They'd been waiting three weeks for a replacement.

"She's here to visit someone," Gibbons said.

Private Gibbons was a simple and good-hearted lad. Everyone liked him. He did as he was told, he worked hard, and he was as dim as the moon on a cloudy night.

"*Who* is she visiting?" David asked.

"Lieutenant Chastaine," Gibbons said. "The pilot with the broken leg."

"Is she his sister, his maiden aunt, his grandmother?"

Gibbons gave him another goofy grin. "I dunno, Captain. Sergeant MacLeod found her at the station, and she needed a ride. Reverend Strong said it was all right with him, so it was all right with me. Colonel Bellford won't like her."

"Won't he?" David asked. "Is she pretty?"

Gibbons blushed. "I wouldn't know that, Captain."

David sighed and let the lad get on with his task, turning to watch the young woman disappear through the flap of the officers' ward. "Lucky Chastaine," he murmured.

He put his empty pipe in his pocket and went to find the chaplain.

CHAPTER FIFTEEN

Louis Chastaine scowled at his broken leg, bandaged, splinted, and hanging in a sling, and attached to pulleys and wires and a pole at the end of his bed. The apparatus reminded him of the rigging of his airplane, the wood and wire contraption that had carried him into the heavens above the battlefield, giving him a bird's-eye view of the world below.

The plane was nothing but a pile of ash now, and he was lucky to be alive.

They'd pulled him out of the burning wreckage in the nick of time and gotten him to an aid post. But that was nearly three weeks ago. Since then, he'd been trapped in this narrow, lumpy, beastly bed, barely able to move. In fact, he'd been warned not to move *at all*, or his dancing days—never mind his walking days, or even possibly *all* his days—would be over. His backside ached from lying in the same position for so long. He'd read all the bloody newspapers and well-thumbed copies of *Country Life* that the VADs—those Very Adorable Darlings—handed round with beguiling smiles, every single issue months out of date. Worse, his mother was prominently featured in almost every issue, photographed doing good works for the war effort. She'd turned Chesscroft into a hospital, and he wondered if some weedy infantry captain was sleeping in his bed, enjoying the clean Yorkshire air and the splendid views of the dales.

There was an article about Cyril's funeral as well, which he refused to look at.

And if he tired of *Country Life*, his godfather, Colonel Sir Hugo Ferris, had sent him the gift of a leather-bound set of Dickens's works to pass the time.

Louis hated Dickens. Jack London was more to his taste.

His mother had sent him books as well, of course, which he'd promptly donated unread to the CCS's fledgling library to be inflicted on other poor sods. They were dull improving tomes, full of lectures on masculine morals, fortitude, obedience, and the responsibilities of the upper classes to set an example for the lower classes. She meant them as a crash course for the next earl, the younger son never expected to inherit the title and the fortune and the ancestral pile. They should load the guns with those books, Louis thought, and fire them at the Germans. The enemy would laugh themselves to death, bringing the war to a swift and amusing conclusion. Of course, Louis would be dead of boredom himself by then. He flipped listlessly through the latest issue of *Country Life*, nearly two months old and featuring photographs of his mother donating a motorcycle to the local regiment and digging potatoes in the victory vegetable garden that had replaced part of the rose garden at Chesscroft. Poor Binns—the old gardener loved the roses so. It must have been a blow to him to see them plowed under for turnips and tatties.

He tossed the magazine aside and looked around the officers' ward for someone to talk to. He'd had Jack Charring-Sandford to natter to for a few days, but Jack been quickly shipped off back to Blighty, his left eye lost to shrapnel. He remembered Charlie Peckerill from Cambridge, but Charlie had been drugged to the gills with morphine while he was here and still screamed for more, insisting that his left foot was in flaming agony. The worst of it was that Charlie's left foot and the whole rest of his leg had been taken off at the hip. The poor bugger had been a champion sprinter before the war, a good dancer, and a damn fine cricketer. The ladies loved him. Would they still? Charlie's dancing days were most definitely over. Louis tried not to consider the possibility that he'd not dance again, either, or even walk without a limp.

And good old Bumpy, Lord Anthony Bixby, the son and heir of the Earl of Hareton, had been here. He'd always been good for a laugh. He was a silver-tongued devil with women, charmed duchesses old and young, shop girls prim and cheeky, and the lovely Lady Arianne Cowper-Martin, the belle of her coming-out season. But Bumpy had seen a dozen men in his command take a direct hit as he was speaking with them. They'd simply vaporized, vanished before his eyes, as if they'd never existed at all, and suddenly he was talking to himself. He'd stood there, stiff as a statue, covered with blood and bits of bone, unable to speak or move. The lucky charm one of his men wore, a wooden four-leaf clover, had been blown off the man's neck and embedded itself in Bumpy's cheek. They'd carried him out of the trench, cleaned him off, and put him to bed, stiff as a pole. He hadn't spoken a word since, and he hadn't recognized Louis. They'd taken Bumpy away with the other shell-shock cases, and Louis supposed he was likely locked away somewhere safe and quiet with doctors poking at him day and night and examining the odd scar of a four-leaf clover on his cheek.

The rest of the poor bastards in the bell tent that served as the officers' ward—and there were only four of them at the moment, all recovering from surgery or drugged insensible against pain—weren't inclined to conversation. Louis understood well enough. Too much on their minds, too many bad memories, too much bloody shame or guilt or simple horror at what had happened to them. The silence was wearing, and it left too much time for Louis to think about the accident that had put him here, to analyze it, to relive it in horrifying detail, from the sight of the bullet holes appearing in his propeller to the first puff of smoke to the sudden hard punch as the next bullet pierced the fuselage and buried itself in his thigh. The plane went down like a dead swallow, heading straight toward a trench full of Frenchies. He'd seen their open mouths, the horror on their faces as they waved him off even as they tried to flee the certain death plummeting toward them. Louis had been so busy trying to control his airplane that he hadn't noticed the pain in his leg. He remembered the sudden flare of flame, orange against the gray sky, and the way it chewed hungrily at the canvas wings, reaching for him.

He'd fought with the damned controls, made bargains with God and the devil and whoever else might be listening. The airplane had cleared the trench, heading instead for a field behind it and a burned-out farmhouse. All he could do was let the plane go where it would and watch as the ground rose up fast. The impact was bone jarring. He'd bitten his own tongue, which distracted from the fact that his leg shattered on impact. He'd had enough wit left to drag himself out of the inferno, one leg useless, blood pouring from his mouth, his left sleeve on fire. He lay on the ground in agony, wondering if he was actually dead. He saw feet rushing toward him but remembered nothing after that.

He was lucky—the farmhouse turned out to be a British Regimental Aid Post, and the doctor was in.

Sir Hugo, his godfather and a dear friend of his mother's, had been by his bed two days later, when he woke here at 46/CCS. He informed Louis that he was a hero and would get a medal for the magnificent landing he'd managed, at least a Distinguished Service Order for gallantry. Then a lemon-faced nursing sister had informed Sir Hugo that he must go at once and let Louis rest. The doctor sternly informed Louis that he must lie still, that it was too dangerous to move him to a base hospital or home to England, and that he'd have to stay put and wait for his bones to knit and stabilize if he wanted to keep his leg. There was still a risk of infection, or of gas gangrene, or that the burns on his arms might cause problems.

He could die.

For once in his life, Louis did as he was told, afraid not of death itself, but of a slow, rotting, painful end.

But after nearly three weeks, almost a month, the pain had lessened to a dull ache, and he was bored.

He wished Sister Spofford would come through the ward. She was the prettiest nursing sister, with big blue eyes and a simpering lisp. She blushed easily when teased, which embarrassed her and amused him. He'd even settle for Sister Dane, who was as sharp as broken glass. She pursed her lips when she was angry or aroused. He'd once caught sight of a lock of blond hair that had slipped its pins and escaped from under her veil. He'd caught it in his fingers as she'd bent over him, stroked the lock gently for a moment, and grinned at her. She'd taken a soft, surprised breath, her eyes widening, her tight little mouth softening, the warm weight of her breast resting on his chest. It had been intensely erotic. She hadn't pulled away. Well, not immediately. If he hadn't been trussed like a goose, he would have caught her in his arms, pulled her under him and kissed her silly. Instead, she'd freed herself and scurried toward the door like a frightened mouse.

He drummed his fingers on the coverlet. He wanted a drink and a cigarette. He wanted to scratch his desperately itchy, aching leg—or his balls. Christ help him if he found himself reduced to *that* for amusement. Perhaps Nurse Spofford would oblige . . . the very idea had him half hard.

He heard voices by the door and looked up eagerly. But it was Matron Connolly who entered, her gimlet eyes roaming the room for anything out of place. Her gaze fell on him, and her brows rose with disapproval. Now there was a sight to wilt the stiffest pecker.

He gritted his teeth and gave her his best heir-to-the-earldom grin as she marched toward him.

"You have a visitor, Lieutenant," she said, her tone cool and oh-so-efficient. She straightened his blankets with a sharp twitch and checked that his pajamas were buttoned. She pleated a knitted sock and put it over the naked toes of his splinted leg. She took a comb out of the drawer in the bedside table and fixed his hair as if he were a lad in short pants.

"Ah, so it's a lady, then," he said. She wouldn't fuss so if his visitor were male. "Or is it just a woman?" Oh, let it be a *woman*, a low, immoral chippy with warm hands and a clever mouth, and not some highborn, whey-faced do-good volunteer bringing sweeties and another stale edition of *Country Life*. Perhaps Edward Atherton had sent someone—good old Edward, his partner in crime, seduction, and misadventure—he'd know what was wanted.

"Yes, you have a *female* visitor," Matron said unhelpfully, stepping back and running a critical eye over him.

"An orderly gave me a bath and shaved me this morning, Matron. I'm as presentable as possible," he said in cold aristocratic tones, tired of being judged and prodded and primped. "Show my guest in at once."

Instead she took her time, calmly moving to check on the other patients and draw screens around their beds, providing them all with a modicum of privacy before she went to fetch his visitor. Louis chafed at the delay.

Maybe it would be someone he knew and liked. Cynthia Meldrum, perhaps—he'd heard the lovely Cyn was serving as a VAD somewhere in France. Lady Anne Dear-oh-Dear Dearing would also be a welcome sight for sore eyes. He hoped it wasn't his mother. She'd made it her cause to worry and fret over him, the new heir to the title, and he wouldn't put it past her to rush here to badger and berate him. Or worse, fawn over him. Neither of them would enjoy that. They had a distant relationship. Cyril had been her favorite, while Louis had merely been the spare. But the Countess of Kirkswell would already have barged in, more than a match for even such a formidable dragon as Matron Connolly. Louis rolled his eyes heavenward and whispered a prayer. "Please, if there is a God, or even a benevolent devil, let it be anyone but my mother."

Anyone at all.

CHAPTER SIXTEEN

Eleanor waited for the nursing sister to return. Would Louis be glad to see her? Surprised? What if he looked at her with disdain, or laughed at her the way he used to with Edward? At least she had no braids to pull. He'd never been quite as quick to tease her as Edward. In fact, he'd often drawn her brother away from tormenting her, citing other, more interesting things to do, as if she wasn't worth the trouble of tormenting. It took a lot to make her cry, for she had learned that crying only made Edward crueler. Stone-faced, her stomach in knots, she'd watched them run away, leaving her behind, longing for another of Louis's dazzling smiles, a crumb of attention or concern, or another gallantly bestowed handkerchief. He was Edward's friend, not hers— but Edward wasn't here, and she, Eleanor, was the friend he needed now.

She took the interval to tuck the loose strands of her hair under her hat and straighten her collar and her skirt, making herself present- able. Perhaps Louis would look at her with male interest, see that she'd grown up to be an attractive, interesting, capable woman, and be intrigued. She gripped the handle of her doctor's bag tighter. It wasn't impossible—Fraser MacLeod had looked at her that way.

But she was supposed to be thinking about Louis.

Her patient.

She'd been asked to wait outside the curtain that guarded the officers' ward, in the supply area by the door of the bell tent. She looked at the shelves—nothing more than crates turned sideways to hold medical supplies, basins and buckets, piles of sheets and towels, and a small stove and the things necessary to make tea. Her stomach growled, reminding her she hadn't eaten since Calais, hadn't had anything to drink since the dreadful cup of tea with Sergeant MacLeod at Arras. And the sip of whisky he'd given her, of course.

She heard the starched rustle of the nursing sister returning. She opened the curtain but did not immediately step aside to allow Eleanor through. "The lieutenant is ready to see you," she said, her lips tight, her eyes traveling over Eleanor with clear disapproval, though she knew nothing about her yet. "I will remind you that our patients need quiet and rest. Decorum on your part is essential. You must refrain from crying, exclaiming, or fainting."

Eleanor's lips parted. "Is he so bad off, then?"

The woman didn't reply to that, not when there were rules and regulations to impart, and she carried on with those. "There is a nursing sister on duty, seated at the desk at the end of this ward. She's here to keep an eye on things and make sure everything is in order—and that they remain in order." She swept Eleanor with another head-to-toe glance, as if she were disinfecting her.

"I was given to understand that Lieutenant Chastaine is suffering from a broken femur—is that still the case?"

The matron looked surprised. "Yes."

"Is there any reason to assume he is not stable enough to endure a visit from a . . . a family friend?"

The matron clasped her hands at her waist. "No. There are burns on his hand and arm as well. Those are uncovered. Such wounds, mild as those are compared to the injuries suffered by others, often shock female visitors."

It was on the tip of Eleanor's tongue to inform the nurse that she was a doctor and she had never fainted in her life. She also considered asking to see Louis's medical chart, but she suspected telling this woman she'd come to assess Louis's medical condition and treatment would be like throwing gasoline on hot embers. She'd speak to the surgeon first, and the commandant.

She met the suspicion and curiosity in the matron's eyes squarely. "I will be sure to inform the duty nurse if the lieutenant needs anything."

The woman nodded crisply and took Eleanor past the curtain, leading her into the ward. It smelled of carbolic and soap, which didn't entirely hide the scent of wounds and male bodies. There was little to see, as every bed was draped and shuttered as if it were laundry day.

The matron paused, cleared her throat, and spoke through the linen wall. "You have a visitor, Lieutenant." She waited for a few decorous moments, then pulled back the curtain. She left it open, tied it back, and, with a final scowl of warning and disapproval, she stepped back and let Eleanor enter.

Louis's right leg was extended in a splint that stabilized his broken leg.

"Why, it's Eleanor Atherton!" His handsome face lit up, and those sleepy-bright blue eyes were roaming over her, making his own male assessment.

She stood before him like a ninny, wondering if she should offer her hand for him to shake. Or should she curtsy? Perhaps she should take his pulse?

Did one curtsy to a viscount, especially if that viscount was her brother's friend? She'd forgotten how beautiful he was, how looking at him made her heart thrill and her stomach come alive with butterflies. The old familiar tingle of her girlish crush made her light-headed and giddy, and she was unable to say anything more than a half-whispered "Hello."

He held out his hand to take hers and squeezed it as if she were an old and dear friend. "What a lovely surprise! I had no idea you were in France. Did Edward come with you?" He raised her fingers to his lips, kissed her knuckles, then turned her palm up to smell her wrist. "You smell divine, like summer roses, like Yorkshire."

He was sniffing her. Eleanor's fingers curled into her palm, and her toes curled in her boots. Laughter fizzed in her breast. He was looking at her with utter joy, *seeing* her, smiling at *her, glad* to see her. "Thank you, L—" She hesitated. Should she call him Louis, address him as Lieutenant Chastaine, or use his title? She settled for giving him a bright smile that felt forced and rushed past all that.

"No, Edward isn't here." Did the joy in his expression fade just a little? "I'm here because your mother—the countess—sent me."

The expression in his eyes congealed, turning cold and suspicious, and he let go of her hand at once. "My mother? What on earth for? I had no idea she even knew I was here. I certainly didn't tell her. But I suppose they notify one's next of kin when these things happen, don't they?"

His eyes roamed over her, from the prim lace at her collar to the muddy hem of her skirt, more wary than delighted now. "How kind of her not to come herself," he muttered, looking as petulant as a ten-year-old.

She looked away and scanned his left forearm. The burn that covered the back of his hand and wrist was crusty and purple, but healing. She noticed a small tattoo on his forearm—a bird with outstretched wings.

Not an eagle or a falcon. "Is that a sparrow?" she asked.

He followed her gaze to the mark. "Yes. Someone's idea of a joke, because I'm a flier. I was drunk at the time, so it might well have been my idea. My mother will be furious, of course. Probably why I did it. And you can see my heroic burns, of course. Now, those will leave a scar that will be hard to hide. I daresay she'll mind that even more. She can't abide ugliness."

"She's worried about you," Eleanor said. "She asked me to come and—"

"Why you, exactly?" he interrupted, shrewd and serious now. "Other than our connection through Edward, of course."

They were strangers, he meant. There was nothing in his gaze now but the question, no flirtation or admiration or delight. She squared her shoulders. "She asked me to come because I'm a doctor. I'm to supervise your care on your journey home. Your mother thought traveling privately would be better, more comfortable, and—"

"Home?" His eyes widened.

She smiled at him the way she'd been trained, tilted her head, and offered bland reassurance and encouragement, with a modicum of coddling. "When you're well enough, of course. I shall have to confer with your doctors here and make arrangements when—"

"What's going on here?" A tall, broad man in uniform marched down the aisle between the beds with the matron behind him, and behind her came Chaplain Strong, looking concerned. He slipped past the nurse with the agility of desperation, his concerned gaze on Eleanor.

"Hello again, Miss Atherton," he said brightly, coming to a stop between herself and the officer. "May I introduce our commandant, Colonel Bellford? Colonel, this is Miss Atherton."

The colonel stopped at the foot of Louis's bed and glared at Eleanor, ignoring the niceties of introduction. She noted the RAMC insignia, the flashes and badges on his shoulders and collar, the gold frogging on his sleeves that marked his rank.

"Colonel, if I may, I fear I might have given you the wrong impression when I said Miss Atherton was a doctor—" the chaplain began, trying to catch the commander's attention, but the matron gasped in horror, as if the chaplain had announced she was a cabaret dancer about to shed her clothing and perform. She added her own affronted glare to the colonel's, piercing Eleanor with it.

"Uh-oh," Louis murmured beside her. "You're in for it now, El, old girl."

The colonel ignored the quip, the nurse, and the chaplain and kept his attention on Eleanor. "Who precisely are you?"

She stood frozen to the spot. She knew that look—the indignation, the annoyance. It was the way her father looked at her, the way he spoke to her. She recognized the bully, the martinet, the kind of man who must always be right and in charge. The kind of man who did not countenance female doctors.

She fought the urge to smile and placate him. She was here at the behest of the Countess of Kirkswell, after all; she had her ladyship's full confidence. She squared her shoulders. "I'm Dr. Eleanor Atherton."

"I understand you think you're a *doctor*"—he said it like it was a sin, his mouth twisting on the word—"but why are you *here*?"

She reached into her pocket, fumbling for the wallet that held the countess's letter of introduction. She unfolded the monogrammed sheet of stationery and held it out.

She remembered Sergeant MacLeod's warning. *The colonel has the authority to send ye home.*

"I have a letter from—"

"I can read, Miss Atherton." He snatched the letter from her and glanced briefly at the crest and the countess's signature, then scanned the rest. His red complexion darkened to plum.

"This is my hospital. *Mine.* This is not some suffragette's lark. We are in a war zone, and this man is a wounded military officer and therefore under my direct care."

There's a war on, he might have said. No time for manners or niceties, no polite couching of harsh words to soften their effect. Military orders trumped the rules of civilian authority, even the aristocratic command of a close friend of their majesties. The colonel could indeed send her packing at once. She watched his mouth open as he drew breath to speak, knowing he intended to do just that. She imagined the smug complacency on her father's face when she came slinking home without Louis. He wouldn't say a word, of course, would simply remind her to turn the light out when she was finished scrubbing the surgery.

Louis spoke first. "If I may, sir, my mother sent her—the Countess of Kirkswell. That's the family crest on the stationery. If you've kept up with *Country Life*, then you'll know my mother is very active in war work. She's quite busy donating motorcycles, cutting ribbons, and supervising the planting of potatoes on the south lawn of the old pile, among other good works." He sent Eleanor a cheeky grin. "I can vouch for Miss Atherton. I doubt she's a suffragette. She's an old and dear friend of the family." He took her hand in his. "Not only that, *Dr.* Atherton is very highly qualified. She is my mother's personal physician and treats my father's gout. In fact, he'll allow no other doctor to attend him."

The colonel looked at her in surprise. So did the matron and the chaplain. Eleanor felt a blush fill her cheeks at the exaggerations, the outright lies. Louis squeezed her hand, and she saw mischief in his eyes. She withdrew her hand from his and lifted her chin. She'd fight her own battle. She looked the colonel in the eye. "I was asked by the countess to provide medical care for Lieutenant Chastaine on his journey home. Her ladyship wishes him to have companionship and medical care. Private care. My care."

"A worried mother," the chaplain said softly, as if the countess were the holy virgin, which would have made Louis—Eleanor swallowed a nervous bubble of mirth at that idea. "That's most understandable under the circumstances, don't you think, sir?" Strong added.

The colonel ignored the chaplain and waved the letter over the splint. "If you are any kind of doctor at all, then you can see for yourself that Lieutenant Chastaine cannot be moved for some weeks yet. He needs rest, and the bones must have time to knit before he undertakes the rigors of travel. If he were jostled roughly on the open road at this point it would cause pain and potentially infection, even death. I am doing everything possible for him *right here*. You may do for treating an earl's ulcer, but the earl is not a doctor, nor is the countess. *I am*—and I do not know anything about you, young woman."

"Gout," Louis murmured. "Didn't I say it was gout?" Eleanor wished he'd be quiet, or at least serious. "Is there a chance I can leave now, today, with you?" he pleaded.

She looked over the splint, the half-healed burns. The colonel was right. "No, not yet." The chaplain let out a relieved breath. The matron made an indignant noise in her throat. The colonel didn't move at all.

Louis's charming grin turned into a petulant pout. "It's been weeks. I am tired of being trussed up like a holiday goose. I thought I'd emerge from the operating theater with an onion in my beak and sausage stuffing up my—"

The matron gasped. "Mind your language, Lieutenant!"

Louis glowered at her. "Then when can I go?" he demanded.

"May I see Lieutenant Chastaine's case notes, please?" Eleanor asked.

The colonel looked like a bull about to snort fire. "The *notes*? Young woman, do you know anything about wounds sustained on the battlefield? Have you seen what gas gangrene can do to a man, how quickly infection can spread, even with a minor wound, and do worse harm than a bomb or a bullet? Have you any understanding of what a triumph it is to save even one badly wounded man, to bring him back from the brink of death, to know he will be useful and able to serve again because of timely and expert medical care? If you do, then the training for female doctors has changed since I was at medical school."

Eleanor felt herself blushing. "I have read everything possible about the new techniques being developed here in France, the new antiseptics and improved methods of care." She glanced at the matron. "I know it was nurses who developed the best treatment for shock." Instead of looking pleased by the recognition, the nurse continued to glare indignantly at Eleanor.

"You have *read* about it," Colonel Bellford scoffed.

"This isn't proper, Colonel," the matron said. "Think of the example it will set for the nurses and the VADs if she stays—"

The chaplain weighed in. "What does Lieutenant Chastaine have to say? Perhaps he does not want a woman prodding and poking at him, or perhaps—"

"Oh, prod away," Louis said brightly. He sent Eleanor a wink. "Just know that I have no tolerance for pain."

"Miss Atherton does have written authority, Colonel," Chaplain Strong said, looking pointedly at the letter in the colonel's hand. Matron Connolly cast a surreptitious look at the paper, reading over the chaplain's shoulder. Her brows twitched, and she drew back with a frown, and Eleanor knew she recognized her credentials as official.

"She does not have *my* authority," the colonel said, turning his wrath on the chaplain. Strong stood patiently in the face of it, like Daniel facing the lions.

"I also have a letter from Colonel Sir Hugo Ferris," Eleanor said quickly, keeping her eyes on the crumpled paper in the colonel's hand. "I believe he has already been to visit Lieutenant Chastaine."

"Ah. So that's how my mother found out I was here. Sir Hugo told her," Louis said. He flicked a glance at Eleanor, his eyes narrowed, assessing her true purpose before he turned his attention back to the colonel. "The colonel is not only my godfather, he's a regimental commander and friend of the king's—and of Sir Douglas Haig." He looked charmingly apologetic. "He outranks you, sir. My mother, of course, outranks us all. Well, perhaps not the king, but most certainly the kaiser." He gave the matron a dazzling smile. "Mater is the dragon of all dragons. If I have no objection to Dr. Atherton's care, why should anyone else? You've done all the important work, Colonel. She needs only to keep an eye on me, take my temperature, rub my back, and see the bandages aren't too tight. My morale will surely be improved by the company of an old and dear family friend, and her qualifications will undoubtedly relieve the nurses of the burden of one more tiresome patient."

He batted his golden lashes at her. "But you should know that I can be quite tiresome indeed, dearest Eleanor—*Dr.* Atherton. I hope you're prepared to be patient, mop my fevered brow, and soothe me when I'm pettish."

Matron Connolly made a strangled sound of outrage.

Bellford folded the countess's letter and handed it back to her. He returned Colonel Ferris's note as well. "It appears you have friends in very high places, Miss Atherton, but look to the lieutenant himself—it is quite possible to fall from high places, even when one has all the cheek and confidence in the world. Make no mistake. This facility and all the other patients within it are forbidden to you. I hope that's clear. I will continue to monitor Lieutenant Chastaine. All decisions regarding his care, even if it's just to prescribe a headache powder, must be approved by me. If his condition worsens or if I feel he's not receiving proper care, I will not hesitate to step in, no matter who has authorized your presence here, is that clear?"

She could stay. She resisted the urge to whoop.

Instead she straightened her spine and nodded crisply. "Perfectly, Colonel. I shall provide you with regular reports on the lieutenant's health. Would you prefer them in writing, or shall we confer in person?" Her attempt at being professional, the way a male doctor would be, fell flat. Bellford's eyes narrowed, and his nostrils flared.

"I shall continue to visit this patient daily to see for myself."

"There now, all settled, then," Reverend Strong said cheerily. "I'd be pleased to see that Dr. Atherton is made comfortable in the guest quarters. She's had a long journey, and no breakfast." He beamed at her as if she hadn't just nearly been flayed within an inch of her life and almost sent packing. "Sergeant MacLeod asked me to make certain you ate."

"Thank you," Eleanor said, as much to the absent Scot as to the chaplain, and moved to follow him, but Louis caught her hand.

"When will you return to me?" he asked, and the admiring look in his eyes, even if it was a mocking one, melted her knees. As good as a handkerchief. Better, even.

"Soon," she murmured. Once she'd had something to eat, a bath, and a chance to comb her hair.

"Make sure you come straight here. You're not to set foot in the other wards. The sight of a female doctor, the very idea of one, would upset the wounded," the colonel reminded her sharply.

She nodded. She'd won her first battle. He was allowing her to stay. "As you wish, Colonel."

Reverend Strong was waiting, and she looked at Louis, waiting for him to release her hand. His eyes were keen on her, lit with male interest. It was the way she'd seen him look at other, prettier girls, girls she'd always envied. Feminine delight filled her. "I'll be back soon," she said.

He let her go. "I'll be counting the minutes."

The chaplain was regarding them with interest.

"No doubt you'll want to hear all the news of home," she said lightly.

But Louis couldn't resist. He'd never been able to resist a chance to be wicked. "Oh, I have *Country Life* for all that. It's you I'm interested in, El." He raised her hand to his mouth again and let his lips linger, his glittering eyes on hers.

She plucked her hand free, unsure if he was flirting or serious, not knowing how to respond. "I'll be back soon," she said again.

He chuckled as she followed the chaplain out, and she knew he'd been teasing her yet again.

But this time it was a grown-up, man-woman kind of teasing. *Flirtation.* Who knew where it might lead? To friendship, perhaps, warm regard, or—

Heartbreak, a small inner voice warned her.

She turned at the door. Louis was still watching her, his eyes heavy lidded, his smile winsome—and completely false.

She bit her lower lip and tasted the faint echo of Sergeant MacLeod's whisky on her skin, and it made her think of him instead. He'd left her less than an hour ago, and in that time the whole world had changed. She could stay. She wanted to find him and tell him, as if he were an old friend, someone who would understand just what this meant to her. The chaplain opened the door for her, and the winter wind hit her hot cheeks, stealing her breath and replacing it with a dose of sense. She'd known Fraser MacLeod for a few scant hours, shared on a dark journey. He'd been good company, and that was all. She closed her eyes as the wind swept a lock of her hair across her face. And when she did, she could see the intense gray stare that was so different from Louis's flirtatious gaze.

She followed the chaplain as she wondered where Sergeant MacLeod was now. She hoped he was safe and had found some breakfast.

She might never see him again, but she suspected—*knew*—that she'd carry the memory of him for a very long time.

CHAPTER SEVENTEEN

By the time Fraser MacLeod arrived back at the frontline aid post it was late afternoon, and nearly dark yet again. He'd found a ride with the lads in the quartermaster's wagon, and he came bearing supplies, mail, and a tin of cake that one of the nursing sisters at 46/ CCS had kindly sent along.

The aid post occupied the cellar of a ruined bakery a few hundred yards behind the forward trenches, where the wounded could reach it easily. It had been a snug billet for the winter, with the old bake oven providing heat and the bombproof thick stone walls.

Fraser climbed off the wagon and swung his pack over his shoulder. He winced as it rubbed at the raw places on his neck and back where the straps of the stretcher bit deep day after day. Out of habit, he paused for a moment to listen to the sound of guns, much closer here, and for the cries of wounded men calling for help, but the gunfire was intermittent and half-hearted. He'd have enough time for a meal and perhaps a few hours' sleep before he had to take his team of bearers forward to support the men going out on night raids.

He let the quartermaster's detail go ahead of him down the narrow stairs into the cellar, carrying tin pails of food for the medical officer, orderlies, and bearers inside. It was cold now, but they'd reheat it on the small stove—not that it would make it any more palatable.

Corporal Max Chilcott, another bearer, looked up and grinned as Fraser appeared in the doorway. "Look who's back, and just in time for supper! Good to see you—not that you missed anything—it's been quiet." He sent a dour sideways look at the soldier carrying the rations. "Did *you* bring anything good to eat by chance, Fraser?"

"Cake from Sister MacKinnon," Fraser said, and he watched the corporal's eyes light up as he put the tin on the table. "There's mail and a few boxes of supplies in the wagon."

Two of the other bearers went out to fetch it, and Fraser stood next to the warm bread oven, holding out his battered hands to the heat radiating from the bricks.

Captain Nathaniel Duncan, the regimental medical officer, was sitting at a small table with some of the bearers and orderlies, playing cards by candlelight to save the kerosene. The cots and treatment tables along the walls were empty save for a few medics, who were using them to catch some sleep. Fred Hammond was snoring like a tank driving through porridge, but no one minded. Sleep was too precious to wake him from.

"Welcome back, Sergeant," Captain Duncan said, glancing up from his cards. "The Germans apparently knew you were away, since they've not bothered to fire a shot at us in two days. I daresay we're in for it now you're here again."

"Any rumors of a spring offensive? Did Bellford say anything?" Chilcott asked, taking a cigarette from behind his ear and passing it to Fraser.

"Not to me. It's quiet on the line, though there's some shelling farther south, near Bapaume." Fraser lit the fag and took a drag.

"And your patient?" the MO asked.

"Guthrie was alive when I left him," Fraser said. "They did an amputation at 46/CCS and asked me to accompany him to Calais, which I did."

"You're a lucky lad, as usual," Chilcott said without resentment.

"Oh, there were plenty of nurses and orderlies who could have gone, but Reverend Strong knew Captain Duncan would be wanting an update when I got back here."

"Still, all the way to Calais! It's not Paris, but how's the big city?" Chilcott asked.

Fraser shook his head. "I didn't see more than the train station. The chaplain asked me to bring back a consignment of supplies, and they were at the station, ready and waiting. I took one train out, the next one back."

He should tell them about the marvelous curiosity that was Eleanor Atherton, lady doctor, but he didn't. He found he wanted to keep her to himself, not answer questions about whether she was pretty, or willing, or prudish. Besides, he wasn't likely to see her again, so what was the point of mentioning her?

"The lads on the line will be glad to hear Guthrie is alive and on his way home to Blighty," Duncan said. "I'll spread the word. Did you get any rest?"

"Some, on the train ride back," he lied. He should have slept—he'd been here long enough to know to grab sleep whenever and wherever an opportunity presented itself, because there was no way to know when the next chance would come. Instead, he'd spent most of those precious hours watching Eleanor Atherton sleep. Even now, tired as he was, he couldn't see it as wasted time. He remembered her pale face, the long copper lashes resting on her cheeks, the long locks of russet hair falling free from the hat that had gone askew after her fight with the soldiers. He grinned at that, even here in the cellar. Then he frowned.

She'd probably had a joyful reunion with her wounded flier and had forgotten all about meeting a grubby Scottish sergeant on the train.

"Sounds like a dull trip," Chilcott said.

"Aye," he muttered.

"You still look half dead, Sergeant," Duncan said, assessing him with a medical eye. "Have something to eat, and sleep for a while. I'll wake you if I need you."

Fraser took a tin cup and filled it with tepid and typical Irish stew from the pail on the stove. Duncan rose to join him, and Fraser filled a cup for him as well. "Ever work with a female doctor, Captain?"

Duncan's brows rose. "That's an odd question. No. There were two in my class at university—well, not *my* class, since they trained separately from the men."

"Were ye in Edinburgh?" Fraser asked.

"London," Duncan replied. "Why? Did you hear something? They aren't suggesting bringing over female doctors, are they? I know we're short staffed, but they could never do the job—shouldn't do the job."

"There was a hospital run by women in Paris," Chilcott said, overhearing.

Duncan frowned. "Aye, I've heard of it. And there are a couple of others here in France as well, at Royaumont and Wimereux. There's even one in London, on Endell Street, staffed entirely by women. The War Office sanctioned it when female doctors wouldn't take no for an answer when they tried to enlist. Mind you, they needed the beds, and the doctors, and I hear they do passable work there at least, safe behind the lines. Most of them go to the French when the War Office rejects them. Some even formed their own associations to fund themselves, and since the women were willing to supply everything from staff to medicines, the French readily agreed to let them. Saves them money, and in the end, the women aren't their citizens, and therefore not their problem if there's trouble. Daft system. I wonder if those women even realize how vulnerable they are. Why are you asking? What did you hear?" he asked Fraser again.

"Nothing at all," Fraser said, staring at the stodgy stew in his cup.

Chilcott nudged Fraser with his elbow and jerked his head at Duncan. "Might be nice to have a woman as MO," he teased. "Prettier than this bloke, and her stitches would leave less of a scar." He mimed the act of sewing, his pinkie extended, his lips pursed sweetly.

"It will never happen," Duncan said. He frowned at the meal as well and set his cup aside. He took a chipped china mug and filled it with tea from the metal pot on the hob instead. It was thick and black as treacle from brewing all day, but hot and strong. "A woman could never face the horrors of the front," Duncan said. "Can you imagine a woman shoving some poor bastard's guts back into his belly while he curses her for a butcher? Or examining a man down with the clap? The poor lad would die of embarrassment, and *she* would faint dead away at the sight of it. No, a woman can't be expected to manage the full duties of a male doctor, entering the trenches and billets of ordinary soldiers. It would be an affront to their dignity—hers and his."

"Hear, hear!" Chilcott agreed around a spoonful of stew. He raised his cup and saluted the smiling photo of English music hall sweetheart Gertie Gitana, cut from a newspaper and nailed to the wall above the table. "Women have their place at home, waiting for us, pining, keeping the kettle hot and the fire stoked. There's where I want to think of a woman, in her bood-whar, her perfumed hair in ribbons, dressed in lace and silk, waiting for me to come marching home."

Fraser tried to picture Eleanor Atherton at a makeshift aid post set up in a shell hole or an abandoned trench, tending patients under fire, risking death. In the past five months, they'd lost two MOs. He couldn't picture her sitting at home in a boudoir, either. He remembered the look of clinical determination on her face as she had leaned over McKie, the gas patient on the platform in Calais, and the sturdy left hook she had planted in the eye of the soldier who'd dared to accost her.

"Are you grinning that way because you agree with me, Fraser?" Chilcott asked him, and Fraser sobered and looked up at Gertie Gitana again, then simply nodded.

"Aye, she belongs at home, where she's safe," he muttered. He made his way toward a cot. He fell on it facedown and was asleep in minutes.

CHAPTER EIGHTEEN

MARCH 6, 1918

Eleanor's days fell into a pattern. In the morning she would visit Louis after breakfast. The matron insisted that she not arrive before eight thirty, since the patients needed to be cared for, fed, shaved, and bathed before then, and she would be a distraction and an affront to their dignity and their expectations of privacy. She was just a visitor, in the matron's opinion, which was the only one that mattered. The colonel may have given her permission to stay, but the matron made the rules where her presence on the officers' ward was concerned, the only ward Eleanor was permitted to set foot in. She spent the early mornings pacing the floor of the small visitor's hut they'd given her as accommodation, since the sounds of the war beyond the thin walls would not allow her to rest past dawn. She woke every time she heard the sound of footsteps on the duckboards. Surely running feet meant an emergency, and she itched to help. She heard the sound of ambulances arriving or departing, the motors chugging, the brakes squealing. There were shouted orders, calls for supplies, and worst of all, the cries of the wounded. She wasn't used to enforced leisure, or to solitude. No one was actively rude to her, but the nurses and orderlies remained distant when she encountered them by chance. They were positively suspicious if they thought she was watching them, observing procedures or techniques. She learned to observe from the corner of her eye, to keep her tongue trapped firmly behind her teeth, and not to ask questions.

When she did arrive to see Louis—usually at 8:31 a.m.—Matron Connolly crisply and briefly updated her on Lieutenant Chastaine's condition. "His leg was examined this morning by Colonel Bellford, and the night sister checked the burns on his arm. He slept well, has eaten sufficiently, and performed his bodily functions in good order. There's nothing of a medical nature for you to do, but perhaps you might read to him. I'll ask one of the orderlies to bring you a chair." There was nothing more to do until Colonel Bellford pronounced Louis fit to travel and released him to her care for the journey.

When the matron left the ward, Eleanor still did her own check on the adjustment of the splint on Louis's leg.

"How much longer will I have to be here?" Louis asked her irritably one morning after she'd been there for nine days and he'd grown bored with the novelty of flirting with her and fell back to teasing her again. "My leg aches, and so does my backside, and I'm bored."

"Just another little while. A fortnight or so." Eleanor looked at the case file and read Bellford's minimal scrawled notes, which said little. "The colonel is very happy with your progress," she told him encouragingly.

"Blair said I was doing well," Louis argued. Eleanor still hadn't met Captain Blair. He was on night duty and did his rounds at dawn, and he was often away, on call to other CCS units, since surgeons were in short supply. Another man was due to arrive from England any day, but medical officers rushed back and forth to the locations where the fighting was heaviest and they were most needed. Since her arrival, it had been relatively quiet in forty-six's sector.

"You're doing *very* well, but healing takes time," she soothed.

"Rub my shoulders, will you?" Louis demanded petulantly, and she obliged.

"You're a lucky chap, Chastaine," Captain Findlay said from the bed next to Louis's as she moved the pillow and began to massage Louis's back. It no longer felt intimate or thrilling. He was tense and simply wanted the knots eased. He wasn't used to sitting still—she couldn't remember him ever walking when he could run, or sitting when he could climb. He liked speed, the thrill of wind in his hair, a dare, danger, and he'd had nearly five weeks of enforced rest. He sent a frustrated frown Findlay's way now, and Findlay laughed. "You are, you know. I haven't got lovely young ladies coming to care for me. How did you manage it?"

"Perhaps if you were a pilot, old boy, instead of just an infantry officer. Women—ladies, matrons, even doctors like Eleanor—love fliers," Louis said, basking in Findlay's envy. "Isn't that right, El?" He gave Eleanor a grin of his own now he had an audience, but she knew the flirtatious smile was more for Findlay's benefit than for hers, a glorious moment of superiority for Louis. She'd come to realize that even when he was at his most charming, his heart remained untouched where she was concerned. She was a friend, and he treated her with familiar ease, though even that felt superficial. Only his frustration was real, his restlessness. Under his careful facade of charm and careless courage, she suspected there was much more. Perhaps he was in pain, or worried that he might not ever heal. She did her best to soothe that, but thus far he hadn't allowed her to crack the hard surface he kept over his true emotions. She supposed she should be disappointed that her childhood hero had feet of clay after all. But strangely, she wasn't. She had come to see Louis Chastaine as an interesting medical case, her brother's friend, the son of her employer and benefactor, and a genuine pain in the backside. She wondered if he was as shallow as he pretended to be. Surely not—he'd won a medal for bravery, had endured and survived. Somewhere inside, she suspected, the real Louis Chastaine was a man worth knowing, worth admiring—or so she hoped.

"Is that 'Elle' from the French for 'she,' perhaps? Is that a childhood nickname?" Findlay asked, still vying for her attention. He'd been at the CCS for two days. His arm was in a sling, and he had several broken ribs. His breathing was shallow, but his eyes brightened when she entered the ward each morning. He had a charming smile and bright green eyes under reddish-blond hair. He was another unrepentant flirt, like Louis. Captain Findlay grinned at the nurses and VADs, asked after their families, and promised to arrange to send them all kinds of treats when he got well again and was back in England. His compliments made them blush and smile and turned even the most professional nurses to putty. Louis competed outrageously with Findlay, and in the heady glow of such intense and charming masculine attention, how could any woman resist? The only woman immune to it was Matron Connolly. Nothing softened her icy demeanor.

Eleanor found it exhausting, constantly trying to decipher the double meaning of their compliments and quips or the precise suggestion meant by a wink, a roguish grin, or a smirk.

She found herself comparing them to Fraser MacLeod. His gaze had been forthright and direct, and he'd made her feel like a person, not a conquest. His admiration wasn't given easily, she suspected, and would be hard won and honest when it came, and all the more precious. It surprised her that she longed for that, not for Louis's meaningless compliments.

She didn't realize she was smiling blankly at Captain Findlay, lost in her own thoughts, until Louis grabbed her hand and squeezed it until she fixed her gaze on him.

"Of course it's a nickname. *Elle*, French for 'she,' woman." He lowered his tone, made the last word a seductive purr. The corners of his eyes crinkled, and his thumb stroked her knuckles. Golly, it felt good. Could a man seduce a woman just by caressing her knuckles? "That makes me *Lui*, 'him,' *l'homme, n'est-ce pas*? Eleanor and Louis, *Elle et Lui, Lui et Elle*."

Eleanor and Louis. How often had she written that in her notebooks as a girl, dreaming of a moment like this? He didn't mean a word of it. She searched his face, the lines around his mouth and eyes, the slight tension in his jaw, met the heavy-lidded eyes, wondering yet again what he was truly thinking, but Findlay laughed and broke the spell. "*Elle et Lui*—very clever. It would be hard to make such a charming play on my name. My parents christened me Lancelot."

"Ah, but in other company, perhaps, Lance?" Chastaine said and gave his comrade a wink. Findlay had the grace to blush. Perhaps Louis thought Eleanor was too innocent to understand the double meaning. She wasn't. She'd faced a great deal of that kind of teasing in medical school, where her male classmates made sport of her just because she was young, female, and virginal. This jest was mild by comparison to some she'd endured. She turned away to pour a glass of water from the carafe on the bedside table.

"Good heavens, you're as pink as a June rose. We haven't shocked you, have we, Eleanor?" Louis asked, touching a knuckle to her cheek. "Perhaps I've been in rough male company too long. Forgive me?" She glanced at him, wondering if he was sincere now, and if she'd even be able to tell. He sent her a wide-eyed, pleading look that made her heart flip in her breast. Her hand shook, and she spilled water on her sleeve. She could understand how a lass would give him anything just for that smile . . . Still, she raised her chin and gave him a sharp look.

"I'm not shocked at all. I'm a doctor. I know all the meanings of the term. I have 'lanced' hundreds of boils, wounds, and unwanted swellings," she said tartly, playing the game. She held up her thumb and finger an inch apart in front of Louis's nose, then snapped them, making him jump. "I reduced them to nothing at all, and the patients were far better for it." She'd learned that at medical school, too, how to hold her own in saucy conversations with male medical students who sought to shock and confound their female counterparts.

Louis's brows rose and he laughed, genuine appreciation for her wit clear in his eyes, and that was better than flirtation.

"What clever repartee, Miss Atherton, though it is quite lowering to be mentioned in the context of boils. You have 'lanced' me to the heart," Findlay said.

She was contrite at once. "Forgive me, Captain. Yours is quite a romantic name. Lancelot was a great hero, a brave knight who loved too well."

"But alas, not too wisely. He chose the wife of his friend and king to love, and such love triangles always bring tragedy and sorrow." Findlay put his uninjured hand over his breast, his fingers dark against white bandages. "Chivalry demanded that poor Lancelot worship the fair lady from afar, but he did not heed the rules of courtly love and honor, whereas I, his namesake, shall keep my distance, unless a certain lovely lady here in this humble CCS bids me approach her, to—"

"Bloody thespian. I thought your father was a bishop," Louis said.

"So he is, but I read English at Oxford. I confess that I spent a summer or two treading the boards in repertory companies. In fact, we did *Morte d'Arthur* in the summer of '14."

"There ought to be a rule—forget sanctioning recruits for flat feet or short stature—I say no bloody thespians," Louis said. "How did you get in, and with a captain's commission?"

Findlay's brows rose. "Same as you, I suspect. My father has friends in high places." He pointed to the roof of the tent. "Not socially, of course, but perhaps having the ear of the angels is of equal use."

"Not here in hell," Louis grumbled. "And I found my own way to high places. My father forbade me to become a pilot. But I was just the spare to the heir then, so it didn't matter so much. Now I'm the heir with no spare." He frowned, shifted in the bed, his good mood clouding over. He glowered at the apparatus that held his leg up. "How long until this damned thing comes off?" he demanded again. He looked across the ward at a VAD who was delivering newspapers to the wounded officers and summoned the girl with a crook of his finger. "You there—go and tell Colonel Bellford I want to see him. Tell him my *doctor* wants to see him." He sounded peevish, and spoiled, and titled.

The VAD looked at Eleanor in surprise, then her eyes hardened as she blamed Louis's rudeness on her. "I'll fetch Matron," the young woman said, turning on her heel to do just that.

"Somerton—" Eleanor began, using his title. She could imagine the colonel's annoyance, his anger, not with Louis, but with her.

"Call me Louis, for God's sake," he snapped. "We were playmates as children."

The comment took her by surprise, and she gaped at him. "We were never that!"

Perhaps it was her indignation that made Captain Findlay laugh.

Then he gasped and began to choke. His eyes widened as he fought for air.

"What the devil? Take a breath, man!" Louis said.

But Eleanor rounded the bed and hurried to the captain's side. His lips were blue, and he was struggling to breathe. She put her fingertips against his neck, where she felt his pulse hammering weakly. He gazed up at her, his green eyes wide and desperate.

She ran for the supply cart at the end of the ward, grabbed a pair of scissors and a needle and ran back again. Lancelot Findlay's complexion was gray now from lack of oxygen. Eleanor flicked back the bedclothes. "It's all right, Captain, I'm going to help you," she said as she cut away the bandages, revealing the horribly battered chest beneath. She carefully searched with her fingers and found the place where a balloon of air had formed between his chest wall and his lungs, making it impossible for him to draw air.

"What are you doing?" she heard Matron Connolly cry as she arrived on the ward with the VAD. "Stop at once! This man has severe wounds, three broken ribs and—" Her voice was high-pitched with outrage and horror, but Eleanor couldn't stop now.

"He has a pneumothorax," Eleanor said calmly. The nurse grabbed her shoulder, but Eleanor flung her off and went back to what she was doing.

"You're going to kill him!" the matron said.

She lunged for Eleanor again, but someone stepped past the nurse. "Step back if you would, Matron. I'll assist if necessary," the newcomer said calmly. Eleanor glanced up at the tall man standing beside her. "Go ahead," he said.

"I'm going to get Colonel Bellford!" the matron spluttered and marched away.

Eleanor picked up the needle. The stranger did nothing to stop her, instead simply observing. She measured with her fingers, found the intercostal space between the ribs, and inserted the needle. Instantly, Findlay drew a hard breath.

"That's done it. Very good," the observer said, and put his fingers against Findlay's neck, measuring his pulse.

"The bandages were too tight," she said. "There was air trapped, you see, and—"

"Yes, I know what a pneumothorax is—one of his broken ribs likely lacerated the lung. Have you done one before?"

She swallowed. "In medical school." And only on cadavers. She read amusement in his dark eyes, as if somehow he'd known that.

"I'm a surgeon. David Blair," he supplied. For a moment his gaze roamed over her. "And you're the lady doctor who's caused such a tempest in our little teapot."

"What the devil is going on here?" She heard Bellford's voice and shut her eyes. Before she could speak, the colonel shoved her aside and bent to examine the patient.

"Couldn't breathe. She—she saved me," Lancelot Findlay said. He reached around the colonel for her hand and squeezed it. "Now it's my turn to hold your hand," he gasped. "Thank you. If I had known that's what it would take to get your attention—"

Colonel Bellford plucked Findlay's hand free on the pretense of measuring his pulse. "This is not a game, Miss Atherton. This is a badly wounded man, an officer and a hero. He deserves the finest care we can give him. He isn't a practice dummy." He ignored the nurses and orderlies who'd gathered to watch. He checked Findlay's wounds. He frowned when he found nothing amiss and that she'd done no harm after all. "Rebandage this patient at once," he ordered Matron Connolly.

"But not so tightly," David Blair said, standing at the end of the bed with his arms folded over his chest, his expression bemused.

"There's a risk of pneumonia if he can't breathe," Eleanor added.

Bellford glared at her. He was purple again, breathing hard from hurrying here to catch her killing someone. Eleanor looked at her hands and hid a smile of triumph, but it was short-lived.

"Young woman, I allowed you to stay despite my doubts. I ordered you to stay away from any patient but Lieutenant Chastaine, and you have blatantly disobeyed that directive. You have letters from those who clearly do not understand that proper, careful, expert medical care keeps morale high and saves lives, and there is no room for amateurs. Need I remind you that I have the power to send you right back where you came from on the next train if I choose to do so?" Behind him, Matron Connolly smirked, waiting for the commander to give the order.

"I'm glad she was here," Captain Findlay said, his voice still rough and thin, his eyes on Eleanor. He drew another lungful of air, as if to assure himself he could. "You have my thanks for saving my life, *Dr. Atherton*, and for keeping my morale very high indeed." He coughed and grimaced. "Are you one of my father's angels?"

"Don't be blasphemous, Captain," the colonel warned. Captain Blair made a sound like suppressed laughter, but turned it into a cough when his commander shot him a reproving look. "Isn't Findlay your patient, Blair? Where were you?"

"I just got back from 32/CCS. By chance, I operated on another man with broken ribs and a lacerated liver while I was there," he said without flinching at the colonel's fury. "I hope he gets care as good as Findlay is receiving. You have my thanks as well, Dr. Atherton. Fine work."

His compliment meant more than all of Louis's insincere words. She glanced toward him now, but Louis didn't smile or offer praise for her quick work. All the flirtation had gone from his eyes, and he was staring at her, slack-jawed with horrified surprise.

Eleanor needed a breath of air. "Please excuse me," she said, though Colonel Bellford looked like he had more to say. She left the ward without waiting to hear it.

Outside, in the chill of the cloudy March morning, she gulped fresh air. She sank down on a bench, a makeshift thing made from two boards and a pair of short logs, and listened to the icicles dripping. She'd done what she was trained for. Another few minutes and Findlay might have suffocated, his lung collapsed, his heart too constricted to beat. It might have gone wrong, but it hadn't. She'd saved his life. Louis wouldn't understand that, of course, but Bellford did.

She shut her eyes, rubbed them. *Do no harm.* The meaning of the Hippocratic oath was a simple one, often incorrectly abbreviated to those three simple words. But harm came in so many forms—mental, physical, emotional . . . The men here had been through so much. Had she done wrong? She wondered what it was that had so dismayed

Louis—was it seeing a comrade gasping for breath, turning blue, or was it the sight of her, a woman he'd once known as a clumsy, moony little girl, stabbing a needle into a man's chest?

She straightened her spine as the door opened, sat up properly, and pulled herself together. She'd learned that at medical school, too—not to show any reaction to rebukes or criticisms that might make her appear weak or overtly feminine. She had to be stronger, braver, better than her male classmates, fully armored.

David Blair sat down beside her. The bench creaked under his added weight, and she gripped the rough boards tight, both to keep the rickety structure steady and to brace herself if he was here to deliver a lecture.

"I meant it when I said you did well. Bellford knows it, too. He's not one for praise—or female doctors. I'm sure you've noticed, since you appear to be quite observant."

She swallowed and nodded but didn't reply. He was very tall, cord-thin. He was dark haired, his face as lean as the rest of him. He wasn't as handsome as Louis or Findlay, but he had kind, clear, intelligent eyes. Surgeon's eyes.

"Findlay lay on the battlefield for nearly four days with three broken ribs and a broken arm. It took a further twenty hours to get him here and to dig two bullets out of him. He survived all that, but he would have died if you hadn't been there and known what to do."

She scanned the tents around her, noted the icy mist that hung over them, though it was nearly spring. "My father is also a doctor. He would have reacted the same way Colonel Bellford did if he were here."

"Yes, well, not all of us are such fossils. There were three women in my class at Cambridge, at least for a time. They were competent and quick, but they were bullied into leaving. I'm glad you stuck it out—so's Findlay, I daresay. I'm David Blair, by the way, captain, surgeon," he introduced himself again.

"Eleanor Atherton, doctor, civilian."

"Not a surgeon? You have the hands for it." He glanced down at her hands, folded on her knee.

"They opened full surgical training at the university while I was there. I took every class I could. Still . . ." She shrugged. "I do understand what Colonel Bellford means when he says how appropriate medical care and the confidence of a patient in their doctor's skill helps heal."

He shook his head. "Don't you dare, not now, so soon after saving a man's life. I've been here for eleven months. I've seen men so badly injured they thought they'd die. They lay out in No Man's Land all alone, waiting for help or death. Once they reach us, they know there's hope, and that they aren't alone anymore. Hope like that doesn't care whether you're male or female."

He got to his feet and glanced at the watch on his wrist. "God, I've been awake for nearly thirty hours. I need sleep, a bath, and food. If I take care of the first two, will you share a meal with me later?"

She let go of the bench, unclenched her fingers, and clasped them in her lap instead, resisting the urge to touch her hair, tuck back an errant strand that had fallen over her eyes. She saw him notice it as well, wondered if he'd reach out and do it for her. She rose to her feet at once, straightened her spine, met his eye with professional frankness. "Thank you, Captain, I will."

He smiled. "Then I'll look forward to it. It was a pleasure to meet you, Dr. Atherton."

She watched him walk away. Now she reached up to brush her hair back. She stopped with her hand halfway to her head and stared at the blood on her sleeve. *There was blood on her sleeve!*

Elation replaced her anxiety.

She'd saved a life.

She went back to her quarters to change.

CHAPTER NINETEEN

D avid Blair had known Eleanor Atherton had a medical degree, but it was to his utter surprise that he realized she was
truly a doctor.

He'd assumed she was simply husband hunting, here to snare the
titled and dashing lieutenant.

She'd acted fast with Findlay, decisively, had known exactly what
was needed. It took her a matter of seconds to assess the situation, a
few more seconds to fetch a needle and perform the procedure. She'd
managed the crisis calmly, her movements quick and precise. If that
was her first time, she'd acquitted herself remarkably well. Cadavers
were good for practice, but they offered no indication that the doctor
had done the job right.

The moment when Captain Findlay dragged in a ragged, desperate breath, David fell in love with Eleanor Atherton, even though he
knew nothing else about her. It was just as his mother had predicted.

"You'll know the right woman when you see her. Your whole life will change in an instant," she'd told her sons. David had thought it a foolish notion then, especially for a doctor with a practical, scientific mind.

But something had bloomed in David's breast as he watched Eleanor Atherton wielding her needle. He'd all but heard angels sing as he watched her. Was that love? It was no medical condition that he knew of. Perhaps his mother had been right after all. But when Bellford had arrived, she'd stood primly silent, her expression flat as the colonel berated her, admonished her. There was blood on her cheek, and on her blouse. Findlay was gulping sweet air, gazing at his rescuer in astonished admiration. Matron Connolly had stared at Findlay, and Eleanor, and at the colonel, stunned speechless for once. It was Connolly's fault that the bandages were too tight in the first place, but Bellford hadn't mentioned that. And poor bloody Chastaine had missed the point entirely, had failed to grasp the true magnificence of his visitor. He'd gaped at her, pale and horrified, clutching the bedclothes to his chin in alarm.

If she *was* here to bag the noble pilot for her husband, she'd failed. The lieutenant had quit the field, retired from the competition, and left the prize for a brighter, more appreciative chap. It was that thought that made David grin as he shaved before the small mirror in his tent. He cut himself with the sharp razor. Some surgeon! He was acting like a schoolboy who'd met a pretty lass on the lea and was giddy as a puppy.

It wasn't the fact that she was pretty that attracted him. Pretty women were a dime a dozen. Several of the VADs were outright beauties. No, there was something else about Eleanor Atherton. It was her eyes, perhaps, keen, forthright, and without an ounce of flirtation. No one would ever accuse Eleanor Atherton of being as giddy as a puppy. He pressed a towel against the bleeding nick and winced at the sting.

He put on a clean khaki shirt, sponged his uniform, and even ran a brush over his boots and set them in place for later, ready to put on before he saw Eleanor again.

He stuck his head out of his tent and hailed a passing orderly. "Wake me in time for tea," he said. "If I'm not needed before, of course."

Then he climbed into bed and slept.

Hours later, dressed and as close to spit and polished as he could get without a barber or a valet, David dropped into the officers' ward and stopped by Findlay's bed. He was fast asleep, resting easily, his color good, his pulse normal. The fresh bandages around his chest were less snug than before.

"She should have waited for proper help," Chastaine said, watching him. "Eleanor, I mean. She was told not to interfere."

"Findlay would be dead if she hadn't," David replied. He crossed to examine Chastaine's leg since he was there.

"When can I get out of here?" Chastaine said peevishly.

"Soon," David said vaguely. He wondered if he could invent a reason for Chastaine to stay, just to keep Eleanor here awhile longer. "Your leg is healing well, but if we rush things, it could still go wrong. Let the bones knit properly and you'll walk with a limp, but at least you'll walk, and you'll still have the privilege of buying your boots in pairs." He turned his attention to the burn on Chastaine's arm, red, scaly, and ugly. The image of a small bird, tattooed just above the charred skin, stared at its own singed wingtips in open-beaked alarm.

"The burn could still be a source of infection if we're not careful," David added.

"Aren't the best doctors at the base hospitals? Perhaps I should go to Paris. Wouldn't I be better off there?"

David gritted his teeth at the man's haughty tone, at the plummy sound of privilege and the kind of wealth that could buy anything.

David's own father had been a senior lecturer in history at Cambridge. He'd inherited a modest windfall from an uncle and had invested it wisely until he had enough money to raise his sons like gentlemen, to help Patrick emigrate and buy the ranch and to pay for medical school for David. Even so, they'd never be gentlemanly enough for aristocrats like Chastaine. He held the flier's eyes without deference. Here in France, at war, social rank mattered less—and David's military rank of captain and his position as surgeon trumped Chastaine's lieutenancy. "If you want a second opinion, you might perhaps ask Dr. Atherton to—"

"No," Chastaine said quickly. "Not Eleanor."

The easy use of her Christian name irritated David, but he nodded. "She is your physician. She should at least be consulted."

Chastaine frowned. "My mother sent her—I had no idea she was a *real* doctor. I thought she was nothing more than a glorified nanny, a nursemaid. She's not the girl I remember. You couldn't say boo to her as a child."

"And now you're surprised she's a doctor?"

"I heard she'd made it through medical school, graduated. Her brother told me. I suppose everyone expected that she'd simply find a husband and marry and give it all up. Will she find one now? A woman who can do *that*"—he glanced pointedly at Findlay—"without blushing or even turning a hair? This is awkward for me, you understand. What must the other chaps in here think of all this? Eleanor is what they used to call an 'original' in the old days, a woman out of place, different, an embarrassment."

"An embarrassment?" David asked. "She saved a man's life!"

"Not my life!" Chastaine snapped. "I didn't ask her to come here. She's my mother's creature, sent to spy on me, to drag me home where I'll be kept safely under my mother's manicured thumb. Well, what if I don't want to go? What if I don't want to be a bloody viscount?" He glared at David, waiting for a reaction, for agreement, perhaps, but

David remained silent. "I need a cigarette. Do you have one by any chance?"

David shook his head. He had cigarettes in his pocket he shared with other patients, but he didn't want to oblige Chastaine, not after all he'd said about Eleanor.

Chastaine rolled his eyes in frustration and scrubbed a hand through his hair. "How long did you say I'd be trussed up like this?"

"Probably another fortnight." He heard the telltale sounds of Matron Connolly coming along the ward, the starched crackle of her pristine uniform, her crisp, quick footsteps. He looked up, noted that her face was set as usual in proper hospital creases. She leaned over Findlay, picked up his wrist, and took his pulse.

"Let him sleep. He's doing fine," David said.

"I intend to keep a close eye on him. I hope *she* didn't do him any harm."

"Dr. Atherton saved his life. The one who did the harm was the person who wound the bandages too tightly in the first place," David said pointedly. The matron's lips pinched tight rather than offer a word of apology or praise.

"Send someone to get me if Captain Findlay's condition changes, but I think we'll see only improvement now," he said to the nurse. He ignored Chastaine completely and walked away, whistling as he left the ward, on his way to meet Eleanor.

CHAPTER TWENTY

Eleanor scrubbed the stain out of her blouse in the small basin in the guest hut she occupied. She gazed at her reflection in the small mirror above the washstand. Her cheeks were as pink as the water.

She'd saved a life.

She'd broken the colonel's strictest rule by helping a patient other than Louis, and he'd been furious. Perhaps justifiably so, but what else was she to do? If she'd waited for someone else . . . She squeezed the water out of her blouse. She was a doctor. She'd reacted to an emergency the way she'd been trained to, the only ethical way possible. It had been the right thing to do.

But if anyone understood inflexible rules and regulations and etiquette, it was she—and the colonel still had the power to send her home for disobeying his directive, and where would that leave her? The countess was a civilian, and this was war, and her ladyship's influence would only go so far. If Eleanor failed, made her look foolish, she'd withdraw her support, perhaps even censure her career instead of helping her rise as a doctor.

And Louis—Louis had been shocked by her actions, stunned. What if he was so upset that he felt moved to ask the colonel to dismiss her at once, send her away? She couldn't insist that he accompany her back to England. She'd leave alone like a naughty schoolgirl, dismissed and chastened.

She could imagine the bland, silent resignation in her father's face when she returned. And her mother—there'd be triumph in her eyes. "Now will you settle down and be a proper woman?"

"But I *saved* someone's life," she whispered to the empty little room. "Isn't that more important?"

She needed a chance to walk. She donned a clean blouse, buttoned it to the neck, and added her thick cardigan over that. It was early March, and still cold. At home there'd be snowdrops, ewes heavy with new lambs, the scent of spring in the air. She looked longingly at the small wood that lay on the southern edge of the CCS, but Sergeant MacLeod had warned her not to leave the confines of the station, which left only the network of boardwalks and paths between the tents.

The CCS was a collection of about forty tents, each housing a ward for sick, or wounded, or officers. There were tents to accommodate nurses, VADs, orderlies, and medical officers. The largest tents served as triage and reception, and housed the operating theater. Another provided a quiet moribund ward for hopeless cases. Buildings that were once farm sheds, barns, and stables now served as the kitchen, storerooms, and the washhouse. Purpose-built huts functioned as the commandant's quarters, guest accommodations, and Matron Connolly's billet. Everything was stitched together by a network of duckboard walkways and gravel paths. She listened to the sound of boots on the boards, the hale and healthy hurrying along and the slower pace of ambulatory patients limping or making their way on crutches. The wind drummed a tattoo on the walls of the tents, and the endless lines of laundry snapped like gunshots. Voices carried easily through thin canvas walls—cries of pain, laughter, the quiet buzz of conversation.

And above it all was the unending crump of the guns.

She followed one walkway, then another, until she came to the road that ran along the front of the CCS. To the northwest was Arras. To the southeast lay the village of Bapaume and the front lines. She stared across the road at an empty field, brown and dry and fallow. Well, not entirely empty—one lonely corner was filled with makeshift crosses. Many of the mounds were black and raw, the soil fresh-turned and unused to the harsh glare of daylight. She wondered what had grown here before the war had planted this sorrowful crop. She let the cold wind chill her as she stared at the small cemetery. She began to count the crosses. Dozens, and more were planted every day to mark the dead. How many men lived for each man who died?

She'd saved Captain Findlay, kept the hungry ground from claiming one more.

How many more can I save? a small voice asked.

None. Well, only Louis, and only if she was allowed to stay—if she agreed to obey the rules, to do as she was told. For now, it was the only way to get what she wanted, be a doctor. Not here, of course, but someday, somewhere else.

She turned away and walked back along the duckboard high street, between the tents, then circled the route again, thinking. Was it worth it, to keep her hands folded demurely, her eyes down, to do nothing if another soldier began to choke? How many could she save later, at home, if she waited, held her tongue, did as she was told now? Could that number ever make up for the dead here? Was she capable of doing as she was told, instead of what her heart and mind and skills demanded of her? She'd never been one to sit and wait and blindly obey. But now, if she followed the rules set out for her by Colonel Bellford and the countess, there'd be rewards in the future, the chance to practice medicine, to save other lives elsewhere.

That would be enough, surely. It had to be.

CHAPTER TWENTY-ONE

David found Eleanor standing outside in the cold, staring down the road toward Arras, and for a moment he thought that perhaps Colonel Bellford had insisted she leave after all, or that she was considering doing so on her own. He watched her, thought her lucky to be a civilian, to be able to come and go as she pleased, to choose to go home, while he was trapped here in uniform and by duty for the duration.

But she wasn't dressed for travel. She was gazing at the cemetery, her face thoughtful and grim. She wasn't leaving. At least, not of her own accord.

"Good evening," he said, approaching her and following her gaze with his own.

She turned in surprise, her hand curled in the thick collar of the god-awful cardigan she was wearing. "Good evening," she said, echoing him.

"Findlay's doing well. I looked in on him just now."

She regarded him for a moment, her expression carefully blank.

"I wasn't checking up on your work. Just rounds."

She nodded. "And Louis? Lieutenant Chastaine?"

"Chafing to be released like a lapdog on a leash," he quipped, but she lowered her eyes.

"He's never liked to be stuck in one place."

"He mentioned he knew you as a girl, that you have a brother. Do you have a history with the dashing lieutenant?" He strove for an insouciant tone, as if he was merely curious. It must have come out more sharply than he intended, because she looked up at him and scanned his face, gauging his interest, or perhaps his right to ask, before she answered. She looked away, scanning the burial ground once again.

"No. Edward and Louis are close friends. I was just Edward's sister, a mere girl, and not welcome on their adventures, though I did try. I was a terrible tagalong. They called me pest, pulled my hair, and threw mud on my frocks."

"How unchivalrous."

"They weren't officers then, just boys."

They still were, he suspected. At least that was true of Louis Chastaine.

The wind was turning cold enough to sting, and he pointed to the lighted refectory tent. "Shall we go in out of the cold and find out what there is for supper? I predict stew. Not that I'm some kind of mystic. It's usually stew on Wednesdays."

"I should check on Louis—Lieutenant Chastaine—first. Would you mind?"

David gritted his teeth and forced a smile. She wished to see if Chastaine had gotten over the shock of watching her perform an emergency medical procedure. He could have dissuaded her, convinced her to eat first, forget about Chastaine, but he didn't bother. Perhaps it would do her good to let her see her hero as he truly was, pettish and shallow, spoiled. It would certainly cast *him* in a better light. "As you wish. It isn't medically necessary, of course."

He wondered if he should offer his arm, but she stayed an arm's length away, her hands in the pockets of her bulky cardigan. "I know. It's just that Louis—Lieutenant Chastaine—is anxious to be out of bed, and his mother—"

David gave her a lazy grin. "His mother? I assumed he was old enough to sign up and come to war on his own. Did he take a wrong turn on his way to buy sweets and end up here by mistake?"

She sent him a sharp look. "Her ladyship is simply concerned. Louis's older brother died last fall. He's his father's heir now—Viscount Somerton. He'll be the Earl of Kirkswell someday."

"God save England," David murmured. He held the door of the officers' tent for her to enter.

In the winter twilight, the officers' ward was lit by a row of lanterns hung down the center of the tent and warmed by a small stove.

The patients regarded Eleanor with a new kind of interest as she entered, less flirtatious or dismissive now, more careful and respectful since she'd saved Findlay. Her actions had had the opposite effect to the one that Chastaine feared—his fellow officers envied him all the more for his association with the fearless lady doctor.

"Good evening, Miss Atherton," one man greeted her with admiration in his eyes as they passed his bed—a lieutenant with a chest wound, awaiting transportation. She nodded politely but didn't stop.

"The heroine returns," Louis Chastaine said dryly as they arrived at his bedside. He flicked a bored glance at David, who stood back and waited.

"Hello, Louis. How are you? I wanted to check on your leg," she said, her color high, her voice almost breathless. She peeled back the sheet that covered the splint to expose Somerton's leg, a long, muscular, manly limb sparkling with golden hairs. There was a small silver scar from an old injury just below the upper ring of the splint. The leg was stretched out straight between two iron bars that ran from the ring to the frame attached to the bed. A linen cradle held the leg, while ties kept it from flexing or moving. The heel was pressed to the frame so the muscles of the calf were properly stretched. David had helped Bellford set the shattered bones, had made the pilot as whole as they could. There was still a danger of bone fragments, of course. They'd cause him pain unless they were removed later—not here, of course, but in some plush, private hospital in England, attended by the finest orthopedic surgeons an earl's money could buy.

He watched Eleanor stare at Chastaine's leg, naked to the hip, the sheet barely keeping things polite, but David saw only clinical interest in her eyes. She examined the angry crosshatch of scars, long and red. She bent to sniff delicately, seeking putrefaction. In any other situation, the gesture might have been erotic, but her eyes were keen and decidedly unaroused as she followed the veins and vessels, looking for infection. "It's healing well."

She avoided Chastaine's eyes, though David knew she was here for the pilot's forgiveness and to gauge how much damage she'd done by showing off her skills, acting like a doctor instead of an adoring and devoted nursemaid.

Chastaine regarded Eleanor with a mulish expression, held his silence, denied her his blessing or understanding.

"Then when can I get up?" Louis Chastaine demanded, just to be bloody-minded, to bully and disconcert her, since David had already given him the answer to that question.

"Soon, I think. Perhaps in a week. No longer than two—"

"I'll run mad by then," Chastaine snapped.

She offered the kind of soothing smile a nanny gives a truculent infant. "We'll check it every day, and if it *can* be sooner—"

"Fuck," Chastaine cursed, and Eleanor colored.

The gas case across the ward cleared his throat. "I say, Captain Blair, one of the orderlies said there's a chance of heavy rain tonight. Heard anything about it?"

He meant bombardment, an attack in this sector, but he was doing his best to spare Eleanor's delicate sensibilities with euphemisms in order to deflect Chastaine's anger and his rough language by changing the subject.

But Chastaine wouldn't play along. "He means the Huns are coming," he told her bluntly.

"They might not," David said quickly. "It's just a rumor. It might be far from here, or not at all."

Eleanor looked at him with wide eyes. "A rumor? How will we know?"

"Oh, if the Huns come a-knocking, you'll know," Chastaine said. "They wear hobnailed boots and use eighteen-pound shells to ring the bell. Are you afraid, El? You must be afraid of *something*."

She sent him a fierce look. "Of course I'm afraid. Isn't everyone?" She waited until Chastaine looked away first.

"No cause to worry," David said, loudly enough to soothe Eleanor and the entire ward, but her forthright gaze demanded honesty. "We'll get as much warning as they can give us, especially if it's our side attacking—um, *advancing*. They'll want us ready to receive casualties. If it's the enemy, the observers will tell us if there are warning signs, like troops moving up, or a heavy barrage, or trench raids."

Chastaine gave a bitter laugh. "Or gas. They'll release that first. There'll be no one left to sound a warning. It chokes, and burns, and blinds, and—"

"Stop it! You'll scare her," the gas case said, his voice gruff, tight with his own fear, the terrible memory of his wounding.

Eleanor looked so concerned that David resisted the urge to pat her shoulder. "Don't worry," he said instead. "The colonel will let us know, and we'll move you back somewhere safe if necessary."

She met his eyes, her expression fierce. "I'm not afraid for myself—it's the soldiers in the field, the ones in range of it all. And the stretcher bearers, like Sergeant MacLeod. Do you know him?" He nodded. "They'd be in the thick of it, wouldn't they? Is there shelter for them?"

"Don't be daft, Eleanor. It's their damned duty," Chastaine snapped. "God, I hate being stuck down here like a bloody sitting duck." He pointed up at the canvas ceiling of the tent. "From up in a plane, you can see the armies getting ready to attack, like insects marching. Trains bring up the biggest guns. They drag them through the mud with men and horses, and when they stop, lift the barrels, and aim them, you know which part of the line will get it. You can see frail little bodies pouring over the top of the trenches like roaches, running pell-mell for No Man's Land, straight toward the damned guns. It's all so pointless. You can watch them fall from up there. They lie in the mud, staring up at me in my plane. Or maybe they're looking at heaven. I've often been tempted to look up myself, see if the sky has opened above me, if the angels are coming, but I don't. I look at *them*. For an instant, their blood is red on the ground, but then the mud sucks it away, drinks it down like nectar to feed the killing field. Then they're as gray and colorless as everything else. They don't even look human anymore. There's nothing to show for their sacrifice, just empty husks."

"Steady on, Chastaine," Findlay murmured from his bed, his voice thin with his own fear.

Chastaine looked at him. "You think I should spare her, this delicate flower of English womanhood, a lass bold and brave enough to pierce a dying man's chest with a needle? I won't. You want to know, don't you, El?"

She swallowed and nodded.

"Then I'll tell her. It's different on the ground," Findlay said. "No angels, no heaven. The men in the trenches always know when there's a show coming—at least the ones who've been here awhile." He turned his head so he could see Eleanor, his hand closed in a fist against the white bandages that swathed his chest. "It's the way the artillery sounds, you see, a feeling they get in their bones. A corporal told me he can read every order that's coming up, even before they're issued to the men, just by looking into the eyes of the officers—well, the officers who care about sending their men over the top, that is." He looked away. "I hate to order them to go out there. I hate the tension, the smell of fear, the way some of them are so bloody cheerful, trying to encourage the others, give them hope. It's harder when they fall." He paused. "Most of the time, they don't even see it coming."

David was watching Eleanor, wondering if she'd cry, or faint, but she was staring at Findlay, listening, her face bereft, but strong and compassionate. Chastaine was studying her, too, his eyes on her white face, his jaw tight, his expression expectant. David knew the bastard was hoping that she'd faint, show some womanly weakness, some emotion he could understand. He wanted her to suffer the way he was suffering, the way they were all suffering. "Did you know we're only eight miles from the front here, Eleanor?" Chastaine said cruelly, but she didn't look at the flier, or at Findlay. She looked at *him*.

"What are the chances it will happen tonight, or tomorrow?" she asked. "Will they come here, since it's only eight miles?"

Findlay replied before David could speak. "Eight miles might as well be eight hundred. Advances are measured in yards. A few yards and a thousand dead, and they call it a success. The more dead, the bigger the success it's deemed to be," Findlay said bitterly. He shut his eyes. "God, I'm glad I'm out of it. I wish we all were."

But Eleanor was waiting for David's answer as a surgeon, a medical officer. He realized she was trusting him to tell her the truth, a professional courtesy between colleagues. "We won't know much until the wounded begin to arrive—that's how we know what's happening, by the kinds of wounds and the regiments the men are from. If you know where the Canadians are posted, or the Australians, or the West

Yorkshires, then you know what part of the line is under fire," David told her. "Have you seen battle wounds?"

She nodded. "In Edinburgh, after the Somme while I was at medical school, in my third year. The wounded arrived there by train on their way to the hospitals. And on the way here, I saw wounded men in Calais and at the station in Arras."

Men already treated, David thought. Not the gory, dirty, terrifying sight of freshly wounded men, screaming, stinking, shell-shocked and bleeding, in agonizing pain or dying. He hoped she'd be gone before she saw such things. Perhaps Bellford understood better than anyone, and his edicts were meant to protect her as much as the soldiers.

"The Countess of Kirkswell has a convalescent hospital for officers at Chesscroft—" she said.

"My mother, my home," Chastaine said sharply, reminding her of his presence.

Eleanor spared him a quick glance. "Yes. She's given use of the dower house for lieutenants and captains. Higher-ranking officers stay in a wing of the manor house."

"Of course they do. Most of them are probably friends of hers. It must be like a weekend house party that never ends," Chastaine muttered.

"Hardly that," Eleanor said. "Some are very bad."

"How tiresome for the staff to have to look after the maimed, and the halt, and the blind," he drawled. "They must hate the extra work."

"No one complains," Eleanor said. "There are plenty of volunteers, and there are doctors on staff, RAMC men."

"Any female doctors?" Chastaine asked. He barked a laugh when Eleanor shook her head. "And I thought my mother was all about that, women's suffrage and the equality of the sexes. She's always longed to be in charge, and now she has her chance. It's all for appearance, the great lady doing her bit for king and empire. I imagine she rules her hospital with an iron fist, the same way she ruled poor bloody Cyril, and my father. What a terrible disappointment I was to her—I never let her tell me what to do, and as long as I wasn't the heir she ignored me. But now things are different. She expects me to come up to snuff, toe the line, do as she bids me. Isn't that why she sent you? Tell me, am I to go home and be one more patient? Once we finish exchanging tales about how we got our respective wounds, am I to play host, tell the other gimpy officers amusing tales of my ancestors and the ghosts that walk the long gallery in the dark of night, warn the ones on crutches about the loose board on the sixth step on the back stairs?" He rolled his eyes like a peevish schoolboy. "How boring."

"It doesn't sound so bad to me. Think of the ones who won't go home at all," David said sharply.

"I'm one of them—I'm not going," Chastaine snapped.

Eleanor gasped. "What? But, Louis, your mother—"

"Oh, just go, Eleanor. Get out." He turned his face away and closed his eyes. "Send the damned nurse in with some morphine on your way."

David took her arm. "Come and eat, let him get some rest," he murmured, and he led her out, silently cursing Chastaine. She'd borne the terrible descriptions of impending battle and personal harm, but her patient's final pronouncement had been the thing that had shaken her.

She followed him silently, her face pale, and he wondered what she was thinking, what he could say, and what she feared most of all.

CHAPTER TWENTY-TWO

MARCH 10, 1918

The big attack didn't come the next day, or the day after that. Wounded and sick men arrived each day in manageable numbers. They were quickly and efficiently treated, then sent on to hospitals farther in the rear or returned to the front.

Or so Eleanor heard. The colonel had called her into his office the day after she'd treated Captain Findlay. She was sternly reminded that she was not allowed to even *look* at patients other than Louis. Failure to comply would result in her immediate removal from the CCS, with or without Louis. She promised to comply.

Louis was guarded and edgy. Sometimes he returned her smile, and other days, he was mulish and cranky.

Today she was reading Louis an article in a censored copy of the *Times*, a piece about the Prince of Wales's recent visit to France. Louis looked at the photographs of the young prince and sighed. "Poor David. I know exactly how he feels. He wants to serve, but they're not going to let the heir to the throne get close to the front. All he can do is wave from the rear and smile and keep morale high."

She'd forgotten he knew the Prince of Wales well enough to call him by the name only his family and his closest friends used, that he attended the same parties and golfed, hunted, and sailed with the prince. Louis knew the king and queen as well, since his grandmother had once been one of Queen Mary's ladies in waiting.

She latched on to that to change the subject. "What was it like to meet the king and queen? Are they—"

The cheerful chortle of a car horn outside interrupted her. It wasn't the usual strident blare of an ambulance pulling up, but something jaunty.

Louis lifted his head. "I know that sound—it's the horn on a Vauxhall D. A colonel's car or a general's—even a field marshal or the king. It's a surprise inspection, no doubt. Perhaps you'd better run away, Eleanor, before the brass hats stride in and make us all stand at attention. The officers always want to line up the medical staff and whatever patients they can prop up so they can take pictures. I wonder what they'd make of you, the redoubtable Eleanor Atherton, lady doctor?"

But it wasn't a cadre of high-ranking officers who strode into the ward. It was a glamorous young woman, elegantly coiffed and lavishly dressed in pink silk, gleaming furs, and a king's ransom in jewels. She was on the arm of a handsome young lieutenant.

Eleanor gaped at the officer. "Edward!"

Her twin brother looked at her in surprise. "Eleanor? What on earth are you doing here? Did you sign up as a VAD or something?"

"She's here for me," Louis said.

Edward looked at his friend in surprise. "You? And El?"

But the young woman on Edward's arm detached herself and squealed as she rushed to throw herself into Louis's arms. "Budgie!

Oh, darling, I was *frantic* when I heard you were injured." She was covering his face with kisses, wriggling against him like a giddy spaniel, and Louis was laughing.

"Budgie?" Eleanor asked Edward, who was grinning at the tender scene.

"A pet name. Didn't he show you his tattoo?"

"He said it was a sparrow."

"Private joke," Edward murmured. For a moment he stood and regarded her, still looking baffled by her presence. She wondered if he'd hug her or peck her cheek, but he merely gave her a half smile, and when she moved to hug him, he quickly stepped past her, out of her reach, to greet his friend, now buried under the woman in pink, who was covering his face in lipstick kisses. Eleanor let her hands drop to her sides, knotting them in the folds of her skirts. She was glad to see her twin whole and safe and in good health, and she should have remembered he'd never liked mixing family with friends. Still, she had a reason to be here, a job to do, and she stood her ground, even if that was off to one side, an observer instead of a participant, or a friend, or even a sister. She was still Louis's doctor.

Louis was laughing. "I'm not *injured*, darling Fanny—I'm *wounded*. Only civilians get injured nowadays. I'm a hero!" His eyes were bright with all the amusement and charm Eleanor hadn't seen for a while. She felt her heart tumble into her sensible black boots, so unlike the fashionable and frivolous pink kid leather heels "darling Fanny" was wearing. Her pink silk dress was the only color in the room, so bright and sweetly feminine amid the gray and black of the ward. Her perfume—something heavy, sweet, French, and no doubt expensive—filled the ward with imitation springtime.

She giggled and kissed Louis again, adding another smudge to his forehead. "Wounded." She purred the word with a delectable pout. "Of course you are. Uncle Douglas sends his regards. I borrowed his car, and dear Edward. Reggie and Beatrice and Maud are outside, but a dreadful dragon of a nurse wouldn't let more than two of us inside, even when I told her Papa was a general and answerable only to Uncle Douglas and the king himself."

Edward glanced at Eleanor. "Uncle Douglas is Field Marshal Haig," he said. "She's Lady Frances Parfitt, the Duke of Winslowe's daughter. She heard Louis was wounded, and she showed up at HQ and insisted on coming to visit him." He looked smug, proud of such high connections. "Uncle Douglas cannot refuse his beloved niece anything, and when she insisted I simply must be the one to escort her here, I was immediately ordered to do so."

Lady Frances shimmied out of her mink coat and laid it over Louis like a blanket. The pink dress clung to lush curves, a garment more suited to tea at Buckingham Palace or a garden party than a war zone. She plopped down on the edge of the bed and regarded Louis's leg. "Is it very bad?" she asked, her eyes wide, her lashes working like fans.

"A mere scratch," he said with a disarming grin.

"It's broken in three places," Eleanor said, but no one was listening, and Louis only had eyes for Lady Frances now.

Lady Frances turned and waved a languid hand at Edward. "We brought three cases of champagne, but the dragon refused to allow me to bring them inside. Not even Edward could convince her. Have we *anything* to celebrate with? I'm utterly parched."

Edward reached into his breast pocket and laid a silver flask in her palm. It was engraved with her brother's initials, and it was expensive. Eleanor had never seen it before. "I've got brandy, darling," Edward drawled, his tone lazy, his plummy accent an exact copy of Lady Frances's. "Quite medicinal, and I say that as a doctor's son. Will it do?"

He glanced at Eleanor from the corner of his eye and had the grace to blush at her look of surprise.

Louis took the flask and drank. "Oh, you're a lifesaver, old chap. I thought I'd die of boredom." Eleanor felt a prickle of indignation. He reached up a hand to flick at the fluffy ostrich feathers that adorned Lady Frances's ridiculously fashionable hat. "Yet another silly hat, darling?"

She giggled as she plucked one of the feathers free and used it to tickle him under the chin. "You noticed! I wore it just for you, Budgie. I did try to get budgie feathers, of course, but the milliner said they don't use those for hats. Something about it not being proper to skin people's pets for fashion. You can get pheasant, or goose, or ostrich, or even eagle if you really want it, but not budgie. We shall have to give you a different sobriquet."

Louis made a face, his good humor fading. "Just not ostrich. They're flightless, you know."

Fanny raised one eyebrow before replying. Then she pressed her cheek to his. "How silly you are."

Eleanor gaped at the giddy scene.

Lady Frances took the flask from Louis, sipped, and passed it on to Edward, who did likewise. Eleanor glared at her brother, and he held it out to her.

She shook her head. "This is a *hospital*," she hissed. Society magazines at home were full of photographs of glamourous and titled debutantes visiting the front to help raise the morale of the troops or to visit wounded relatives. A number of upper-class ladies had volunteered as VADs or served at hospitals set up by their noble mamas or aunts. Some wore elegant uniforms that looked as custom tailored as a tea gown, wore pearls, and posed for pictures. Some worked as hard as anyone else. There were photos of the Prince of Wales in uniform, leaning on a cane with elegant insouciance as he chatted with white-clad aristocratic female friends at the Duchess of Sutherland's hospital here in France. Some ladies visited the front to spread cheer and gifts on goodwill tours. Most of those scurried home as soon as the mud sprayed their frocks or they saw things they wished they had not. Fraser MacLeod had imagined she was precisely that, the delicate, curious, fainting kind. Looking now at the glamorous Lady Fanny, Eleanor suspected she was the type of visitor Colonel Bellford wished to bar—a frivolous, rule-breaking, outspoken, and titled female. It appeared she was here to raise Louis's morale the way she might have done in England if he were bedridden with a slight cold.

Sir Douglas's flamboyant niece had not even glanced at the other patients, though she looked around now, her expression imperious, as if seeking a servant so she could order tea or looking for a phalanx of idle footmen to carry in the aforementioned champagne. Her blue eyes fell on Eleanor and slid over her briefly, taking in her plain blouse and dark skirt. Her lips tightened, her dismissal of Eleanor instant.

"And who is this?" Lady Frances asked, looking down her pert nose at Eleanor. "Another dragon?"

Edward chuckled uneasily, but didn't reply. Louis did. "Almost. This is Eleanor, Edward's twin sister. Eleanor, may I present Lady Frances Parfitt?"

Lady Frances didn't hold out her hand, and Eleanor didn't curtsy. They simply regarded each other across the width of Louis's bed. "I didn't know you had a sister, Eddie," Lady Frances said, her tone serious now, almost imperious. "Are you a nurse, then?"

"She's a doctor, as a matter of fact. *My* doctor," Louis said brightly.

"No!" Lady Frances said, looking horrified.

"'S'truth—Mater sent her to check up on me," Louis said.

Frances's eyes narrowed again, and her nose wrinkled. "Like a *nursemaid*?"

"More a valet," Louis quipped. He had the audacity to wink at Eleanor. She regarded him soberly, not finding his jest at all amusing.

Lady Frances laughed, a sound like silver spoons tinkling against fine bone china. "Really, Budgie, you're too funny." She kissed him again, on the lips this time. "It is good to see you able to make jokes. I feared—" She pouted and blinked hard until glossy tears sprang to her eyes. "I feared you were . . ." She swiped at the tears with a monogrammed handkerchief that was lavishly trimmed with alençon lace. She gave him a watery smile. "But you're not, of course, so all's well."

Louis smiled back, his lipstick-stained mouth almost as red as Lady Frances's.

"Miss Atherton, these visitors are disturbing the other patients," Matron Connolly said, gliding up behind her shoulder with a terrifying glare.

Dragon indeed.

The matron's eyes flicked over Lady Frances's position on Louis's bed, and the fur coat. Her lips rippled with disapproval.

Edward quickly pocketed the flask and gave the matron a dazzling smile. "Good afternoon, Matron. I'm Lieutenant Edward Atherton, aide to Lieutenant Colonel Lord Petrie at HQ. This is Lady Frances Parfitt. She's Field Marshal Haig's niece and the youngest daughter of His Grace the Duke of Winslowe. Lady Frances is a very dear friend of Lieutenant Lord Somerton."

Edward was looking at Matron Connolly as if she were the most enchanting woman in the world, but his practiced charm didn't raise so much as a half smile from the dragon.

"He means me, Matron," Louis said. He looked at Edward. "It's still plain Lieutenant Chastaine here."

Fanny gasped. "Budgie! You don't use your title?"

He frowned. "Cyril's title, rather. I didn't want it when my brother was alive, and now . . . Well, it means a lot of unwanted attention and expectations."

"But, Louis—" Lady Frances began, but Matron Connolly cleared her throat and fixed Edward with a commanding glare.

"Lieutenant *Atherton*. Are you a relative of Miss Atherton's?"

"Brother," Edward said, looking sheepish.

"They're twins," Louis said brightly.

"Though they're obviously nothing alike," Lady Frances added tartly.

Nothing at all, Eleanor thought.

Matron Connolly kept her eyes on Edward. "Lieutenant, I must insist that you curtail this . . . this *visitation*. These are wounded men, and they need quiet. You may return tomorrow between ten and eleven o'clock, one at a time." She glared down the length of the ward, where two other elegant young women and another man in uniform stood peeking through the curtain, waggling their fingers and blowing kisses at Louis. He waggled back.

"Oh, we're not staying," Lady Frances said. "Not here. It's too ghastly, and Uncle Douglas fears we're too close to the front. We're going on to Paris."

"Paris?" Louis's smile faded wistfully.

"Yes. Do come with us, darling Budgie," Lady Frances said. "I have a motorcar outside."

"He's not able to travel. He's still recovering," Eleanor interrupted. Lady Fanny rolled her eyes and sighed. She didn't bother to look at Eleanor.

"Then when *can* you come?" Fanny demanded.

Louis smiled, but it didn't quite reach his eyes. "Soon, darling girl, soon. Just as soon as Eleanor says I might go."

Fanny looked at her now, haughty annoyance simmering in her eyes. "Really?" she drawled. "My, but your mater really does have you on a short string."

Eleanor saw the muscle in Louis's jaw tense.

"Perhaps we should take our leave for now," Edward said, eyeing the matron.

Louis looked at Eleanor. "Are those your orders, Doctor? Must they leave?"

Eleanor felt everyone's eyes on her—Edward's, Lady Frances's, Louis's, and Matron Connolly's. "I think it would be prudent if you got some rest, and perhaps later—"

But another horn sounded outside, this one harsh and tinny, followed by the squeal of brakes and the rough rumble of a motor. No, it was more than one vehicle. Eleanor heard voices calling for assistance and cries of pain. There were running footsteps on the duckboards outside. Every patient in the ward, every nurse and VAD, turned toward the door, wide-eyed and expectant. Eleanor felt a prickle run through her.

"What's happening?" Lady Frances asked. "What's that noise?"

Matron Connolly barely glanced at her as she hurried past. "Ambulances. There's wounded coming in."

CHAPTER TWENTY-THREE

Eleanor's mouth dried. *Wounded coming in.* An attack, then? *The* attack?

The staff rushed out, following the matron, and the patients fell into solemn silence. Even Louis was frowning. Everyone left on the ward was still listening to the sounds outside: the rumble of motors, the squeal of brakes, the shouted orders and calls for help, the cries of wounded men. The hair on the back of Eleanor's neck rose.

Lady Frances broke the spell. "Do go find out what's happening, Eddie," she ordered, wrapping her satin-clad arms around her body, her eyes wide.

Eleanor followed her brother out of the tent. David Blair ran past without a glance, nearly running straight into her. Edward pulled her back just in time. "Steady on, mate! Have a care where the bloody 'ell you're going," he yelled in his old Yorkshire drawl, but David Blair ignored him and ran on and disappeared around the end of the tent.

"You're blocking the walkway, Miss Atherton," Colonel Bellford said, coming along the duckboards from his office, pulling on a white surgical gown as he went. "Go and wait in the guest quarters. Do not, and I repeat, *do not*, get in the way!" He sent Edward a sharp look, and Edward snapped to attention and saluted, but by then the colonel was gone.

"Martinet," Edward muttered, still holding her elbow. "We'd best go back inside out of the way." But Eleanor pulled free and followed David Blair and the colonel. "El, wait—"

She didn't stop. She picked up her skirts and followed a nursing sister moving at a dead run along the boards, carrying pails of bandages and supplies, her white veil flapping behind her.

Eleanor rounded the end of the tent and stopped. Her heart climbed into her throat. The road and all the space in front of the triage tent were filled with ambulances and walking wounded as far as she could see. The noise was even louder here. Screams and horns and shouted orders filled the air. She could smell blood and smoke and vomit—and gas. She remembered the terrible smell from Calais, when the hospital train had opened its doors. It had been nothing like this, nothing as bad.

Ambulances were pulling in around Lady Frances's huge touring car like farm geese surrounding a swan. The drivers jumped down and cursed the fancy vehicle for being in their way. One man kicked at the front tire as he passed it.

"Watch what you're doing! That's Lieutenant Colonel Lord Petrie's motor!" Edward called, but everyone was too busy to take any notice. Her brother might as well have been invisible.

Orderlies and bearers streamed past them, swung open the doors of the ambulances, and began unloading the wounded. They, too, had to take a detour around the car, through the muddy ditch.

Eleanor caught her brother's sleeve. "Move the car," she said through stiff lips, but Edward was staring around him in horror. Eleanor shook him. "Edward, move the bloody car!" she shouted, and he snapped his eyes back to her, pale and helpless. He looked as if he might be sick. He swallowed hard and shook his head.

"I can't. There's too much traffic. It might get scratched." He grabbed her arm. "Come back inside." He dragged her away, back to the officers' ward, and pulled her inside, and she allowed it, too numb to resist. The patients turned to look at her. "What's happening, miss? How many?" one of them asked Eleanor.

"I don't know. A lot . . ."

Someone had drawn the curtain around Louis's bed, but she could hear laughter. There was a loud bang, and Lady Frances screamed. One of the wounded officers flinched and cried out, clapping his hands over his ears.

Eleanor feared the worst—Louis had fallen out of bed or broken the splint and was lying on the floor in terrible pain. She shoved back the curtain.

Lady Frances was pouring champagne. A picnic hamper lay open on Louis's bed, disgorging a lavish feast across the fur coat. Louis's other visitors were here as well, two young ladies, and another man in uniform—a clean, crisp, expensively tailored uniform that had never seen battle.

Not like the scene outside. She wondered if they were all mad.

One of the women yelped at the sight of Eleanor. "Is that the dragon?" she asked Frances.

Lady Frances looked at her. "She's Eddie's sister. Come and have some champagne. There's plenty to go round," Lady Frances said, holding out a glass to her. Eleanor recoiled, but Edward pushed past her and took the glass. The other officer opened a second bottle and the cork popped with a sharp report, and another patient cried out in alarm, writhing in his bed, trembling.

"Stop it! The corks—they sound like gunshots. It's frightening the patients. You can't open them here!" Eleanor cried.

"Don't be silly—it's a 1911 Bollinger, and a 1911 never frightened anyone," the officer quipped. He grinned at his friends. "Quite the opposite, in fact."

Eleanor met Louis's eyes, pleading silently, but he stared at her as someone filled the glass in his hand, his eyes heavy lidded. He *knew* better . . . She held his gaze until he flushed under her glare. "Fanny—" he began. "Perhaps we'd best not—"

"Look, we can share with all of them if you'd like," Fanny snapped, following his gaze to Eleanor. "There's enough."

"It's not that," Eleanor said. "It's shell shock."

"No such thing," the dapper young officer said. "Cowardice, you mean. Drink up, all—here's a toast to good old Budgie. Long may he fly!"

She turned to her brother. "Edward, do something!"

"What would you have me do, El?" he asked, looking annoyed. "What *can* I do? We're all tired of this bloody war. Live a little for a change, and stop being such a *stick*."

She stared at him, at the bland insouciance in his eyes, the careless aristocratic stance he'd learned and now used to perfection. He regarded her as if she were a stranger—an embarrassing stranger trying to make a connection where there wasn't one, to presume upon an old and half-forgotten acquaintance.

She turned away and began to gather the bottles that hadn't been opened to carry them away, get rid of them, and she heard laughter and whispers.

But Edward stepped in front of her, snatching one of the bottles out of her hands. "Stop it. You're embarrassing yourself. It's just a bit of fun. Why do you have to take everything so damned seriously?"

She stared at her brother in his crisp, perfect uniform. Even his nails were manicured.

"There's a war on," she snapped, making her tone as aristocratic as his. "Do you not know that? There's. A. War. On."

"Miss?" one of the patients called. "Captain Graham is in a bad way."

She looked at the patient across from Louis. The man was curled into a ball, shaking, muttering, crying out.

"Coming," Eleanor said.

Edward made a sound of frustration, or annoyance, perhaps, and went back to his friends.

Eleanor crossed the ward to the shattered captain and gripped his hand, holding it tight.

Across the room, the gay celebration continued on without her, or despite her. She caught Louis's eye, and for a moment he looked back at her, and she read regret and helplessness in his eyes. Then he turned away.

CHAPTER TWENTY-FOUR

David Blair felt the familiar horror rise in his belly—familiar even though he never got used to it. The wounded pouring in, the blood and pain and stink made him feel helpless and small in the face of an impossible task. He wanted to freeze, to hide, to run. Instead, he forced himself to reach for the nearest patient, to make a start. Once he did, the horror would pass, and he wouldn't feel anything but the need to work, to do whatever he could to *fix this*, even knowing the whole fucking mess was utterly unfixable.

A dawn attack had cut three battalions to ribbons, like so many pounds of stew beef and offal, and it was up to him to pay the butcher's bill, to stitch the pieces back together, reassemble them, make them human again.

And these poor buggers were the lucky ones.

The walking wounded streamed along the road toward him like ghosts, their eyes hollow, carrying or leading staggering comrades. He listened to the bellowed calls for help, to the grind and growl of an endless parade of ambulances coming up the road, trying vainly to go gingerly over ruts and potholes for the sake of the poor buggers in the back.

Triage gave him a place to start—take the worst ones first and get them to surgery or send them to be resuscitated. The nurses would handle the rest. They were short staffed. They needed ten more doctors to deal with this—or twenty. But there was only Bellford and himself . . . Clean them up, warm them, bandage them, put them to bed, send the hopeless cases to the moribund tent to await the end . . . Make space for the next ambulance and the next lot of wounded . . . Continue. Don't stop, or give up, or take too much time. Move on, and on, and on.

The fact that the ambulances left again as soon as they finished unloading meant more casualties were awaiting transport at aid posts and field ambulances. Was this the big push that had been a rumor for weeks? Everyone was whispering that question now. No one knew. They'd had no warning—or not enough. David wondered if there was enough of everything—ether, bandages, antiseptic, morphine, beds. And time. Just himself and Bellford in theater, and the colonel was already scrubbing for surgery.

Urgent cases first.

Nurses and orderlies were bending over the wounded, reading the tags attached to each man's tunic, taking note of the treatment and diagnosis given by the medical officers at the frontline aid posts.

Chaplain Strong was directing traffic, doing his best to help, but they were already overwhelmed. Stretchers were lined up along the edge of the road in a double row outside the reception tent. There were forty or more already, and twice that many walking. David felt his belly curl against his spine.

The first three—one gut shot, moribund. The second was shot through the jaw, but still breathing, still conscious. His eyes pleaded with David to save him, to let him live. As if it were up to him. He nodded, a silent promise to try his best. The third man was in shock, his arm shattered below the elbow. He gave orders and moved on.

The orderlies were bringing the worst cases straight to him, piling them around him, hemming him in, waiting for his decision, life or death.

How many times had he done this, waded through blood and mud and broken bodies? It should be routine by now. He should be able to turn off his emotions and just get on with it, but it never got easier. A slippery hand gripped his wrist, three fingers missing. "Help, please," the lad croaked. "Help me." David looked down, saw the boy's shattered legs.

"Surgery," David ordered, pulling away, moving on as they carried the lad away.

He could see at least five more surgical cases from where he stood. Bellford was likely already elbow-deep in some dreadful belly wound, with other critical patients waiting on the tables and outside for him to finish. David should be in there, too, but someone had to manage this chaos, funnel patients into the system in an orderly, professional manner.

He noted that some of the patients were missing tags, which meant they'd come straight off the field and their injuries hadn't even received basic treatment. It meant the aid post was overwhelmed, or worse, that the medical officer had been wounded or killed.

Someone caught his arm, and he looked into the fierce eyes of Fraser MacLeod. The big stretcher bearer was muddy, his uniform stained with the blood of other men, his face lined with worry. "Captain Duncan took a piece of shrapnel in the belly. Can ye come?"

David shut his eyes for a moment. There it was—he'd been right. A medical officer had been hit, and it would have to be Duncan, one of the best.

"I left Corporal Chilcott at the aid post, but beyond a dose of morphine and a bandage, there's not going to be much he can do for anyone. I ordered him to send everyone straight here."

"What about 38/CCS?" David asked.

"Full. They're directing wounded here. And you're closer."

"I need a doctor!" Matron Connolly yelled over a row of stretchers, her white apron covered with blood, with more pumping from her patient's thigh.

"Pressure," David said to her.

"This one's urgent!" Reverend Strong called to him.

"Captain Blair!" an orderly bellowed at him.

He looked at Fraser. "Can you help with triage?"

Fraser looked around him. "I can help, but I'm not a doctor. Ye need—"

"I need assistance!" someone else screamed.

"There is no one else. You'll have to do your best," David snapped and turned back to Fraser.

The stretcher bearer looked around, his granite features bleak. "Aye," was all he said, and David moved on to the next patient.

CHAPTER TWENTY-FIVE

E dward, *please* stop!" Eleanor pleaded again, looking from her tipsy brother to Louis. "Louis, you can't have a party here, not while there are men out there, wounded and even—"

One of the young ladies looked at Eleanor and screamed. Well, not at Eleanor, but at something behind her. The woman's eyes rolled back and she swooned. Edward leaped to catch her.

"Maud! Eleanor, fetch some smelling salts!" Edward ordered.

Eleanor stared at the society beauty. She'd seen Lady Maud's picture in *Country Living*, part of the smart set, wealthy, titled, and pretty. Now her mouth hung open, her lipstick was smeared, and her fashionable hat was tipped askew. Edward lifted her in his arms and held her out to Eleanor like a sacrifice. "Help her, Eleanor." *Now* he appreciated that she was a doctor. But no, that was unkind. He looked honestly distressed.

"Dr. Atherton!"

She spun at the harsh voice and found herself staring up at Sergeant MacLeod, big, dirty, and bloody. He was frowning, and Eleanor instinctively took a step back. He caught her elbow, held her still, loomed over her.

"Ye need to come with me. We need another doctor."

Behind her, Lady Frances gasped, perhaps at his rudeness, perhaps at his disheveled condition, or maybe at the way he addressed Eleanor without so much as removing his cap.

The sergeant glanced over Eleanor's head and took in the silk-clad ladies, the fur coat, the champagne and caviar, the dandy young officers, and the limp woman in Edward's arms. He flicked his eyes back to Eleanor. "We need another doctor," he said again.

"Well, we bloody well need a doctor here, too—Lady Maud has fainted," Edward said in the arrogant tones of a superior officer.

But Fraser MacLeod ignored him, keeping his attention on Eleanor. His grip on her arm tightened, and he pointed toward the door with his free hand. "There are wounded men out there who need help, more than Blair and Bellford can handle. You're needed."

She stared up at him miserably. "I'm not allowed to help—the colonel said . . ."

He made a small sound of frustration, muttered something guttural in Gaelic. He gripped her other arm as well and leaned close to her face. "I don't give a damn about the rules, nor do those poor bastards waiting out there for help, dying. Ye told me ye were a doctor. Can a doctor stand here drinking with her fancy friends and do nothing?"

"'S'truth, man, you cannot speak to me that way," Edward said, though Fraser hadn't said a single word to him. He still held Maud in his arms. "Stand to attention! What are you anyway, a sergeant? I can't even tell under all the mud and the, um— Go and get cleaned up at once! Eleanor, come and see to Maud."

Fraser didn't come to attention. He frowned at Edward and at poor Lady Maud. "My medical officer took a piece of shrapnel in the gut. He needs surgery, and so do a lot of others. We need Miss Atherton—*Dr.* Atherton—to help. Now. Slap the lass's cheek to wake her. Put her head between her knees if she swoons again."

"Now wait a minute, you," Edward tried again, shifting Maud's limp weight awkwardly, but Fraser MacLeod turned back to Eleanor.

"Will you come or no?"

She stared up into his eyes and read concern and urgency. This was what she was trained to do. It was against the rules. If the colonel found out, he'd send her home. She didn't look at Louis. The choice was hers.

"Yes."

Fraser let out a breath and strode toward the door, her elbow still in his grip, and she had to run to keep pace with his long strides.

"Eleanor!" Edward called after her. "You can't! What about Maud?"

Eleanor paused. "Do as the sergeant said. Chafe her wrists and loosen her collar. Rub a little champagne on her pulse points. She'll be fine."

She paused at the door to wash her hands. "What can I do?" she said, rolling up her sleeves.

He grabbed one of the buckets used to carry supplies and filled it with bandages and towels. She followed his lead and took another, added basic medical tools—scissors, forceps, a scalpel, tweezers, and bandages.

She felt as dizzy as Maud, and she took a deep breath. "Where do I start?"

He looked down at her, his gray eyes bright and serious. "I'll show ye."

Eleanor gasped as she came around the end of the tent. Every inch of ground was now covered with stretchers, dozens of them, dozens of dozens, perhaps, and the ambulances were disgorging more. Still more bloody, shocked, bandaged men were propped together like broken dolls on benches or on the muddy ground. And up the road came an endless parade of more. Eleanor stared at the smashed faces, the missing limbs, the broken bones canted at impossible angles. The smell was terrible, even in the open air, and the unholy buzz of moans and cries vibrated in her chest, turned her knees to water.

"My God," Eleanor murmured. "Why aren't they inside? They should be inside."

"The reception tent's full. Ye need to triage them, sort them, get them the help they need," Fraser said.

"I can't," she said. She was a doctor. She should know how to help, what to do. She should be able to fix this. But she didn't know anything, couldn't think or move. She couldn't even breathe. "There's too many. I've never . . ."

He squeezed her arm. "Ye can because ye have to. There's no choice. They need a doctor, and there's no one else but you." She tore her eyes from the grim scene and looked up at him. She read determination in his eyes. There was no fear or panic. He looked down at her as if he was sure she could do this, had confidence that she could manage this horror. She drew strength from him and nodded.

"What do I do, where do I start?" she asked again.

His shoulders eased. "One at a time," he said. He guided her to the first stretcher.

"What have ye got?" Fraser asked the nurse bending over the patient. Her white pinafore was bloody. She looked up, and her lips parted in surprise at the sight of Eleanor.

"But—"

Eleanor dropped down beside her. "I'm here to help."

"Gunshot wound, left thigh. He's in shock," the nurse reported.

Fraser turned the patient gently. "Look to see if the bullet went straight through." It had.

"It will need cleaning and dressing," Eleanor said. "Irrigate the wound with disinfectant and warm him against shock."

Fraser moved toward the next stretcher. Under a makeshift bandage, half the lad's skull was gone, and blood oozed from his ears. Eleanor swallowed hard. "He needs surgery at once—" But Fraser shook his head.

"There's nothing you or anyone else can do for this lad now. He won't last the night. He's for the moribund ward." She stared at him in horror, and he held her gaze calmly. "The chaplain and the VADs will make sure he isn't alone. Ye have to concentrate on the men ye can save, the ones who have a chance."

The orderlies stood waiting for her pronouncement. "Moribund." The word was thick and ugly on her tongue. The orderlies carried the stretcher away to a tent that stood apart from the others in a quiet corner of the compound. She blinked away tears.

"Ye need to move on," Fraser said. "Can ye do it?"

She was struggling to breathe, the stench nearly unbearable. Her stomach had crowded up next to her heart, crushing her lungs. Her hands shook. The bearers placed another stretcher in front of her at MacLeod's beckon, and she looked down into the soldier's wide eyes, huge in a face white with fear and pain and too little blood. She moved automatically, her brain already working, her eyes seeking his wounds, her hands reaching for him.

"First check for—" the sergeant began, but her hands moved automatically, her mind noted the wounds, the medical protocol.

"I can do this," she said through gritted teeth, in part to Fraser, but more to herself.

She knelt in the mud, felt the cold wetness soak through her skirt to her skin, and ignored it. She lifted the blood-soaked bandage around the soldier's thigh, and hot blood spurted from a damaged artery, spraying her face. She swiped it away, and the wind cooled and stiffened it on her cheek. Fraser clamped a hand over the wound and applied a tourniquet.

"We're trained to stop bleeding as soon as we can in the field." He showed her the paper tag tied to the button on the man's tunic and handed her a stub of a pencil. "Write 'tourniquet' and the time so the surgeon knows."

Eleanor made the note and turned to the waiting nurse. "Stabilize him with fluids and get him to surgery. He'll need a transfusion."

The next man lay so still that she put her fingers against his pulse. "He's only sleeping," Fraser said. "Most of them fall asleep as soon as they know they're safe."

"He looks—peaceful," Eleanor said, though the soldier's face was spattered with blood and dust and sweat. She examined the long gash on his leg and felt the chill in the boy's limbs. He was soaked to the skin, his flesh ice-cold. "The laceration is just a deep scratch," she said to the orderly who arrived to look at the patient. "But he needs to be warmed up. Treat him for shock, get him dry and clean, suture and bandage him, and let him sleep."

The orderly scowled at Fraser. "I can't take orders from her. She's a civilian, just a visitor."

Fraser moved to interfere, but Eleanor met the orderly's insolent glare. "What's your name, Corporal?"

"Swiftwood," he said tersely.

"I'm a doctor, Corporal Swiftwood, fully trained and certified. Are you a doctor?"

He stiffened. "No, but—"

"Do you think I'm wrong in my diagnosis and recommendations?"

The orderly cast a quick glance at the sleeping soldier, at the wound on his chest, at his pale, sleeping face. "No," he said again, just as grudgingly.

She got to her feet. "Then do as I say. There are others to see to."

She walked away, suspecting that behind her he was looking to Fraser, but when she glanced over her shoulder at the stretcher bearer, he was following her, ignoring the stunned corporal, leaving him to carry out her instructions. She felt a surge of gratitude—another rush of surprise at Fraser MacLeod's confidence in her.

In the next hours, she sent dozens to the dressing tent, and dozens to surgery, and far too many to the moribund ward.

She looked up as another ambulance pulled up next to them, and Fraser moved to open the back doors as the driver climbed down, his face grim. "No hurry, Sergeant—it went quiet back there a few miles back. This lot will want the chaplain now, not the doctor."

Eleanor swallowed, but Fraser simply nodded and pointed to the next vehicle. "Let's save the ones we can," he said again. He caught the arm of a passing VAD. "Has Captain Duncan gone to surgery yet?"

The girl shook her head. "He's still in resus."

He looked at Eleanor. "Can you carry on here without me?"

She nodded.

"Are ye sure?"

She wasn't sure at all. She was terrified, but she nodded again, more crisply this time. She squared her shoulders. "I'm sure."

T he Reverend Captain Hanniford Strong wondered how they were going to manage the deluge of wounded, already lined up in their terrible multitudes waiting for help, with more coming. They were all frightened and in need of comfort and care. The surgeons and nurses were trying hard to keep up, and God and His angels surely had their hands full.

Worse, he'd heard that Captain Duncan, the 51st's regimental medical officer, was among the fallen, badly wounded. For a moment the chaplain looked skyward, asking the Almighty for help. They couldn't afford to lose good doctors like Captain Duncan. Strong joined the nurses, orderlies, and bearers in the triage area, knowing they'd need every pair of hands, even his, to make it through this day. "Let this war end, Heavenly Father. Send a miracle, or an angel," he murmured aloud. As he peered heavenward, he noticed the clouds were thickening, rushing in over the horizon like another belligerent army. "And if you could keep the rain off for just a few hours, Lord, we'd be most grateful," he added. But it never hurt to offer the Almighty a helping hand. He'd break out waterproof tarpaulins to cover the unfortunate soldiers, just in case. He looked around for Private Gibbons.

Instead he saw Miss Eleanor Atherton. The young woman's red hair burned like a flame against the gray light. Her face was white, her eyes wide pools of horror. He knew what she was seeing—a vision of hell on earth, all the corruptions and evils and tragedies of war. He frowned. She didn't belong here. In a moment she'd faint, need to be carried away, tended to, soothed. And what, he wondered, was the best Bible verse for that? There was no explanation, no forgetting, after seeing this. Forgiving one's enemies seemed impossible some days.

But she didn't faint.

With Sergeant MacLeod beside her, she crouched beside the first stretcher. Her eyes sharpened as she unwrapped the bandages, looked at the wounds, and assessed them. She looked up at the waiting orderly and gave instructions, and he saw the lad nod and jump to. And when that patient was sent inside, Miss Atherton followed the sergeant to the next man. She lifted the bloody bandage, and Strong winced as blood sprayed her cheek, dyeing her pretty blouse gore-red. He held his breath. Now she'd faint.

But she didn't. She kept going, her movements quick and definitive. He marveled at the calm determination in her slender frame. He watched as a patient clasped her hand in gratitude, then saw her smile at him and move on. It didn't matter a jot after all that she was female—not to the patients, at least—they were just glad of someone to help them.

Her face and hair and blouse were soon streaked with blood and her skirt was heavy with mud, but she didn't seem to notice. She kept on, doing her best. To him, she looked every inch a doctor—or an angel.

Sergeant Fraser was talking her through the process of triage. She examined a man with half his jaw missing and one with his arm blown off. Someone had lovingly laid the poor lad's severed limb on the stretcher beside him. She grimaced, blinked, instructed the orderlies and moved on. She swayed on her feet for a moment, and the sergeant gripped her arm, and she went on.

The warm glow of gratitude for a prayer answered filled Strong's breast, and he reached for the crucifix that hung around his neck, closed his hand over it, and sent up a word of thanks.

"You're needed, Reverend," a nurse said quietly, and he turned.

"I'm just coming, Sister Ellis." He pointed toward Eleanor Atherton. "I was watching Dr. Atherton work. Can you go and fetch a surgical gown to cover her clothes? Not that it will help now, but better late than never."

The chaplain looked once more as she bent over another patient, checking the tag and the bandages as if she'd done it a thousand times instead of just a dozen. God's mysterious ways were a marvel, even here in the midst of war.

CHAPTER TWENTY-SIX

Fraser found Captain Nathaniel Duncan in the resuscitation tent, waiting his turn for surgery.

"How bad?" the medical officer murmured. "Don't spare me, Fraser." He paused. "Moribund?"

"Stop blethering and let me look," Fraser said. A VAD was pressing a pad of blood-soaked cloth against Duncan's belly. She lifted the cloth, and Fraser's own stomach did a barrel roll at the sight of it. It was severe, probably fatal, but if Duncan had lived this long, had made it here to a CCS, was lucid enough to ask questions, then perhaps there was a chance . . . Ah, but how many times had stretcher bearers carried a man out of danger, off a battlefield where he'd survived in the open for days, only to learn that he died when he finally reached the Casualty Clearing Station?

Duncan was pale and sweating, his eyes too bright. Fraser forced a smile.

"Och, it's just a Blighty."

The VAD was choking back tears, her hands shaking. He realized that he didn't know her name, that she was new, and probably fresh from England. This was probably the first intake of casualties she'd seen. She was as pale as milk and glassy-eyed. He should send her outside, tell her to go and get some fresh air, but it was just as bad out there as it was in here. He squeezed her arm, made her look up.

"Go and find Dr. Atherton. Do ye know who she is?" She nodded. "Tell her I've sent ye to help her. Do everything she says, and don't faint, do ye understand? No one will have time to revive ye," he said, giving her a task, a purpose, making her focus. He used the same method with new stretcher bearers, green lads afraid of the noise and smell and sight of the battlefield, horrified by the wounds, the sucking mud and the bullets and the long, heavy carries. If they focused on one task at a time, they made it through.

Duncan quirked a smile as the girl left.

"Poor chit mistook you for an officer," he said. "She doesn't know you're far better than that." He coughed, and there was blood at the corners of his mouth. Fraser wiped it away.

"How are the lads I brought in?" he asked before Fraser could speak.

Duncan had done a foolishly heroic thing when the dawn attack went badly. He'd gone out onto the battlefield to help bring in some of the wounded, and he'd strayed too far and was hit. He shouldn't have been there at all, but they were short of bearers—four killed in action, three down with trench fever, seven others wounded.

"You saved three men," Fraser said to him. "You'll get a medal for it."

"God, I hope not," Duncan said tiredly, his voice a mere thread of sound. "You're the one who deserves the medal for carrying me in. I wasn't unconscious, you know. I heard every word you said, every curse. I put you in danger. I shouldn't have done it."

"Aye, but ye'd do it again, wouldn't ye?" Fraser asked.

Duncan was a good man, a good officer, the kind who'd do anything for his men, which meant the men liked him. When Fraser had carried the captain back to the aid post, a wounded private gave up his place on the ambulance to make room for Duncan.

Fraser looked under the dressing again and saw the hard glitter of the chunk of shrapnel. No, it was a button, blown off Duncan's shirt and into his flesh by the explosion. "I'll get ye more morphine."

"No. I've had enough. I want to be clearheaded," the captain said. "I won't go quietly into the night. Tell my wife—"

"No one's going into the night," Fraser insisted, and he caught a passing orderly. "Tell Captain Blair I need him right now."

"I'll tell him, but he's in surgery."

"Will it help?" Duncan asked Fraser. "It means taking Blair away from some poor bugger who has a better chance than me."

"Blair's a good surgeon. You'll be home before you know it."

"Thank you for that." Duncan shut his eyes. "Will you stay with me for a while? Just till they take me in for surgery. Do you have time?"

"I've got all the time in the world," Fraser said, and he pressed a fresh pad against the hole in the medical officer's chest and hoped Blair got there soon.

David Blair looked at Nathaniel Duncan as they carried him into the theater. Fraser MacLeod was carrying one end of the stretcher, his expression grim. Duncan's eyes were glassy with morphine, but still he gasped in pain as they laid him gently on the operating table.

"I do hope you'll mind my shirt, Blair. The laundry lads will be hard-pressed to clean it as it is. Any more bloodstains and they'll likely change sides and find some nice, tidy German officer to do for instead."

"Perhaps ye can make their job easier by buttoning your shirt on the outside next time," Fraser quipped. "Do ye want us to save the button so ye can sew it back on?"

"Yes. Thrifty," Duncan whispered.

There was a crash as the nurse assisting Colonel Bellford with anesthesia fainted from the fumes. The colonel frowned at her prostrate form. "Swiftwood! Take her out, get her some air. Get someone else to give ether before this man wakes up."

The orderly who'd been ready to assist David hurried over to the other table.

"Uh-oh," Duncan said. "Looks like I'll have to do my own anesthetic."

"I'll do it," Fraser MacLeod said, his eyes meeting David's. "I've seen it done often enough. Talk me through it."

Duncan groaned. "Nearer my God to Thee," he said, rolling his eyes and trying to grin. It came out a grimace. He caught Fraser's hand. "I trust you. Lucky bearer and all."

"Put a mask on, and don't breathe too deeply," Blair told Fraser. "Hold the mask over Duncan's face and give a drop at a time, slowly and steadily."

"Who's doing triage?" Bellwood demanded, looking up from the patient in front of him.

"Eleanor Atherton," Fraser whispered to Blair. "And she's doing a damned good job." He watched David Blair's eyes widen, then he nodded.

"It's being managed, sir," Blair called to the colonel.

"Good, good," Bellford said and turned his attention back to his patient.

"Ready?" Blair asked Duncan, and he nodded slightly.

The MO clasped Fraser's hand. "If this goes south, give my best to the men, and get yourself home before your luck runs out, won't you?"

"I'll see ye when ye wake up," Fraser said, and he put the ether mask over Duncan's face. He held his breath and added the first drop carefully, watching Duncan's eyes drift shut. He was no longer a praying man, and he didn't believe in luck, but he hoped both God and good fortune were on Nathaniel Duncan's side.

CHAPTER TWENTY-SEVEN

It was long past dark when Fraser walked out of the operating tent, having done anesthetic for Duncan and four other patients. He crossed the now-empty compound, picked up a bucket, and helped the drivers clean the ambulances, pouring soapy water over the benches and floors to wash away the blood and mud and make them ready for the next cargo. He worked until he was sweating and the urge to vomit was gone, subsumed by exhaustion.

He emptied another bucket and turned to find David Blair standing behind him. "Got a cigarette? I'm out of pipe tobacco."

Fraser reached into the pocket of his greatcoat and took out a flat metal tin, opened it, and held it out. The surgeon sat down on the fender of the ambulance and lit the gasper, drew deeply on it and puffed smoke into the clear night air. "How many hours was that?" he asked. "Is it still tonight, or already tomorrow night?"

Fraser sat down beside him. "Fourteen hours, give or take. It's a little past ten."

They sat in silence for a moment, the blue smoke of the cigarette rising around them like one more ghost in a place already filled with ghosts. Fraser pictured the departed as roaming the field behind the white tents of the CCS, lost, confused by what had happened to them, bending low to look into the faces of their living comrades, invisibly pleading . . . He didn't want to think of Duncan's restless spirit. He reached for the flask in his pocket, the last of his precious Highland whisky, the last taste of home. He drank, letting the spirit numb his tongue and burn a path down his throat, before he passed the flask to David Blair. "Here's to Duncan."

Blair raised the flask before he drank. "To Duncan."

"We'll need a new MO at the front," Fraser said somberly.

"I know. We're two men short here as well. We've been waiting weeks for a new surgeon."

Fraser scanned the tents, the sky, the boardwalk. "Eleanor Atherton did well today. She knows the way of things now, could be of use here. It would free a man—you, probably—to take over the aid post for a few days."

Blair took a long drag on the cigarette. "Bellford would never go for it."

"Does he have a choice?"

"His word is law. And *she* has a choice. This is no place for a woman."

"She's not just any woman."

Blair looked at him. "You're serious, aren't you?"

"Aye. The nurses manage, and most of the VADs are gently raised lasses, and they cope—" Fraser broke off as one of the VADs, her uniform bloody, hurried out of the moribund tent to be sick. "Well, most of them do." He wondered how the lass he'd sent to help Eleanor had fared. "Why not Eleanor Atherton?"

Blair grunted. "Won't do, MacLeod. She's leaving. Chastaine will be ready to travel within the week, and Bellford would be apoplectic at the very idea of her staying."

"Chastaine." Fraser drew out the word, his Gaelic burr lengthening the word to a growl.

"What? You don't like the gallant hero? Golden-haired, blue-eyed, cleft-jawed, and nobly born?"

"Do you?" Fraser asked.

Blair frowned. "Not in the least. She deserves better." They passed the flask once more. "Is it love, do you think?"

"It's his mother," Fraser said. "She wants him home."

"I wish my mother wanted me home, at least enough to send a pretty woman to carry me there."

"Aye."

"On her part, well, I think she'd like it to be love," Blair said. "It's in the way she looks at him."

"Like the sun rose out of his—"

Fraser stopped when Reverend Strong stepped out of the moribund tent, his white stole around his shoulders, his prayer book in his hands. He saw the glow of David's cigarette and came to join them.

"Seventeen dead," the chaplain said, adding his weight to the bumper. He looked around, his sorrowful gaze stopping on the make-shift cemetery, at the burial detail carrying the shrouded bodies out to new graves. "Such a waste. How many have we already laid to rest here?" he asked.

The gravediggers were "disgraced" patients, men recovering from venereal diseases, sentenced to do the most disagreeable jobs the army could find for their sins, including burying their fallen comrades.

Fraser had heard there were infected women who'd lay with soldiers for an extra fee to give them the disease so they could stay safe behind the lines for a time. It still counted as a self-inflicted wound. Soldiers with the clap went without pay, and the harsher commanders sent letters home to their kin informing them precisely why their pay had been stopped. But staying alive was worth the risk and the humiliation for some, as were a few weeks safe behind the lines. They handled the dead without resentment, laying them down with gentle reverence.

"Better to think of all the ones we've saved, Padre," Blair said.

Fraser thought of Duncan. He flicked the end of his cigarette into the mud. It hissed as it went out. "I'll help dig the graves."

The chaplain smiled tiredly. "Thank you, Sergeant, but I didn't come to ask for that. I came to say there'd be even more dead if not for your Miss Atherton. She's been a godsend, a fine doctor."

"*Your* Miss Atherton?" David asked Fraser, and Fraser noted the sharp edge of jealousy in the casual comment.

"Nay, not mine. I simply found her at the train station in Calais and helped her get here."

"Perhaps you shouldn't have. Perhaps you should have sent her home," David said, his tone sharper still, a bayonet of indignation now.

"Or perhaps Sergeant MacLeod was simply an instrument in a higher plan, and she was meant to come," the chaplain said.

"God sent a woman *here*?" David Blair scoffed. "Cruel of Him."

"Mysterious ways, Captain, mysterious ways," the chaplain replied. "Who's to question His plan?"

"I was just telling Captain Blair that we'll need a new MO at the aid post." Fraser shifted the topic before it became a debate, keeping his tone casual.

Strong's eyes widened. "Are you suggesting sending Miss Atherton *there*?" He looked at Blair. "A woman, Captain? A lass of such tender years?"

"Mysterious ways, Chaplain," Blair said harshly.

"Not there," Fraser said quickly. "Blair'll have to go, but she could help here at the CCS. She's qualified, and ye need a doctor."

"But she's not *entirely* qualified—she's still a woman," Strong argued. He glanced at the venereal gravediggers. "She can't be asked to . . . to . . . treat—or even diagnose—certain conditions!"

"She can do triage. She can remove shrapnel and give injections and perform basic procedures," Fraser said.

"Yes, I suppose so," the chaplain murmured. "She did all of that and more today."

"She saw far worse things than the clap," Fraser said.

The chaplain closed his eyes at the crudeness. "Sadly true, but—"

"It seems to me that you've been praying for weeks—months—for divine intervention," Blair interrupted. "For help for the sick, relief, for an end to suffering. Perhaps Eleanor Atherton is the answer to your prayers."

"I don't question that, Captain, but I doubt Colonel Bellford will have the same appreciation for the Lord's sense of—unique solutions."

Blair rose. "I'll speak to him."

"And Lieutenant Chastaine?" the chaplain asked. "What happens to him if she stays?"

Blair shrugged. "I haven't the faintest idea, but I have a feeling he's the kind of chap who'll land on his feet with or without Eleanor Atherton by his side." He stretched his shoulders. "If no one needs me, I'm going to try and get some sleep. All this can wait until morning."

Fraser watched him walk away and got to his feet. "I think I'll go and get a cup of tea," he said to the chaplain, and he went toward the triage tent, the last place he'd seen Eleanor Atherton.

CHAPTER TWENTY-EIGHT

Fraser found Eleanor sitting on a bench by herself in the triage tent, staring at the wasteland of bloody bandages, vomit, and the remains of filthy uniforms that had been cut off and discarded. Only three men remained now, lying on stretchers with hot-water bottles tucked around them as they stabilized.

"Are ye all right?" Fraser asked, sitting down beside her. She still had dried blood on her cheek, and her hair was tumbling out of the tight pins, long locks of it framing her pale face. Her hands were folded on her knee, and her skirts were covered with a bloody hospital gown. She looked exhausted and alert, her eyes wide, taking in everything. He knew her mind must be ticking like a stopwatch.

She looked every inch a proper doctor.

She focused on him slowly and scanned his face, her eyes softening at the sight of him. "I'm fine. Your medical officer?"

He shook his head, unable to speak over the bitterness in his throat. She reached for his hand, squeezing it.

He stared down at her fingers against his. The rest of her was a mess, but her hands were clean, ready, though it had been fourteen hours since the first ambulance arrived. She hadn't stopped, or broken down, or given up. He closed his hand around hers and held tight, drawing on her strength.

"Miss Atherton? Surely it's not you. Not here." Colonel Bellford stood in the doorway, glaring at them in alarm.

Eleanor withdrew her hand from Fraser's and rose to her feet. The colonel looked over her bloody attire. "You were told to stay away from the wounded."

"I was asked to help," she said simply. "I couldn't say no, sir. There were . . . so many." She stepped in front of Fraser, not mentioning his name as the one who had brought her here and insisted she help.

Bellford's face darkened. He was as exhausted as everyone else, his eyes bloodshot. He opened his mouth to speak, to command and rail and forbid. Fraser met the commander's eyes, ready to defend Eleanor, to take the blame, the bloody field punishment, or the court-martial, or whatever else Bellford had in mind.

But Eleanor began to push past the colonel. He grabbed her arm. "I am not finished, young woman."

Eleanor pointed. "That man is choking."

"Of course he is—the West Kents were caught in a gas attack. Sister Kelly, go and see to that man at once. Jeffers, find Captain Blair and tell him I need to see him." Bellford looked back at Eleanor. "Do you know anything at all about treating a gas victim?"

She regarded him. "I do now. After today."

The colonel looked at her in dull surprise, then released her and stepped back. "You've done enough," he said crisply. "Go and get some rest." He turned and walked away to check the gas victim without a backward glance. Eleanor watched him go.

"Come on," Fraser said. "He's right—ye need to eat, and sleep." He resisted the urge to reach up and swipe at the blood on her cheek. In truth, he was sorely tempted to kiss her.

She swallowed, then looked around her, taking in the aftermath once more, making sure no one else needed her.

"I liked it," she told him softly. "Not because men were hurt, but because I was useful—I helped, I made a difference. They *needed* me." Her eyes met Fraser's, and he saw the flame burning there, the sense of purpose and determination, the realization that she was alive amid the carnage, had come through it. "*Was* I useful?"

"Aye, lass, ye were useful," he said. Faint praise, but he couldn't say more—his tongue was too thick, his throat too tight. He couldn't touch her, it wasn't allowed, but he reached for her hand anyway and brought it to his lips, planting a quick kiss on her knuckles. Admiration, thanks, grief—he included it all in the press of his mouth on her skin. Her knuckles were rough and red, and she smelled of carbolic. She drew a sharp little breath and squeezed his hand, stepping closer to him. It had been a long day, emotionally and physically draining, probably the hardest day she'd ever had, the worst. If he needed comfort, she needed it just as badly. He wanted to pull her into his arms, hold her, make them both feel human and whole again.

"Miss?" Private Gibbons said softly, and Fraser dropped her hand and stepped back. Eleanor blushed, her pale face heating, and Fraser knew her thoughts had been the same as his own. "The colonel said I was to see that you ate something," Gibbons recited his orders. "Then I'm to escort you to your quarters and see that you have plenty of hot water. I'm to tell you that you are ordered to rest, and then to report to the colonel in the morning in his office." He gave her a sweet, vacant smile. "There's hot tea and sandwiches in the refectory if you're ready, miss."

She looked at Fraser. "Will you come with me?"

He clenched his fists against the desire to follow her. "Nay. I've got to get back. We've no MO at the front, and any fresh wounded will have to get by with what the bearers can do for them."

She scanned his face for a moment, and again he felt the desire to touch her, to wipe away the dried blood on her cheek or tuck the errant strands of hair back behind her ear. He put his hands in his pockets. "Thank ye for what ye did today."

She scanned his face as if she were memorizing it. "I'm the one who owes you my thanks, Sergeant. I wish . . . I hope I'll see you again. Not under such dire circumstances, of course, but . . ." He watched her lips move, saw the color rising in her pale cheeks, but Gibbons was waiting. "Stay safe," she said softly.

He watched her go, feeling as if he'd been given a blessing.

Or a curse.

CHAPTER TWENTY-NINE

Another medical officer killed in action," Robert Bellford muttered to David Blair in the privacy of his quarters when things were finally quiet. It was not quite dawn, a bit early for a drink, or a bit late, but one long hellish day had turned into night and was about to become another bloody day. It seemed most appropriate to share a drink now, and surely it counted as medicinal.

He took out the bottle of exquisite cognac he kept for such occasions, for times when the war threatened to overwhelm him. He poured two glasses, considering the events, the cases, the successes and failures of the past twenty-four hours. He handed one glass to Blair and raised his own. For a moment he regarded the dark amber liquor. The rare and excellent spirit was forty years old, a gift from his wife. It had been bottled in 1874, when the world was at peace and he was still in short pants and carefree.

"To Captain Nathaniel Duncan," he said, and David Blair raised his glass in return. They both sipped, and the mellow heat of the cognac flowed through Robert's veins like molten honey.

The moment of bliss was over all too soon. There wasn't enough cognac in the world to keep from being overwhelmed by this damned war, eaten away and destroyed from the inside out, heart and mind and soul. But he was an officer, a surgeon, and a gentleman, and there was nothing for it but to carry on, do his duty, and lead, no matter how long it took.

He looked at David Blair. The surgeon's shoes, and the hems of his trousers, were still spotted with blood, as were his own. Neither of them had been to bed yet. He wondered if he looked as bad as the captain did. The man needed shaving, a bath, and sleep. Food, too. In the seven months Blair had been at 46/CCS he'd lost at least twenty pounds. Dread and overwork made everyone lean and gaunt. Surgeons and soldiers and nurses and orderlies were all hollow-eyed and hollow-cheeked, their bellies caved against their spines. He remembered Blair when he had arrived, rosy, earnest, and eager. Blair was a good surgeon, relentlessly patient with the wounded and the staff, and he kept his head in a crisis. Bellford was grateful for that—he just needed two or three more doctors as good as David Blair.

Robert leaned back and rubbed his hand over his face. He needed sleep himself, weeks of it, in his own bed at home, in England. He wondered if it was just age that made him feel the exhaustion and futility of it all more than younger men, or if it was because this was his second war. His bones ached. With the shortage of doctors, he couldn't even get leave. Today he'd lost count of the surgeries he'd performed in fourteen hours, setting shattered bones, cutting off limbs, picking shrapnel out of once healthy young bodies that would now be forever twisted and scarred, despite his best efforts.

He looked at the folding frame on his desk, the photographs of his wife and his children, Colin and Elizabeth. Thank heaven Colin was only twelve, too young to join up. Elizabeth was only four. He'd missed most of her life. The bloody war went on and on, bloody, terrible, and—

"Pointless," he said aloud. He looked at Blair. "I've been informed it will take at least a week to get a replacement for Captain Duncan. They've asked us to send someone to take over the aid post until then. As if we can spare anyone."

He met Blair's eyes, but there was no surprise there. He had probably known when his commanding officer had sent for him and pressed a glass of fine cognac into his hand that he'd have to be the one to go to the front.

Blair studied the contents of his glass for a moment. "Are we expecting anything heavy?"

Bellford sighed. "Not that I've heard. Not on our side, at least. I've had no word about what the Huns have in mind."

Blair looked up again. "It will leave you rather shorthanded, Colonel."

Alone, the only surgeon, the only doctor.

"Yes."

"You'll need someone to replace me while I'm replacing Duncan."

"I'll ask 4/CCS at Doullens if they can send someone."

"They're as short staffed and stretched as we are." Blair leaned forward, the glass cradled in his hands, his elbows resting on his knees. "I have a solution to suggest, sir."

Bellford frowned. "Oh?"

"Dr. Atherton."

Bellford felt his blood pressure rise and blow like the whistle on a steam kettle. "That woman?"

"She's good. She, um—stepped in—today. Yesterday, actually," he said. "We could ask her to stay. Temporarily, of course."

"She was ordered not to interfere," Bellford said. He squeezed his glass until the cut crystal points pressed into his palm. "She doesn't listen, she's impetuous, and impertinent, and—"

"She's also efficient and quick thinking, sir. In her defense, Sergeant MacLeod asked her to help when he saw we were overwhelmed," Blair said. "She agreed at once, and she managed well. Once MacLeod showed her the way things work here, she took to it."

"Sergeant MacLeod is a stretcher bearer, not a doctor."

"Which is why he insisted we ask Dr. Atherton to help. She *is* a doctor, and she was the only one available to us, sir. She saved many who might not have made it without her."

"There are sound reasons why the War Office refuses to allow female doctors to practice on the front lines, Captain, reasons I fully support. Women are too flighty, too likely to be shocked or startled by war. And some of the wounds, the illnesses—they're nothing a lady could—or should—cope with."

"They're nothing *anyone* should have to cope with. She managed triage all day, and her diagnoses were all correct. Her manner was calm and professional. She didn't faint or turn squeamish at the sight of blood," Blair said.

"She's young, unmarried. She's probably never even seen a naked man."

Blair grinned. "Perhaps not a live one, but—well, you remember dissection class."

"Our patients are not for experimentation!" Bellford snapped.

Blair's smile faded to earnestness. "Of course they are, sir. Think of the things we've had to try, to improvise, to make do with since this war started."

"How do I know what her qualifications are? She's very young. She might have no experience beyond midwifery and children's sniffles."

"Not often a midwife needs to cope with a pneumothorax."

Robert resented the reminder. He remembered seeing Eleanor Atherton in triage after fourteen hours of work. She'd been on her feet, bright-eyed, not sobbing in a corner. *Do you know anything at all about treating a gas victim?* he'd asked her. *I do now,* she'd replied. In that moment, he understood all she'd seen and done that day, what she'd managed to accomplish—and on her own, too, since both he and Blair had been in surgery. He'd felt shamed, as if he were less of a doctor or a soldier or a man for not being able to cope without the help of a mere slip of a lass. He was protective of women, but he hadn't protected Eleanor Atherton. She hadn't needed his protection, he realized. Perhaps the guilt he felt came from the need to know he could still control something, keep one precious thing safe and sacred in this terrible place—a single, innocent woman, a girl.

He raised his chin. "I'm sending her home to England tomorrow."

"With respect, sir, I think that would be a mistake. Think of what might have happened if she hadn't been here, how many more might have died."

Bellford scowled at him. *His* masculinity, his authority, weren't being threatened by the female doctor.

"When I go up to the front, there'll be only you, sir," Blair said. "And if I don't make it back, and I might not—there've been two MOs killed in the past three months—you'll be unable to cope if there's an attack. Dangerously so. The alternative—"

"I know what the alternative is!" They'd have to close, join with another CCS farther away, a longer journey for the wounded, more crowding. He wouldn't be in command any longer. Still, he was stubborn. "This isn't my first war, Captain. I daresay I can find a way to manage."

But they both knew this war was different, the weapons and the terrain, and even the wounds were different, and the treatments—gas, gangrene, men blown to pieces in an instant, shell shock. To Robert, having a female doctor in a war zone, especially a young woman like Eleanor Atherton, was unthinkable, an insult to his Victorian sensibilities. Had the world changed so very much? His aging bones ached with fatigue.

"We're down to asking the chaplain to handle anesthesia in the operating theater," Blair said. "We can't stretch ourselves any thinner and still do what we're here for. Can we truly turn away qualified, willing help and call ourselves doctors?"

"Chastaine will be ready to travel within the week. She'll leave anyway."

"But even that week would help, sir," Blair pleaded. "That week might very well pass quietly. It may not even be necessary to use her if there isn't another attack. It's just in case."

Or that week could be filled with days like today, days that ran together, drowned in blood and toil and an endless stream of broken bodies. She'd be by his side. He'd have to trust her.

David Blair held his tongue, waited. The damned pup was no doubt thinking that his commander had no choice, and he was right, damn his eyes. She was here, and she was competent.

"She was hired to see to Chastaine's care. Even if I were to ask her to, to—help out—she'd likely refuse after today. If she has sense, she'll *insist* on going home as soon as possible." He paused, sighed. "*If* she stays, I'll make use of her only in emergencies, and she'll have rules to follow—and she bloody well *will* follow my orders from now on, or I'll send her home with or without Chastaine."

Blair nodded. "Of course, sir. It *is* possible she might refuse, but I don't think she will." He set his empty glass down on the desk and got to his feet. "I'll go and ask her—"

Bellford rose himself. "You will not. I'll be the one to speak to her when I've made a decision on this matter, Captain."

Blair scanned his face. No doubt he thought his commander was a stubborn old goat, but he was still in charge. "Very well, sir."

Bellford sighed. "I suppose you should at least go and see how she's faring," he said shortly. "Now that it's all over and she's had time to think, she's probably scared, shell-shocked. It would serve her right, of course—" He broke off, felt that fatherly, chivalrous sentiment again. "Just make sure she's all right."

"Yes, sir." He hesitated, and Bellford frowned again.

"Well, Captain, what is it now?"

"You'll be—less gruff—when you ask her to stay, won't you, sir? She's a colleague now, a fellow doctor."

Bellford's frown deepened. "One week, Captain. Then she goes home."

Blair offered a wry smile. "I wish we could all be that lucky."

CHAPTER THIRTY

The minute Fraser arrived back at the aid post, the waiting bearers knew by the look on his face that Duncan was dead. There
was no need to say it aloud. For a long moment Chilcott and others
stood or sat silently, their faces strained and tired. Another good officer, a fine doctor, a good man, gone.

"Anything happening?" Fraser asked. He noted the half dozen
lightly wounded still waited for transport, but they'd been given basic
care and something hot to drink, and there was no cause to worry.

Chilcott shook his head. "It's gone quiet again," he said softly, his
usually cheerful face crumpled with sorrow. "Thank God. So when do
we get a new MO?"

"Blair might come," Fraser said. He poured a cup of tea, black as
sin and thick as treacle, before sinking down onto a chair with his cup.
It was undrinkable, but it warmed his hands.

"Are you hungry?" Chilcott asked. Fraser looked at the half loaf of bread on the table, the open tin of plum-and-apple jam. He couldn't bring himself to eat it, though he hadn't eaten since morning, when he'd grabbed a meal at the CCS.

"If that's all there is to eat, I'll eat my boots instead."

"Probably a better choice," Chilcott agreed.

A corporal came down the stairs, fresh off the line, muddy and cold. He held up his hand to them. "I cut my trigger finger on a bit of wire when we were out on patrol. Lieutenant sent me back to get it patched up properly, me being a sniper and all. Where's the doc?"

"Dead," Chilcott said dully. "You'll have to make do with us." He turned to collect the necessary supplies. "We've no commanding officer. For now, Sergeant MacLeod's in charge—at least until we get a new MO."

The corporal frowned. "Crikey. Then I hope the bloody rumors aren't true."

"What have ye heard?" Fraser asked.

"That patrol I was on. We were supposed to capture a Hun, bring him back so our lads could ask him a few questions, if you know what I mean. The lads in our listening posts have heard some funny things lately. The Huns are bringing up troops. The men in our own forward trenches can hear 'em talking and scurrying around like rats across from them."

Fraser felt the back of his neck prickle. Soldiers were sensitive to rumors, learned to listen and to observe, to be prepared for what was coming. He'd learned to do it, too. It was habit now. If he survived, made it home—*if*—he'd always be on high alert for trouble, one ear forever cocked for a shift in the sounds around him, one eye on the horizon, watching. As Chilcott once said, *It's a hell of a way to live, but not when you consider the alternative.*

"Did you get a Hun prisoner?" Chilcott asked, indicating that the corporal should sit at the table across from him.

"Aye," the corporal said. He leaned in. "He didn't say nothin', but his uniform was clean, almost new." He tapped the side of his nose with his forefinger. "Even when they don't say a word, we get the story, eh? Means he's fresh meat, hasn't been up on the line before. Young, too—maybe sixteen." Chilcott held the corporal's hand over a basin and poured disinfectant solution over it, and the patient swore at the sting. He looked at Fraser. "If they come, there's a rumor they'll come through our lines here first—that's straight from our lads. Means you chaps will be in the line of fire if we have to fall back." He looked around at the snug basement. "My lieutenant said to tell your MO that it might be best to scout for a new spot for your aid post, farther back, just in case." He grunted as Chilcott took the first stitch in his torn flesh, but he kept still. "But you don't have an MO."

"Ah, the happy signs of spring," Chilcott said with sarcastic cheer. "You can always count on daffodils and snowdrops and brand-new bloody offensives, regular as the sunrise and the bells of St. Mary's back home. I used to love the spring, but not anymore. I'd hate to have to move house. It's a snug little hole we've got here, and it serves us well."

"There's a farm up the road a mile or so that might do," Fraser said. The bearers were used to keeping an eye out for alternative sites. You never knew when an aid post might have to move back fast, since they were barely a hundred yards behind the firing line here, where the wounded could easily find them. The farm he had in mind was a landmark. The house had been bombed to a roofless shell, but there'd likely be a useful cold cellar, deep and relatively bombproof. There'd be no bread oven like in this one, though—which meant it would be cold, summer and winter. Fraser hoped the German medical team appreciated it if—when—they took this place over. He suspected yesterday's attack was just a sign that there was indeed a major offensive coming. The enemy was testing for soft spots in the British lines. They were all soft, every unit under strength with no fresh recruits coming, and the politicians back home arguing over the wisdom of sending more men into the meat grinder of the Western Front.

Chilcott wrapped a bandage around the corporal's hand. "Keep it clean and dry," he said, and the corporal laughed.

"I'll do my best to stay out of the mud," he said sarcastically and left.

Fraser couldn't sleep. He tossed on a cot for an hour before he got up again. He reached for his greatcoat and shrugged into it.

"Where the devil are you going?" Chilcott asked. "It's raining out there."

"I think I'll take a look at that farm." He pulled his collar up around his neck and headed out.

CHAPTER THIRTY-ONE

"May I have a word, Miss Atherton—*Dr.* Atherton?" the colonel called to Eleanor as she hurried toward the officers' ward to see Louis. She'd only meant to sleep for a few hours, but she'd dragged off her blouse and skirt and had been asleep before she'd even dropped onto her bed. She'd woken twelve hours later groggy, stiff, and very late. She'd rushed to wash and dress, tossing her bloodstained skirt and blouse into a pile and choosing a plain dark gray skirt and a pale blue blouse. She wanted a very long, very hot bath and a chance to shampoo her hair and brush it by the fire as it dried, then rub rose oil into it until it shone. She'd settled for combing the dried blood out of it and washing it in cold water with carbolic soap, and now her crowning glory was itchy against her neck. When she looked into the mirror, sure she was pale and tired, a new face stared back at her. Her eyes *were* puffy, but they were also bright and keen. She'd saved lives, given hope, eased pain under dire circumstances. But Louis was her patient, and he was waiting.

And now Colonel Bellford stood before her on the boardwalk, his hands clasped behind his back, his expression flat, his stance rigid. "I'd like a moment of your time."

Eleanor's belly tightened. She was sure another dressing-down was coming. She clasped her hands at her waist. "I know you told me not to, to—" She fumbled for the right word. Interfere? Intervene? Assist? "*Help*—but there were so many men, so much suffering." She raised her chin. "As a doctor yourself, I'm sure you could not stand by and watch someone suffer, knowing they might die if you did not *intervene*, use your skills and training to *assist* . . ."

"Captain Blair and Reverend Strong have made me fully aware of your contribution. Thank you." He said it as if it choked him to do so, but still Eleanor smiled.

"It was—" Educational? Enlightening? Breathtaking? "*Good* to be of service, sir."

"One of the men killed yesterday was a doctor, a medical officer who was serving at the front."

Her smile faded. "Yes, Captain Duncan. I'm sorry."

He scanned the camp. "We've lost far too many doctors in this war, too many good men. Now I've been ordered to send Captain Blair to the aid post to take Duncan's place for a few days." He peered at her. "A week at most, I'm assured, until a replacement can be found."

She pictured David Blair wounded, dying, and her throat tightened.

"Unfortunately, that will leave us shorthanded. As you saw yesterday, we were barely able to cope. If there's another attack—" He paused again and rocked on his toes, making the leather of his boots creak. "We'll have to turn men away, send them on to other facilities, delay care and leave them to face the risks of infection, hemorrhage, death."

"I see," she said.

"Do you?" he asked. She nodded solemnly. He scanned her face, his expression grim. "I find I must ask for your assistance after all, Miss—*Dr.* Atherton. *If* there is another influx of wounded while Captain Blair is away, and only if, would you consider pitching in again?" His face flushed red and he frowned. "It is strictly against regulations, as you know. It would not be an official role. It would be considered—a favor—since you're here—"

"Yes," Eleanor said at once. "Yes, of course." She clasped her hands together more tightly. Surely she shouldn't be elated, but she was. "I do want to help, I'm willing. More than willing," she babbled.

"There will be strict rules, of course, and you will be called upon only under extreme circumstances. Of course, at this point Lieutenant Chastaine is more in want of amusement than of a doctor. It's a simple matter of keeping him still for a little while longer."

She hadn't thought of that. What on earth would Louis say? "Yes," she said again.

He stepped back. "I shall inform you if or when your assistance is required. We should go over the rules, of course."

"Of course, sir."

"Very good, then. Attend rounds this evening. I'll have a list of expectations and restrictions ready for you then. Carry on with your day."

He turned on his heel and walked away without another word, and she knew what it had cost him, or suspected she did—the colonel, a man of her father's generation, believed a woman's place was at home, safe and silent.

But she was here, and she had proven herself professional and capable, a good doctor after all. If she was needed, she'd be ready to help.

But for now, Louis was expecting her.

CHAPTER THIRTY-TWO

W here have you been?" Louis asked shortly. He looked peevish and bored, and Edward and Lady Frances and his friends were gone, to Paris, maybe, or perhaps her brother had returned to duty. He hadn't said goodbye, but she'd been rather busy. She hadn't thought about Edward, or Lady Fanny, or even Louis, for that matter, since the influx of wounded had claimed her attention. She felt no guilt. The wounded had needed her more than Louis or his visitors. Still, she would have liked to have had a word with Edward before he left, if only to ask if he'd had any news from home.

"How are you feeling?" she asked Louis now, ignoring his question. How could she even begin to explain to him how she'd spent the last two days?

"Hungover. Can you make the dragon give me a headache powder?"

Eleanor leaned in to examine the whites of his eyes and feel his forehead, just in case it was something more serious. She looked at the splint and examined the tension of the wires. All was well. "You didn't refer to Matron Connolly as 'the dragon' before your friends visited."

"But she is, isn't she? Is there any reason to deny me comfort for my pain? I suppose she thinks I should suffer for my sins. She probably considers this a self-inflicted wound, or she's peeved that Fanny didn't offer her any caviar."

"Or because you frightened the other patients and made too much noise," Eleanor said. She looked around the ward, full after yesterday. There were ten patients, two of them critically wounded. Private Gibbons sat beside one of the worst cases, a captain, patiently watching over him.

"Are you listening to me?" Louis demanded, drawing her attention back. "You haven't heard a word I've said, have you?"

"I'm sorry. I—I, um, had a conversation with the colonel this morning."

The vicious delight in his eyes surprised her. "Sending you packing, is he? I heard all about you mucking in yesterday. Just be glad you're not in the army—they shoot soldiers for disobeying direct orders. Not to mention my mother's orders. Or mine." He snapped his fingers in her face, and she flinched in surprise. "I want a bloody headache powder!"

She felt indignation rise in her breast. "They needed me. There were so many wounded, and you had plenty of company—"

"Were you *jealous*?"

Her cheeks heated with annoyance. He really was as thick as a bloody brick. "Not everything is about you, Louis. A medical officer was killed yesterday, a good man."

"What do I care? I didn't know him."

"But it does affect someone you do know—Captain Blair must go and take his place at the front until they can get another doctor," she said sharply. Nothing changed in his expression. She lifted her chin. "The colonel asked if I would—help out—while he's away."

"You?" Louis threw his head back and laughed. "You, heal wounded men, perform surgery, chop off limbs, pull shrapnel out of ruined bellies with your bare hands? Oh, they must be desperate indeed! Well, I won't have it. You're *my* doctor, or companion, or whatever it was my mother called you when she hired you."

She felt the sting of his cruelty. There was no charm in Louis Chastaine now. She resisted the urge to snap at him again. Instead, she reached out to smooth the covers as she kept her expression flat. "You'll be fine, Louis. It will only be for a week, and only if there's another push."

"Another 'push.' Picked up the lingo, have you? What's next, bobbing your hair, asking for a fag, chatting with the lads as you singe lice, or singing "Hinky Dinky Parlay Voo" with your skirts kilted up to amuse Tommy Atkins?"

Eleanor turned away and picked up the chart hanging on the peg, her hands shaking. "Colonel Bellford has ordered another seven days of bed rest to let your leg mend. The burn on your arm is healing well. You are showing no signs of illness or fever—"

"I have a headache!" he insisted.

She put the chart back. "When you are ready to leave, I will be here to escort you home. I will be your *doctor* when—"

He grabbed her hand, suddenly contrite before her stiff tone. "Just my doctor? Not my friend?" He gave her a dazzling smile. "I was only joking, El. Come now, don't be sharp. Read to me."

But the curtain at the end of the ward parted, and David Blair walked in. He was dressed for travel, wearing his greatcoat and his cap, his boots and puttees. He looked every inch a soldier.

"There you are," he said to Eleanor.

"Off to play hero at the front?" Louis asked him.

David flicked a bland glance over the pilot. "May I speak to you outside, Dr. Atherton?"

Louis gripped her hand tighter, holding her. "Don't go! I've been without you all day."

"I'll be back directly," she said, feeling David's eyes on her. She plucked her hand free, her cheeks burning.

"Bugger it," Louis cursed. "At least bring a headache powder when you come back, and a cold cloth, and see if you can find a copy of the *Times* that isn't a month old!"

"He isn't normally so—imperious," she said to David outside. She wrapped her arms around herself, as much out of humiliation as from the cold.

"No need to explain. I wanted to thank you for agreeing to fill in while I'm away," David said.

"I was just telling Lou—Lieutenant Chastaine—that you were going, and I—" She paused. "He doesn't approve, I'm afraid."

"Does it matter so much to you that he does? Do you have hopes of him?" Blair asked bluntly.

She looked up at him in surprise. "What? No! I had a crush on him when I was a girl, but I'm—"

His eyes cut into her like a scalpel. "Do you still? Is that why you came here, hoping?"

"The Countess of Kirkswell asked me to come!" she objected, flustered. "As her son's doctor." She was blushing. She could feel the hot blood burning in her cheeks. "She promised that—" Tongue-tied, she fell silent. It seemed trivial now, when David was leaving for the front, and danger.

Blair folded his arms over his chest. "Chastaine doesn't need a private doctor. You're clever enough to know that. And if the countess had checked, she would have found out that Bellford was one of the top orthopedic surgeons at the Royal London Hospital before the war. He's done the very best for your flier. All Chastaine needs is someone to hold his hand, tip the porter, and mop his brow. He doesn't need a doctor to do that."

"It's not like that," she said. "She—the countess—knew he'd be stubborn, would refuse to come home if she came. She's just concerned, you see—he's the only heir now, and it's time for him to take his responsibilities seriously, to go home and do his duty."

He shook his head. "But that's not medicine—it's a carrot on a stick. You make a very pretty carrot, to be sure, but it's a poor use of your skills. Why did you *really* come to France, Eleanor? Surely you weren't so foolish as to pin your hopes on winning Chastaine, war hero, playboy, rascal, and earl's son—unless you just wanted a bit of a fling." He looked at her critically, with speculation, as if to determine whether or not that was true. She held his gaze, her expression flat. He looked away first and sighed. "No. You're not the type for that, are you? Not from what I've seen. You want to be a doctor, a real doctor."

She raised her chin at his rebuke. "And I will be. Her ladyship promised she'd help me when I got home, recommend me to her friends. I will be a real doctor."

"You'll be a society quack."

Suddenly it felt like a shameful reason to have come, especially when she stood surrounded by men in pain, dying, broken. "What other choice do I have? The options for medical women are limited. You know that. I would be expected to work with women and children, in public health, and always under the supervision of a male doctor. With the countess's help, I'll have a practice of my own."

He studied her again, frowning. "I have a friend in psychiatry—fascinating to see how people tick," David said. "The way the mind works—especially the female mind—is an interest of mine. You're different from most of the women I know. You're stronger, braver, keener than most. You don't back down, or faint at the sight of blood and death. You carry on. I can't quite figure out what it is you truly yearn for. It isn't really Chastaine, or you wouldn't have helped yesterday and left him alone with other company. You'd be playing by his rules if that was the case. You'd be content to fluff his pillow and hold his hand.

And I can't see you running homeward to dose titled biddies with patent tonics and calling it medicine. I suspect you'd never be happy with that, not now you've had a taste of real medicine, and nothing you do will ever be as real as this. It doesn't matter that you're a woman. No one can use that argument against you now. You're good enough to be a surgeon, a fine doctor in your own right—and if anyone can change the minds of the men who say that a woman isn't good enough, it's you, Eleanor. So is that it? Have I figured out what makes you tick, Eleanor Atherton? Is it this?" He indicated the CCS with a wave of his hand. "Have you found what you really want?"

Every nerve in her body quivered. Yes, she wanted this, all of it. She looked up at him. There was a keen light in his eyes, so different from the witless flirtation in Louis's insouciant blue gaze.

"And what will you find, at the front?" she asked.

"Oh, mud, blood, terror," he said with sangfroid, but she noted the tension in his jaw. "You know, you're very pretty when you blush."

"That is not how one colleague speaks to another," she said tartly.

"Ah, but yours might be the last tender blush I ever see."

"Don't say that," she whispered. "Aren't you afraid?" She listened for the sound of the guns, gauged the direction like an old pro now that she'd been here for nearly a month. She'd learned to ignore them unless the cadence changed. For now it was flat and low, far away, and only half-hearted.

"Oh, I'm afraid, and I'll continue to be afraid, every second. Will you worry?"

"Of course."

He smiled. "How fine you are, Eleanor Atherton. Don't waste your time hoping for Chastaine. Don't settle for less than you deserve. Choose someone worthy of you, someone who respects your talents, your brains, and your bravery, all of what and who you are."

She scanned his face, saw something sharp and hopeful in his eyes, and it made her breath catch. She looked away.

He caught her hand and held it. "Look, I'll be back before you leave for England. We'll have a chance to talk then. Don't worry about me too much. It will only be a few days, and—" He glanced at the ambulance waiting to take him to the front. "Oh, bugger it," he swore. He swooped in and kissed her firmly on the mouth, his arm coming around her waist to pull her close for a brief instant. Then he stepped back and grinned. "That's for yesterday, for helping out, for worrying, and just because I've wanted to kiss you since the day you saved Findlay." He grinned. "Goodbye, Eleanor. I'll see you when I get back. I fully expect you'll be in command of this post by then."

She gaped at him, speechless, her mouth still tingling from his kiss and the surprise of it. He smiled again and jokingly came to attention and saluted her before turning smartly on his heel and marching away. She watched as he swung up into the ambulance and drove away.

"Miss?" Private Gibbons caught her sleeve. "Captain Greaves on the officers' ward is looking poorly. Will you come and see? Chaplain's with him, but he's wondering if there's anything more we can do to make him comfortable."

"Of course." Eleanor hurried after him to check on the dying man. She glanced at Louis as she hurried past his bed. "Private Gibbons, will you ask one of the VADs to get Lieutenant Chastaine a headache powder? And plenty of water."

An hour later, Captain Greaves died, the rattling breaths in his chest falling silent at last, his hand going slack in hers. Eleanor closed his eyes with her fingertips. Private Gibbons clapped his hands together and mumbled a prayer with the chaplain.

"What happens now?" she asked. She watched as Gibbons took a cloth bag out of his pocket and solemnly handed it to the chaplain.

"We gather his belongings—his watch, and his glasses, the book he had in his pocket when he came in," the chaplain said sadly. "We pack everything up and send it home to his loved ones." He sighed. "Greaves was engaged to be married, I understand. I'll write a letter, tell them he died quietly, without pain, a hero." It wasn't true—he'd died slowly and in agony, despite morphine and the best efforts of the surgeons and nurses. "Some men struggle against dying if they have something important to live for. Still, we tell their loved ones that they were at peace, and that their last thoughts and words were of home and family."

"I'll write to his fiancée," Eleanor said. "I saw him yesterday when he came in. Her name was Rosy. He kept saying it over and over again."

"I heard him call you Rosy, miss," Gibbons said. "He thought you were her at the end." He held out a pocket watch and opened it so she could see the photograph of a young woman under the lid.

The chaplain nodded. "It comforted him to think so. Thank heaven you were here, Miss Atherton." He turned to Gibbons. "Go and fetch the orderlies, lad, and we'll take him out." He took off his spectacles and rubbed his eyes. "Three more to bury this evening. It will be at sunset if you'd care to come."

"I'll be there," she promised.

She took the photograph out of the watch. "I think he'd like to keep this close by," she said, tucking it into his breast pocket next to his heart.

The chaplain smiled. Eleanor pulled the winding pin on his watch to stop it and mark the time, then she handed it to Reverend Strong to put in the muslin bag with the rest of the captain's belongings.

CHAPTER THIRTY-THREE

Louis was reading a book when she returned to his bedside. He looked up at her, his expression neutral. "Dickens," he said. "*David Copperfield*. It's better than I thought it would be. Either that, or I've truly lost my will to live."

"Don't," she said, her mind still on Captain Greaves's death. "Don't joke. You're alive, Louis."

He looked past her, watching the orderlies carry away the shrouded stretcher.

"I was a cad, wasn't I?"

"Yes," she said. She looked down, saw something under the bed, and picked up a pink silk scarf, heavy with perfume.

"Fanny's," he said. "I doubt she'll miss it. She has a hundred others."

"Will she be coming back?" She moved to hand the scarf to him, but he shook his head.

"I don't want it. Keep it. It's a pretty color. Wear it if you want. It would suit you."

Eleanor stared at the pink silk. It was soft in her hands, unlike the rough blankets and boiled sheets, the washed and rewashed bandages that smelled of carbolic and disinfectant, or the plain wool and linen of her own clothing. It was the one extravagant spot of color in the room, the color of a June rose, and it smelled feminine, exotic, and glamorous.

Eleanor folded it and set it on the table beside the bed. "You keep it," she said.

"She'll come back with a new one—bright blue, or yellow as a buttercup, straight from Paris, with a dress and hat to match, and shoes as well," Louis said. "Not red. That would remind her of blood. She does have a soft heart, you know. She gives money to crippled soldiers, supports the war widows and orphans on her father's estates."

"Is she in Paris now?" Eleanor asked.

He grunted. "She's off looking for more champagne. Other than silk, and perhaps me, that's the one thing she can't live without."

"There's a war on, you know," she said with a rueful smile.

"Is there? I've been lying in this bed, bored witless, for weeks. How would I know what's going on out there?" He tossed *David Copperfield* aside, looking peevish again.

"If the weather stays fine, you can get up in a few days' time, go outside in a wheelchair, get some fresh air."

"A wheelchair? Why not a pushchair? You really are my nanny, aren't you?"

She remembered what David Blair had said and turned away to fidget with the splint. She turned back to find Louis staring at her— not with admiration, but with bafflement.

"Don't you feel ill, or faint? Doesn't it make you want to cry to see wounded men? How can you touch them, stick needles into their chests, operate on them?"

"It makes me feel *alive* and *useful*. I feel compassion, and a desire to help, to use my knowledge and my training to ease their suffering."

He frowned. "How brave you are, then."

"No braver than David Blair or Sergeant MacLeod—or you."

He looked at her as if he were seeing her for the first time. There was no flirtation in his eyes, no mirth. There was something else there, something akin to terror, or guilt. Her breath caught in her throat. "Louis?"

He forced a grin. "Come now, let's not be serious," he said brightly, sounding more like Lady Fanny. "As you said, there's a war on. We owe it to ourselves to enjoy every day, just in case—" He paused and the grin faded again, and he glanced at the nurses busy changing the sheets on Greaves's empty bed across the ward. He swallowed hard. "God," he muttered.

"Were you afraid?" she asked him. "When you were shot down?"

He studied her for a long moment before replying. "Do you want to know if my life flashed before my eyes as I tumbled out of the sky, if I felt like a hero, if I called out my mother's name, pissed myself?"

She held his eyes. "Yes."

He looked toward the door. "Where the devil is Fanny with that champagne?"

"Louis," she said softly.

He turned his attention back to her. "You really do want to know, don't you? Then yes, I was afraid. Only a fool isn't afraid here. Death is everywhere, and you only get so many lucky breaks. Did you know pilots in the Royal Flying Corps have a life expectancy of less than eighteen hours of flying time? My time was up weeks ago—*months* ago. Yes, I was afraid. I heard my leg break. Do you know what that's like, hearing your own bones breaking?"

She shook her head.

"And no, I didn't call out for my mother. Oddly, the last thought I had before I passed out was of a wolfhound I once had named Beowulf. He was old, and he died when I was eleven. I called him Bo, and oh, how I loved him! He was the last thing to go through my mind when I crashed. I've wondered about that ever since—was a dog the love of my life? Wouldn't it make more sense that I'd feel regret for my misspent youth and all the times I disobeyed my parents, chose the wild road over the safe, dutiful one? Instead, I thought of Bo. I didn't think that I should be married by now, should have left the requisite heir and spare to take my place, strapping sons who'd honor my family history better than I've done. I thought of a *dog*. Does that surprise you?"

"No."

"Well, it bloody well surprised me. I don't regret it, you know—not choosing the safe path. Not a minute of it, especially if I'm to die young." He caught her hand, breathing hard. "Don't do it, El. Don't be dutiful. Take your chance while you can. Do something daring, break the mold. Be a doctor if you want, but do it on your terms. Don't let anyone tell you how, or say no. Not Bellford, or my mother. Not even me."

She bit her lip. "I didn't think when Sergeant MacLeod asked me to help. I didn't consider you, or my father, or anyone. What if I'm not being compassionate, but selfish?"

"Edward once told me it was pigheadedness that made you want to be a doctor. It's not pigheadedness, though. This is what you truly want, isn't it?"

She wondered if her brother was jealous, if he regretted that he hadn't studied harder and passed the exam. It had made her feel guilty at times. She recalled Edward's silence after the test, and her own, sure she'd done poorly, and her father's fury with his son when the results were posted. She'd vowed at that moment that she'd become the best doctor she could be. "Yes. This is what I've always wanted," she murmured now.

"Then is that truly why you came? Not for me?"

She felt a blush rising from under her prim collar. "Yes, for you—

and for other reasons. I hoped that . . ." She swallowed. "I didn't expect they'd ask me to help. If David hadn't had to go—"

Louis chuckled. "*David?* Not 'Captain Blair,' or 'that surgeon chap'? Have you made a conquest, El? And here I am telling you to go and do something daring. What a fool I am! Or is it simply an *affaire du cœur*? I never would have thought that you'd . . ." He stopped.

She raised her chin. "That I'd what?"

"Oh, don't poker up, El. It's just that you've always been so serious, so . . . so . . . dutiful, and *good*."

"You say it as if it's a bad thing."

"Not at all. Blair is probably right for you. Edward always said you'd marry a man just like your dear papa, a country doctor or a sober man of the church, someone older, widowed, with seven motherless brats to raise. A sober, teetotal, church-on-Sunday sort—a vicar, perhaps. We had a wager, in fact."

"You had a wager about me?" she repeated, suddenly cold. She stared into Louis's handsome, careless face.

"It was all in fun, of course. Don't be cross. I bet on you marrying someone much more interesting than that. Blair's a surgeon, so I suppose if you marry him, I win." He winked at her. "There's something of the dash about the good captain. Edward and I had a wager about your going to medical school, too. He said you wouldn't go, or if you did you'd run home in tears before the first week was out. Everyone thought so. But I bet you'd stick to it, and I won. Of course, we didn't think—" She drew a sharp breath and he stopped. "Uh-oh. Have I said too much? It was all in fun, of course."

Fun? They'd wagered on her, mocked her? "Didn't think what?" she said through wooden lips, prompting him to continue.

He looked sheepish. "We didn't think your father would even allow you to go to medical school, or that you'd really be brave enough to do it. But you did. You really did."

Guilt rose in her throat. Was Edward so bitter, so resentful? She choked the emotion down, swallowed it, as she pinned Louis to his pillow with an angry glare. "I'll have you know I graduated near the top of my class!"

He held up his hands in surrender. "Don't take on at me! You're rather a marvel, aren't you? I had no idea." He turned serious again. "Don't settle, then, El. Take the best life has to offer. Do your damnedest to thwart your father's expectations, and Edward's, and my mother's. God, I hope Blair knows how magnificent you are, and that he's worthy of you." He regarded her with a new interest in his eyes. There was no flirtation, no laughter. He took her hand. "Have you ever even been kissed?"

She thought of David's farewell kiss. "Yes, of course I have."

He caught her chin in his hand and made her look at him. "No, I mean *really* kissed, properly, with passion and desire, the way a man kisses a woman he wants to bed." His voice had turned husky, dropped to an intimate purr. "I've wondered for weeks what it would be like to kiss you like that." He took her hand and drew her toward him. For a moment she was mesmerized, caught in that seductive, heavy-lidded blue gaze. Her lips rippled. But he wouldn't mean it. She drew back, freeing her hand from his. "El?" he asked, waiting, so sure she'd come back.

She took a breath and shook her head. "I think—"

The curtain surrounding his bed flew open, and Eleanor jumped back.

Lady Frances Parfitt stood there with a look of glee on her face, holding two bottles of champagne aloft. "Darling—look! Two more bottles! A farmer had them hidden in his barn. I had to pay the earth for them." She nestled the dusty bottles in the bed beside Louis and sat next to him, taking the kisses that might have been Eleanor's. The duke's daughter had barely even glanced at Eleanor, but Louis cast her a single look over Fanny's frivolous feathered hat—robin's-egg blue today. Was there regret in his eyes, or relief? He turned his attention to his visitor before Eleanor could decide, his familiar look of dissipation and mirth back in place.

"Good job, Fanny, darling! If I were a cavalry officer, I could use my sword to open them, but alas, I am a mere flier!" he drawled. *Never serious, never afraid*, Eleanor thought.

"Did you bring any more caviar?" he asked, and Eleanor realized she was superfluous at a party just for two.

She slipped away from the low intimacy of Louis's voice and the fairy chime of Fanny's answering giggle, leaving them together without a single regret.

Don't do it, El. Don't be dutiful. Take your chance while you can. Do something daring, break the mold.

She paused to check on one of the new patients, a man with a wound in his jaw, and beckoned to the nursing sister on duty. "This patient requires morphine, sister." She adjusted his bandages, murmured to him, and made him more comfortable. He couldn't speak, but the gratitude in his eyes was worth a dozen of Louis Chastaine's kisses.

She looked around the ward at the other patients.

Yes, this was what she wanted.

CHAPTER THIRTY-FOUR

M iss Atherton is interfering with the function of this hospital. It is confusing my nurses and disrupting protocol," Matron Connolly said.

Bellford looked up at the career military nurse. She stood in the middle of his office, precisely halfway between the door and his desk, as if there were an *X* painted on the floor to mark the place. Her uniform was spotless, her scrubbed hands clasped at her waist under her red capelet. Sarah Connolly reminded him of portraits he'd seen of Queen Victoria, or even the present consort, Queen Mary, their spines as stiff as iron, their faces haughty, smug, and tightly closed. Any secrets, softness, or femininity were locked away deep inside their dour bodies, the key lost.

"She has my permission to assist us if casualties get heavy. As a doctor."

The nurse's pale eyes popped. "She cannot serve as a doctor here!

It's strictly against the rules. What would the director of Army Medicine say?"

And who would tell him? But there was no need to ask the question aloud. The answer was clear enough. The matron grew taller before his eyes, a starched pillar of indignation.

He set his pen down. "In ordinary circumstances I would agree, Matron. But we're woefully short of qualified doctors, and woefully long on wounded. We must find a way to provide proper care."

"But she's a woman!"

"I am aware of that," he said tiredly. "She's also a qualified physician."

"Colonel, I have been a nurse in Queen Alexandra's Imperial Military Nursing Service for sixteen years. I have served here since the very start of this war. I was at Mons, Ypres, the Somme, and Arras. I have seen the toll the war takes on young women who are gently raised and unprepared. How many eager members of the First Aid Nursing Yeomanry or VADs thought themselves brave and capable, only to collapse at the things they're forced to witness, to cope with, to endure? So few of them can hold a man's hand and calm his fears while there are bombs falling. So many of them can't bear to look into the half-gone face of a dying man and offer a smile of reassurance. They do more harm than good, and then they scurry back home again with all their hopes and good intentions shattered, their time and ours wasted."

Matron Connolly felt she knew best how to run a hospital, and perhaps she did. There was no doubt that she'd be a commander if she were a man. She managed her nurses and volunteers with military strictness and discipline, but without kindness or tolerance for human frailties like fear, exhaustion, or inexperience. She cared for her patients the same way, with excellent care, but no coddling—they were men, and this was war. Everyone, wounded beyond bearing or not, must do their part to keep order.

As commander and surgeon, he appreciated her insistence on the highest standards of cleanliness, organization, and care, of course. But in war, there was also a need to remain flexible and adaptable and to seek victory in unlikely places.

Like making use of Eleanor Atherton.

He looked at his chief nurse and saw the conviction in her eyes, the justification. Why was it that women were hardest on one another, harder even than men at times?

"I'm afraid there's simply no choice in the matter, Matron. Dr. Atherton was pressed into service during that last crisis, and she acquitted herself well. With Captain Blair away, we need another doctor. There is a shortage of medical officers."

"But a woman—a very young woman, a civilian—"

"I think it would be a far more serious breach of our duties if we were unable to provide care to our wounded men, don't you agree?"

The matron's sharp glare didn't soften one whit. "There are rules for a reason. Her inexperience might kill someone."

"Or she may save lives."

He was tired. He didn't disagree with her arguments, and yet . . . "Thank you, Matron. I will make note of your concerns."

"Not concerns, sir—*objections*," she said, not moving an inch. His irritation grew, making heat prickle under the tight collar of his tunic. He got to his feet.

"My decision stands. If there is a situation like the one yesterday, where we are overwhelmed with wounded men, I expect you to work with Dr. Atherton, to support her medical orders, is that clear?"

She hesitated, her lips so tightly pursed there was a white ring around them. "Colonel, I—"

"Dismissed," he said, and she turned on her heel and was gone.

Bellford sank back into his chair. There'd be trouble, of course, and it would fall upon him like a bomb. He just hoped that Eleanor Atherton, and everyone else, was back in England when it hit.

CHAPTER THIRTY-FIVE

MARCH 11, 1918

The farmhouse must once have been a fine place. Fraser looked at the damage the bombs and bullets had done, at the broken walls and splintered gates, and tried to imagine it whole again, a comfortable, prosperous home situated in green fields that came alive with wildflowers in the summer and turned golden with autumn's kiss. He wondered where the farmer was now, and if he'd come back when the war ended, rebuild, and begin again. After so long, it was hard to remember peace, or even imagine it. Lately, he'd felt a constant yearning for it in his chest, a terrible tightness, after years of forcing himself to feel nothing, want nothing. Duncan's death had brought it on, he told himself, regret at losing a good man, a good officer. But that was a lie. It was Eleanor Atherton's presence that had unsettled him, made him long for something again, want it badly when he knew better. The future was a distant place he was not likely to reach. He'd seen too much suffering and death to believe that his turn wouldn't come, that he wouldn't die here. He'd held the hands of men who fought death, even knowing they couldn't beat it, men who regretted leaving someone behind to mourn them, someone they'd made promises to, had sworn they'd come home to. It made dying all the worse. No, he'd learned that it was far better to empty your heart and your head of expectations and hope, not to plan for a future that might be snatched away in an instant by a bullet or a bomb or a slow and agonizing death.

And yet Eleanor Atherton had made him imagine things he had no business thinking about. Not that any future of his could ever include a woman like Eleanor. They were from different worlds, worlds that had just happened to collide in war, a chance meeting. He might never see her again, but he'd not soon forget her. Would she be his last thought as he died, if—*when*—his luck ran out?

He pushed the thought away and concentrated on assessing the place before him as a potential aid post.

The farmhouse was near the road, so ambulances could get close. The stretcher bearers would appreciate that—their bodies ached from carrying men for long miles through mud and over broken ground. And the sick and walking wounded would find an aid post here easily. A stone fence still surrounded the yard, offering protection from wind and stray bullets.

Fraser walked through the gates, nothing more than twisted scraps of metal hanging crookedly on posts riddled with bullet holes, and walked into the yard. The house resembled a dollhouse, three walls still upright, and the floors were still in place. The fourth wall was missing, exposing the rooms inside. He could see broken furniture, and weather-stained wallpaper still decorated the sitting room and the bedrooms. In the kitchen, the ruined stove was still in place, though the table and anything else made of wood had long ago gone for firewood. Above the sink, there was a tattered, weather-stained calendar from a soap company. The faded picture showed a smiling lass with russet curls washing her hands in pure white froth while a kitten played with the rainbow bubbles coming off the soap.

The lass reminded him of Eleanor Atherton, clean and pretty, and he smiled, feeling his face crack and stretch. The wind riffled the pages, and Fraser shook himself.

Again he was wasting time on emotions he couldn't afford. He had duties to see to. If Duncan hadn't been wounded, or if they had anyone on the bearer team or at the aid post of higher rank, they'd be here checking the farm, but it had fallen to Fraser until a new MO arrived, and at the moment, he was glad of the distraction. He dragged his eyes away from the calendar and turned to trudge across the yard to the well and looked down into the deep hole. His reflection stared back at him. There was water, and that was good. It would have to be tested, hauled up by the bucketful, boiled, made clean.

The entrance to the cellar yawned next to the kitchen, a black hole with broken stone steps that led down into the earth. The steps were steep and narrow, and they'd have trouble getting stretchers down, but they'd manage.

"Hello?" he called before entering, and waited for a reply, just in case, but there was no answer.

He descended the steps carefully and found himself in a storeroom with a mud floor. The ceiling was low, and he had to stoop slightly, but he was tall. Others, like Max, who was ten inches shorter than he was, would be able to stand upright. He let his eyes adjust to the gloom. The space was generous—three rooms. Shelves, empty now, had been cut into the chalky soil to store wine or apples or potatoes. The holes in the beams above probably held hooks once for hanging hams and dried beef. They'd need cots and benches and tables, supports to put stretchers on, a stove.

What they needed most, of course, was a doctor.

The space would do, he decided. It wasn't cozy like the cellar of the bakery, but it would be a suitable place to set up if they needed to retreat. It was just two miles or so from the bakery, but the front lines had been static for so long that even when they did move, the change was more easily measured in inches than miles.

He climbed into the farmyard again. The sky had turned moody and gray, promising wet spring snow or icy needles of rain. He stood still, breathing in the gunmetal air, and longed for the fresh, heady fragrance of a brisk Highland breeze. His arms and shoulders ached, and the weight of exhaustion pressed on him. He felt it most when there was a lull in the fighting and he wasn't busy—weary to his very bones. He rubbed his palms over his face, felt the sandpaper roughness of his own hands, full of splits and splinters and scars. The mud was ground so deep into his flesh that he couldn't get his hands clean anymore. He thought of Eleanor Atherton's hands, white and neat and pure as snow, the clean, capable hands of a doctor, the supple, delicate hands of a lady. All of her was supple and delicate—strong, too, like a fine ash bow that bent without breaking. He felt another wave of yearning wash over him, to be clean, safe, and warm for a change.

Instead, a bitingly cold gust of wind chilled him, finding gaps in his clothing, tearing at his hair, reminding him that he was daydreaming again.

"*Cac*," he swore aloud in Gaelic, and he took shelter behind the wall of the kitchen and lit a cigarette in cupped hands.

He stared up at the calendar, swaying in the wind like a come-hither beckon, and saw Eleanor again in the girl's printed smile. On a whim, he climbed over the rubble and tore the picture off the wall.

He heard the crack of a rifle and felt a sharp sting on the underside of his arm. He jerked back, instinctively ducking, but the rubble under his feet gave way and tipped him sideways, sliding him into a jagged crater. There was more pain as he landed hard, and something sliced into the soft flesh above his wrist. He put his hands over his head against falling debris and more bullets, not daring to move, unable to look, until he was sure the shooting had stopped and the rest of the building wasn't going to fall on him. He felt the hot rush of blood running down his arm and watched it drip from his cuff. He felt surprise, but no pain yet.

How bad? Is it a Blighty?

He shook off the thought and stared at the sky and the debris above him, waiting, wondering if his luck had run out at last, but the ancient bones of the house stood firm, even sheltering him from the worst of the debris.

"*Faigh muin,*" he cursed, daring to draw a breath. He looked at the scrap of paper still clasped in his hand, at the lass's smiling face and the rainbow bubbles. His arm was burning now. The sleeve of his coat was torn, and he could see a jagged splinter of wood embedded in his flesh, black against the white of his skin and the red of blood. A lot of blood, but not so much he feared the shard had pierced an artery, which was good. But the wood was old, and dirty, which was bad.

"'Tis what ye get for daydreaming," he muttered to the lass in the illustration. He should toss the foolish thing away. Instead, he shoved it awkwardly into his breast pocket and began to climb out of the rubble, ignoring the pain, the blood, the shock of being wounded.

He heard a stifled, shaking gasp from somewhere close by and paused, his ears alive to the sound of fear and pain.

"Hello? Are ye in the rubble? Are ye hurt?" he called out.

His stayed still and listened, scanning the debris for signs of a wounded man—a hand, a foot, or a face in the debris.

"I'm here," a voice sobbed at last. "For the love of God, help me, get me out!"

Fraser saw him. He was half buried by the fallen debris, his eyes rolling white with terror in a dirty face.

He ignored the pain in his own arm and the blood trickling down his sleeve and went to help the soldier. He saw the rifle clutched in a shaking fist.

Now he knew where the bullet had come from.

CHAPTER THIRTY-SIX

Good afternoon, chaps," David Blair said as he entered the cellar of the bakery with a pack of supplies on his back. Private Gibbons followed behind with more crates.

Blair looked around the cellar. "Why, this is nicer than the CCS," he said. "Very snug."

Chilcott grinned. "All plush and pleasant aside from the bullets and bombs. Pull up a chair by the fire. We've got an hour before sick parade. There was a lad from the forward trench who came with a cough yesterday, but we couldn't do more than give him a cup of hot tea and promise there'd be a doc to see to him soon. He'll be back today."

"My condolences on Captain Duncan," David said.

Chilcott's smile faded. "Yes. Everyone loved him. Good doc, kind to the men. That's all some of 'em need now and then, just someone to be kind to them, offer a cup of tea instead of a Number 9 laxative pill and an earful."

"I'll keep that in mind," David said. "Which bunk is free?"

"They're all free at the moment. Take your pick. You'll have to give it up if things get busy, but here's hoping they won't. We've heard rumors from the lads on the line. Haven't heard anything, have you, Captain?"

David shook off the shiver of dread that coursed down his spine. "Colonel Bellford would have warned me if he'd had news of an attack anywhere in our sector." He dropped his pack on the nearest cot, shrugged out of his greatcoat, and went to pour coffee from the pot.

Chilcott grimaced. "Oh, I wouldn't drink that, or you'll be on your own sick list," he said. "I'll show you how things are set up, then we'll see if we can scrounge up a pot of what passes for tea instead. We've heard a few ugly rumors here, even if they haven't reached the rear yet. Sergeant MacLeod is out scouting new digs in case things heat up and we have to move house in a hurry."

The ragged blanket that covered the doorway opened suddenly, letting in a cold gust of wind.

"Close that bloody—" Chilcott began, but Fraser MacLeod staggered in, half carrying a wounded man. Chilcott hurried forward to take the soldier.

"This is Private Cooper. He's suffering from exposure and a gunshot wound in his hand."

David frowned. "Self-inflicted?" There were rules about that sort of thing, protocol, punishment, court-martial. As medical officer, he'd been trained to diagnose such wounds and report them.

MacLeod looked away. "I didn't examine him. I brought him in because he needs help."

The young soldier let out an agonized sob as Chilcott tried to unwrap the dirty strip of cloth stuck to his shattered hand. He was shivering with both fear and cold, David suspected. He crossed to look at the wound. It stank—it was badly infected.

Fraser MacLeod slumped into the nearest chair. "The farm will do as an aid post," he said to everyone present. "The house isn't safe, but there's a stone wall around the yard, and a well, and a good, deep cellar."

David glanced at the Scot. He was smudged with dust and soot. Then he saw the fresh blood dripping from MacLeod's sleeve.

"You're hurt. What the devil happened to you?"

"Cooper mistook me for the enemy. With his hand in that state, and as scared as he was, his aim was off, and he missed. Mostly. There's a splinter in my arm that hurts worse, and that's my own bloody fault."

David lifted the bearer's arm and looked at the wood embedded in his skin. The shard was dirty and crumbling. It would need to be removed carefully, preferably somewhere cleaner than the aid post. "Where'd the bullet hit you?"

Fraser grunted. "Right side. Minor. Barely hurts at all." Which meant it hurt a lot, David suspected. MacLeod was pale, his face drawn and stoic.

Fraser shifted, trying to take his greatcoat off. "No, stop," David said. "If that splinter is in the artery and it comes loose with your coat . . ." He paused. The Scot was already pale, his forehead beaded with sweat from the effort of carrying Cooper.

"We can take it out here," Chilcott said. "Shall I get the tweezers?"

"No. I want you to go back to the CCS," David said, his eyes on Fraser. "The ambulance is still here, and they can see to it in nice, sterile conditions. You won't be able to lift anything with that arm for a while, so there's no point in staying here at the front."

MacLeod's eyes were ice, his jaw locked into iron lines of determination.

"The lads on the line think there's going to be an attack. I'll be needed. Do it here."

"When was the last time you had a tetanus shot?" David asked.

"A few months back," Fraser said. "I cut my knee on some barbed wire. I survived."

David looked at the sergeant's tight jaw and the puddle of blood on the floor. There were hollows of exhaustion under his eyes and deep lines around his mouth. He was too tense, too thin—he looked a dozen years older than he probably was. Still, the man was on alert, ready if anyone should need him.

"How long have you been here, MacLeod?" David asked.

"Since June of '16, just before the Somme."

"How much leave have you had?"

MacLeod's lips quirked. "None. Stretcher bearers are like MOs—they have a bad habit of getting killed, and there's never enough trained men to replace them."

David fashioned a sling and carefully eased Fraser's arm into it. "We'll have to do without you for a while. I'm sending you back to forty-six for treatment and putting you on light duties for a week. I'll reassess the wound when I'm back there. Or Bellford can."

MacLeod started to get up. "A week? But if the rumors are true—"

"Go, Fraser," Chilcott said. "You're of no use to anyone like that. And the lad—Cooper—he'll need to go back. His hand is infected." He looked at David. "He's got the wind up—he's nervous. He can't go back on the line like this. He'll shoot himself or someone else." He nodded toward Fraser. "And it might not be the enemy he takes a crack at. I'm not sure what kind of officer you are yet, Captain. Captain Duncan would have wished to save this lad's life. He'd likely have done the amputation right here, since the hand is infected anyway, and sent him on without anything to make anyone suspicious, if you know what I mean."

He meant there'd be no proof the wound was self-inflicted. David looked at Fraser. "He shot you. That might have gone very badly."

"I survived," Fraser said again in the same laconic tone.

"Let it go, Captain," Chilcott pleaded. "This war has gone on too long, taken enough men. This lad's just seventeen. Surely a little mercy is called for now and again."

The young soldier's pinched face was stark white under the dirt that covered it. His eyes were huge, and they darted around the cellar in terror. He was trembling hard enough to shake the chair he sat on. David looked at his hand and nearly recoiled at the smell. It was badly infected, the bones and tendons shattered. If he sent him back like this, Cooper would certainly die, and he'd die in disgrace, executed for cowardice. David looked at the simple operating area. "Can you do the anesthetic?"

Chilcott nodded with a relieved smile. "Yes, sir."

He looked at Fraser. "Are you agreeable?"

"Easy to get separated from your unit when you're looking for an aid post. Must have cut his hand on some barbed wire in the dark."

Blair nodded grimly and began to prepare for surgery.

"Can I help?" Fraser asked.

"With one arm?" Chilcott asked. "I'll do it. You get ready to go."

"What am I to do with myself for an entire week?" Fraser asked, looking at the sling.

"Sleep," David said. "Even on light duties, I'm sure you'll still find a dozen ways to make yourself useful. I know you're not the kind to sit still, but this time, it's an order." He wrote out a ticket, but Fraser snatched it from him before he could attach it to his coat.

"See? I always said you were lucky," Chilcott said cheerfully. "It's not a Blighty, but oh, what I'd do for a soft bed, and the softer hands and warm smile of a pretty nurse. Shall I send a Number 9 pill along with him, Captain, just for spite?"

Fraser glowered at his comrade. "I'll be back if you need me."

Fraser gathered his things, using his left hand instead of his injured right one, his movements awkward. "Is Eleanor Atherton still there?" Fraser asked casually—too casually—and David felt a sharp needle-prick of jealousy.

But MacLeod was just a sergeant, a poor Highlander, while he was a surgeon, an officer, a man of her own class and profession. If there weren't a war on, Eleanor would never have met Fraser MacLeod, nor looked twice at him if they chanced to pass on the street. Still, he felt a twinge of uncertainty. She'd come to France. Here, things were different. He recalled the way Fraser had showed Eleanor how to do triage, how she'd looked at the big Scot. It wasn't how she looked at Louis Chastaine, or himself. He let out a long breath—resignation, perhaps. Fraser would be at forty-six, and he was stuck here. A man could make a lot of headway with a woman in a week.

"Do you believe in fate, Corporal?" he asked Chilcott.

Chilcott watched Fraser climb the steps. "Don't know, but when I look at Fraser MacLeod, I believe in luck, and that's good enough for me."

CHAPTER THIRTY-SEVEN

Eleanor stared down at the letter she was writing to her father, trying to explain that she'd been asked to stay a little longer, to practice medicine—well, *potentially* practice medicine—and that she intended to do so. It was a letter of telling rather than asking permission, and it wasn't going well. Her parents would not approve of or understand her decision, and she couldn't seem to find the words to explain.

The knock on the door of the spartan guest hut took her by surprise, but the distraction, whatever it might be, was welcome.

She opened it to find her brother leaning against the sill.

"Edward. Is everything all right? Is it Louis?"

"In a way," he said, stepping into the tiny one-room visitor's hut. He looked around with minimal interest. He looked directly at her. "He wants to leave."

She smiled. "I know. It will only be a few more days, a week at—"

"No, now, today. He wants to go to Paris."

"That's impossible."

He held out a form to her. "We just need your signature, releasing him."

"I can't go to Paris!"

His brows rose. "Not you. Just Louis."

Her mouth dried, and she stared at him. "But I'm his doctor."

He crossed and set the paper on the desk and picked up her pen. "There are doctors in Paris. He'll be fine, better than fine. Just sign it. Someone has to, Blair's away, and I can't very well ask Bellford." He held out the pen to her.

She didn't take it. "Of course not. The colonel would refuse. It's just a few more days, Edward. I'll speak to him, explain—"

"God damn it, Eleanor, you owe me this! Sign the order!"

"I *owe* you this?" she asked slowly, surprised at his anger, his haughty insistence.

"You know what I mean. You must know."

"I don't!"

"You wouldn't be here playing doctor at all if it weren't for me."

"Playing? I'm not playing at anything. I am a doctor."

He narrowed his eyes. "A doctor. You couldn't even pass the damn medical school entrance exam."

Her heart froze in her chest. "But I did pass! You were the one who failed, Edward."

He smirked. "I didn't fail. I passed that exam with top marks."

Tears sprang to her eyes. "No! That's—" *Impossible.* But it wasn't.

"Yes, Eleanor. I lied for you, cheated. I saw you at the end of the exam. I knew you'd failed. You, sure you were so clever, the one who read every book, studied night and day. You were so sure you'd do better than me."

She'd frozen the day of the exam, had sat numb and nervous, unable to think, to remember anything, though she knew it all. She'd been sure she'd failed. And so she had. It had been a surprise when the results arrived, a miracle. "No," she murmured again.

"All I had to do was make one little change on the cover of the booklet. We all signed in by first and middle initial and last name. We're twins, adorably and rather predictably called by names that begin with the same letter, both of us E. Atherton. I simply wrote 'Miss' before my initial.

"It was a mistake," she said breathlessly. "You wrote it on the wrong booklet."

"No, I didn't," he said coldly. "I made sure of it—I changed the middle initial on my paper as well. The *C* for Charles became a *G* for Grace. I did it intentionally. I did you a favor." He held the pen out like a dagger. "Now do me a favor and sign Louis's release, or I'll expose you as a fraud. I'll tell father, and Louis's mother, and Bellford. I'll write to the university. I'll tell anyone who'll listen."

"Why?" she managed to croak. "Why would you do this?" Tears stung her eyes, but she refused to blink, to let them fall.

"Louis's well enough, and he's bored, and there's no reason he should be trapped here when he could be in Paris with Fanny. There are better doctors than you there. He's a bloody viscount, and Fanny will see he gets the best care her fortune can buy, far better than you can give him."

"But you're a doctor's son, a soldier. Surely you know what could happen to him—" she began, trying to reason with him still, though she was shaking.

"He doesn't care. He can't bear another minute of this bloody place, and I promised I'd get him out. It'll be good for both of us. I have a week's leave, and being with Fanny's set will further my own career. Can't you see that? *That's* what you owe me, the same opportunity I gave you, the chance to do what you want with your life. I can take that away from you now. You have no choice. You're a fraud and you shouldn't even be here. If you want to keep what little dignity you have left, then you'll do as I wish and sign the release."

Her tears were pouring down her face now. She could barely breathe, let alone reach out and take the pen. She shrank away from him. *A fraud.* "But I am a doctor!" she said fiercely.

He shrugged. "Apparently not. Not really."

He took a step toward her, but there was another knock on the door. "What is it?" Edward snapped.

Private Gibbons entered with a shy smile. He saluted Edward, then turned to Eleanor. If he noticed her tears, he didn't say anything. "Sergeant MacLeod is here, miss. He's wounded, and the colonel is busy. Will you see him?"

"He's— Oh, no. Not . . ." She pictured Captain Duncan's pale face, his terrible wounds, and in her mind it became Fraser's face, Fraser's broken body. "How bad?"

"His tag says he's *WW*, walking wounded, and *FW*, flesh wound, and *G* for gunshot," he said, listing the wound ticket abbreviations. "*T* for tetanus, too. Captain Blair signed it. They brought him from the aid post with another patient, a private with his hand amputated. The matron is seeing to him."

"I'll come," she said, grabbing her cardigan.

"Eleanor." She heard the warning in her brother's voice, the low growl, but she couldn't look at him now. She wanted to be away from him. She left him standing behind her, the pen still in his hand. She was relieved when he didn't follow her. She wiped away her tears with the heel of her hand as she walked, and Gibbons followed. "Is that your brother, miss?"

"Yes," she said through tight lips.

E. Atherton.

Gibbons didn't comment further or ask what had happened. Her whole life had changed in an instant, that's what had happened, and what did it mean, exactly? Was she even still a doctor, still *anything*? Her head buzzed, her stomach ached, and she was aware of the wind on her face, knew it was cold, but she was numb, didn't feel it.

You must have known. Had she? She'd wanted to be a doctor all her life, wanted it so badly that it felt as if nothing could stand in the way of it, as if it was destined, fated, what she'd been born to do, to be. And now?

She kept on walking with Private Gibbons along the duckboards. Someone needed her. Fraser MacLeod needed her. What would he say, do, if he knew the truth? *She was a fraud.*

Sergeant MacLeod was seated on a bench outside the triage tent. His eyes were closed, and his face was turned up to the long fingers of pallid sun that struggled to part the clouds. His right arm was in a sling, loosely bandaged and protruding from the blood-soaked sleeve of his greatcoat. Her chest contracted. Little things could turn septic quickly here, her medical brain said. Fraser's left hand was curled against his knee, the wound tag clutched in his fingers.

He didn't move as she approached, and she realized he was asleep. He looked younger, like a lad who'd wandered in off the battlefield to rest, utterly peaceful for once. And yet he was wounded, and the colonel was busy.

There are wounded men out there who need help, Fraser had said the day of the attack. *I don't give a damn about the rules, nor do those poor bastards waiting out there for help, dying. Ye told me ye were a doctor.*

She'd graduated seventh in her class, and she knew what to do.

Fraud, liar, cheat.

There was blood on his greatcoat.

He needed help.

She carefully pulled the wound tag from his hand and took a moment to decipher David Blair's appalling scrawl. *Gunshot, splinter, both right side. Light duty for seven days, reassess.* A more personal note said, *See that he gets some sleep and eats well.*

She touched Fraser's shoulder. "Sergeant?"

His eyes opened at once and he sat up, instantly on alert. He looked around for a moment, searching for danger, then focused on her.

He stared at her, his gray eyes heavy with the scant sleep he'd had and the need for more. "If Blair hadn't insisted I come, I'd think I was dreaming. 'Tis a good dream," he murmured. He looked away. "Och, I'm babbling." He lifted his hand to rub his face and frowned at the sling. "Blair sent me back. There's a wee splinter in my arm. A lot of fuss about nothing. I just need it cleaned up and bandaged properly."

"I believe I'll wait and determine what's required once I've examined your wounds, Sergeant," she said, more sharply than she had intended. "The tag says you were shot."

"Just a graze. Don't take on. I only meant to save ye time, let ye get on with your patient." He meant Louis, and she ignored the comment.

"Would you prefer to see Colonel Bellford? He's busy, but I'm sure—"

His brow furrowed. "Nay—I didn't mean that. Do ye think I don't trust ye?"

"No. It's just . . ." She swallowed. "It's one of the rules the colonel has insisted I follow. He fears some men will be uncomfortable with a female doctor, so I must ask their permission before I treat them."

"Not me. I saw ye in action. I know well enough you're a good doctor."

"I wasn't fishing for compliments."

"Aye, but I suspect ye get few enough of those—where your medical skills are concerned, I mean, not about yourself. No doubt ye get plenty of—" His eyes flicked over her, and he blushed. "There I go, babbling like a green lad again. I must be hurt worse than I thought."

"We'd best check that," she said.

He rose to his feet, towering over her, a foot taller than she, a quintessential Highlander. Her belly tightened. What would he look like at home, in plaid?

"You don't wear a kilt," she said, speaking the stray thought aloud. Now she was the one babbling. She turned to lead the way inside to the treatment area.

"Nay. If the wool gets muddy, it turns the pleats to razors when it dries, and they slice into a man's legs, and the cuts get infected. And gas attacks the damp areas of the body first."

The throat, then, or the inside of the nose, or . . . Oh. *Oh.* It was another lesson she'd learned in Edinburgh, precisely what Highlanders wore—or didn't wear—under their kilts. She felt her cheeks grow hot again thinking of what Fraser MacLeod had under his uniform.

Inside, she led him to one of the tables set up for simple procedures. The tent was nearly empty, and the linens on each examination bench were fresh and crisp as new snow, ready for the next influx of wounded.

He sat on a small stool next to the table and gingerly slid his arm out of the sling. He frowned at the torn and bloody sleeve of his greatcoat. "I suppose you'll have to cut it off. The splinter is in the way. I hate to lose this coat."

"Surely they'll give you another."

His eyes were bright as he looked at her, silver instead of gray in the muted glow of soft daylight inside the tent's canvas roof and walls. "It's not that. I've sewn extra pockets inside this one for supplies and things I might need to tend a wounded man—cigarettes, a bit of rum, extra bandages, and such."

"Comforts," she said.

"Aye."

She used the heavy shears to cut the sleeve enough to expose the splinter, long and black and deeply embedded. "Are you in pain?" she asked, touching his flesh, looking for signs of shock or deeper damage, warning signs.

The muscles in his jaw were tense. "Nay. Well, not very much."

She cut through the thick wool of the coat's shoulder and helped him remove it. It weighed nearly as much as she did, or so it seemed as the thick garment fell into her hands. There was more blood on his tunic, high up under his arm. She could see the dark eye of the bullet hole in the fabric.

"Your tunic will have to come off as well," she said. "And your shirt—"

"Nay!" The word was as sharp as a knife. She looked up at him in surprise at the ferocity in his eyes—or perhaps it was modesty. "Do what ye want to the tunic, but I'll be keeping my shirt." He kept his left arm clamped across his chest.

"We'll see to the splinter first," she said. He nodded crisply and laid his arm down.

The splinter was black and jagged against the sterile whiteness of the linen that draped the table. It had missed arteries and tendons or bone, thank heaven. His head was bent close to hers, and she knew he was making his own assessment. "You'll have a scar," she said.

"Aye." His voice was low and husky, male. "I've already got plenty of those. What's one more?" She looked at the old scars and half-healed cuts and blisters that marked his hands and wrists and forearms. So many . . . She thought of what he'd endured, and she looked up at him.

His face was inches from her own, his eyes on her, not on his wounds. She felt a blush rise in her cheeks, and she turned away and busied herself gathering the supplies she needed, taking antiseptic, clean towels, forceps, tweezers, sutures, salve, and bandages from the shelves.

"How did it happen?"

He grunted. "A house fell on me, or what was left of it. I was scouting for a new aid post. I lost my footing when the bullet hit me."

He stuck his left thumb through the holes in his tunic. "It went straight through. The damage can't be too bad." He tried to sound unconcerned, but there was an edge to his voice.

"But if it had been an inch to the right, or the left—" she said, but he shook his head.

"I ken. An inch to the right, the bullet would have shattered the bone, and I probably would have lost my arm. An inch to the left, and—" He stopped, his mouth tightening. She knew what followed. Shattered ribs, a punctured lung, or even death. Another casualty, killed instantly, or left to bleed out in agony. "But didn't happen, so there's no point in brooding over it."

"Lucky," she murmured, and he frowned.

She scrubbed her hands, then poured clean water into the bowl and cleaned the skin around the splinter with disinfectant. He bore the sting silently, without flinching, the tension in his body the only sign it hurt.

She looked at the shard of wood, and her clinical brain considered the veins and nerves and tendons under the skin. *She'd memorized every one of them for the exam.* She knew how the injury might affect them, if hemorrhage or infection or damage to nerves might occur. *She'd known all of it.* She felt Fraser's pulse beating under her fingertips. She traced the lines of the blood vessels, noted his raw knuckles, the older cuts and bruises on his arm, the long, scarred length of his fingers.

"Ye have such wee hands," he murmured, watching her. So close to her ear, the comment felt intimate, as if he were assessing her as well.

"And you have fine hands as well," she said. "Artistic hands."

"I was a musician before the war, played the pipes. I carved things and tied fishing flies. I don't draw or paint." His voice was a low, pleasant burr, and her stomach slid sideways, and she felt breathless for an instant, but when she looked up, he was staring down at his hand.

She reached for the forceps.

He looked up then, and she met his gaze, ready to warn him that there'd be pain, but his eyes were as gray and deep and unfathomable as the North Sea. There was no fear there, only trust. His fingers closed over her own for a moment, his skin rough on hers.

"You should wear gloves," she murmured. "In the field, I mean."

He chuckled at that. "Gloves? I've lost more pairs than I can count. Ye have to take them off to apply a dressing or give morphine. Ye set them down, and they sink into the mud, or get left behind. Scissors, too, if ye drop them." He was still looking into her eyes as he spoke.

"So what do you do?" she asked, not just to distract him but out of genuine interest.

He reached inside his tunic and pulled on a long string and dangled a small pair of surgical scissors.

"A good solution. Are you ready?" For an instant he curled his fingers around hers and squeezed gently.

"Aye," he said. He met her eyes, his gaze flat. "Do it."

She gripped the end of the splinter and pulled it free. She dropped it onto the towel. She heard him exhale the breath he'd been holding. The wound bled freely, cleansing itself, and she washed it with saline, then an antiseptic solution. She examined the ragged hole for debris. He watched her without moving and without comment. She leaned over his arm and began to suture, feeling his breath on her hair, smelling the salt heat of his body, the tang of wool and winter wind.

"Ye sew like a seamstress," he murmured. "I'll hardly have a scar at all."

"My mother wanted me to learn to knit. I took up embroidery instead."

"Now was that just to be contrary or because ye knew ye'd be a doctor?"

She glanced at him, surprised he understood that. Her mother didn't. "A bit of both, I suppose."

"You're a good doctor," he said.

"For a woman?" she added automatically. She smeared a thick antiseptic paste carefully over the stitches and wrapped his arm in bandages.

"For anyone. You were brave the other day, with triage. It can't have been easy for ye, but ye didn't give up."

"Is that why you stayed close? In case I fell into hysterics?" *Or panicked, froze, couldn't think* . . .

"One reason," he said honestly. "I've seen a number of VADs and even a few seasoned male doctors lose their nerve. They can't take the terrible things they see day after day."

"How do you manage?" she asked.

He shrugged. "Training. That and knowing that if I don't get the wounded off the field, they'll die, add to the number already dead, and that's high enough."

She asked him what she'd asked Louis. "Are you afraid?"

He quirked one eyebrow. He had a dimple in one cheek when he smiled, even if it was a grim smile. "Only fools aren't afraid."

"Then you just . . . just get used to it, the wounded and the dead, the blood, the fear?"

He sobered. "Never." He hesitated. "A week ago I helped the chaplain bury another bearer. He was new, here only a month. He took a bullet in the sleeve of his coat on his second day. It passed straight through, didn't touch him." He glanced at his own tunic again. "He showed it off, talked about how lucky he was." He shut his eyes. "He told everyone he was as lucky as me. The bullet that got him went through his helmet the very next day."

"I'm sorry."

"Now we're short another bearer," he said gruffly, but she read grief in the tight line of his jaw, in the bitter set of his mouth, in the tension of his hand gripping hers like a lifeline.

"Let's see to your bullet wound," she said softly. "Then you can rest."

. . .

He'd gladly endure the extraction of the splinter all over again, Fraser thought, and the sting of the antiseptic, and the pinch and tug of the stitches, just to stay near her a few minutes more, to smell the sweet, feminine scent of her hair, to watch the way her lips tightened with determination, pursing, when she was considering how best to treat a patient. He'd noticed that the other day, too, during triage. She was easy to read, probably because of her youth and inexperience of the world, though she tried to hide it by being bold and brave. She blushed easily, too, her cheeks turning as rosy as sunrise, and her eyes were the exact color of the Highlands at this time of year, gold and bronze and fragile green. She looked up at him again, her eyes like a touch, a balm, a caress, and his breath caught in his throat. *Pretty* was his only thought now. *Nay, beautiful.*

"I need to look at that bullet wound," she said again, like a mother coaxing a stubborn bairn.

The soft, muzzy warmth of attraction turned to horror in Fraser's gut as she reached for the buttons of his shirt and began to undo them. He clapped his hand over hers and pushed her away, shrinking back. The stitches in his arm objected, and the untended bullet wound stung, leaving him panting.

She'll see . . .

"Careful, Sergeant, or you'll tear those stitches. Let me help," she said brightly. She reached for him again.

"No! I'd like an orderly," he said. "Get Bellford."

She looked surprised and hurt.

"I'm—dirty."

"Oh." Her brow cleared. "Don't worry. We'll get you clean once we've seen to the wound." She said it with gentle insistence. She gave him a "be-a-big-boy" smile, and it was his turn to blush. He felt the hot blood rise in his ruddy Scottish complexion. The wound ached like the devil was gnawing on it now, but his dignity was at stake.

"I'll tend to it myself."

She regarded him sternly. "That won't do. You need a doctor to see to it—"

"I won't take my shirt off," he insisted again.

"Come now, Sergeant," she said as she picked up the shears, and he waited, his heart pounding. "We'll start at the bottom, cut it open only as much as we need to." No doubt she thought him prudish or shy, or she was imagining he didn't trust her after all. So be it.

She slipped under his arm to take the first snip. The wool of the frayed hem parted easily, and he nearly cried out. She paused to examine a scar on his lowest rib.

"That's old. A sheep bit me," he said. "I stitched it up myself."

"With your left hand? Did you not have a doctor look at it?" She continued cutting, was approaching his armpit now. She'd see the wound and stop. He relaxed. His secret was safe.

"Highlanders are used to tending our own ills. We do have a doctor in the glen, though. When my mother saw what I'd done, she dragged me all the way to his surgery by the ear and made him lecture me."

"I can imagine what he said," she murmured. "He told you that it might have become infected, you might have died, you should have come to him, and—"

He grinned. "As a matter of fact, he told me that I'd made a fine job of it. I'd disinfected it with whisky, cleaned the needle and thread—I used a strand of my own hair, which was longer before I joined up. If the stitches weren't pretty, at least they were secure. He asked me if I'd ever considered becoming a doctor myself one day . . ." his voice trailed off.

For an instant the shears stilled. "Have you?"

"Nay. My da's a gamekeeper. I'm expected to be a gamekeeper

after him. With a dozen of us in the house, there's no money for fancy schooling, and no patience among the local folk for lads who think to jump above their station." He knew that well enough, had learned that lesson the hard way. He had another scar, this one under his jaw, where a fist with a fancy ring on it had cut him open.

"So when you joined up—"

"I joined the infantry, just like every other lad in the glen. Our doctor wrote to the RAMC officer at the training camp, told him I'd be better suited to a posting as an orderly instead of a foot soldier. They took one look at the size of me and decided I'd make a good stretcher bearer."

"And what will you do after the war?" she asked. He was staring at her again, noticing the freckles across her nose, the length of her neck, her ears, even.

He focused on what she was saying. "After the war? I'll go home and be a gamekeeper's son again."

"Everyone says there'll be new opportunities after the war," she said. "There might be scholarships, or—"

He hadn't noticed she'd cut through the neckband until that side of his shirt fell forward, exposing his arm and his shoulder and half his chest. With a shout he leaped to his feet, tried to cover himself.

Too late.

He saw the horror in her eyes at the sight of his body. He knew it was bad. He had seen other bearers with the same deep scrapes, scars, and bruises on their chests and backs and shoulders caused by the straps of the stretcher. It was ugly, and painful, and not something any woman, even a doctor, should see.

Corporal O'Neill, one of the bearers who'd been on the line when Fraser had first arrived, had won a pot of money in a card game. He'd written to his wife, asking her to come and spend a furlough with him in Dunkirk, and the lads had seen him off on his holiday with much teasing. O'Neill was back long before his leave was up. His wife had recoiled at the sight of his naked body, had refused to let him touch her with his scarred hands and damaged flesh, as if the marks were contagious, as if he weren't her husband and the man she loved. O'Neill shot himself, and unlike Cooper, he'd made sure it was fatal.

"Were you beaten by someone, or kicked by a horse?" Eleanor Atherton asked, staring at his body. He clutched at the ruins of his shirt, trying to hide himself from her eyes. He was lumpy, misshapen, abhorrent. Anger rose, and he opened his mouth to tell her to go, to leave him alone and not pity him. He'd decided long ago that he'd keep his clothes on, and not show anyone what lay beneath them. But it wasn't horror he read in her eyes, or disgust. It wasn't even a doctor's clinical interest in a medically interesting case.

It was something else, something protective. Concern. For him.

"It's the straps of the stretchers. They cut into the skin, slide against our necks, bite deep, rub the flesh raw. We use feedbags to pad them but it doesn't do much good. Our carries are heavy men—heavier still when they're unconscious, or wet, or muddy. We have to concentrate on finding the way through the mud, not tipping them off the bloody stretcher. We haven't got time to think of ourselves, or our pains." He looked up, pleading with his eyes. "I'd have spared ye the sight of me if ye'd let me. I did try to. Go and fetch an orderly, or I can wait for Bellford if ye'd rather that."

Instead she came closer. Carefully, she ran her fingers over the worst of the welts. "I'm not offended."

He shut his eyes, enjoying her touch, though he had no right to, and it wasn't appropriate to take pleasure in it. He pulled away. "I'm dirty and scarred and I stink. I'm not like—" He didn't want to bring up her flier, rich and titled and clean, an old friend, a hero, a man she admired.

She ignored the comment and drew the curtains around the table, closing him in, giving him privacy. "Wait, please," she said, and she left him alone.

She'd fetch Swiftwood, or some other male orderly, to tend to him now.

He was surprised when the curtain shifted a few minutes later and she came in carrying a basin and a pitcher of steaming water. She had a folded shirt with her, along with a sponge and clean towels. She filled the basin and dipped the sponge into it.

He tensed at the first swipe across his chest, but the water was warm and soothing, and she was gentle. She dipped the sponge again, washing his chest, his arms, his back, going carefully around his wounded side, his injured arm, the worst of his bruises. He shut his eyes and felt his body edge toward ease, and the pain ebbed. She bathed him the way a mother bathes a bairn, or a wife might wash her husband.

Her husband. He wasn't that, and could never be.

"I wish I had some of the lanolin ointment the farmers in Yorkshire use. It helps heal their skin—they get plenty of bites and cuts, bruises and scrapes. The women make it."

"We use similar stuff in Scotland. My gran makes ours. She adds heather and a few ingredients she keeps secret. Every woman in the glen has her own secret salve she swears by." She smiled at him, and his heart did a slow roll in his chest. He looked at her and tried to see her as just a doctor, a civilian, a stranger, but he couldn't. The steam from the basin had risen and curled the loose tendrils of her hair, made her cheeks rosy.

She blushed under his scrutiny and lifted his arm to examine the long, narrow groove Cooper's bullet had torn into his flesh. It had only nicked his skin, narrowly missing his ribs. He peered at it with her. "Doesn't look too bad. Just a scratch."

She gave him a sharp look, and her face was inches from his own. *Close enough to kiss.* He swallowed.

"It's bad enough, and it could have been—" she began, but he put a finger on her lips.

"Nay. Don't think that. Ye can't count the near misses, or wonder what might have happened if ye'd turned at that moment, or stepped to the left instead of the right. It would drive ye mad."

For a moment they stared at each other, eyes locked, and she turned rosier still. He lowered his hand from her mouth, dropping it into his lap.

She stepped back as well, the spell broken. "It needs disinfecting, and I'll check it daily while you're here."

"Not a Blighty, then," he said, his tone matter-of-fact.

"No." She frowned. "I'm sorry."

He watched her clean the wounds. "Don't be. It's not that I don't want to go home, it's just—"

"Just what?" she prompted, but he held his silence.

He didn't expect to go home again. He'd learned not to hope for it, not to want it, knowing it would drive him mad, dying here in the mud when he longed for the Highlands. "We're short of bearers. I'm needed here," he said instead.

He heard the jaunty tootle of a car horn outside, and she looked up.

"Is that for you?" he asked.

"Who cares?" she murmured, her attention all for him. She finished the sutures in silence and bandaged him. "All done. You can get dressed," she said at last.

He nodded at the shirt she'd brought him. "I can't wear that. It's an officer's shirt."

"It's lighter than a woolen one, and it won't chafe the wounds or your bruises," she said. "The buttons will make it easier to get on and off."

"Whose is it?" he asked, hesitating as she held it up to help him into it. Not Duncan's. Maybe one of Blair's?

"Louis's," she said. "Lieutenant Chastaine. It's the very finest, softest cotton, and fresh from the laundry, clean and waiting until he's ready to be discharged."

He grabbed the cuff and looked at the monogram embroidered there, the family crest. "And he doesn't mind?"

"No, he won't mind. He has dozens of them."

She held it up, and he put his arms into it, frowning. It fit because he was thinner than he should be, though it was still snug across his shoulders and too short in the sleeves. He rolled up the cuffs, tucking the damned monogram out of sight. "I'd like to help where I can while I'm here. I can't just sit still while—"

The curtain parted, and Corporal Swiftwood peered in. He looked at Fraser, then at Eleanor, and noted the bloody basin, the bandages, and the shirt. His dark little eyes narrowed suspiciously.

"What is it, Corporal?" Eleanor asked.

"Matron wants to see you on the officers' ward." He handed her a sealed envelope. "And there's a note for you," he added, his tone arch, as if it contained something highly suspicious. Fraser watched as Eleanor took the note and glanced at it. He could see the words *E. Atherton* scrawled across it. He saw Eleanor flinch, go pale, and slip the envelope into her pocket without opening it.

Swiftwood was still there, taking note of the flier's fancy shirt. "Go," Fraser growled, and the corporal snapped to attention for an instant before he turned and walked away as if he had important duties to see to, though Fraser knew he was going off to spread gossip.

"Your patient?" Fraser said, pointing to the pocket that held the letter.

She looked stricken, fearful, before she turned away, busying herself by tidying things. "My brother."

"Then you'll need to go at once."

She shook her head. "It can wait. Edward has come to visit Louis. They're old friends."

"And can *he* wait, your *Louis*?" he asked sarcastically, the sound of the French name thick on his Gaelic tongue.

"They can all wait until I'm finished here," she said tartly.

He lifted one eyebrow. "I'm honored," he said dryly, though he meant it.

"Any pain?" she asked, changing the subject. "I can give you something for that."

"No. I'm fine. Better."

"Captain Blair has ordered you to rest while you're here," she said. "And eat."

She avoided his eyes and glanced at his body again, probably noting that under the fine shirt he was too thin.

"Eat?" he said, as if he'd forgotten what it meant. He was clean and warm, and getting sleepy now.

"Three meals a day," she ordered. "Thick porridge, steak and eggs, and toast with jam for breakfast, stew for luncheon, and a pie for supper." He noted the slenderness of her figure, like a reed, delicate.

"Will you eat with me?" he asked, surprised by the words even as they fell from his lips, like a beggar lad asking a duchess to tea, but she looked up at him and scanned his face before she nodded.

"I'd like that."

He felt ridiculously happy. When was the last time he'd actually been happy? Months. Years. He hadn't even realized it until he met Eleanor Atherton. Her eyes softened as she gazed at him, as if they were friends and she liked to look at him, found comfort and pleasure in his features.

"Sleep heals as well, Sergeant. Now, let's find a bed, somewhere quiet."

He wished she hadn't said that, but it was too late. The thought of bed and Eleanor brought a surge of desire. He'd all but forgotten what lust felt like, too.

For a moment they stared at each other, and he remembered her brother and the lieutenant were waiting for her. "Thank your flier for the shirt."

Her eyes widened for an instant, as if she'd forgotten them entirely. Was she so pleased with his company? It made him smile to imagine that could be true.

He reached for his stained greatcoat with his good arm, picked it up, and opened the curtain. "I think I'll go find a needle and thread, see if I can save this." She reached out and touched the battered wool, running her finger over the rough stitching on the inside pockets he'd added. He felt it as if she were touching his skin. She was so close he could see the gleam of the lamplight on her hair and smell the scent of flowers under the carbolic and canvas and wool. He shook himself and stepped back, clutching the coat tighter. "I'd best go," he said gruffly. "Thank ye. I'll see you later."

She nodded, and he watched her walk away with that purposeful stride of hers and realized that for the first time in a very long while he had something good to look forward to.

CHAPTER THIRTY-EIGHT

Eleanor paused outside the officers' ward to pat her hair and straighten the cuffs of her blouse. She hadn't read Edward's note because she dreaded what it might contain. She felt the weight of it in her pocket. If he'd told Louis, or anyone else, she'd know soon enough. She took a breath and entered the ward, scanning it with a glance, looking for her brother.

He wasn't here.

Worse, Louis's bed was empty.

One of the VADs was changing the sheets. Matron Connolly was removing the books and papers from the table beside the bed and putting them into a box.

"Where's Lieutenant Chastaine?" Eleanor asked her.

The matron's brows rose as her lips tightened as if a pulley connected them. "Didn't you *know*?" she asked Eleanor mockingly. "He's gone."

Eleanor's mouth dried. "Gone?"

"An officer presented an order for his release. It seems military authority still supersedes yours, *Miss* Atherton."

Her belly caved against her spine. "Whose authority? What orders?"

"They were signed by an officer from Field Marshal Haig's staff, I believe, an adjutant to a lieutenant colonel."

"Not Edward—was the order signed by E. Atherton?"

The matron tilted her head. "Yes, I believe it was."

Another prank, a cruel trick. But this time the joke wasn't on her, it was on Louis. Eleanor shut her eyes.

The matron tsked at the VAD making the bed. She bent to adjust the sheet herself, pleating the corners so they stood at precise military attention. The VAD blushed at the silent correction.

"They were off to Paris, I believe, to see the field marshal's personal physician—or so the orders said. I saw no reason to question them."

"Did the colonel know? Did he approve?"

Matron Connolly folded her hands at her waist like a plaster saint. "I don't know. It hardly matters. The colonel has no authority to countermand orders from headquarters." Her gaze was as sharp as a scalpel, and she pierced Eleanor with it, smirking in triumph. "You'll have to go yourself now. There's no longer anything or anyone to keep you here." She turned to walk away, dismissing Eleanor.

"I overheard one of the young ladies say there was a party in Paris they were eager to get to," the VAD whispered when she thought the matron was out of earshot. "She was most displeased they'd run out of champagne again."

"Miss Miller." The VAD jumped as the matron called her name. "If you do not have enough work to do, I can find more."

The VAD bowed her head in meek contrition and stepped away from Eleanor. "Yes, Matron."

"There is a bottle under the bed. Retrieve it at once and dispose of it."

"You should have called me, asked me to come before—" Eleanor said to the matron as Miss Miller dove for the champagne bottle.

"I sent Corporal Swiftwood to find you. He said you were busy with *other* patients. Lieutenant Chastaine was most insistent on leaving at once." She cast a scornful look over Eleanor. "You could go off to join the fun, since there is no longer any reason for you to stay here. Or were you not invited?" A hot flush of humiliation rose from Eleanor's toes to the crown of her head, and Matron Connolly smirked. "Ah, I see. Well, whatever you do, you cannot stay here."

"But the colonel—"

"Colonel Bellford has no authority to allow a civilian doctor—a *female* civilian doctor—to practice here. If the director general of the Royal Army Medical Corps was to hear of it, or anyone in the War Office, the colonel would be in a great deal of trouble. And civilians who are caught where they shouldn't be can be shot as spies. Did you know that?"

"I'm not a spy!"

The matron shrugged. "You have no right to be here, no rank, no official permission. You are not subject to military control or protection. In fact, you seem to be determined to disobey orders and thwart protocol and rules at every turn. There are rules for a reason, and they must be obeyed."

"That's preposterous! I'll speak to the colonel myself," Eleanor said, moving past the matron.

"And I shall send my report to the director general," Matron Connolly called after her.

Eleanor strode along the duckboards toward the colonel's office. Damn Edward. Did he not know the harm he could do, that Louis's leg wasn't fully healed, and that there was still danger of disrupting the knitting bones, of pain and infection? Perhaps she *should* go after him, follow him to Paris. She stopped walking, breathless. She imagined bursting in on a grand society party to find Louis with Lady Fanny and their smart friends, demanding that he return to hospital—not this one, of course—or allow her to take him home to Chesscroft. Amid the smirks and titters of the other guests, Edward would set down his champagne with a frown to take her firmly by the elbow and hiss in her ear that she was making a spectacle of herself and embarrassing him dreadfully. Then he'd announce that she wasn't a doctor at all . . .

Nausea rose, and she dashed away tears of frustration and betrayal, of loss. Oh, not of Louis, but of the future, of the chance to be a doctor at last, to make a difference. And she had. *She had.*

It was all a lie.

She stopped walking. "No," she whispered aloud, fiercely.

Her desire to be a doctor had led her here—her own determination and her skills.

She stood still and listened to the distant guns, felt the cold March wind on her hot cheeks. She thought of David Blair at the front, in danger, counting on her to stay and help if she was needed. Without her, they'd have only one doctor if there was an attack. The wounded, desperate for treatment and comfort, for a chance to be safe and clean and out of pain, would have to wait, would suffer, die. Surely even Matron Connolly understood that.

She damned her brother again, then Louis, then Edward once again. This wasn't a game. This prank had terrible consequences that went far beyond hurting her.

I don't regret it, you know—not choosing the safe path. Not a minute of it, especially if I'm to die young, Louis had said. How could she ever have thought him bold and dashing? She'd been here for a short handful of weeks, and she knew that war wasn't a game. Life was fragile, precious, easily snatched away, and snuffed out in an instant, and luck was fickle. Louis had been lucky and squandered it. He'd end up forever addicted to laudanum for the pain in his half-healed leg, living in twilight, bitter with regret, wishing— What would he wish? That he'd stayed, chosen *her* over his friends? Never that. It wasn't his style. He'd probably forgotten all about her by now.

She knocked on the colonel's door and entered at his command. He was seated at his desk, writing letters. He frowned over his spectacles at her, then set the pen down and looked up at her with a guarded expression. "Dr. Atherton."

She clasped her hands before her, stood at attention the way a girl did when called before the headmistress—or her father—to discuss a misdeed.

He folded his hands on the desk and peered at her, waiting. "Lieutenant Chastaine has—left," she said.

The colonel removed his spectacles altogether. "Left? On whose authority?"

"There was an order. It was signed by . . . by . . . E. Atherton."

He glared at her. "You?"

She swallowed, shook her head. "Lieutenant E. C. Atherton. My brother. He's an adjutant at headquarters, on Lieutenant Colonel Petrie's staff."

"I saw no such order. I gave no approval."

She blinked, holding back tears, too proud to let them fall. "Matron Connolly saw the order and approved it. He—Lieutenant Chastaine has gone to Paris."

"Paris."

Eleanor noted the pile of letters on the colonel's desk, and she knew he'd been writing to the families of the dead, trying to explain, give comfort, ease their pain with mere words since he'd been unable to save their lads with all his medical skills. That was the true torment of this war—skill could never be enough, and young men would continue to die, and more and more letters would need to be written.

"It means you cannot stay."

"I'm willing to, of course—"

He shook his head. "No, not now. I still need a physician. We cannot do without one. But under the circumstances, I cannot keep you here. Before Lieutenant Chastaine's departure, there was a reason, but now . . ."

"I don't wish to return to England."

He frowned. "You are without a doubt one of the most stubborn, difficult, bloody-minded women I've ever met." She didn't reply, and he sighed. "You're also a good doctor, and there aren't enough good doctors. If you wish to stay in France, there are several hospitals run by female surgeons at the behest of the French Red Cross. You could continue to do good work, I believe. Important work. There are plenty of refugee women and children to tend to. It's a bloody disaster." He regarded her. "It's just something to consider, but if you take my advice, you'll go home, forget this place and the terrible things you've seen. I suggest—*I hope*—you will. I hope you will have a long career healing the most mundane of illnesses, somewhere safe."

She hesitated. "If I stay, I can help make sure others can go home, too."

"Is your sanity worth that?" he asked. He looked tired, a mountain worn down.

She looked at the letters on the desk and at the little piles of forlorn personal belongings, all that remained of individual lives and loves and ambitions. "I think it's why we choose to become doctors."

"We're still human, Dr. Atherton. A medical degree doesn't change that. We bleed, and suffer, and feel pain just like our patients, and when we fail them—" He lowered his eyes to the items on his desk. "When we fail them, with all our skill and our training and cleverness, we suffer even more. I remember the face of every man I've operated on. I think they'll haunt me for the rest of my days. This war has gone on too long." He drew himself up and looked at her again. "I'll bid you good night, and if I don't see you in the morning, have a safe journey."

He sat down again and picked up his pen, and there was nothing to do but go.

CHAPTER THIRTY-NINE

Eleanor ducked into one of the ward tents. She took the letter out of her pocket and made use of the lamp hanging above the supply cupboard. It was addressed to *E. Atherton*, not *El* or *Eleanor*, or *Miss*. The pointed reminder wasn't lost on her. Her fingers shook as she tore open the envelope and took out the letter.

> *We've gone on to Paris. I gave the orders to the dragon myself, duly signed and official. Lt. E. C. Atherton, this time. The dragon was most willing to accept the orders, and to release Louis at once into my care. There is no need for you to follow or raise a fuss. Fanny will ensure that Louis receives the best medical care possible from here out. I daresay Louis will be able to talk his way out of any bother in Paris, being a hero and the son of a peer of the realm, and Fanny will convince her dear uncle Douglas to excuse any difficulties this might*

cause with the Flying Corps. Don't poker up— If Louis is going home anyway, then what's the real harm? I can read a medical chart as well as any doctor's son, (or any doctor's daughter), and the reports have all been good, so we saw no reason to leave our hero lying there fretting. Erringdale (another of Fanny's admirers, and also a lieutenant) and I carried him to the car and saw him settled comfortably in Fanny's lap, with her furs tucked around him.

Mother wrote to me at HQ and asked me to convince you to come home. Since there's no further reason for you to remain in France, I suggest you do exactly that.

It was signed simply *E*, without regards or love.

There was no message at all from Louis.

Eleanor stared at the supplies on the shelves in front of her—bandages and basins, splints and syringes in orderly array. What was she to tell the countess? *Dear Lady Kirkswell, this is to inform you that your son, Lieutenant Lord Louis Chastaine, has found a prettier, richer, more amusing caregiver, and she has taken over all matters relating to his care, prescribing champagne thrice daily, as much merriment as possible, and the company of his own kind . . .*

Eleanor resisted the urge to tear Edward's note into a thousand pieces. She folded it instead, precisely and crisply. *Mother asked me to convince you to come home. Since there's no further reason for you to remain in France, I suggest you do exactly that.*

She could still go back, still take up her life. It wasn't too late. Her mother would find her a husband. Her father would allow her to clean the surgery . . .

But it would be an ordinary life, and she knew she couldn't go home and be that woman again, couldn't try to step back into shoes that no longer fit.

The colonel was right about her determination to practice medicine. But her father would never forgive her if she stayed and took a posting with the French Red Cross. Someday the war would end, and what then? Would she even be able to go home? Would her mother ever speak to her again if she stayed now? Who was she, *what* was she, if she couldn't practice medicine? The questions made her breathless, and she put a hand to her chest, like Findlay, but there was no one to save *her*. She was alone, and any decisions were now hers and hers alone. She stood stiffly, Edward's letter clutched in her hand, looking at the scrawled address, the cruel reminder that she'd failed yet again.

"Miss? Doctor?" She turned to find a VAD standing behind her. "Is everything all right?" She pointed at the letter in Eleanor's hand. "Is it bad news?"

Eleanor blinked at the young woman and the concern in her eyes.

She wiped away her tears with the heel of her hand. "No. All is well," she lied. "Thank you for asking."

The young woman smiled at her. "I saw you with the wounded. It made me feel proud to see a woman taking charge, pitching in. I've decided that when I go home, I'll ask my father if I can go to medical school and become a doctor."

"It's not easy."

"But it will be a different world after the war ends. My cousin works in a factory, and my sister is in the Women's Army Auxiliary Corps. She says there'll be lots of opportunities for women after the war."

"Miss!" a patient called, and the young woman smiled as she hurried away to see to her patient.

Eleanor watched her go, then slipped out of the tent. She stood in the chilly darkness for a moment. *A different world.*

Perhaps it already was.

CHAPTER FORTY

Fraser made the plate of soup last, sipping it slowly, watching the door for Eleanor. She was late, or perhaps she'd changed her mind and wasn't coming. Perhaps there was an emergency, or her flier needed her, or just wanted her. He pictured their heads together, hers red, his blond, laughing at some intimate joke. He pushed the cold soup away.

And why wouldn't she choose an aristocrat over a gamekeeper's son? A woman like Eleanor Atherton wasn't for the likes of him. He'd climbed above his station again. It wasn't as if he hadn't been reminded of his place before over a woman. He rubbed the wee scar under his chin. He'd fallen hard for the laird's youngest daughter, the fair Catriona, when they were both sixteen. He'd spent weeks making eyes at her whenever they chanced to meet. She'd smiled back at him, too, and he'd stupidly imagined he had a chance, that she felt what he felt. At the next village ceilidh, he'd worked up the courage to ask her to dance—just that, but it was enough. Her brothers caught him by the collar and dragged him outside. Catriona MacLeod was meant for a much better man than the son of a gillie. They'd punished Fraser's presumption with a beating that blackened his eyes and bruised his ribs before Angus MacLeod, Catriona's eldest brother, had knocked Fraser out with a hard punch, splitting his chin open with the jeweled signet ring he wore, leaving the scar to remind Fraser to stay where he belonged.

When he married, he'd choose an ordinary village girl of his own kind, someone plump and plain. Perhaps he'd wed a war widow. There'd be plenty of those. If he married at all, of course—he'd never felt the kind of attraction that would carry a man through a lifetime with one woman. Well, not until now.

He worried a bit of bread between his fingers. Ach, he was still daft, still pining for lasses meant for better men. The crumbs got caught in the bandage. It would need changing if he got it dirty. Perhaps he should dunk it in his soup just so Eleanor would have to tend to it. He could watch her do it, smell the sweet, feminine scent of her hair as she bent close to him, imagine . . .

No, better not to.

"Fool," he grumbled under his breath, sure she wasn't coming. He needed sleep. He rose to go.

"Hello." She was nearly breathless, as if she'd been running. Just the sight of her made his heart kick, and his own breath turned ragged. Looking her in the eye had the intensity of being struck by a bullet, a hard punch of awareness, the sudden heating of his flesh. Time stopped, and he stood there, struck dumb and staring across the table at her like a ninny.

"How's your arm?"

"Fine, just fine," he said, sinking back onto the bench as she sat down. "Have you eaten?" He could have cursed himself for the daftness of that question. "Ach, ye probably ate with your lieutenant."

"No, I didn't. He's gone."

He gaped at her. "Gone? What, *dead*?" he blurted. It happened. One moment a man seemed fine, and then—

"No, gone to Paris."

He frowned. "Paris? And you're not with him?"

"I wasn't invited," she said quietly. She tried to keep her face blank, but he could read her emotions anyway, in her blush, the hard set of her jaw, the glitter that showed through her lowered lashes. *Hurt*, he surmised, *shocked, and disappointed.*

He swallowed, considered what to say. "What will ye do now? Surely Bellford will be glad to—"

She shook her head. "No. It's against regulations for me to stay. I'm to leave tomorrow."

"Tomorrow?" He gaped at her, struggling to contain the raw outburst of his own disappointment. "But surely that's good news," he said at last. "Anyone would envy your good luck, and—" He saw that the shimmer of tears in her eyes was brighter now. "Are ye not happy to go?"

She wiped away the tear with an angry swipe of her wrist. "No. Yes. I don't know."

He closed his fist on the table. The stitches in his forearm pulled, and he forced himself to relax. "But you're needed here, surely. Ye promised to stay until Blair came back. Nothing's changed because one patient has gone." Perhaps his tone was too raw, too gruff. She looked hurt, indignant.

"It is not my choice. I gave my word to the colonel, and the countess, and to Captain Blair. I would keep it if I could."

She was pale, and lovely, and he wanted her to stay. She looked so stricken, so damnably fragile that he leaned in. "I didn't mean it that way. I'm just—" *Disappointed? Frustrated?* He settled for "Tired. What if there's an attack? There's talk of something coming, something big, and soon. Can Bellford truly do without ye?" It was selfish of him. He knew it even as he said it. Her eyes widened, and he saw torment in the soft depths.

He wished he could touch her, take her hand, but that was strictly against regulations. "I'm sorry. I shouldn't have said that. I don't know why I did. Perhaps because I've never met a woman like ye, and I wish—" He knew he shouldn't go on, shouldn't say it, but she was leaving tomorrow, and he'd likely never see her again. "I wish I had time to know ye better, Eleanor Atherton."

She stared at him in surprise, so still she might have been carved out of wax. He'd offended her, he thought, biting his tongue. He began to rise. "Look, if I don't see ye in the morning, I wish ye a safe journey home. You're a fine doctor, and—"

"Don't go." Her hand shot out to catch his, a staying touch on the fingertips of his bandaged hand. He stared down at those fingers in surprise as he felt electricity and heat run through his body. He glanced around to see if anyone was looking, but the tent was nearly empty. He stayed perfectly still, holding his breath, as if a wild creature had come to him, one he didn't want to frighten.

"I—I can't bear to be alone just now," she admitted. "Perhaps we could talk awhile—if you wish to. You're supposed to be resting while you're here, and I should pack, but—" She looked up at him, the fierce desire for his company clear in her eyes. He felt the same longing, but he could only stare at her in surprise, the silence stretching between them. Her eyes flicked to their joined hands, and she tried to withdraw hers, but he held it tight as he sat down again.

A flash of uncertainty flickered in her eyes. She gave a nervous laugh. She had all the confidence in the world as a doctor, was bold and brave, but under that armor, she was as shy as any lass.

"Of course, if you truly are tired, or in pain, or if you have other things to do, letters to write, or . . . or . . ." she said again, as if she'd forgotten she'd already said that, as if she was flustered in his company. She shut her eyes, but not before he'd seen the glitter of tears.

"What is it?" he asked. "Is it your pilot?"

She opened her eyes and scanned his face as if she was searching for something, her eyes bereft and clear and, for once, utterly lost. "Not Louis. I had . . . a disagreement with Edward."

"No one fights like family," he said. "The closer the kin, the more bitter the arguments."

He waited, giving her space to tell him what had happened. For a long moment the silence grew between them, pregnant. Then she shook her head slightly. "I don't want to talk about it tonight."

"Then what shall we talk about? Tell me about Yorkshire."

"I don't want to talk about that, either. Home. Or me. I want to forget the rest of the world, and tomorrow, and . . . *everything*." That last word was heavy, full of bitterness, or sorrow, or something deeper than that. If anyone understood the need to forget the war, the sights and sounds and smells of it, the tragedy of the whole damned thing, he did. Dwelling on it only made it worse. It was why soldiers sang and whored and made terrible jokes. He squeezed her hand instead, offering comfort and understanding in that simple touch, and the sharpness in her eased, became round and soft and feminine, and she forced a smile. He felt a ball of heat in his chest, an expanding of his heart and lungs. It was the way he'd felt standing on a high cliff over a deep glen, the world spread out before him, with the sun warming him at the same time as the wind chilled him. It was the purest joy, connection to the land and to himself. He'd never felt it with another person before, but he felt it now. He realized he'd felt it the first moment he met her.

He stared at her in surprise, and she stared back. Perhaps she felt it, too, and was just as surprised by the heat that flowed through their joined hands and was reflected in their connected gazes. He felt her sorrow that it could not be more, that there was no time, and that there was a war on and all was lost, not just for them, but for the whole damned world. They had minutes, a scant few hours at best, but he'd take it, use it wisely, snub everything that stood against them. Instead of withdrawing his hand, and himself, he ran his thumb over her knuckles, gave her a smile. "You're pretty," he said instead. "More than pretty."

"You as well," she said, and blushed. "No, that's the wrong thing to say. Handsome? Braw? Bonny? What *is* the right word?"

He laughed. "Ye babble when you're nervous."

"I'm not very good at—at flirting. I've never really done it before. I mean, flirting is an expression of—of interest, isn't it? I—" She bit her lip. "I haven't had very much experience—well, none, really. With flirting, that is. It feels . . ." She turned serious again, as if she were considering a medical issue.

"Nay, lass. Ye can't diagnose or cure this. It's attraction. Nay, don't *think* about how it feels, lass. Just *feel* it." He was gratified that her fingers tightened on his, and her smile turned his heart upside down.

Oh, Fraser MacLeod, you're a daft lad, he chided himself silently as he felt her charm and beauty and sweetness seep past his own armor and into his bones, even though he knew she would leave and he would return to the front. He was tempting fate, pushing his luck. There was no future for them. But for the moment, he was warm and clean and safe, happy in her company, and she was all that mattered.

Just for now, and nothing more. His heart gave a lurch of longing and regret.

"Would you like a cup of tea, Eleanor? Or a bite of supper?"

She smiled at him, and that was warmer and sweeter than any cuppa. "I'd like that very much," she said without specifying which she wanted, and he let it lie, and smiled at her again.

W hat on earth was she doing? She should be packing, writing to her parents or the countess, getting her life back in order, making decisions. Instead, she sat at a simple plank table with Fraser MacLeod, sharing thin soup and tepid tea, basking in his smile and smiling back. Hours passed. Or minutes. She didn't care. His eyes softened when he spoke of his home, told her stories about his kin and the village he came from. He made her laugh. He was handsome and charming, and for the first time in her life she felt the thrill of a man's company in her breast, a delight and desire and yearning that was entirely different from a girl's crush, and yet brought out the same butterflies to flutter against her ribs.

He held her hand all the while they sat together, leaning across the table, the dim lamp above casting a warm glow over them. It felt as natural as breathing to have his fingers clasped around hers, their palms together. She could feel his pulse under her fingertip.

When Corporal Swiftwood walked into the tent and fixed his sharp eyes on them, Fraser pulled away at once and dropped his hands into his lap. His smile faded to wariness as he nodded at the orderly. Swiftwood poured himself a cup of coffee and sat down, not to join them, but close enough to listen and watch. The orderly was a notorious gossip.

They fell silent.

"It's late," Fraser said. "I'll walk ye back to the visitor's quarters and say good night. Ye still need to pack."

So soon?

She felt bitter regret as they rose and walked out of the tent.

Fraser walked beside her, his hands at his sides. She measured her pace, counting her footsteps. The visitor's hut was past the sick ward, just beyond the officers' ward. She stared at the tiny building, wishing it were a dozen yards farther away, or a hundred, so she could have Fraser next to her for just a little longer. He'd made her forget Edward and Louis and the whole world. Nothing else had mattered. There was nothing to prove, and nothing to fear.

They reached the door all too soon.

She turned to look up at Fraser. A lock of dark auburn hair had fallen over his brow, casting a shadow across his eyes. Without thinking, she reached up to brush it back. He caught her hand, brought it to his lips, and kissed her palm. Warmth flooded all the way to her toes.

She stepped toward him, or perhaps he stepped toward her, but suddenly she was wrapped in his arms, held tight against his body, his heart beating against hers, and his mouth was on hers, and she was kissing him back and never wanting it to stop.

He broke away, stepped back. "Someone might see."

She didn't want to let him go, watch him walk back down the duckboards and away. Tomorrow they'd have no choice, but now, tonight, they did.

She reached behind her, found the latch, and opened the door. The hinges gasped as it swung wide. "Then come inside."

He was silent for a long moment standing there on the doorstep, in the dark. She held her breath and waited.

"Oh, lass," he said softly at last. He made no move to step inside or to go, just stood looking down at her.

She took his hand in her own and stepped over the threshold, and he followed. Inside, she held up her arms, and he came into them, kissing her again, harder this time, as desperate as she.

She reached for the buttons on his shirt, her skilled fingers clumsy now.

He broke the kiss and caught her hand in his. "Are ye sure?" he murmured. "I mean, I want ye, want this, but—"

"I'm sure," she said. She curled her hand against his naked chest and felt the hard muscles under his warm skin, the steady beat of his heart, the softness of his breath on her hair. Her body throbbed, turned liquid.

He turned away, and her heart sank, but he only closed the door and locked it. For a moment they stood in silence and darkness, with only the faint glow from the lamps in the ward tents lighting the small room. He leaned on the door, halfway across the room, watching her, or waiting.

"I don't know where to start," she said. Her face flamed in the dark. She was glad it was dark. "I mean, I know *how* it works, of course, but I haven't—" She stopped.

He walked toward her and cupped her cheek in his hand. "*Och,* it's not a medical procedure, lass. It's . . ." He took a breath and spread his fingers wide enough to reach her mouth, ran the tip of his little finger over her lips. "It's more akin to dancing, or poetry, or music. Even magic, if ye do it right."

"I want to . . . do it right. Is there time? I'm—uh, I'm not much of a dancer."

She saw the gleam of his smile in the dimness. It faded almost as quickly as it had come.

"I wish I had longer to show ye. Not that I'm an expert. I—" He looked helpless.

"We only have tonight," she said. "Is it enough?"

"It will have to be. That's all there is," he said, his voice ragged. "Are ye sure?" he asked again.

She reached up to undo the pins in her hair. "Very sure. Show me all the poetry, music, and magic you can, Fraser. Teach me how to dance."

And when he drew her back into his arms and held her, she felt like this choice was the right one, the best one, and for a time she forgot the war, and Louis, and the whole rest of the world, and only the two of them mattered.

CHAPTER FORTY-ONE

THE RITZ HOTEL, PARIS
MARCH 13, 1918

S omerton!"

Louis tried not to grit his teeth at Fanny's call. She insisted on using the title—he was a viscount, the heir to an earldom, a hero with two medals pinned to his chest. She believed he'd earned the right to it. But had he?

Cyril had been the one raised to all the pomp and pride and responsibility. Louis had simply had it thrust upon him, and being a viscount seemed so much less important than being a pilot, or a soldier.

The suddenness of his brother's ignominious death had hit him hard, shocked him more than he let on, hurt him more. He couldn't just step into Cyril's shoes, suddenly be all that history and the future demanded. It made him sweat. He was an imposter, not a real viscount, and not a real hero, either. But his whole life had changed the moment Cyril's bloody horse unwisely put its foot into a rabbit hole, and now the rightful heir was moldering in the family crypt, and like it or not, Louis Patrick Allenton Henry Chastaine was Viscount Somerton.

Toll the bells, lower the curtain, snuff the candle, The End, dust to dust, nothing to be remembered for. Poor bloody Cyril. And poor him.

Louis looked around Fanny's grand Hôtel Ritz suite—his was right next door, luxurious and huge, fit for a viscount, made for indolence and the pursuit of pleasure and pretending that there wasn't really a war going on less than seventy miles from the hotel's gilded front doors.

"Somerton!" She said it again, more insistently, and still he ignored her.

He didn't want it. Not the title, not more champagne, not more caviar, and not her. He drew on the cigarette, sucked the smoke into his lungs, and remembered the flames as his plane went down, the acrid smoke, the fear. He was the one who should be dead, not Cyril.

Every day here was a party. Champagne flowed like water, and there was steak and fresh eggs for breakfast, and gâteaux of the kind he hadn't seen in nearly three years. It wasn't even noon and he was drunk. Again or still? Did it matter?

"Which is the illusion, the war, or all this glamour?" he asked Fanny.

She looked up from considering a list of invitees for tonight's do. "Don't be silly, darling. This is what's real, of course. The war won't last forever."

God, he'd die of boredom if this was how he was to spend eternity! He read the newspapers, current ones, saw the reports of skirmishes and battles, and scanned the casualty lists when Fanny wasn't looking. She didn't like to be gloomy. He wondered if Eleanor had made it home to Thorndale safely and what she'd told his mother. He felt a twinge of guilt—her ladyship didn't like it when she didn't get her way. What might she do to Eleanor in reprisal? Poor El—she'd never get Mama's patronage now. Quite the opposite. She'd likely be lancing boils on the backsides of the tubercular poor until the end of time if the countess had her way. He should write at once, tell her his escape from 46/CCS wasn't Eleanor's fault, but he was a poor correspondent. Edward had signed the order for his release in the end. Eleanor wouldn't do it. Her stiff-necked sense of honor and duty was inspiring—or shaming, perhaps. He hadn't cared which. Edward said it would make a fine prank, and Louis was so bloody eager to leave the CCS, come to Paris, return to wine, women, and song, and get away from the dead and dying. Still, as they'd fled in the night, he'd realized he hadn't even said goodbye. It didn't matter. She was a big girl, and not his concern. He frowned and took another drag on his cigarette and blew smoke—palest blue, not black—into the air.

"Is there more champagne, darling?" he said, holding up his empty glass. There was nothing bloody else to do. Fanny retrieved the bottle from the bucket and filled the delicate flute to the brim.

She was clad in some lovely slip of a dress made of clouds and stars, and she smelled divine. He was stuck on the chaise, his splinted leg stretched out before him, well padded with satin pillows stuffed with swansdown. He curled his hand around her calf and let it slide slowly upward.

"Shall we invite Dinsy Montrose tonight?" she asked, unaroused.

Louis removed his hand. "He's a subaltern at HQ. He might find it hard to get away."

She smiled archly. "I'll simply ring Uncle Douglas and ask if Dinsy can drive in with Edward. Sunny Kerridale is coming. Edward will like her."

"Sunny? What happened to Maud?"

Fanny rolled her eyes. "It was all too much for her. She's gone home, too saddened by the sight of the wounded. She's thinking of training to be a VAD. Can you imagine Maud a VAD? She'll never do it. She hates dirt and blood and the downtrodden poor."

"I'm not sure Edward could see Maud as a VAD, either. He can't even see Eleanor as a doctor," Louis replied.

Fanny's smile faded. "Poor Eddie, having a sister like that."

She crossed to wind the Victrola and put on one of the cylinders. The jumpy, jolly, tinny sound of American rag filled the room. No sad, patriotic songs for Fanny, no "Danny Boy," or "Keep the Home Fires Burning," or "Tipperary." You wouldn't even know there was a war on here in Fanny's cocoon if not for the uniforms her bright, elegant, titled companions wore to her parties. All officers, of course. If they'd seen battle, or blood, or the ugly side of things—and most of them hadn't—they never let on. They were as gay as a sunny summer day in England. Well, he'd seen it, and firsthand, on the front lines, the sharp end. He was starting to hate them all. Every night they filled this room, dancing, drinking, and laughing while Louis lay on the chaise like an effigy, unable to dance, his aching leg stretched out in front of him, his burned wrist chafed by the gold cuff link and the starched and monogrammed linen of his shirt. The ladies paid homage to him by tying colorful silk scarves around his splint and pinning them with diamond brooches until he glittered like a cancan dancer. He gritted his teeth, smiled, and charmingly kissed their fingertips. He missed his uniform and felt out of place without it, or perhaps just out of sorts. Christ, he couldn't believe he'd lived for these puerile pleasures before the war, for nights of wild drunken abandon and endless merriment.

He lit another cigarette, one of the good ones, proper Turkish tobacco that Fanny bought on the black market. He blew another plume of smoke into the air and saw more clouds, imagined aircraft.

He should be there, not here.

"All right, Budgie, darling? You've turned pensive again," Fanny said, and he forced a grin and raised his glass. He could still play the game, and surely the game was a damn sight more palatable than reality. There was no chance of dying here, unless it was *la petite mort*. Even inside his head, that joke fell flat. When had he become so stodgy, so dreadfully dull?

Fanny put another disk on the Victrola, and Billy Murray's fine tenor voice filled the room, crooning "I Wonder Who's Kissing Her Now." He should have kissed Eleanor when he had the chance, should have taught her how, made sure she'd never forget him. She'd probably go to the marriage bed of some worthy chap like David Blair or Lancelot Findlay, an untouched virgin, prim and proper and far too smart for her husband. If she married at all, of course—she could end up as a bluestocking spinster, a do-gooder running a charity hospital in some dank city, the kind of careworn crusader no one would want to kiss.

"More champagne, darling?"

"No thank you, I'm flying," he murmured, even as he let Fanny refill the glass. The clouds and the planes and the thoughts of Eleanor disappeared, and he was all quip and no substance once again. "I think I'll go to my own room and take a bath," he said.

Fanny had turned to the guest list again, and she barely glanced up. "Yes, do. Shall I order oysters for luncheon?"

And what were the poor lads at the front eating now? Maconochie's tinned meat, and bloody Tickler's plum-and-apple jam on stale biscuits that tasted more of gunpowder and mud than anything else, with rats the size of badgers for dining companions.

"Whatever you like," he said. He shoved the crutch under his arm and hobbled out.

In his own room, he limped over to look in the mirror, where he saw the lines around his mouth and under his eyes, the new light of sober care in his gaze. He wasn't the carefree, adventuresome lad who'd joined up. He was all grown up, or halfway to old, rather. Like all the other young men in this war, he stood with one foot in the grave while the bell tolled.

He rang for the concierge and sat down to wait.

This dissatisfaction, this restlessness, was all Eleanor's fault. She'd made this life—his life—seem small next to her own.

She hadn't turned a hair when she stuck the needle into Findlay's chest. She'd looked as avidly interested in stabbing him as Fanny looked when contemplating a tray of sweets or a book of the latest dress designs.

Eleanor was prettier than he had remembered. A beauty, in fact, even with that needle in her hand. If she changed her hair, wore more fashionable, less conservative clothing—and lost the needle—she'd be stunning.

Even more so than Fanny?

Fanny had seven generations of aristocratic breeding on her side, and she'd inherited her mother's beauty. But long nights of drinking and dancing and going from party to party took their toll, and he suspected she now owed her fresh-faced loveliness more to her maid's clever tricks with paint and powder than nature.

Perhaps seeing Eleanor after so many years apart and then being close to her for all those weeks, it was natural to think about her, to notice that she'd grown up slender and strong, clever, elegant, and keen.

Fanny was soft everywhere, well curved, lushly feminine, and purely decorative. Aside from riding to the hunt or dancing, she was a languid creature. She ruled her world with a charming word and a coy smile. Her wit was invisible until she needed it, like a dangerously sharp blade in a hidden sheath, suddenly drawn and pressed to your throat.

Eleanor had a kind of restless energy, something to prove to the world. Even when she sat still, he could tell her mind was moving at a hundred miles an hour. Did she ever allow herself to be languid? He couldn't picture it. He suspected that if she ever was properly set alight, the intensity would burn a man to cinders.

He'd caught a glimpse of that fire when the brash sergeant had stalked into the ward and demanded she help with the wounded. It was as if a trumpet had sounded. Eleanor had mounted her chariot like Boudicca and rushed away to meet the challenge, purposeful and sure, her eyes bright.

She mucked in, got dirty and bloody, and saved lives.

It had rather shamed him to see Eleanor Atherton as such a marvelous heroine. Edward had been embarrassed by his twin. Fanny had giggled and made a tart little jest about Amazons and suffragists and poured more champagne. They'd laughed, and drunk, and stayed where they were. No one had gone with Eleanor to help. Would *he* have, if he could walk? He didn't know. She frightened him. No, it wasn't fright—it was awe. She had *courage*. His medals were earned for a lucky accident, but her mettle was innate, and as true as any blade, and never, ever hidden.

There was a gentle scratch at the door, and the concierge entered. "A bath and a shave," Louis ordered. The concierge—a man well past the age of retirement, since there was a war on—bowed with arthritic stiffness and left.

Louis lay down on the bed to wait and shut his eyes. Feathers cradled his spine, his head, his leg. He pitied the poor blighters back at the CCS, wrapped in scratchy sheets on lumpy palliasses.

Ah, but perhaps they were the lucky ones after all—they had Eleanor to tend them, to stick needles into them when they couldn't breathe, and to show them what bravery really looked like.

That evening, Louis sat on the chaise and watched Edward and Sunny performing a graceful tango. Edward had doffed his khaki tunic in favor of a garish brocade smoking jacket. He was so very different from his twin.

Louis was willing to bet Eleanor couldn't dance more than the most basic box steps, or a polite waltz—nothing new or modern for Eleanor. Except medicine, of course—she'd be right up to date on that. *Have you heard the latest?* he imagined her saying, and then describing a surgical procedure that would horrify and baffle him. David bloody

Blair would understand her perfectly, of course, with his sharp surgeon's eyes and his long white hands. Eleanor had looked at Blair quite differently from the way she looked at him—with interest in his mind, his conversation. Louis had known for years that Eleanor had a crush on him, but he suspected she'd been disappointed when she saw the real Louis Chastaine. He'd been peevish, cruel, toplofty, and asinine. It was lowering in the extreme, and yet, seeing himself in her eyes made him *want* to be better, be *more*, just to see Eleanor look at him even once the way she looked at the damned surgeon.

"Penny for them," Fanny purred, and she blew in his ear as she arranged herself artfully beside him on the chaise and tickled his chin with her long, lacquered nails. "You're a million miles away, darling. You must be exhausted. You'll be better when we get you home to—" He drew a sharp breath at the thought, and she paused. "What is it?"

He met her pretty blue eyes. She was playing the coquette tonight, charming him, wooing him expertly, tightening her snare. Her cap was set, his fate sealed. Still, he made a last bid for freedom.

"I'm not going home."

Her smile faded. "What?"

"I'm going back to my squadron."

Out came her stiletto glare, bright and sharp as a blade, to pin him to the chaise. "And when did you decide that?"

"Only just now," he said, realizing it was true. "But it's what I want." His chest felt lighter, his mind clearer for the decision.

She frowned at him, her eyes hardening. "You've done your bit, Louis. You have the wounds and the medal to prove it. You're a hero. Let someone else take a turn."

He forced himself to smile at her, though his teeth were gritted. He wasn't a hero. Not for tumbling out of the bloody sky, being lucky enough not to kill himself or anyone else. "But I'm good at it, darling," he said, more sharply than he meant to. "And I like it."

She pouted, and he picked up her hand and kissed her fingertips.

Her fingers remained limp in his, and her body stiffened with disapproval. Fanny didn't like to be thwarted or disappointed. She thought of herself as a modern Athena, manipulating the warriors in this Trojan War, making them dance to her will. If she wished, she could have higher gods, like dear Uncle Douglas, ground him, or ask her esteemed father to have a quiet word with the Air Council, or the RFC, or her mother's dear friend General David Henderson, who would arrange a cozy and safe backwater posting for him somewhere in England for the duration.

"I know a dozen young men who've died in this bloody war. I don't want to lose you, too," she said, her eyes clear, sober, with no pretense or flirtation. She truly cared.

He forced a laugh. "Me, darling? I'm not going to die. Not if I haven't already."

Something dangerous sparked in her expression, turned her up brittle and stubborn, Athena at her worst.

He had to head her off, win free, and he could see only one way to do that. He took a deep breath. "Darling, what do you say when I come back, we get married? Will you do me the honor of marrying me?" Again, he felt the rush of the plane diving out of control. This time he didn't think about Beowulf. He thought about the title, the expectations of family, and the full weight of aristocratic tradition that chained him, held him fast, left him with no choices of his own.

He wasn't ready to marry, but he'd make a deal with the devil—or Lady Frances Parfitt—for one more chance to fly, one more hour of freedom, a last adventure, a chance to prove he was a man, not just a title.

Fanny's eyes went as wide as china saucers, and there were tears as brilliant as the diamonds pinned to his splint glittering on her lashes as she blinked. Oh, she played the game well. It couldn't be a surprise. Had she ever failed to get what she wanted? Or perhaps she truly hadn't expected him to propose, here, now, before he'd even spoken to her father.

"Yes! Oh, darling, yes!" She threw herself into his arms, and he caught her, felt her breasts pressed to his chest. He tasted champagne and lipstick and perfume when she kissed him.

Then Fanny was on her feet, shouting the news, and the entire party was offering gleeful congratulations. The gentlemen grinned and shook his hand, but their smiles didn't quite reach their eyes, and no doubt they were wondering why now, why here.

For freedom, lads, and a funny kind of honor. And Fanny wasn't so bad. She was good company, and she'd make a highly suitable wife for a viscount, and an excellent countess when the time came. She'd been raised to it. Even his mother would approve of the match. He laughed and let them refill his glass, drink toasts to their health and happiness. It would be a grand wedding.

If he lived, of course.

But for now he was free.

CHAPTER FORTY-TWO

MARCH 14, 1918

Eleanor heard the soft tap on her door and woke with a gasp. Morning light was peeping around the edge of the curtains. She was tangled in the sheets and blankets and Fraser's embrace, entirely naked. Fraser's bandaged arm rested lightly on her waist. Had she done him any harm? The night had been . . .

She blushed, smiling quietly. Was there even a word to describe it? Wonderful, marvelous, delightful, and—

The knock came again. "Miss?"

Over.

It was morning, and she had to leave.

"It's me, miss, Private Gibbons. There's a transport of wounded going to the station soon. The colonel asked the chaplain to save room for you."

She glanced again at Fraser, but he didn't wake. At long last he'd relaxed enough to sleep deeply. He needed it, deserved it. She blushed. Not because . . . She looked at the rumpled sheets, the hastily discarded clothing that scattered the floor of the tiny hut, and felt her heart flutter.

She should wake him, whisper her farewells, promise to write, to see him after the war, to, to . . . She felt tears spring to her eyes. What if he didn't want that? What if he didn't want her? She had only to wake him, to shake his shoulder until he opened his eyes and saw her in the light of day, and she'd know. She reached out, but stopped with her hand in midair. What did *she* want? She didn't even know where she was going when she left this place. Not home, and not Paris . . . She didn't regret this. She couldn't bear to discover that he did, that things were awkward between them. Not now. She drew her hand back again and let it fall on the pillow.

Wonderful, marvelous, delightful, and over.

She carefully slipped out of bed so she wouldn't disturb him, grabbed a blanket, and wrapped it around her shoulders. She opened the door a wee crack and peered at Gibbons.

"I overslept," she whispered. "I need a few minutes, Private, and—"

He gave her his shy smile. "I can wait, miss." He turned around, his back to the door to give her privacy, and she shut it, gathered her clothes, and slipped into them as quietly as she could. Her body ached a little, but it felt soft, pliant, and womanly, too. Loved.

She looked at him. *If only* . . . She willed him to wake up, to look at her, to reach out for her and pull her back into the cocoon of tangled sheets. But Gibbons was waiting, and she could not stay. She hadn't stopped to think of what the consequences might be for him if he—they—were caught. Fraternizing was strictly against the rules.

Better to let him sleep while she slipped away, went without tears or awkwardness. She bound up her hair with nervous fingers, her eyes still roaming over him, memorizing him. She could smell him on her skin, still taste him. Another flush of longing made her shiver. She stared down at him, memorizing him, every detail. As if she could ever forget. Fraser MacLeod would stay with her forever, part of her.

At last she turned away. She put on her coat and hat and took her case to the door. Still he didn't wake. She set her hand on the doorknob, ready to go. She paused to looked back at him, his long limbs relaxed in sleep, his hair splayed against the pillow, his jaw stubbled, his bandages white against the gold of his skin. Her heart climbed into her throat. She crossed the room, bent over him, and softly kissed his brow.

Then she opened the door just a crack and slid her case through to Gibbons. If he thought it odd, he gave no sign of it. He picked it up. "All ready, miss?"

No. She wasn't ready, didn't want to go. But she must. She forced herself to step out and shut the door firmly and quietly.

"Ready," she said to Gibbons, her tone husky, and let him lead the way.

CHAPTER FORTY-THREE

E leanor didn't recognize the tall soldier walking along the duck-boards ahead of them. He turned at the sound of their footsteps behind him, glanced at Gibbons, and tipped his cap to her.

"I'm looking for Captain David Blair. Can either of you tell me where I might find him? It's urgent." He spoke with a flat drawl that marked him as Canadian, and the maple leaf on his cap badge confirmed it.

"He's not here," Gibbons said.

The news seemed to hit him like a blow, and he swayed on his feet. "Are you wounded, Sergeant, or ill?" Eleanor asked.

He squared his shoulders. "Me? No, I'm just fine, thank you. It's—" He rubbed his hand over the grim lines of his mouth. "Will Captain Blair be back soon?"

"Not for a few days. He's at the front, temporarily serving at an aid post."

The soldier frowned. "I've been to two CCSs where they said I might find him. Now he's at an aid post." He looked at Eleanor. "I need to reach him as soon as possible. It might already be too late. It's his brother, miss, Captain Patrick Blair. He's with the 31st Canadians. He's . . ." He swallowed. "He's wounded, and not expected to live. He asked to see his brother before . . . Can you give me directions to that aid post? Our Captain Blair is a good man, you see, a good officer. He saved the lives of five men, and now he's going to lose his own for it. We want to give him his last wish and bring his brother to see him, give them a chance to say goodbye."

Eleanor sighed. David was close to his brother, and he'd be devastated that Patrick had asked to see him, that he hadn't been there.

But David couldn't leave the aid post, not without a doctor to replace him.

"We're close by, miss, near Arras, at the Canadian CCS there. It wouldn't take long. Our Captain Blair doesn't have very long."

She looked at Gibbons. There was calm sympathy in his vague blue eyes, acceptance that this was the way of the war, that good men died, left behind brothers to mourn them. She remembered Nathaniel Duncan, and Captain Greaves.

She made the decision in a heartbeat. "Can you wait for just a moment? I'll take you to him. Go and have a cup of tea, or food—"

His face brightened. "Thank you, miss, but if it's all the same I'll wait right here. I've got a truck out front, ready to go."

Eleanor turned to Gibbons. "Private, I need a favor." There were butterflies in her belly, and they seemed to be wearing thick-soled army boots.

Could she do this? Did she dare?

She had nowhere else to be, and David did.

"I need a uniform about the same size as your own," she said to Gibbons.

He didn't ask why. He simply led the way to the supply tent. Inside, folded uniforms were stacked up, most of them used, but laundered and clean, ready to resupply the wounded who needed new clothing.

He reached for a folded bundle. "Will this do?"

She unfurled the garments and gauged the size. "Yes."

"Who's it for, miss?" he asked.

She met his eyes. "For me, Private Gibbons. Captain Blair must go to Arras to see his brother. I'm going to take his place for a day or so."

His smile faded to a look of surprise. "Should I tell the colonel?"

"No, Tom, don't tell him. I'll be back before he knows I'm gone."

"But it's bad at the front, miss. Dangerous."

She felt fear rush along her limbs, but she ignored it. "I know, but this is urgent. Now turn around and watch the door while I change my clothes."

He faced the door, his back stiff, and she unbuttoned her skirt and pulled on the woolen trousers. They were loose at the waist and baggy in the seat, and the wool was scratchy against her skin. She took off her blouse and pulled the woolen undershirt over her shift, added suspenders to hold up the trousers, and shrugged into the tunic. It was too big at the shoulders, too long in the sleeves, and tight over her breasts. She buttoned it with effort and pulled it straight.

"You can turn around now, Tom," she said to Gibbons.

He turned and stared at her.

"How do I look?"

"You'll need a cap and boots," he said. He found a cap, and she put it on, tucking her hair into it as he searched for boots. He held a pair out and she put them on and laced them. He bent to wind the puttees around her ankles and calves.

"Now you look more like a soldier, but you haven't got orders, miss."

"I'm a civilian," she said. "I don't need orders."

"But you're in uniform," he pointed out.

"It will have to do. Would you take my clothes back to my quarters—

no, don't." Fraser was there, fast asleep and naked. What would he say if he saw her now, knew what she was going to do? She didn't have time to think about that. "Leave my things here. I'll just take my medical bag."

She picked it up and stepped outside, the uniform feeling odd on her body, itchy, too tight in some places, too loose in others. Without the bulk and drag of her skirts, she felt free. She took long, unhampered strides toward the road where the Canadian sergeant was waiting beside his vehicle, smoking. He flicked the end of it into the mud when he saw her coming, pushed back his cap, and regarded her in surprise.

"Dangerous up there," he said. "I thought the private might be coming."

"He's needed here," she said. "I'm ready to go."

For a second longer he hesitated and looked to Gibbons, who stood behind her, but Gibbons's face was flat and calm, offering no assistance. The Canadian looked at her again from head to toe and shook his head. "I don't know if you're the bravest woman I've ever seen, or the dumbest."

It was on the tip of her tongue to tell him that she was neither, that this was the equivalent of running away—or running *to*—something, a place where she'd be useful, where she could be a doctor for a little while longer. It was selfish, not heroic. She didn't deserve his praise. She walked around him and got into the truck. "I'm ready to go."

CHAPTER FORTY-FOUR

Fraser woke slowly, surfacing from a deep sleep. He stretched without opening his eyes, trying to remember the last time he'd slept so well. He felt a grin rise, filling his face, and realized it was the first time he'd smiled, truly smiled, for a long time as well. Eleanor was responsible for all of it. He felt human again, fully male, and right in his own skin. He rubbed at the stubble on his jaw, felt the pull of the stitches in his arm, and stared at the bandage. He should thank Cooper for shooting him, or he wouldn't have been here at all. Nay, he should thank Eleanor. He rolled over and reached for her, but he found the bed empty, the sheets cold.

The grin faded to a frown and he sat up and looked around the room, taking in the wee desk and the chair beside it, the empty clothing hooks on the wall. Her case was gone, her clothes, her doctor's bag, everything.

"No," he said softly.

He shouldn't have fallen asleep here, should have returned to his assigned cot in the orderlies' tent. What if Swiftwood or someone else had noticed his absence? There'd be gossip. It wouldn't matter so much to him, but Eleanor would mind. And he'd mind for her. He was a private man, and she . . . He'd been her first, her only.

Had he frightened her away? He'd tried to be considerate, gentle, *good*. He'd wanted her badly, needed her with a passion he wasn't sure he'd known with other women before. But then, it had been a long time, and she was beautiful, and as eager as he. He remembered the soft sounds she had made, the urgency in them, the insistence on a second time, then a third, until they'd both slept. His last thought as he'd fallen asleep with Eleanor in his arms was a hope that morning wouldn't come.

But here it was.

He stared at the empty pillow beside him. He would have liked to have told her that it was special, that *she* was special, that he'd always— no. It was over. It was never meant to be more than one night. She was gone, and he'd never see her again. Perhaps that's how she wanted it. No entanglements, no farewells.

He got up and washed his face, then pulled his clothes carefully over the bandages. His ribs were still tender, and his arm felt heavy with the weight of the wound and the binding linen. The rest of his body felt light, his skin comfortable again.

He slipped out of the hut into the bright light of day. It was warmer, and the ice was melting and dripping. She was probably half-way to Calais by now. He remembered her trip here, the soldiers who thought she'd be easy prey. He wondered how that young private had explained his black eye. He silently wished her an easier journey home as he walked along the duckboards, tried to picture her in her wee village, Thorndale, waiting for him. He pushed the idea out of his mind. That way lay madness and obsession. He wished she'd never told him the name of the place, made it possible to even think of going there, of finding her again. He wouldn't, of course.

He came around the front of the tents, and the cold wind hit him like good sense. He needed something to do to occupy his hands and his mind and keep him from dwelling on things he couldn't have, to help him forget that he felt soothed and raw, replete and ravenous all at once.

Swiftwood passed him with a load of dressing trays, and Fraser held his breath, bunched his fist, waited for the smirk, the knowing look, the crude quip, but the corporal continued on with just a crisp nod.

Gibbons came out of the supply tent. "Hello, Sergeant," he said. "How's your arm?"

"I'm well, Tom. Is Reverend Strong around? I need something useful to do."

"He's gone to the station with the wounded."

Fraser scanned the empty road. "Did he . . . Did he take Dr. Atherton with him?"

"No, she was already gone."

"But how did she— She didn't walk, did she?" The thought struck him, the image of a tearful Eleanor hurrying down the road on foot, filled with regret.

"No, a Canadian sergeant took her to the front."

"The *front*?" Fraser asked.

Gibbons nodded. "Aye, to the aid post to see Captain Blair."

"Captain Blair?" The explosion of jealousy hit him first, followed by concussive waves of concern for her. Of all the dim-witted, hare-brained things she could do, going to the front was the dimmest. He cursed, first in Gaelic, then in English, and added a few words of French for good measure while Gibbons patiently watched him.

"*When* did she go, Gibbons?"

"A few hours ago."

Fraser gritted his teeth. "*Why?* Did the Canadians ask for a doctor?"

"No, they just wanted Captain Blair. His brother was wounded.

He's at the Canadian hospital at Doullens, dying. He asked for Captain Blair to come before—" He paused. "Of course, our captain couldn't leave his post, so Miss Atherton decided she'd go up herself and let him go to his brother."

Fraser stopped listening. "Ye let her go? Did Bellford approve it? What about the chaplain? They let a woman go alone to the front? What the devil were ye thinking?"

Gibbons shook his head. "Not a woman. She borrowed a uniform."

Fraser looked around in a panic. "Get me a truck, or an ambulance—some way to get to the bloody aid post."

"There isn't anything right now, Sergeant. There's wounded coming in, and the ambulances are out."

"What units? Where's the attack?" he asked.

"South, near Bapaume. Gas. Chap with a broken arm says the Huns are testing the lines, looking for soft spots."

"But that's close to the aid station!" Fraser turned away, staring at the road and listening to the guns. He had to get to her, to bring her back. An attack was coming, and she was right in the line of fire.

And all he could do was wait.

CHAPTER FORTY-FIVE

Another patient was carried down the stairs into the cellar. "Leg wound, critical!" the bearer called to Eleanor, setting the stretcher on supports and positioning a small brazier under it to keep the patient warm. The cellar was already full of wounded, and more kept coming. Two bearers were doing their best to assist her, but there was too much work, too much blood, and every patient needed urgent, immediate care.

"Just patch 'em up and send them back to the CCS," David had instructed her before he left. When she'd walked into the aid post, newly moved to a ruined farm, he'd been surprised to see her, amused by her uniform—until his eyes had fallen on the Canadian soldier behind her.

"It's your brother, sir."

"Go," she'd said as his smile melted to sorrow. "I'll be fine."

How long ago was that? Hours? Days? Deep in a cellar, she

couldn't see the sky to know if it was day or night. Barrages came at dawn, didn't they? Like everyone else, she'd learned to tell time by the sound of the guns.

She flinched as another shell exploded, a direct hit on the already shattered farm above them. She stifled the urge to scream as the beams over her head shuddered, and she folded herself over a patient's open wound.

She blinked dust out of her eyes, gulped air that tasted of dirt, smoke, blood, and sweat, and carried on, pulling a long shard of shrapnel from a soldier's leg. Another bomb exploded nearby, and the patient moaned. She grabbed his hand, squeezed tight. "It's all right," she said, trying to convince herself as much as anyone else. "Bandage him and send him on," she said, and the orderlies moved the stretcher and the bearers set another in its place.

Another bomb shook the cellar.

"Ha—missed me again, even if it was a close one," the patient said in a broad Yorkshire accent.

She barely recognized his face under the mud and soot and blood that covered it, but his voice was the sound of home. "Charlie? Charlie Nevins?"

He lay on the stretcher staring at the ceiling and sucking on a cigarette, waiting for her to undo what the guns had done and make a torn, broken, ruined man whole again. Not a man, a boy—someone she'd grown up with in Thorndale, had known all her life. She'd played on the village green with him on market days, had seen him in church on Sundays. He was sweet on Daisy Blenkin . . . She thought of his mother, and the fear his father had expressed for his youngest son that day at Chesscroft. *No, not this . . .*

Charlie gave her a faint smile. "Is it really you, Eleanor? Funny meeting you here like this. I took one in the leg—just like Da that day." She flinched again as another shell landed. "Have you been here long? No, of course not, not any longer than me. Don't worry. You'll get used to it," he said, trying to console her. He coughed, and grimaced in pain, but drew harder on the fag, his hand shaking, and bore it. She looked at his leg. The bone was shattered below the knee, his foot hanging on by a mere scrap of sinew. Her stomach climbed into her throat.

The bearer who'd brought Charlie in cleared his throat to get her attention. His face was grim as he met her eyes. He gave a small shake of his head. "The leg's not the worst of it. He's got a belly wound," he said through tight lips. Eleanor's heart clenched.

"Never mind, Ellie," Charlie said, consoling her. "There's no need to whisper. I already know."

"No," she said. "You hang on. We'll get you patched up, send you back to the CCS—"

"Will you tell my parents you saw me, that I was brave? I saw my brother Will last month. He's a gunner, y'know. Fred's dead, like Matt—he was killed near Ypres. His face crumpled. "Ma will be grieved. And Da . . ." He looked at her. "Who'll help him on the farm now? Tell him to hire one or two of Joss Knaggs's sons. They're dumb as oxen, but they're all big, strong lads, and they know sheep. They'll do."

Her hands were busy, trying to find the damage and stop the bleeding. "You can tell them yourself, Charlie. You'll be home again in no time."

"Nah. It's no Blighty," he said. "It's nice to see someone from home, although you shouldn't be here. You should be somewhere safe and clean."

"We should all be somewhere safe and clean," Eleanor replied. He needed surgery. There wasn't enough light here. They were low on antiseptic and time. He needed Bellford and a sterile theater.

She turned to the bearer. "Corporal Chilcott, I need your help. It won't take long—I'll amputate his leg here, get him back to the CCS—" She saw the pity in the corporal's eyes, and he shook his head. "It's no use, Doc, and I'm needed out there. The yard is full, and there are a hundred others, men with a better chance—" She silenced him with a furious glare.

Charlie brushed her hand with the back of his own, careful not to touch her with the cigarette. His skin was slick with blood and mud, and it marked her. "Don't take on, Ellie. There's no need for it now. Let me die in one piece, aye? I knew when I was hit that I was done. Just unlucky, I guess. I thought maybe when they brought me here . . . Well. Will you tell Da that I was brave?" he asked again. "He'll want to know that. Tell Ma—" He swallowed. "I promised her I'd stay alive and come home safe. I promised." He shut his eyes, and a tear leaked through his lashes, rolled down his cheek. "Tell her I'm sorry I couldn't keep my word. I'm glad you're here, someone from home. You're a fine doctor, and I couldn't ask for better. Tell Da I said that, too."

She grasped his hand, squeezed tight. "Hold on, Charlie," she said. But he scanned the beams of the ceiling as he took another puff, determined to finish his last smoke. She watched as the tip of the cigarette flared red between his dirty fingers, glowed briefly in the dim light of the dugout, then faded to black.

He gave a long exhale and watched the thin plume of smoke rise above him. "Been a good life, all things considered. I would have liked to wed Daisy, but I was too shy to ask her. Wish I'd . . . stolen a . . . kiss at least." Then Charlie's fingers slackened in hers, and the end of the cigarette fell to the dirt floor. She watched the light fade from his eyes.

Her body was numb. She was exhausted—beyond exhausted—after unknowable hours of tending an endless stream of wounded, and now Charlie Nevins— She was crying, tears rolling down her face, and she swiped them away with the back of her hand.

"Eleanor."

She turned to see Fraser standing behind her. He was so tall his head nearly touched the ceiling. She stared at him, wondering if he was real or if she'd wished him here, if she was hallucinating. His brow crumpled, and he gripped her arm, and she knew he was waiting to see if she'd fall apart and stood ready to catch her if she did. "Lass?" he said softly.

"Charlie Nevins, from home," she murmured, looking at Charlie's body again.

"I'm sorry." Fraser reached out to close Charlie's eyes, and he nodded to the bearers. She watched as they carried him out, making room for the next patient. She shivered, and Fraser reached into his pocket and handed her a flask.

"Whisky?" she asked, taking it.

"Rum, now."

She sipped, letting it burn her tongue and throat, explode in her belly, heat her fingers and toes. It was raw and harsh, like everything about this bloody war. "I prefer whisky."

"When did ye last eat, or take a break?"

"There's too many, more outside, and all of them—" She looked around the cellar. So many. She fought back grief and fatigue, suddenly heavy with it, overwhelmed.

"Bellford knows you're here. He said he'd find someone to come as soon as he can."

"Uh-oh," Eleanor said softly.

"Aye. He isn't pleased."

She scanned his face, looking for his own feelings on the matter, but his expression was flat and unreadable.

"I'll help ye where I can. Go outside for a few minutes, get some fresh air," he said gruffly. "Keep your head down."

She longed to be taken into his arms, held, kissed again, but the bearers carried another stretcher between them, and she jumped back, schooled her face to dead calm so he couldn't read her feelings in her eyes, and squared her shoulders. She looked at the patient instead. "Shock. Warm him up, get him on the next ambulance."

She moved on, lifting the temporary dressing on a shattered shoulder. "Fresh bandage, tetanus shot, send him back to the CCS."

She was all efficiency, all determination, her emotions in hard check like a bottle of foaming beer that was stopped too tight and ready to blow. She didn't look at Fraser, couldn't, though he didn't leave her side, and he obeyed every order she issued. She worked and worked and worked, ignoring the ache in her legs and back, her body's demands for food and rest. There wasn't time.

"The guns have moved off," Fraser said, hours later.

She looked up in surprise. She swayed and bumped against a table, light-headed.

He caught her elbow before she fell. "Sit down for a moment." He handed her a cup of water, since there was no time to make tea and the coffee had all but run out, having been fed to men in shock by the spoonful, mixed with rum. She sipped the water and scratched her temples, then frowned. It was unladylike to scratch, but she couldn't help it.

"I'm itchy all over. It must be the dust. I want a bath, and—"

"It isn't dust. It's lice," Fraser said.

She looked at him in horror. "Lice? But lice cause typhus!"

She picked up the long, thick braid that hung over her shoulder and examined it. The russet glow of her hair was dimmed by dust, and the loose strands around her face felt sweat-stiff.

"They like long hair best," Fraser said. "That's why so many VADs and nurses cut their hair short. They get infested by the wounded."

In dismay, she gaped at her hair, her crowning glory, her pride and joy. It was ugly now, crawling with vermin.

She saw the heavy shears on the table and reached for them with shaking hands. She grabbed hold of the braid, but she couldn't make herself do it. Her hands shook, and tears blurred her vision.

Fraser gently took the shears. "Ye did a dozen amputations today, pulled shrapnel out of a hundred men. You're covered with dirt and blood and vomit, but ye can't cut your own hair." He ran his hand over her braid. "Turn around. I'll do it for ye."

She turned her back to him and closed her eyes. She heard the muted click of the scissors and felt the weight of her hair suddenly gone. Short locks fell around her face.

"It's done," he said, and he held up the long braid, the end still tied with ribbon. It reminded her of severed heads and tales of unwanted Tudor wives. She still felt her scalp creeping with lice. She'd have to wait to wash them away with carbolic.

She reached up a hand to touch her neck, bared now. The cut ends of her hair were sharp, and her head felt too light, like it belonged to someone else. She took the braid and stared at it, her own amputation. Tears welled, spilling over, and her shoulders shook. She watched them splash on her hand and on the long locks of infested hair.

He wiped her cheek with the pad of his thumb. "All this fuss over hair?" he said softly.

His eyes were warm, soft as a bed, and he was her Fraser again, her lover. "I must look dreadful."

"Nay, ye look fine. It will be easier to wash now."

"My hair was— It was what made me pretty."

"Nay, it isn't. It's your courage that makes ye beautiful, your spirit and your skill, and your wits, all the things inside ye. And now ye look—" He paused, took in her ill-fitting uniform, the baggy trousers, and the blood on the tunic, and stopped on her short hair. "Ye look even more beautiful, lass." He reached out and coiled his finger in one of the springy curls that lay against her cheek. "I've never met a woman as beautiful, or as fine, or as brave as you, Eleanor Atherton. I wish—" He stopped.

"Fraser," she whispered. She let all the love in her heart show in her eyes.

A dozen emotions crossed his face. She read surprise and regret, fear, and even, for a brief instant, an answering love, but he shut his eyes and stepped back with a soft groan. "We can't do this. Ye can't *feel* this, not for me, not here."

There was a lump in her throat. "Fraser," she said again, a plea.

She heard boots on the stairs, cries of pain, and a call for help, and an exhausted team of bearers carried in two new patients. For a moment she stood still, her eyes locked on Fraser, and he stared back. "More outside," one of the men said to him, and he looked away and left the cellar.

"Doc?" Someone spoke to her, and she turned, saw the patient and the blood, and moved toward him. Somewhere close—too close—another shell landed, shaking the earth, and the war went on.

CHAPTER FORTY-SIX

MARCH 16, 1918

Louis tried not to limp as he got out of the car and walked across the small airfield. He was healed, mostly, the crutches replaced with a cane—a silver-topped one that Fanny had purchased for him, bearing the image of a winged woman, like the masthead of a ship, an angel of protection, a winged Athena. *To Budgie from Fanny* was engraved on it. It was a gaudy thing, but he needed it for now. He wondered how long it would be before he could throw it away, walk across the field with long, sure strides the way he used to. At least he could leave the cane on the ground when he flew. Up there he wasn't a cripple, crawling over the earth, feeling the sickening ache and pull of every halting step.

He scanned the airplanes on the grass—Sopwiths, Nieuports, and Bristols—and felt his breath catch the way it always did when he thought of flying.

"Squadron Leader Lord Somerton?" a corporal asked, approaching him and saluting smartly.

"Yes," Louis replied, still gritting his teeth at the title and the salute, but determined that Squadron Leader Lord Somerton would be a better hero than Lieutenant Louis Chastaine. A true hero. He'd bribed Fanny's fancy French doctors to let him go the day after he'd proposed to her. He'd left the morning after that, leaving Fanny a fond note of farewell and a single red rose.

He inhaled the sharp smell of new varnish on the wings of the planes and listened to the wind singing through the struts—his siren song, calling to him. It felt like coming home, free, renewed, himself again, no one's heir or fiancé.

"I'll see the commander first," he said to the waiting corporal. "Take my things to my quarters."

The lad saluted again and hurried to obey.

Ah, but it was good to be back.

He stroked the shining wingtip of a Sopwith Camel, exactly like the one he'd crashed. It was like an extension of his own body—his own wings. "I'll do better by you," he promised the plane. "We'll fly into history together, eh?"

The plane didn't answer, but he noticed the bullet holes in the fuselage and wondered what had happened to her last pilot.

CHAPTER FORTY-SEVEN

G ood afternoon, lads. Who's in charge here?"

Eleanor looked up from the wound she was bandaging. An officer stood in the doorway of the cellar. His face crumpled into a frown as he looked around. "Am I in the right place?" He was young, and the RAMC badges on his crisp uniform were so new and bright that the glitter of them hurt her eyes. He looked like he'd arrived straight from his tailor in London. He was freshly shaved, his hair neatly trimmed, and she could smell his cologne over the darker smells of the cellar. It made her wonder what she smelled like after being at the aid post for six days.

"Hand me those forceps," she said to him without bothering with an introduction.

He crossed to place them in her bloody hand, and she concentrated on removing a bullet. He leaned in to watch, and she dropped the bullet into the bucket under the table and pressed a clean pad over the wound to stem the bleeding.

"Good work, lad. What are you, a private or a corporal?" Eleanor looked up at him, and he started. "Good Lord, you're a *woman*!"

"I'm Dr. Atherton," she said, and she reached for a blank wound tag, filling it out with quick efficiency. "This is Private Kerr. Bullet wound, left thigh," she said, introducing the patient as well. Kerr didn't bother to salute. He took a drag on his fag and nodded.

"I'm Captain Angus Dalrymple, RAMC, the new MO," the newcomer murmured, still staring at her. She must indeed look a fright. "I'm not sure if I should salute you or kiss your hand."

"My hands are rather bloody, I'm afraid, and I'm a civilian. The uniform is borrowed, though I doubt anyone will want it back now."

"What the dev— I mean, what *are* you doing here?" he asked, checking his language for her sake. She supposed she should be flattered.

"Waiting for you, or for Captain Blair's return. What day is it?"

"It's Thursday."

Then she'd been at the Regimental Aid Post for only five days, not six. It felt more like a month, or a year. She glanced at Fraser, who was bandaging one of the walking wounded for transport. They hadn't spoken since he cut her hair. There hadn't been time.

Dalrymple was still staring at her in astonishment.

But another stretcher arrived. "Dawn attack," one of the bearers said. "Shot through the jaw and the upper arm. Morphine in the field." They left the dugout as quickly as they'd come, going back for more wounded. Eleanor moved toward the patient, but Dalrymple held up his hand. "I'll do it. Got to start somewhere."

Eleanor nodded and washed her hands in the basin. She'd done it so often that the carbolic soap was rubbing her skin off. She now had the hands of a stable boy to go with her shorn hair. Dalrymple had taken off his coat and folded it and was looking for somewhere clean and safe to set it down. She almost laughed. "It's going to get busy," she warned him like an old hand. "I'll go out and do triage in the yard and send the ones who can travel directly back to the CCS."

He blinked at her as if she'd said it in a foreign language.

It was the first time she'd been outside in days. There were signs of spring at last, and it was milder now. At home, the air would smell of thawing earth and green shoots and resound with birdsong as returning flocks sought mates and built nests. Here, the thawing mud blowing off the battlefield stank, carrying the fug of decay, the bitterness of smoke, and the terrible smell of the unburied dead at the front.

Here in front of her the farmyard was choked with dozens of wounded men, fresh off the line. They rested against the stone wall, or sat on piles of debris, or leaned against the old well, waiting for a doctor to tend their wounds. Some smoked, their hands shaking. Others slept, sprawled on the ground. Some silently clutched at their makeshift bandages, their eyes flickering back and forth as they stared at ghosts, or at nothing at all.

Someone caught her arm, and she turned. A lieutenant stood behind her. His face was stark white, the front of his uniform soaked with blood from his chest to his boots. He held his hand over his belly, and more blood oozed between his fingers. "If it's no trouble, might I have some water? I must get back," he said politely.

She wondered how he was able to stand upright, to talk. She caught his arm and tried to guide him toward the door. "Come and sit down, Lieutenant. Let me have a look at you."

He sighed. "I dare not, or I fear I won't get back up. Rather tired at the moment. Just some water, if you please. My men will be looking for me. Our captain was killed yesterday, and they need—" He swayed, and Eleanor put her arm around him.

"Come inside," she said, but he steadied himself, his eyes on the not-so-distant front lines.

"No, thank you, I must get back," he said again. There was a pail on the lip of the well, and he took the dipper out of the pail and drank deeply. "There, now. That's better," he murmured. He straightened his helmet and began to limp back toward the gate.

"Wait—" But a shell landed nearby, and Eleanor flinched. When the smoke cleared, the lieutenant was gone. Then a hail of bullets ricocheted off the stone wall next to her, sending dust and chips of rock into the air. Someone grabbed her arm and hauled her to the ground.

"Get down before they shoot you, you bloody fool!" She looked at the soldiers who surrounded her. They were used to being shot at, had fallen to the ground at the first bullet, made themselves small. Another streak of bullets hit the wall above her, and she shrieked as she clapped her hands over her head and cringed behind the stones.

"What's happening?" she asked the nearest man.

"Fritz has our number," he muttered. "He won't stop until he's killed the lot of us or he's out of bullets."

"But this is an aid post!"

"Maybe he don't know that. Maybe he's color-blind, can't see the red cross," the soldier snapped.

"What do we do?" Eleanor asked.

"Unless you've got a rifle or a Mills bomb and good aim, there's nuthin' to do but sit tight and hope our side gets him."

"Help me," a voice moaned, and Eleanor looked around her. Despite the enemy fire, men still needed care and medical aid.

"I'm coming," she called, and she began to crawl toward the patient.

"Wait a half a mo'—you'd best take this chap's tin hat before a bullet goes through your napper," he said, nodding toward the man beside him.

The lad looked peaceful, appearing to be fast asleep despite the gunfire. "But I can't take his helmet," she said.

He shrugged. "Don't matter a whit to 'im. He's turned up his toes and gone west." She stared at the blank eyes of the dead man and accepted the helmet, putting it on her head. It was heavy. "Now you look like a proper soldier," he said. He held out his wounded arm, and she looked at the long graze. "Is it a Blighty one?" he asked hopefully.

She swallowed. "I don't think so."

He frowned. Another burst of machine-gun fire sounded, and he howled as he took a bullet in the ankle, just inches from Eleanor's own foot.

He forced a grin through gritted teeth as he stared at the shattered bone. "Now, *that's* a Blighty!"

CHAPTER FORTY-EIGHT

Louis looked down at the battlefield below from the front cockpit of the Bristol two-seater. The wind was ice-cold, making his cheeks burn and his teeth ache, but he didn't care. He was glad to be airborne, giddy with it. He'd been assigned to fly reconnaissance missions for now, until his commander was sure he could manage with his gamy leg.

He grinned and leaned over the side. He had a bird's-eye view of the scarred earth below, raw and ugly, but off in the distance, he could see green grass, a bit of hope, a place the war hadn't destroyed.

"We'll fly over C sector first, Cosgrove," he said to the observer seated behind him, holding the heavy camera steady, taking photos for the chaps at HQ. What they made of them Louis didn't know. The ground below was churned to soup, any landmarks blown away by nearly three and a half years of war. The trenches meandered across the blighted land like Frankenstein scars, haphazardly sewn. He thought of all the green, manicured, productive acres at Chesscroft and wondered if the farmland here would ever recover, if the picturesque villages would rise again.

"A little lower, if you please, sir," Cosgrove called. "Toward that farm."

Louis saw the place he meant, just a chimney and a heap of charred rubble. He saw men in the stone-fenced farmyard, wounded men, bandaged and bleeding and lying on the ground. There was a flag planted at the gate, and he could see from here the red cross on it that marked it as an aid post—a busy one, poor blighters, but they were so close to the front that they could spit and hit the trenches from here. A long row of stretchers lay like railway tracks across the yard, the lads on them staring up at him. He swooped down in a graceful dive and waggled the wings, gave them a salute and a cheery wave. Such stunting was forbidden, but if giving the poor wounded buggers a bit of a show would brighten their mood, then he'd happily break the rules. He knew what it felt like to be in pain, to wonder if you were going to live or die or lose your leg. He dropped lower still, ignoring Cosgrove's yelp of objection until it was too late.

He saw the puffs of dust kicked up by the bullets as they traced a dotted line across the farmyard. Those who could cower behind the stone wall did so, or took what cover they could behind the well in the center. Another stream of bullets hit the wall, shattering the top row of stone.

Louis climbed and looked around, seeking the source of the bullets. He spotted the ruins of an army truck, then the red flare of muzzle beneath it as the gunner fired again, giving his hiding place away. It was a scant twenty-five yards out from the farm, close enough to see that it was an aid post, that the soldiers here could do them no harm. "Filthy cowards," Louis muttered.

Cosgrove screeched as the German gun spun, turned in the direction of the plane, and fired.

A bullet whizzed past Louis's face and lodged itself in the wing above his head. Another hit the edge of the cockpit, sending splinters of wood into the air. "There's a gun behind that truck. The bastards are firing at us!" Cosgrove informed him unnecessarily.

"I see him," Louis replied tersely. "But better us than the wounded."

"Sir, are you *trying* to draw his fire?" Cosgrove squawked in horror.

Was he? He thought of the wounded men he'd seen at the CCS, at the destruction of life by distant guns. He thought of Eleanor Atherton and David Blair and all the other doctors and nurses trying to put the wounded back together.

He looked down again. He could see a medic below, crawling around the farmyard on hands and knees like a beetle, head down, rump in the air, tending to the wounded under fire, risking his own bloody life for theirs. The man fell flat as another line of bullets hit the dirt a few feet in front of him. Another minute and they'd have him, Louis thought.

"Yes," he answered Cosgrove. "I'm trying to draw their fire."

He watched the slight figure of the medic rise again and scurry toward a wounded man lying in the open. Now, there was a hero, he thought. Would he let himself be outdone now? "No," he muttered through gritted teeth.

He turned the plane, banked back over the aid post, and flew straight toward the gun, diving as he went. More bullets struck the fuselage of the plane, rocking it, but he kept it steady.

"What the devil are you doing?" Cosgrove screeched. "I mean, what the devil are you doing, *sir*?"

"I'm going to take out that gun," Louis replied calmly.

"*What*? Sir, with all respect, that's not our mission. We're on reconnaissance only. We can go back and give the lads on the ground the coordinates, let the artillery take care of it."

"Not good enough," Louis said. "They'll all be dead by then, or the damned artillery might miscalculate and take out the aid post. We can take care of it ourselves, do some good. Please, take all the pictures you want, old boy. The farm makes a good landmark."

Cosgrove let out a whimper of objection.

Louis concentrated on the machine gun. It was pointed straight at him now, and he saw the deadly staccato flashes as they fired. At least the aid station was being spared. He hoped they'd take the respite to find better shelter. He had just one bomb strapped under the fuselage in case of emergency, one single chance to hit the truck and the gun. He unbuckled the pistol at his hip as well. He'd shoot the bastard's eye out as he flew past if he had to. He focused on his target, ignoring the bullets that sang as they went by, whining. He kept the plane steady, his fingers tight on the lever, waiting for the right moment. Cosgrove was cursing now, wailing, pleading. "This is bloody suicide!"

Was it? No Fanny, no earldom. The medal would be awarded posthumously. But this time, he'd deserve the honor. It would mean something. He gritted his teeth. He was twenty-five, then twenty, then a dozen yards away from the gun, still diving. Bullets checkered the left wing, and he used that to correct his course, knew he was in the crosshairs of the gun.

Five yards. He could see the Germans below, three of them, their mouths gaping black holes of surprise and fear, and he grinned.

Three yards. He pulled the lever, felt the plane lighten as the weight of the bomb dropped away. He pulled up, heading skyward, waiting to hear the explosion, hoping he'd be out of range by then.

It was almost deafening when it came. Cosgrove screeched as a chunk of metal hit the tail, nearly tearing the controls out of Louis's grip. He concentrated on keeping it steady, forcing the nose back up, getting the hell out of there. "How'd we do, Cosgrove?" he asked when he'd gained a little altitude. He had no time to look behind him.

"You got him, sir!" Cosgrove said, his tone filled with disbelief. "You got him!" Louis grinned, hard, sharp, and fast. His leg ached, and he straightened it gingerly.

"One more look," he said, and turned the plane. The controls were sluggish, the tail sloppy. The mechanics would curse him when he got back.

He flew over the farmyard. The medic was on his feet now, hand shading his eyes as he looked skyward. Then he waved, and his helmet fell off. Louis caught a flash of red hair, a white face smeared with dust. He blinked. It couldn't be . . . He was imagining things. She was no doubt safely home in Yorkshire by now, angry as hell at him.

He grinned. At least imagining Eleanor was a damned sight better than seeing a dog flash through his mind.

The engine spluttered, and there was no more time for sightseeing if he wanted to make it back in one piece. With a jaunty salute to the men below, he turned the battered plane back toward the airfield.

CHAPTER FORTY-NINE

Eleanor watched the airplane fly away. "Cheeky bastards, those pilots, but good on him," one of the wounded soldiers said. "Deserves a medal."

"Yes, he does," Eleanor agreed. She wrote the patient's diagnosis on the ticket and pinned it to his tunic.

"Eleanor?"

She turned to see Fraser crossing the yard from the gate, the arm of a wounded man over his shoulders. He lowered the man gently to the ground. "We were pinned down outside the gate. Are ye all right?" He put his finger through a bullet hole in the loose fabric of her shirt. "Christ, lass—"

"I'm fine," she said quickly.

"Was that your pilot?" Fraser asked.

Was it? *Impossible.* "I doubt it. Louis is probably still in Paris."

She turned to the wounded man and recognized him as the lieutenant who'd wanted a drink of water so he could return to his men. He peered up at her now, his eyes glazed and heavy lidded. "Must be hurt worse than I thought," he murmured.

She moved his hand away from his wounded belly. The ragged hole went straight through. She could see his ribs and spine, and she wondered how he'd managed to keep going, to walk in off the line. She met Fraser's eyes for a split second. There was nothing to be done.

"Tell my men—" Red bubbles frothed on the lieutenant's lips. "Tell them—" She took a vial of morphine from Fraser and injected the patient, then clasped his hand in hers as it took effect, easing his pain.

"Lie still, Lieutenant," she said gently.

Fraser reached for the metal disk around his neck and read his name. "Joseph Williams," he said. She swallowed and nodded.

"Lie still, Joseph. I'll tell your men you died a hero."

He smiled faintly, and then he was gone, and there was nothing to do but hurry on and try to save the next man, for Joseph Williams's sake, for the sakes of all the ones who couldn't be saved.

When the flood of wounded let up at last and three ambulances were full and ready to go back to the CCS, Captain Dalrymple handed her a sheaf of papers. "I've saved you a place on one of the ambulances," he said. "Go while it's still quiet." He looked her over from head to toe and shook his head. She knew she was muddy, bloody, and filthy and that she stank. And her hair— She didn't want to think about that.

"Thank you for your help, Dr. Atherton. I never imagined I'd say this to a woman, and certainly not here on the front lines, but you're a fine doctor." Someone called him, and he hurried away.

Eleanor looked at Fraser. "Will you be coming back to the CCS as well?"

He shook his head, his expression flat. "No. My week of light duty is up. Dalrymple can take my stitches out. I'm needed here."

"Oh," she said. "Oh, I see."

He made a sound low in his throat. "Don't do that, Eleanor. Not now. You can't stay, and I can't go. We should never—" He swallowed and looked away. "What happened between us—it can't happen again."

She met his gaze bravely. "Do you regret it, then?"

He shut his eyes. "No, of course not."

She followed his gaze to the ambulance. They were waiting for her, and there wasn't much time. She wanted to stay, even here, if it meant being with him. It was a woman's decision as much as a doctor's. More, perhaps. She pulled him behind a stub of broken wall. It offered scant privacy, but there was nowhere else. The yard bustled with wounded, with men watching others, looking for danger, or something to distract them from pain and war.

"Fraser, I want to stay in France. Not at the CCS, of course, but with the Red Cross. We could see each other now and then, perhaps, and—"

His eyes snapped back to her, and he scowled. "Don't be daft. Ye could be killed, and I'll have that on my conscience, too." He looked at her sleeve, at the bullet hole. "That one was close. Too close. If not for ye, then for me. The next one— Look, this is no place for ye. Go home, Eleanor. Forget all this, and me. Especially me."

She gritted her teeth. "I don't want to forget. I'm tired of secrets and half-truths, and I can't go home, not now. What would I be? 'All this,' as you call it, has changed me. You've changed me. Fraser, I lo—"

"No!" He made a gesture to cut her off, to keep her from saying it, but she let it show in her eyes, saw him read her love there and understand. He groaned again.

"Damn it, lass, this isn't the time or the place." He lowered his eyes to her lips, and she swallowed, remembered his mouth on hers, his body surrounding her, inside her, and knew by the way his jaw tightened that he felt it, too. She wanted him to hold her, to kiss her, to touch her, but he stared at the ground and said nothing. He didn't walk away, and that was something.

"When something is right, even amid something so terribly

wrong, I've learned to find it, to feel it. You taught me that. I want more than one night with you, Fraser—I want everything."

He scowled. "You think we have a future? Here? That night only happened because we both thought it was goodbye. What else could it have been but goodbye? No, there's a war on, and there is no future, not for anyone."

"A kiss should never mean goodbye. For me, kissing you was the start of something, not the end." She swept her hand around the ruined farmyard. "There has to be a reason why I'm here, why you're here, don't you see that? We might never have met, but we did. I've done things, seen things here I never thought I'd see. Not just terrible things, but kindness, and bravery, and hope. And love, Fraser, that as well."

He looked ragged. "Love?" The word came out rough, as if it hurt him to say it. "There's no place for love in the middle of a war. If you've learned nothing else here, surely ye can see that. God, ye should never have come here. It will destroy all that ye are even if it doesn't kill ye."

She swallowed. "None of us are what we were, but after the war ends, the world will change—"

"What if it's never over?" he muttered bitterly. "What if the killing and the dying never stops?" He pointed to a wooden door, once painted bright blue, but faded now, hanging off its torn hinges and riddled with bullet holes. "What if next time a bullet finds its mark, it's me, or you? I couldn't bear it, not now. And seeing ye here in this place, at the front these past few days, under fire, riddled with lice, in constant danger, has been torment." He shut his eyes. "I don't want to fret for ye, worry over ye, or anyone. I've spent all the months—years—I've been here making sure I don't have attachments, that there's no one to mourn me when I die, no one I'll regret leaving behind. I've lived longer than most bearers. I've been lucky so far, but luck runs out here. I doubt I'll see home again, and I'd made my peace with that." He scanned her face. "That was before ye came, before I—" He turned his head away and looked around him, scanning the devastated farm and the ambulance, visible through a shattered window in the broken wall. Men watched from the loaded vehicle, bandaged, waiting, and curious. He glared at them, moved so Eleanor was concealed behind him, the way he'd done on the train. It made her love him all the more. "Go," he said over his shoulder. "There's no place here for love. There's only death here."

She walked around him and stood before him, forcing him to look at her, to ignore the waiting ambulance, the stares, the activity on the other side of the wall. "Seeds take root in the worst ground, where the earth has been scarred and burned almost beyond bearing. Poppies and wild roses grow on the graves here, life amid death. And love—the men who die don't curse the enemy, they speak of loved ones, of home, of friendship." He flicked a glance over her, hopeful for an instant before he closed his eyes tight.

"Not all. Some fight death, Eleanor. They don't slip away quietly, they rage against the frailty of their own bodies, the injustice of this bloody war. They suffer, mourn the living. I don't want to die like that, knowing I'm leaving someone to heartache and torment, wondering if I died a hero or in agony. Even heroes die in agony. Ye know that. You've *seen* it."

She stepped closer, tried to touch him, but he pulled away. She dropped her hand to her side. "All I know is that no matter what happens, I won't forget you. You will be my first thought in the morning and my last one at night, always, for as long as I live. I will love you, and wait for you, and look for you once this war is over—"

"When it's over," he interrupted bitterly. "If we'd met on the street, in Edinburgh or London, or anywhere else, ye'd have passed by me without a second glance. I'm naught but a gamekeeper's son, and you're a doctor. You'd never even have looked at me."

"I'm looking now, Fraser MacLeod, and I won't look away again."

He scanned her face. "Ye think ye mean it, but what of your family, your friends, your pilot?"

Frustration welled in her breast. She was exhausted. She wanted a bath, and bed. More than that, she wanted Fraser MacLeod. They were both bloody and dirty and unfit for any other company, but they were fit for each other. More than fit—right, perfect—and he couldn't see it, or refused to. "I don't care a whit about class or fortune or what other people think. We can make a new future, our own future. I want to live life on my own terms. Don't you see? *You* taught me that—courage, and bravery, and compassion." She met his eyes. "You taught me how to love."

There was agony in his eyes as he reached out and touched her cheek gently, then dropped his hand. "I should have left ye alone for both our sakes. It's not real, lass. Those qualities were always part of ye. It's what I lo—" He stopped himself. "Don't stay. Go home, lass. Let me have that, the knowledge that you're safe," he pleaded.

She shook her head. "I won't leave you."

"Then go to Paris, find your flier."

She gritted her teeth. "He's not *my* flier."

"Then Blair. He's a good man, a suitable man, of your own class. This is because I was your first, that's all, because we're here, and ye think ye see a friend, an ally. I'm not that. I used ye. I used ye when the wounded came in, and I used ye the way a soldier uses a convenient woman." His voice was ragged, raw. His eyes were full of anger and pain. How unlike the cool, flat, guarded way he'd looked at her the first time they'd met.

"No."

He made a sound low in his throat, frustration, loss. "You're the damnedest woman I've ever met, Eleanor Atherton. Goodbye. Wherever ye go from here, I wish ye luck."

He tried to turn away, to go, but she caught his sleeve and held on, shaking his arm like a terrier until he looked at her. "I love you," she said again. He scanned her face as if he wanted to memorize it, to hold a piece of her with him.

He loved her, and he couldn't hide it. Her heart bloomed under the dirty soldier's tunic.

"You won't die, Fraser. Don't you dare. Promise me."

"I can't promise ye that." He touched her cheek, a brief brush of his knuckles. "I wish— Lass, if ye love me, then make me a promise. Promise me you'll go home."

She reached inside his open greatcoat and laid her hand on the rough wool of his tunic, over his heart. "I am home, Fraser."

A soldier stepped around the building, his eyes darting over them. He cleared his throat. "Driver's ready to head back, Doc."

Fraser grabbed her wrist and moved her hand off his chest. "She's coming."

The soldier turned and left them.

"Will you kiss me, Fraser MacLeod?"

He stared down at her for a moment, and she held her breath, waiting, but he stepped back, out of reach, and looked at her with bitter anguish in his eyes. "Better not. Better to leave it. Otherwise you'll be in my thoughts, in my blood, a distraction. I can't kiss ye, lass, not for goodbye."

"Sergeant?" someone called him, and he lifted his head, his eyes on her for a moment more.

"Coming," he replied.

He turned and walked away from her without looking back.

CHAPTER FIFTY

MARCH 20, 1918

Someone shook Eleanor awake when they arrived at the CCS, and she climbed out of the ambulance, her body stiff and sore and weary. She'd left Fraser at the aid post. She'd been at the front for six days, and here before that for three weeks, and her entire life had changed. The CCS felt as familiar to her as home. A number of patients sat outside the tents, enjoying the mild air of the last day of winter or waiting for transport back to the front or onward to other hospitals and the next step in their long journey home.

"What have we got?" a doctor she didn't know asked as the orderlies began to unload the wounded from the ambulance she'd arrived in. She scanned his unfamiliar face. Some things had changed here after all.

"Broken leg, tibia," she said. "Treated with antiseptic, splinted in the field, tetanus shot given."

He looked at the splint. "Someone up there did a damn fine job."

"That would be me," she said, and he looked at her in surprise.

"Good God, you're a woman!"

"And a doctor."

"Are you really? I'm Captain James Wilmot by the way, surgeon, fresh from England. I was assigned to Number 4 General Hospital at Amiens, but no sooner did I arrive there than they sent me here. I'm to stay until your surgeon returns."

"Captain Blair isn't back yet?"

"No. Delayed, I understand," Wilmot said.

"Miss Atherton," she heard Matron Connolly say, her tone sour, and she turned to see the matron leading a phalanx of nursing sisters out to tend the new casualties. "Into more trouble, I see. One can be hanged for impersonating a soldier—or a doctor, for that matter."

"Impersonating? I say, where did you attend medical school?" Wilmot asked.

Eleanor ignored him, keeping her eyes on Matron Connolly. "Captain Blair's brother was dying. I merely took his place for a few days so he could go to him—"

Wilmot frowned. "There *are* rumors of German spies impersonating medical personnel. Where did you say you're from?"

"I'm from Yorkshire," Eleanor said, glaring at him. "I've been at a frontline aid post for several days. We were busy with patients for all that time. There are a number of men who saw me there—Sergeant MacLeod, Corporal Chilcott, and Captain Dalrymple, to name a few. Dalrymple's the new medical officer—"

"Angus Dalrymple? From Aberdeen?" Wilmot said. "Old classmate of mine. Fine fellow."

Curious eyes were watching them even as the patients were being unloaded from the ambulances, and Eleanor turned to the men she'd treated at the aid post and began with the first in the queue. "This man needs a bed, Matron, and—" Eleanor began.

"I don't take orders from you!" the nurse said. "I'm going to get the colonel at once."

Wilmot whistled softly as she strode away. "Why are matrons always so bloody fierce? So what's it like up there at the front? I've never been."

She looked at his jolly face, the cocky half smile, the easy way he stood as if he were on holiday, as if the wounded could wait.

She thought of Charlie's death, and the agony and terror of trying to save lives while bombs fell and bullets flew. And she thought of Fraser. She felt a lump form in her throat, and she moved on to the next patient without answering his question.

"This man's been blinded. There's mud embedded around his eyes, and it will need to be cleaned out under anesthetic," she said, keeping her comments to the treatment of the wounded.

"I say," Wilmot muttered, frowning as he stared at the soldier's horribly swollen eyes.

"There are three gas cases in the second ambulance," she added, moving on. "Two fractures—a collarbone and a rib, and four amputations that will need to be checked and monitored. There are six men in shock, and three sick."

"Sick? Is it influenza?" Wilmot asked.

"Or trench fever, or typhus, or any number of other things," she said.

"Dr. Atherton!" Reverend Strong was leading the gas cases. Their eyes were bandaged, and they held one another's shoulders in a slow, shuffling parade. The chaplain held the elbow of the man in front, guiding the queue. "How nice to see you back safely." He barely glanced at her clothing. "Captain Blair sent word he'll be returning in the morning."

"His brother?" she asked.

He shook his head. "The captain was with him at the end, but there was nothing to be done. At least he got to say goodbye, thanks to you. It was a kind thing, but rather a dangerous one. The colonel was most concerned about you."

"Dr. Atherton!" She heard the colonel's bellow clear across the CCS. He was striding toward her with Matron Connolly following.

"Uh-oh," Wilmot murmured. "Looks like more trouble."

She waited for the colonel to reach her side. He gaped at her, red-faced and affronted, taking in her rumpled uniform, her baggy britches. "You've managed to thwart the rules and raise holy hell yet again."

"Really, sir, I must object to such language in front of a woman," Wilmot said, and Bellford glared at him.

"Dr. Atherton has been here for several weeks. I daresay she has heard all the inappropriate language there is. In fact, it is entirely likely that a number of new words have been coined just for her."

Eleanor blushed, and she jumped aside as a stretcher was carried past.

Bellford looked at the patient, then at the others coming off the ambulances. "Bad, was it?" he asked her quietly.

"Yes, sir," she said soberly.

"Don't blame Dr. Atherton, Colonel. It took a great deal of courage to do what she did," Reverend Strong interrupted. The gas cases cocked their bandaged heads to listen. "Captain Blair's brother—"

Colonel Bellford held up his hand. "Yes, I know, Reverend." He turned to the matron. "Looks like we have wounded to see to. Prepare the surgical cases for Captain Wilmot. I'll be along shortly." He waited for her to obey his orders and move away before he turned back to Eleanor.

"I may admire the sentiment that caused you to undertake such a foolish, dangerous mission, and the skill it took to provide medical care in such a rude place, under fire, but not from you, not from a woman. Can you imagine the difficulties it would have caused if you'd been killed?"

"Yes, sir," she said again, as if she truly was a soldier.

"Your brother sent a letter. He agrees with Matron Connolly. He threatened to report you and me and to have me relieved of my duties and court-martialed if I didn't send you home at once. You could also be arrested, imprisoned by our side, or even hanged by the enemy."

"So Matron tells me," she murmured. "Did my brother say—"

"I promised to send you home the moment you arrived back—*if* you arrived back. I could not spare anyone to go and fetch you. I am relieved to see you safe, but I cannot allow you to stay any longer. You must leave at once."

"If I may, sir, it's late. It will be night soon," the chaplain said.

"Is it?" one of the gas cases said. "No wonder it's dark."

"I daresay Dr. Atherton could use a meal, and a chance to bathe and change her clothes. By the look of her, I'd say a night's rest wouldn't go amiss, sir," Strong added.

Bellford took in her filthy uniform and her dirty face and paused at the ruin of her hair. He sighed. "You will leave at first light, is that clear?"

Corporal Swiftwood appeared. His sandy brows rose at the sight of Eleanor in trousers. "You're wanted in theater at once, Colonel."

"Very well, Corporal," Bellford said. He gave Eleanor one last look. "First thing in the morning, Dr. Atherton," he reminded her. "I am so very tired of saying those words. This time I expect to be obeyed, or I will arrest you myself. For the final time, this is goodbye." He turned on his heel and strode away.

"And good riddance," Swiftwood whispered under his breath, just loud enough for Eleanor to hear, before he followed his commander.

Reverend Strong touched her arm. "The colonel was worried about you. Fortunately, you're back safe and sound, and we'll have Captain Blair back shortly as well. Go and get cleaned up, my dear, have a hot meal, and get some rest." He turned back to his gas cases. "Come along, lads. We'll bathe your poor eyes, and get you washed and fed, too. You'll feel better in no time at all."

Eleanor stood beside the ambulances and looked up at the darkening sky, watched the stars come out one by one. She listened to the wind, to the sounds from inside the tents—the moans of pain, the bark of medical orders, the soothing whispers. She heard the sluice of water as the orderlies and drivers washed out the backs of the ambulances. But something was different. She cocked her head.

The guns had fallen silent.

CHAPTER FIFTY-ONE

4:45 A.M., MARCH 21, 1918

The first shell exploded before dawn. Eleanor woke with a cry, and for a moment she thought she was back at the aid post, under fire.

She took in the walls of the visitor's quarters at the CCS. She saw her suitcase and her black doctor's bag by the door, ready for her departure. It was just a dream—or a nightmare, perhaps.

But another shell howled overhead before landing in the field somewhere beyond the triage tent, or perhaps closer. The concussion shook the walls of the hut and knocked the wind from her lungs, replacing it with stark terror.

She forced herself up, searched the dark with shaking fingers, found her clothes, and dressed. She shoved her feet into her shoes and hurried out to find someone who might know what was happening, why they were shelling a hospital.

The next bomb came closer still, and clods of dirt rained down on the duckboards, on the ward tents, and on her. She ducked into the first tent she came to, but another explosion ripped the canvas wall, and a chunk of shrapnel soared past her face and buried itself in the floor a few feet away, sending up a hail of splinters. Around her, the clean and orderly ward was suddenly in chaos.

A nurse rushed past her, fleeing in terror. Others were struggling to control wounded men who were climbing out of their beds to find cover. So many people were screaming, calling for help, shouting orders. The next shell drowned it all out. The acrid smell of smoke and hot metal hung in the air, and the lamps swung on their hooks, casting swirling shadows, illuminating faces white with fear, the slick red ooze of fresh blood, the semaphore wave of torn canvas flapping in the wind. She knew there must be screaming, but Eleanor could only hear the pounding of her own heart and the ringing in her ears. The explosions were endless now, one after the other, making the earth shudder. She stumbled against a bed and pushed her way along the ward.

Someone caught her sleeve, and she spun. Private Gibbons stood behind her, his face placid, even now, in all this. *Dumb as a sheep*, David Blair called him. *Not a sheep, but a lamb of God*, the chaplain said.

He leaned close and shouted, "The colonel said to find somebody in charge. Is that you, miss? I'm to say the Huns are advancing and we're to evacuate as many wounded as possible, and the nurses are to go with them. What are your orders?"

Her orders? She gaped at him. She wasn't in charge. She was *leaving*. "Where's the colonel? Where's Captain Wilmot?" she asked. She cried out and ducked instinctively as another shell exploded, but Gibbons didn't even flinch. "It's all right, miss. They're shelling the artillery posts behind us. They'll get the range in a minute or two and we'll be safe."

Safe? She looked at the madness around her. They didn't have a minute or two. She heard the whine of another incoming shell and grabbed hold of the nearest bed frame. She saw the little table in the middle of the ward begin to topple, watched as the cracked vase on it slid toward destruction. It was a piece of Limoges, something Gibbons had found in the ruins of a farmhouse. It had probably been a treasured heirloom once, but it was badly chipped now, almost worthless. Gibbons had rescued it anyway, brought it back, and filled it with paper flowers to add a bit of cheer to the ward. "A symbol of hope and survival," Reverend Strong had said with a smile when he saw it. Eleanor leaped forward, caught the vase before it could hit the floor, and cradled it in her hands.

"Where is Colonel Bellford?" she asked Gibbons again.

His smile faded. "He's hurt, miss. Shrapnel in his back."

"And Captain Wilmot?"

"Dead, miss. I saw the chaplain cover his face."

She stared at him. Bellford was the commander, a surgeon. The *only* surgeon, if Wilmot was— She swallowed. Was there no one else— a major, a captain, any medical officer at all? But she knew the answer to that. They needed someone in charge, a doctor. If the colonel was wounded, then there was no one to see to all this, to manage. As the head nurse, the matron held an officer's rank. Surely she could take command. Eleanor looked around again at the panic. Where *was* the matron? She saw nurses struggling and crying and cringing at every shell, but Matron Connolly wasn't among them. Patients wailed, afraid that this time, here where it was supposed to be safe, death had found them after all. They needed order, a calm, steady hand, someone to take charge, to *manage* all of this. Was it even possible? She was afraid, too, terrified. But Gibbons was still next to her, still waiting.

"Where are we to go?" she asked him. "Did the colonel say?"

"Aye, miss, to the railhead."

Four miles away.

"Wounded coming in!" Corporal Swiftwood shouted from the doorway.

"We can't!" a nurse sobbed, wringing her hands. Another shell soared overhead, and she screamed and dropped to her knees with her hands over her ears. The tent shuddered, and the nurse screamed again.

No, they couldn't manage any of this. And yet they had to. The wounded were coming, counting on them.

Eleanor looked at the shaking, crying nurse, at Swiftwood's frown as he surveyed the chaos in the tent, at Gibbons's placid expression.

"There are at least fifty wounded men outside already, and more coming," Swiftwood said. "There'll be a counterattack, hundreds more . . ."

Hundreds? Eleanor swallowed.

She turned to Gibbons first. "Organize the walking cases and get them on the road to the station at once. Ask Reverend Strong to divert the ambulances to another CCS if possible, tell them we can only take those who can't be transported any farther. Send as many as possible directly to the railhead," she ordered. She grabbed the sobbing nurse still curled on the floor and hauled her to her feet. "Go and gather supplies—bandages and morphine and surgical instruments, anything we might need. I need a nurse and an orderly here, but everyone else must go to the railhead. Set up a dressing station there. The rest—" She stopped and looked around, feeling hopelessness threaten to cave her in. She took a deep breath, gathering herself. "We'll have to do our best."

She looked at Swiftwood. For once the orderly wasn't sneering at her because she was a woman and a civilian. He was listening, nodding, ready to obey, glad to have someone in charge—even her.

She needed to speak to the colonel. She hurried toward his quarters, skirted a shell hole in the middle of the camp, ran past walking wounded and men lying on stretchers. One man was screaming, fighting the nurses, and she paused to check. "Morphine," she ordered, and hurried on.

One wall of Bellford's hut was gone. She saw the commander lying on the floor, facedown, his back slick with blood. Matron Connolly was beside him, pressing a dressing to his torn flesh, trying to stop the bleeding, her face gray. Eleanor knelt beside her, took the cloth, and looked underneath. Shards of shrapnel stuck out of Bellford's back like quills.

"He needs surgery."

"And who's to do it?" Connolly snapped. "Captain Wilmot is dead and the colonel won't live to see the nearest hospital. We've no surgeon, and we're under fire."

Eleanor held her breath for an instant. "I'll do it."

Connolly looked up, her lips curled back in disdain. *"You?"*

Eleanor felt calm determination fill her. She'd been at the aid post and managed. She'd saved lives, had stayed steady, sure, and competent through all of it. There was no one else; no choice. She met the nurse's glare with one of her own.

"Me," she said firmly. She held the nurse's icy stare until the matron looked away first, knowing what would happen if the commander was sent on without treatment. Infection would set in, gangrene, and he'd die in agony. Surgery was his only chance.

"Then I'll assist," the matron said. "You'll need someone to give anesthesia." Eleanor began to rise to make ready, but Matron Connolly caught her wrist. "You will not let him die," she said fiercely.

Eleanor stared down at the nurse's hand on her skin, staining her with the colonel's blood, marking her. Like a blood oath she'd once seen Louis and Edward perform. "I won't let him die," she promised. "Now help me get him into the theater."

The matron nodded and got to her feet.

CHAPTER FIFTY-TWO

Reverend Strong pushed aside the curtain and peered into the operating theater. Matron Connolly looked up from the anesthesia mask.

"How's the colonel?" the chaplain asked.

"Holding his own. Nearly done," Eleanor said. "Is there news?"

"It's a major offensive. The Germans are advancing fast. Our troops are retreating. We haven't much time. We've got orders to gather what supplies and equipment we can and leave at once." His eyes fell to the unconscious man on the table. "The orders say the wounded must be divided into two groups—those who can walk to the railhead, and . . . and those who can't."

"When will transport arrive for them?" Eleanor asked.

The chaplain's brow furrowed. "It won't. There's no time. The poor lads who can't walk are to be left behind. We must trust that the Germans will behave decently and care for our wounded."

Eleanor's heart kicked, but she kept her hands steady and took a breath behind the surgical mask. She met Matron Connolly's eyes. The nurse had held the ether mask for nearly two hours, watching Eleanor like a hawk watches prey.

"How much time have we got?" Eleanor asked the chaplain.

"None at all. There's an officer outside, a major, insisting we go at once. He wants us to leave the colonel if he's—" The chaplain's eyes flicked toward the man on the table.

Eleanor shook her head. "I won't leave him." She glanced at Matron Connolly and saw the same determination in her eyes. "Ten minutes more. Tell the major that," Eleanor said.

The chaplain nodded and left.

An hour later, Eleanor emerged from the operating theater to find the CCS in an uproar. Reverend Strong was trying to sort the patients into two groups—the walking wounded and the ones who'd have to stay—but they refused to allow it. "We're not leaving anyone behind," a soldier called to the red-faced major in charge.

"That's insubordination! Orders are orders. There's nothing else for it. We'll all suffer. Can you not see that?" the major bellowed. "The Huns are coming!"

The guns had shifted, and the noise was coming from the other direction. It meant the Germans were bombarding the forward trenches. *Fraser* . . . Panic tightened her throat and made her tremble. No. He was lucky, smart—he couldn't die. She couldn't bear that. She looked around her at the men waiting for someone to *fix* this. Fraser would if he were here. He wouldn't leave anyone behind.

She looked at the lightly wounded soldiers supporting their bleeding chums, or carrying badly wounded comrades in their arms, or crouched beside men lying on the ground, barely conscious.

"The Germans have already taken our front lines," the major bellowed. He stabbed a finger toward the front. "Any moment they'll come up that road and capture us all."

"We're not leaving our mates!" one man insisted again, even as he looked along the road, following the major's point, looking for Germans. Nurses and orderlies stood silent, wide-eyed and grim.

Eleanor looked at the wounded and saw fear as well as brave determination. They needed an officer, and hope, in the face of disaster. They hadn't fled, they'd stayed for their comrades. Eleanor felt fierce pride course through her tired body, giving her strength. What would Fraser do? What could she do? "There are stretchers and gurneys in the supply closets," she called out. "We'll take everyone. There's an aid post at the railhead." It wouldn't be easy.

"You'll what?" the major bellowed at her, but everyone was moving, jumping to, flowing around the officer like a river, ignoring him, going to gather equipment.

A soldier grinned at her. "I can carry my mate, Sister," he said. "There's a bullet in his leg, but I'll get him there."

"Not 'Sister,' Private. This is *Dr.* Atherton," the chaplain told him proudly.

He helped two men lift a semiconscious soldier onto a stretcher. They were both wounded as well, and tired, but they carried their friend gently.

"How many men can your lorries take?" Eleanor asked the major.

He gaped at her. "Those trucks are to take supplies so they don't fall into German hands, and for transporting the nurses and VADs—and you."

Eleanor raised her chin. "I can walk."

"So can I," a VAD said, coming to stand behind her. "You can give my place to one of the lads."

"And mine," a nurse said. "If Dr. Atherton can walk, then I can, too."

"We could be overrun on the road," the major spluttered. "Do you know what the Huns do to women? Do you remember Edith Cavell? It didn't matter to them that she was a woman and a nurse. They executed her as a spy. *A spy!*"

The women stayed where they were.

The major stared at Eleanor, his face red with fury. "This is mutiny!"

"This is honor, and courage," Eleanor replied. She looked at the VADs. "The colonel will need to be taken in the first vehicle. Tell the orderlies—"

"You can tell us what you need, miss," a soldier said, crowding forward eagerly with a dozen others. "We'll do whatever you say."

Eleanor nodded. "Then we'd better get on. I'll gather a few supplies—"

"Only what you can carry," the major snapped.

"I have pockets, miss, and my pack," a soldier offered.

"So have I."

"Load me up with boxes, heavy as you please, and I'll haul 'em for ye," another said. "I'm used to carryin' boxes of ammunition."

Half an hour later, the little convoy of trucks was on the way up the road, leaving the CCS behind, the tattered tents and broken huts sitting forlornly in the field, waiting for the Germans. Eleanor took only her medical bag and walked behind the ambulance that carried the colonel, who was still unconscious, but alive. Matron Connolly sat beside him, monitoring his vital signs. Three other badly wounded men lay beside the colonel, well dosed with morphine so they wouldn't feel the terrible jolting of the rough road.

The major marched up beside her, walking with the rest of the able-bodied. "I don't know how you managed to do this. It's against orders, and regulations. Damn the RAMC."

"But every man is safe," she said. "Isn't that a good thing?"

"We've left the tents. I had orders to bring the tents," he said fretfully.

"Were you at the front, Major? The 51st Highlanders—"

She stopped at the look on his face. "The Germans came through their part of the line first, poor blighters."

She felt her stomach tense. "There's an aid post there, near Sauvigny, in an old farm. Do you know if they're safe, if they got out?"

The officer sighed and shook his head. "It's chaos all along the front. There's no way to know. Bloody bad business. Field ambulances and aid posts move with the troops. If not—"

She stumbled, and he caught her arm. "Don't you dare faint on me now, not after all the trouble you've caused. We haven't got time for an attack of the vapors. This is precisely why I was ordered to get women out first."

"She won't faint," Matron Connolly called down to him from the back of the ambulance. "She's a doctor, and a good surgeon. My rank is equivalent to that of a lieutenant colonel. I outrank you in medical matters. You will address her with respect, Major."

For a moment the major frowned at them both. Then he strode away, bellowing orders to move faster.

"Colonel Bellford is in pain. Will you come up and check on him?" Matron Connolly said calmly, though her brow was furrowed with concern.

Eleanor climbed into the back of the truck and bent over the colonel. His pulse was fast and thin under her fingers. He flinched at her touch. "He needs a transfusion," Connolly muttered. "Are you certain you got all the fragments? Of course you did. I didn't mean—" She looked at Eleanor. "I meant what I told the major. You're a good doctor. I was perhaps . . ." She let the rest of the apology trail away. Every line of the matron's body was stiff with pride and duty. Her veil was askew, and locks of salt-and-pepper hair straggled over a tired face streaked with dust. Her usually pristine uniform was smudged and bloody, but her eyes were alive, burning like brands, determined and brave—the coldness had thawed for a moment. "Thank you," Matron Connolly finished. "I was wrong."

Eleanor gaped at her, wondering for a moment if it was sarcasm or a true compliment, or an olive branch. She suddenly felt the weight of everything press in on her. All the horror and exhaustion of the aid station, the dying faces, Charlie Nevins, the soldier with the Blighty ankle, Wilmot, and Captain Greaves all filled her mind and overwhelmed her with crushing grief. And worry for Fraser—was he alive, safe, or was he lying somewhere on the battlefield, wounded and alone, possibly dying? She couldn't bear that.

She looked out at the ragged caravan valiantly struggling toward the railhead, and hope. Behind them, she saw the terrible black pall of smoke, and she felt the impact of every shell that shook the world.

She thought of Captain Wilmot, who'd been in France for less than a fortnight, and the four nurses and three patients who'd died along with him at the CCS. She grieved for David Blair's brother, and for David, caught in this maelstrom somewhere. Was he gone, too? And beside her, Colonel Bellford moaned, hovering somewhere between life and death.

They all were.

Now she was gripped by the sheer terror of waking in the night to find bombs falling around her. For a moment she thought it was simply the weight of fear crushing the air from her lungs, but it was so much more than that. The matron's compliment, laid atop the terrible danger, suffering, and death, tipped the scales and shattered her.

You're a good doctor. Was she? She didn't know anymore. The terrible secret, the loss of everything she thought she was, fear for Fraser, and the horrors of war had taken her pride, her strength, her nerve, and left her hollow. It wasn't enough—*she* wasn't enough. Tears slid down her cheeks, and she let them drop unchecked. She felt shame and fear and she was so terribly tired.

"Buck up. It's just shock. I meant it," the matron said. "Without you, Colonel Bellford would be dead. So would Lieutenant Findlay, and many others, I suspect."

But Eleanor felt everything rushing upward. "But I'm not. I cheated," she said, the terrible admission bursting out at last. Had she known all along, suspected what Edward had done? Was the sin hers after all? She *should* have realized . . . "I shouldn't be a doctor—shouldn't be here."

If she expected the nurse to call her an imposter, to rail at her, it didn't happen. She simply waited for her to continue. Now it was out at last, and there was no taking it back. The admission had tumbled out, shaken loose by everything she'd endured, as if the bombs had opened her soul and exposed the truth to light at last.

"I've wanted to be a doctor for as long as I could remember. I'd watch my father heal the sick, listen as he spoke of it. He taught us—my brother and me—how the body works, spoke of setting bones and new medicines. He taught us that there is no nobler calling than medicine, no better way to serve humanity, and I believed him.

"I didn't realize he didn't mean me, a girl. He meant my brother, Edward. He intended all along for Edward to be a doctor, to follow in his footsteps, make him proud. I was simply expected to *marry* a doctor. But I didn't know that. When my father spoke of university and medical school, I assumed I'd go with Edward to take the entrance exam, that I'd train beside my brother, that we'd both become doctors." She studied her hands. "I found out later that my father only allowed me to write the exam to prick Edward's pride, to shame him into working harder so he wouldn't be outdone by a mere girl. My father only let me write the exam because he was sure I'd fail, learn my place at last, and that would be the end of it."

"But you didn't fail," Matron Connolly said.

Eleanor shut her eyes. "I did fail. I studied, I was ready, I knew *everything*. But when I walked into the examination hall with Edward, I was the only woman there. The proctor tried to send me home. The men around me hated me on sight, just for being there, for daring—"

She swallowed. "I—I lost my nerve. I couldn't remember anything. I struggled with the simplest of questions, things I *knew* the answers to. I froze. When the exam ended I knew I'd failed."

"So what did you do?"

She clenched her hands into helpless fists, just as she'd done that day. "My brother was waiting for me after the exam. I knew by the look on his face he'd done well. Edward has always been so sure of himself, so charming, so good with people, all the things I'm not. What could I do? I set my booklet on the pile with the others and left the room. Edward said he'd forgotten something and went back. I was devastated, and I barely noticed. Then we went home to wait for the results. It took a month, and I spent all those days wondering what I was going to do now, who I'd be if I couldn't be a doctor. I didn't know. I still don't know what I would have done, or what I'll do if . . ." She swallowed hard, her throat closing.

"And?" the matron prompted.

"And the results arrived, and somehow I'd passed."

"How?" Matron Connolly asked.

Eleanor shut her eyes. She remembered Edward's face as he'd told her, the terrible haughtiness. "My brother and I have the same first initial, you see, and a similar second one. Both of us are E. Atherton. He went back in and wrote 'Miss' in front of his own initials. They mistook his examination for mine."

"And you had no idea?"

She shook her head. "I should have suspected, I suppose. I knew I hadn't done well, but I *wanted* to go to university. I was . . . surprised . . . to say the least, but it felt like a miracle, a sign that I was, indeed, meant to be a doctor. Edward took the terrible dressing-down my father gave him for failing. He didn't say a word to me. I didn't think—perhaps I didn't want to know. I promised myself I'd make it up to Edward somehow, and to my father, that I'd become a good doctor, a great doctor, and prove to everyone that I could do it. Edward left for Cambridge a few days later with Louis Chastaine. They've always been close friends."

"When did you know?"

"Not until recently. Edward wanted me to sign the order for Louis's release from the CCS. He said if I didn't, he'd tell everyone, write to the university, to our father, tell Colonel Bellford that I'm a fraud."

"As I recall, it wasn't your signature on the order he handed me," the matron said.

"I refused to do it; I couldn't. Louis wasn't ready to go, and I feared he'd suffer permanent damage, even death. Edward signed it himself."

The matron's eyes were cool, her expression flat and unreadable. Eleanor felt her cheeks flame. What had she expected? There could be no absolution for such a sin. Rules were rules, and she'd broken all the ones the matron held most sacred.

"I suppose you'll use this in your report," Eleanor said. She realized it didn't matter, not now, not after she'd proven she was a doctor, a good doctor, despite fear and war and guilt. The weight lifted.

The matron's eyes narrowed. "Do you think you're the only woman who's had to fight for what she wants? Every nurse, every female doctor walks a fine line. Those who blunder over that line into a man's preserve face scorn and worse. You can't afford to be less than perfect, or they'll eat you alive." She raised her chin. "Why did you tell me this, Dr. Atherton? Do you expect me to offer you forgiveness, to say it's all right? It's not my place. You can save a hundred lives, prove you deserve to be here, but still you'll never be accepted." The nurse was silent for a few moments. "If you were a military nurse, I'd send you home at once, report you, and make certain you could not work in the profession ever again—but you're not a nurse. Truly, I don't know what I will do. I shall have to consider the matter."

A patient behind the matron gasped for air, and she turned to check on him. "Doctor? Patient needs you," someone called to Eleanor, and she nodded and climbed down from the vehicle. She adjusted a bandage on a wounded leg, gave the patient morphine and said a few kind words, and the column shuffled on. For a long moment she stood by the side of the road, listening to the sounds of the war and the approaching enemy and watching the wounded, the volunteers and orderlies, and the nurses of 46/CCS flow past her.

"All right, miss?" a soldier on crutches asked, stopping beside her, following her gaze back toward the front lines now bearing down upon them. "They're in the thick of it now, up there," he said.

"Do you suppose we'll lose the war?" Eleanor asked.

"Oh, I don't know about that. The Huns are winning for now, but that's been the way of this war. As long as we've got the strength, there's hope. We'll push back. It's not the falling down, miss—it's the getting back up." He glanced at the wounded men hobbling past, men who needed treatment and care, and hope, and fell back into line.

Eleanor had no idea what Matron Connolly would do now, or Edward. She couldn't change the past, or the future. She could only do her best, here and now. She'd proven to herself that she *was* a doctor. She'd saved lives. She could save more. She'd go on and do her best.

She took the arm of a faltering soldier with a wounded hand and carried on toward the railhead.

CHAPTER FIFTY-THREE

MARCH 25, 1918

David Blair followed the retreating troops to the new location of 46/CCS, now housed in the storage sheds at the railhead. He could smell the blood and the sweat and the unwashed bodies mixed with the heavy stench of gas and gunpowder as he approached, perched on the back bumper of an overloaded ambulance. A legion of casualties waited on the platform and alongside the tracks for evacuation or treatment.

Corporal Swiftwood was picking his way among the wounded, giving out water and checking dressings. He smiled tiredly at David. "Welcome back, Captain Blair. We'd almost given up on you, but you've come just in time." He looked around. "We're working flat out, and more keep coming. There's no space left, no supplies, and the bloody hospital train is delayed—bomb damage to the tracks. They've been evacuating the nurses along with the wounded, and we're short of able bodies."

David wondered where the hell to even start. "Where's Colonel Bellford?"

Swiftwood shook his head. "He was evacuated with the other wounded three days ago."

"Wounded?" David had seen the destruction of the abandoned CCS, had passed by it shortly before the Germans had pushed through. There hadn't been time to stop. By now the enemy had probably taken over the site and whatever supplies had been left behind. He'd heard the line was holding firm less than three miles away and the British were still in retreat, if not here, then at other places along the front lines. Reliable information was scanty.

"Who's in charge?" he asked.

"Dr. Atherton. Or you, I suppose, now you're back."

"Eleanor?" He recalled joking that he half expected her to be in charge by the time he returned to the CCS. He hadn't meant it.

Swiftwood nodded. "Aye. She operated on the colonel, saved his life. I think we might have been wrong about her." *Not "we,"* David almost said.

"Where is she?" David asked, looking around for the glint of red hair.

"Inside."

He pointed to a storage shed, and David went toward it, threading his way through the wounded to reach it. Inside, almost every inch of floor was covered with men sitting, standing, or lying. Gibbons and two orderlies were shifting stretchers, trying to keep a path clear for the nurses to move between the rows. David gaped. They needed a whole battalion of surgeons and doctors to cope with just the most urgent surgeries, and three trains to evacuate all the wounded. The hospitals behind the lines must be struggling as well, choked with casualties. He'd heard rumors that at least one hospital had been bombed, doctors and nurses killed. Still the barrages went on, bringing more business, more broken bodies. Half a dozen CCSs had been forced to close or move back; the whole system was in chaos under the German onslaught.

"Captain Blair." He turned to find Matron Connolly behind him, as calm, stiff, and starchy as ever, though her uniform was wrinkled and stained and there was blood on her apron. Did nothing ruffle the woman? "It's good to see you back with us again. We need help."

"I can see that. I understand Eleanor is—"

She puffed like a grouse. "*Dr. Atherton* is operating." She pointed to a curtained area at the end of the building. "Reverend Strong is giving anesthetic. There are dozens waiting for surgery. I've just sent two orderlies up the line to look for transportation, be it trains or trucks." She paused a moment. "We've had orders to move back, but there's no way to leave. Where have you arrived from? Is it bad? Are the Germans—"

"They're close," he said. "For now, the Canadians are holding the line a few miles away, but . . ." He looked around, wondered how in the hell they could get everyone out before they were overrun. The women would have to leave first, starting with Eleanor, as a civilian. The rest— he made his way through the stretchers to the makeshift surgical theater and peered around the curtain. Eleanor Atherton, gowned and masked, was standing over a desk that had been turned into an operating table. Reverend Strong was patiently dripping ether onto a mask over the patient's face.

David stopped an orderly. "I need water to wash with, and get me a gown."

"We haven't got any gowns left. We're using the ones we did have for bandages, and as for water, there's some in the pot on the stove, but not much. We're nearly out. We sent a pair of men out to look for a well an hour ago."

"It's like the bloody Middle Ages," David grumbled. "Alcohol then, or carbolic—or rum, even—anything to kill germs."

Eleanor looked up at the sound of his voice, her eyes widening above her mask. "David!" she said. He watched relief bloom in her eyes and felt like a hero.

"What have you got?" he asked, coming to the table.

"Broken jaw. There's shrapnel embedded in his back teeth."

"No time to be fancy. Take the teeth out and bandage him for transport."

"What transport?" she asked dryly.

He looked down at the ruins of the patient's face. He was young.

"His boots are still new," Eleanor said. "He hasn't been here long."

The chaplain nodded to David. "Praise be you're safe, Captain."

Matron Connolly was already directing the construction of a second operating table, jerry-rigged from a pile of crates with long boards stretched across the top of them. The last board was scarcely in place before the orderlies carried in a patient with a blood-soaked dressing over his belly.

"I'll do anesthetic," Matron Connolly said, and she took her place at the head of the table.

"Are we safe?" Eleanor asked when the patient was unconscious.

David kept his eyes on the belly, assessing the damage. "For now," he murmured. As long as their side was able to slow the German advance, and if the rail lines were repaired, and if miracles were still possible. They fell silent, concentrating. Outside, the battle lines continued to shift. Men fought and died, the wounded kept on coming, and the bloody war went on.

CHAPTER FIFTY-FOUR

APRIL 10, 1918

As spring brought warmer days, the German offensive continued.

The staff of 46/CCS became expert at loading up trucks or trains
or carts and moving back at a moment's notice, day or night, saving
themselves, the wounded in their care, and whatever supplies they
could carry. Everyone was exhausted, afraid, and desperate for good
news.

But the news grew worse—there were reports of German planes
firing on clearly marked hospitals behind the lines, killing doctors,
nurses, and patients.

Eleanor worked side by side with David Blair and Matron Connolly and the orderlies and nurses from 46/CCS. They moved into

whatever space they could find—a school, an abandoned dairy, an open field next to a road where they set up in patched, battle-scarred tents and drew red crosses on them with iodine.

A new enemy appeared. Influenza indiscriminately claimed soldiers, civilians, doctors, and nurses by the score. Someone who was healthy in the morning might collapse in the afternoon with fever and die before the next dawn.

Retreating units of all the allied armies came through their doors— Australians, Canadians, French, and Americans. Surgeons and doctors came, too, helped when they could, and moved on with their own men far too soon. The hospitals in the rear were entirely overwhelmed. Understaffed CCS units amalgamated to make the most of limited resources, and forty-six merged with a Canadian CCS in early April.

Eleanor heard the British casualties had been counted in the tens of thousands in the first week of the attack, with just twelve under-manned British divisions facing over forty German divisions of crack troops, all specially chosen and trained for this final assault, a last attempt to break the stalemate and win the war. The French casualties were higher still. The civilian costs were inestimable. Women and children, sick and wounded, frightened and malnourished, flooded the CCSs looking for safety, medical care, and food.

Eleanor watched every incoming ambulance, every convoy of walking wounded for Fraser. She held her breath as she watched them unload their terrible cargo, hoping to see his tall, rangy form jumping out of the first vehicle, or the second, but he wasn't among the bearers or the wounded. Three weeks had passed since she'd seen him at the aid post, watched him walk away from her. The war made it feel like a lifetime.

"Have you seen a stretcher bearer named MacLeod, a Scot, tall, with red hair?" she'd ask every wounded man who could speak.

"Aren't all Scots tall and red-haired?" exhausted soldiers would ask.

Others shook their heads solemnly. "No. It's chaos up there. Have you seen my mates, miss? We're West Kents." Or Liverpool Scottish, or 31st Canadians . . .

She wanted to go herself to look for him, but she was needed here, and there was no question of her leaving. She doubted HQ knew or cared now that there was a female doctor treating the wounded. No one had time to file complaints or reports. No one asked what she was doing here or reviled her for being female. She was competent, a vital pair of hands, and that was all that mattered.

Men were muttering about losing the war, and Field Marshal Haig ordered the British to stand fast where they were, fight to the last man, and not retreat even one more inch.

"No word about Fraser?" David asked her one day. She sat on a broken cart in the sun, taking her first break in uncountable hours. It was spring at last. Well, the air was warmer. More deadly things than spring rain fell from the sky. She shook her head.

"Have you heard from home?" he asked.

"Not a word," she said, scanning the tops of the trees, newly crowned with a fragile mist of leaves. "How long have we been here?"

He sat beside her. "You mean at this particular location? Three days. Ten days at the place before that—the dairy, I believe. And seven days or so at the school, and—" He paused. "I've lost count of the rest. The only reason I know day from night is if I'm operating in daylight or by lantern."

She did her best to smile at his dry humor, but failed, too tired.

David lit a cigarette, drew on it, and blew smoke into the air. He held it out to her, and she took it from his fingertips, put it between her lips, and inhaled. She coughed, and he slapped her gently on the back and took the cigarette back without comment.

"I heard Bellford made it home to England. He's going to recover, thanks to you," he said.

It was good news, but she had become numb to all news, bracing herself, holding herself ready for word of Fraser when—if—it came.

"You need sleep, Eleanor."

She ran a hand over her face and was surprised to find it wet. How long had she been crying? David reached out and took her hand, and she stared down at his fingers wrapped around her own.

"I never even offered my condolences on your brother," she said. "I'm sorry, David."

He frowned at the distant trees on a small ridge to the north. "He took a machine gun round across his chest. He was a strong man— he had a ranch in the west of Canada, worked horses and cows before he joined up with the Canadians. He left England six years ago be- cause he had asthma and needed dry air. He loved the west, used to write to me and ask me to join him, but I had a life in England, our mother to care for, medical school." He paused and drew on his ciga- rette, then flicked it, still only half-smoked, into the mud. "He was conscious when I got there. He talked a lot—about the ranch, mostly. He spoke about it like some men talk of women they love, with such passion I could almost picture it." He rubbed a hand over his eyes. "At the end he was delirious. I should have left then, gone back to the aid post, when he no longer had any need of me. We'd said our farewells. But I couldn't leave him." He squeezed her hand. "I'm sorry. I would have come sooner if I'd known you were still at the aid post. Was it terrible?"

"I managed."

"You cut your hair. Lice, I assume."

She didn't bother reaching up to touch it. She'd grown used to the short curls, and it was lighter and easier to wash. "Yes."

He scanned her face, his eyes keen.

"Patrick left me his ranch. I'm going to Alberta after the war. It's in the foothills, and the grass is green and gold, and the land rolls on endlessly toward the mountains. The rivers run clear as glass, and the sky is so blue and so wide—Pat said it's a different blue than English skies, a color so intense and pure it takes your breath away. You can ride out under that sky and watch the weather roll in and out again, feel the wind in your very bones, scrubbing you clean, and the earth is alive under your feet, breathing." He made a fist, flexed it. "It's hard work, but at the end of the day—" He paused and swallowed. There were tears in his eyes, and she knew he saw Patrick, heard his voice. "At the end of the day you have blisters on your hands and your backside. You fall asleep under uncountable stars set in skies as black as ink . . ." He fell silent, his eyes distant, not seeing the shattered landscape of France, but green hills, a place with no war, no guns, no wounded men.

"Captain? You're wanted," an orderly said.

David sighed and got to his feet. "Did I mention that there's not another person for miles?" He scanned her face. "You should get some sleep while you can. You look exhausted."

She nodded and got to her feet. Then she heard the grind of gears, the squeak of wheels as another ambulance convoy arrived. Hope replaced exhaustion, and she scanned the walking wounded, watched the men pouring out of the backs of the vehicles, peered at the haggard stretcher bearers unloading the worst cases and setting them down on the new spring grass.

He wasn't among them.

Eleanor swallowed the bitter taste in her mouth and went to tend the first patient.

Corporal Max Chilcott looked up at her from the stretcher, his arm wrapped tight against his chest, the dressing bloodstained and dirty. He smiled faintly. "Hello, miss. Keepin' cheery?"

She checked the wound. His arm was shattered. It would need amputation at the shoulder. "Is it a Blighty one?" he asked.

She nodded. "We'll take care of you. Is Fraser with you?" she asked, feeling hope at last.

But Chilcott shut his eyes and shook his head. "They've listed him missing in action," he said, his tone hollow. His face told her it was worse than that.

Eleanor stared at him in numb horror as the orderlies picked up the stretcher and carried the corporal away for surgery.

She felt hands on her shoulders, lifting her. "I heard. Come on. There are others who need you now. We'll make enquiries about Sergeant MacLeod later." Matron Connolly held her up for a moment, looking into her eyes, lending her strength. "Can you manage?"

Slowly Eleanor nodded. Her body was quivering liquid, and her head buzzed as if it were filled with bees. For a moment she couldn't move. "Dr. Atherton?" the matron said, her tone as stern as a slap.

Eleanor pulled away and looked at the wounded surrounding her. Ten stretchers and a long stream of walking cases, limping, battered, and hurting, their eyes hollow, dark, and empty. She knelt by the next stretcher, ignoring the ache in her belly as she lifted the grimy field dressing. "Surgery," she said, and moved on. "Clean and re-dress this wound . . . Resuscitate this man . . . Treat for shock . . . Fever . . . Gunshot . . . Broken femur, tibia, ankle . . ." The words dropped from her lips like stones, and each patient was carried away and replaced with another. "Trench fever . . . Amputation, left arm . . . Head wound . . . Influenza . . . Moribund . . ." Somehow her brain and her hands still moved, even though her heart lay dead in her breast.

A headache started behind her eyes and spread until her whole body hurt. She needed sleep and food, she thought, passing her hand over her tired eyes. They'd operated for nearly twelve hours, and word had come that there were more wounded on the way.

She found her way to Max Chilcott's bed. His eyes were heavy lidded after surgery, his ready smile absent now. "They took my arm off.

Now I'll never play the violin," he tried to joke, but it fell flat. He plucked at the cover with his remaining hand. "I suppose I'm lucky it's not my right hand. That's what Fraser would have said."

She sat down on a stool next to the bed. "Tell me about Fraser."

He lowered his eyes. "His luck ran out, I guess. We were out in No Man's Land, under fire. The Germans were advancing, and our lads were retreating. He wanted to save them all. 'One more,' he kept saying, and then there'd be one more after that. We'd been ordered to retreat, but we heard there was a lad who'd been lying out there all day, wounded, and Fraser insisted he could get him in. He did, too—he brought that lad in right enough. But that one told Fraser there were two others in a shell hole a few yards farther out." Chilcott stared at the ceiling of the tent. "There were bullets flying everywhere, and the Huns were so close you could hear 'em talking. We were pulling back, and I tried to convince Fraser to stay put and help me get the ones we'd already saved back to our own lines, but he gave me that look—you know the one, miss, the steely one, sharp as a bayonet, that tells you he's made up his mind and nothing you say will change it. Well, off he went. I saw him coming back. He was right there. He had two men on his shoulders, carrying them. He was almost safe, and then a shell landed. There was mud everywhere, and Fraser—" He looked at Eleanor. "I didn't see him after that. He was gone, and so were the men he was carrying." Max's face crumpled. "They listed him as missing in action, since there wasn't a body."

"Then there's hope?" Eleanor asked.

Chilcott shook his head. "He's dead, miss. I'm sure of it. I've seen men vaporized by shells, blown to bits. There one minute, then gone. It was that way with Fraser. At least it was quick. He didn't suffer, wouldn't have had time to think—" He let out a sob. "I'm sorry to be the one to have to tell you. I got the idea he was rather sweet on you."

The bees in her head were louder now, the pain behind her eyes a shell burst. She forced herself to her feet, and the room spun. "Miss?"

Max called. "Miss?" She swallowed, but her throat was sandpaper. She gasped for breath, put her hand against her chest, trying to still the pain. Black spots swam in front of her eyes.

"Eleanor?" She heard David Blair's voice from far away.

But before she could answer him, the world turned black.

CHAPTER FIFTY-FIVE

Write to her parents . . . too weak . . . no hope . . ." She heard voices from a distance. She was hot and thirsty, and her limbs ached. She couldn't breathe. She dreamed that her arms and legs had been amputated, that she was limbless. The sun burned her skin, and she walked through flames, or through mud that hindered her every step, making it impossible to move forward. Then it was cold and dark, and she shivered uncontrollably. She was deep underwater, fighting for breath. She tried to swim, to push for the surface, but something held her limbs. She felt the swipe of a cloth on her forehead, cool and soft, and heard a voice in her ear, crooning nonsense, singing. "Mama?" she croaked, but her mother had never sung to her.

"The fever is higher . . . she's not responding."

She felt a hand grip her own. "Fight," she heard a voice order, close to her ear. "D'you hear me? Fight, Eleanor. Don't give up. I've never known you to give up."

"Fraser?" she tried, but her voice was a broken thread. Was he here beside her, alive after all? The hand squeezed her own, tight, and she tried to squeeze back, but couldn't. She twitched her fingers. He wasn't dead; he couldn't be. She'd know, wouldn't she? His ghost would haunt her, wait for her. But he wasn't here in the dark with her. She was all alone.

She felt a soft hand on her brow, sweetness amid the terrible struggle to breathe, the burning agony, and she turned her face toward it and forced her eyes to open.

David Blair stared down at her. "At last," he said. "When Matron Connolly sent for me, I thought—well, never mind. How do you feel?"

She opened her mouth to speak and managed only a rusty croak.

"You've had influenza. It was touch and go for a while. We didn't think you'd—well, it doesn't matter. The fever's broken. You'll be fine."

"How long?" she managed.

"Five days."

She felt her eyes drifting shut. "F-Fraser?" she asked. "Is there any news?"

David looked away. "Sleep now. We'll get you some broth when you wake up."

W hen she woke again she was in a strange room with walls and ceilings of whitewashed stone. The window was flung wide to let in sun and fresh air, and she lay in a white bed, cocooned in blankets and shawls. There was a VAD sitting in a chair beside the bed.

"Where am I?" Eleanor croaked, and the young woman jumped up.

"You're awake!" She put a hand to Eleanor's forehead, then opened the door. "Tell Matron she's awake."

She returned. "You're in hospital." She spoke slowly, as if Eleanor were daft.

"I had influenza, nearly died."

"Yes!" the girl said, smiling. "I mean, yes, you did, but you're going to be all right."

"Is anyone else sick?"

The smile faded. "A great many people, I'm afraid. You're lucky."

Someone else came to the door, a matron Eleanor didn't know. She smelled broth and saw steam rising from a bowl on a tray she was carrying.

"Good morning, Dr. Atherton. How are we feeling?" the head nurse asked with a thin smile.

She felt like a rag doll. Even turning her head or blinking seemed an effort. "I'm . . . How did I get here?"

"You were transferred to our care to convalesce. Now you're awake, we can send you home to England very soon. Captain Blair's orders."

"Where is he?" Eleanor asked, taking the spoonful of broth the nurse held to her lips.

"He visits when he's not busy at the base hospital. It's a few miles away."

Eleanor felt her eyelids grow heavy. "I need to speak to him," she said as she drifted off again. "Tell him."

CHAPTER FIFTY-SIX

MAY 20, 1918

D avid was beside her when she woke again. The sunlight had slipped itself deeper into the room and rested now in long late-afternoon lines across the bed. David was dozing in a chair, his head back, his legs stretched long before him.

"David," she said.

He was awake at once, jumping to his feet, crossing to look at her. He put his hand on her forehead, looked into her eyes. "How do you feel?" he asked.

"Tired."

He grinned. His mustache was thicker, bristling with gray hairs she didn't remember. How long had she been here?

"You've been here for nearly three weeks," he answered her question without her having to ask it. "You're in a lovely old convent, a perfect place to convalesce."

"Three weeks?" She looked up at him in alarm. "Surely I can't have been here as long as that." She pushed back the covers and tried to get up. Her head swam, and he pressed her back into bed.

"Lie still. You're not well yet. Give it time. You had influenza and pneumonia. We didn't think you'd make it. Your brother came briefly, but it's a trifle busy at HQ just now. He said he'd tell your parents. Your father asked for a full medical update, which I duly sent to him."

She felt tears sting her eyes. "What's happening?"

"Do you mean the war? It's still there. Nothing has changed. We take ground, they take ground, men die. I don't keep track. I've been seconded to a Canadian hospital—three of their surgeons died of influenza, but I haven't had even a sniffle. Let's see, what else can I tell you? Colonel Bellford was invalided back to England. Last I heard he was recovering at a hospital in Sussex, all thanks to you. His wife sent a letter, thanking you. Reverend Strong has a new post in Doullens, and Private Gibbons is with him. Swiftwood was also down with influenza, but he recovered."

"And—and, is there any news of . . ." She paused and bit her lip, wanting to ask about Fraser, but fearing the answer. "Matron Connolly?" she said instead.

"Assigned to a British general hospital a few miles from here." He grinned at her and took her hand, rubbed his thumb across her knuckles. "You look truly awful. You've lost at least twenty pounds. I had my doubts, but Matron Connolly nursed you devotedly. She took care of you night and day until you were out of danger and well enough to move here."

"She did?"

He smiled again, a warm, sweet smile. She lowered her gaze and drew the topmost shawl around her for courage. "And is there any news of—of Fraser MacLeod?"

His thumb stopped, and he withdrew his hand from hers gently. "He was listed as missing in late March, Eleanor. It's May now."

"Yes I know, but I'm sure he's not—not—"

He rose and went to the window, where he stood leaning on the frame, looking out. "I can make some new inquiries if you like, but—"

She forced herself to sit up. She swung her legs over the edge of the bed and gasped at the dizzy, fluttery sensation of weakness the effort caused. "I must get up."

He sprang away from the window. "No, you must not. You need rest. If you get up now, you'll make yourself ill again."

She reached for the robe that lay across the bottom of the bed and tried to put it on. "Look, I'll get a wheelchair if you want to go out."

"Don't be silly. I can walk," she said stubbornly. *Fraser.* She felt tears sting her eyes, and pain crushed the air out of her weakened chest. She wanted to walk, needed to move or run. *Find him.*

"Eleanor, you're not well yet."

She shook her head, looked up at him. "I have to know for myself."

He swallowed, his expression shuttered now, his jaw tight. "Look, I'll do everything I can to get some information for you," he said in a tone that suggested he held no hope. "He was a good man, and a brave one."

"He was," she said. "He *is.*"

"Eleanor . . ."

She got to her feet, and he put his arm around her waist, held her up on her boneless, useless legs. She clung to his shoulder. "I think I might need that wheelchair after all," she said breathlessly.

CHAPTER FIFTY-SEVEN

JUNE 1918

The convalescent hospital had a fine garden, and there were even roses growing, though no gardener remained to school the riot of unruly blooms to strict order. Eleanor liked that, preferred it, watching the flowers find their own way to the sun, a wild, determined profusion of color and scent. Reds and pinks and greens, real color, after so many months of gray and black. It was quiet here, peaceful, though the guns still raged and thumped like toddlers in a tantrum locked in a distant nursery. Would it ever end?

The Germans had come within fifty miles of Paris, she heard, but the Americans had driven them back. Everyone around her was saying that the tide was turning at last, and it would be just a matter of months until the Germans were beaten. Still, casualties mounted daily, tens of thousands, then hundreds of thousands. How many dead? Could anyone even count that high?

She'd written to her parents, telling them simply that she was recovering. She'd also written to the countess, informing her that Louis had taken himself out of her care and had gone to Paris in March, where he had access to the best doctors. What more was there to say? If the powerful Countess of Kirkswell couldn't make Louis do anything he didn't wish to, then how could she? There'd been no reply to either letter.

"Magazine, miss?" a VAD asked, coming around with an issue of *Country Life*. Eleanor took it. How long had it been since she'd read anything? For weeks she'd been too busy, but now she was unable to do anything else but read. "It's two months old now, but it's all new to us, isn't it?" the young woman said cheerfully.

Eleanor longed for something transporting and ordinary, advertisements for garden seeds or spring frocks and new hats, for coming-out portraits of this year's titled debs and society wedding announcements.

She drew a breath when she saw that Louis's picture graced the cover. He was grinning, waving from the seat of an airplane, wearing his flier's cap and leather coat.

"Handsome devils, those fliers, aren't they?" the VAD said with a sigh. "Especially him—he's a true hero."

Handsome indeed. Eleanor flipped to the article inside the magazine, where there were more photographs. "Viscount Wins Distinguished Flying Cross for Saving Aid Post," the headline read. The next photo showed Field Marshall Haig presenting the medal. Lady Frances stood next to him, smiling proudly. "Field Marshall Haig presents the DFC to Squadron Leader Lord Louis Somerton as fiancée Lady Frances Parfitt, daughter of the Duke of Winslowe and Sir Douglas's niece, looks on."

His *fiancée*? Eleanor stared at the photo and noted the smug pride on Fanny's pretty face. She turned the page to see more photographs of Louis and his beaming copilot.

She read the article. Louis hadn't gone home after all. Nor had he stayed in Paris drinking and romancing Lady Frances. He'd returned to duty. In the next photo, Louis stood beside his plane, pointing out bullet holes in the fuselage. She noted the walking stick propped behind him, half-hidden, saw the way he leaned to one side to favor his injured leg. She looked at the familiar devil-may-care grin that had once made her heart thump. It merely made her smile rather ruefully now.

According to the article, the recently wounded Squadron Leader Lord Somerton had returned to duty despite still-healing injuries. On his first mission back, he'd spotted a German gun firing on a British aid post near the front. Though he was only on an observing mission, he'd managed to destroy the gun and save the lives of countless British wounded. Eleanor smiled. "Louis," she whispered, remembering that day, the plane flying above them, and the cheers that went up when the pilot managed to blow up the gun firing on the aid post, a true hero.

The story went on to quote the Earl of Kirkswell, who declared himself intensely proud that his son and heir was doing his duty. The countess added that Somerton's dedication was a shining example of the kind of British fighting spirit that would win the war. The countess confirmed that her son was indeed betrothed to Lady Frances Parfitt. It was glowingly described as a love match—a war hero and his lovely bride, the premier belle of English society, the toast of Mayfair. Her debut portrait was reproduced in the magazine, showing Lady Fanny in a ruffled gown with roses in her hair and a sweet simper on her face. "For this we fight—heroes, true love, and dear old Blighty," the caption gushed. The next picture showed Fanny wearing a VAD uniform, standing with the countess in the hospital at Chesscroft among the convalescent officers.

The article said that Louis was still flying missions over the Western Front—at least he was in April when the magazine was printed— and was still the terror of the skies to the Huns and the hope and glory of grateful England.

Was he still afraid, or in pain? It was no longer her concern, of course.

She wondered if the countess had simply discarded her letter when it arrived at Chesscroft and considered the matter closed.

"Live, Louis," she whispered to his photograph. "Live and go home and be happy."

CHAPTER FIFTY-EIGHT

The neat figure of Matron Connolly came up the pathway, her scarlet cape buttoned over her gray dress, her collar, cap, and cuffs impeccably white. The heels of her shoes clicked on the convent's ancient cobbles in a precise cadence, neither too fast nor too slow. She regarded Eleanor directly as she approached, her expression set in professional lines that gave no hint of her thoughts or emotions.

She paused before Eleanor's seat on the bench and took her in with a medical eye before she sat down. "You look better than when last I saw you. I trust you're recovering well?"

"Yes, thank you." Eleanor saw the new medal pinned to the matron's cape, a Royal Red Cross, awarded for exceptional nursing, devotion to duty, and professional competence. Florence Nightingale had been one of the first nurses to receive the medal. "I see congratulations are in order."

The nurse's hand went to the medal for a moment, then returned to her lap, "I've ordered tea and biscuits. Nothing too heavy. You are still on a light diet."

"You're keeping tabs on me?" Eleanor asked in surprise.

"I simply wished to make certain you were doing well." The matron looked away for a moment. "Sister Ames died the other day. Do you remember her? She was engaged to a lieutenant in the 2nd Durhams."

The young woman who'd spoken to her with such hope the night Louis had left, the one who wanted to be a doctor, who hoped the world would change after the war. Eleanor swallowed the bitterness of yet another soul to mourn, another young person who'd gone before they could make their mark on the world. "Yes, I remember her. How sad."

"There are dozens—hundreds—of others who've died of this terrible flu," the matron said. She sat on the chair across from Eleanor's, her back stiff and straight. "We feared you would—" Her lips rippled. "You're still quite pale. I shall ask the nursing sisters here to give you a glass of stout to build you up."

"Captain Blair told me you took care of me during the worst of it."

"Does that surprise you?"

"Somewhat. I hadn't thought we were friends."

Matron Connolly's chin rose. "I'm a professional nurse, Dr. Atherton. I know my duty." The flare ended as quickly as it had come. The nurse studied her hands. "Actually, I wanted to nurse you. I could easily have ordered someone else to care for you, but—" She paused as a young woman arrived with the tea tray. "Thank you. I'll pour out," the matron said, dismissing her.

"But?" Eleanor prompted once the girl was gone.

"But you deserved the best care. For Colonel Bellford, for Lieutenant Findlay, for Captain Blair, and so many others. You were—are—uniquely brave." She touched the medal again. "You're the one who deserves this, or something like it." She picked up the teapot and poured, adding two spoonfuls of sugar and a fortifying dollop of cream to Eleanor's cup without asking. She placed two biscuits on a plate for her.

"I owe you my thanks," Eleanor said.

The matron poured her own tea. "David Blair said you wished to see me. In truth, I wanted to come and see how you were doing. I'll admit that I'm curious about what you'll do now. Do you intend to continue practicing medicine when you return home to England?"

"Home," Eleanor said. "I haven't even decided when I'm going home. Or even if I can be a doctor . . ."

"Because of what you told me? I haven't told anyone. It's not my tale to tell." She set her cup down. "I did wonder what to do about what you told me, and I considered reporting it. Then I watched you in the days after the offensive, saw how you handled the worst cases without flinching or resting. You kept your head under fire. I saw how good you were." She paused, and the breeze blew the scent of roses through the garden.

"I wanted to be a doctor once. My father was a surgeon, and he assisted a female doctor who worked with poor women and children. I wanted to be just like her. My father said it was no life for a woman and refused to allow me to attend medical school. There were even fewer choices in my day, so I became a nurse instead. I gave up everything for my career—the chance of a husband and children, love, a proper home. I had to work hard to earn the position of matron, prove myself over and over again. It took many years, and in the end, my promotion was given at the whim of a man who thought my *age* made me suitable, not my skills as a professional nurse, or my training. My patients would see me as a mother figure, not a desirable woman, and I would not tempt any soldier to impropriety. I've risen as far as I can in my profession, and still I am subservient to male doctors, even inexperienced or incompetent ones. I hold the rank of lieutenant colonel, and yet I can be overruled and berated by any captain with a medical degree. Your father was braver than mine. You are braver than I."

"My father thought I'd fail. He wanted me to, I think."

"From what I've seen, you don't give up easily. Does anything frighten you? I've seen bad doctors and good ones, and ones that would have done the world more of a favor by becoming dustmen instead of physicians. You have a gift for healing. You're smart and compassionate and courageous. Whatever the results of that exam, you made it through medical school, and you've saved many lives here, in the middle of a war. There are reports that you acquitted yourself admirably at the aid post, under fire." She scanned Eleanor's face. "I want you to know that I have written to the director general of Army Medical Services, not to sanction you, but to ask him to recognize your service. I'm still awaiting his reply, but I came to tell you that you have my thanks—and Colonel Bellford's—and that your contributions have not gone unnoticed or unappreciated. I understand the commander of the Canadian CCS we paired with has also written to headquarters to commend you. I have no doubt your brother will see those letters, your initials being the same."

Tears stung Eleanor's eyes. "I don't know what to say," she murmured. "Thank you. It is still up to Edward to decide what he'll do."

Connolly nodded. "We'll have to wait and see, I suppose. You needn't thank me. It is for me—and many others—to thank *you*. Now eat those biscuits and regain your strength. The world cannot do without you."

The tears slipped down Eleanor's cheeks unchecked. "I'm not ready to leave France, Matron," she said. "I want to stay, to—" She wanted to find Fraser, or find out what had happened to him. She could not go home without knowing.

"You may call me Sarah if you wish. Not many people do. That's another problem with being a woman in a position of knowledge and authority—few friends stand by you. I'd like you to think of me as a friend, or at least an ally. You *should* stay, if your health allows. You could do a great deal of good at one of the general hospitals. The French welcome competent doctors of either sex. But first of all you must get better. Come, I'll walk you back inside." Eleanor took her arm, and together they strolled along the path together toward the yellow stone building and spoke of the glory of roses.

CHAPTER FIFTY-NINE

I t's been hours since you took a break. And when was the last time you ate?" David Blair asked Eleanor. He looked around the ward at the convalescent patients, mostly Canadians at the moment, strapping colonial men missing arms or legs or faces, men shattered by their experiences, or by illness, or by too much bloody war.

"There's a lot to do," she said with a smile. David had gotten her a posting here, and they worked together. He was good company, spoke of his cases, and listened to her speak of hers. He'd helped her make inquiries about Fraser. She looked at him hopefully now. "Is there any news?"

He gave her a half smile and shook his head. "Come on, we'll go down to the local estaminet for a bit of bread and cheese and a glass of wine. The fresh air will do us both good, even if the wine will rot our bellies."

He waited while she fetched her hat, then held out his arm. "What's the war news?" she asked.

"It seems we've turned a corner. The German frontline troops are deserting. They're starving, sick, and tired. Our side is retaking all the ground the Germans gained in the spring and driving them back. The officers on the ward are speaking of victory. Still far too many wounded, and even more sick with flu, of course, but there's some hope that it will all come to an end soon."

"Not soon enough." Eleanor sighed.

It was the perfect late summer day, warm and sunny. A plane droned overhead, and Eleanor looked up.

"Is that your viscount?" David asked.

"I don't know," she replied, wondering herself if it was. It didn't matter. David paused, leaned over a stone fence, and plucked a daisy.

"I used to take these for granted. They grow everywhere in England, but I haven't seen one in years." He handed it to her. "Pretty, isn't it? In fact, I'm noticing a lot of things are pretty. Not that I didn't before, of course."

He took her forearms gently and turned her toward him, and she looked up. David's eyes were brown, intelligent, and usually full of mirth or compassion or the keen-eyed certainty of his diagnoses. That was replaced by something else now, something deeper, less sure. She recognized that yearning. "Eleanor," he whispered.

She knew she could find peace and perhaps even happiness with this man, be his partner, an equal, loved for exactly who she was.

But she pressed her hand to his chest. "I'm not ready."

He didn't ask what she meant, or who. He knew. "I'll wait, then," he said simply. He took her arm, started walking again, and changed the subject. "Did you know the Russian revolutionaries shot the tsar and his family? One more tragedy in a world overwhelmed by tragedy." He was trying to change the subject, striving for a pleasant tone, but she heard the underlying regret.

"There has to be some hope," she said. "Or we'd all go mad."

"Perhaps we have already gone mad," he said, scanning the road ahead, the little half-destroyed village. "All I know is that nothing will ever be the same again."

CHAPTER SIXTY

OCTOBER 1918

It was another crisp, short, brutally formal letter. There was no news about Sergeant F. MacLeod, stretcher bearer, 51st Highlanders, last seen near Arras, and declared missing in action on March 29, 1918.

Eleanor put it with the others.

There was also a note from her mother. Edward had given them happy news—he was engaged to Lady Maud Sheridan, the youngest daughter of the Earl of Edgemont, and they would wed in the spring, when the war was over.

Every conversation started with the hope that it would soon be over. The Germans had requested an armistice in early October, and tentative negotiations were underway.

Eleanor was happy for her brother, and for her mother's pride in the match. Her father sent no message at all, but her mother had written that the dreadful Spanish influenza had arrived in Thorndale, and as the only doctor, her father was very busy tending the sick and dying. Even some of the officers recovering at Chesscroft were ill.

Edward came to see her one afternoon. She stood and watched him walk across the ward toward her, tall, stiff-backed, and serious. He didn't smile as he took off his cap and tucked it under his arm. He scanned her pale face and her thin, sickness-ravaged body. She waited for him to speak first, wary.

"You look dreadful," he said.

She ignored that. "There's a place to sit on the veranda." She led the way. "Would you like anything? Tea, perhaps?"

He was frowning at a soldier propped up in bed, his face and chest swathed in bandages. "No. I can't stay long. I'm expected back at HQ tonight. I just came to see how you are. You—you didn't go home." His tone had softened, and he scanned her again.

She sat down, her back stiff, her mouth dry. He was her twin, her brother, and yet a complete stranger. "No," she said, and didn't elaborate.

He had the grace to blush, and he rubbed a hand over his mustache, new since the last time she'd seen him. It suited him, made him look dashing and elegant, mature. "Look, about the last time we spoke—" He hesitated as a nurse wheeled a patient past him, blanched at the soldier's burned face. "God," he muttered. "How do you stand it?"

"I'm a doctor," she said quietly.

He looked at her, and she wondered if he'd dispute that, tell her again that she was a fraud, a cheat, that she had no right to call herself a doctor. She held his eyes, determined, bold, sure of herself. "Even if I have to start all over again, I am and always will be a doctor. Nothing can change that, Edward. Nothing."

He frowned. "I wish you'd never come to France. People talk, you know, and you don't consider how it affects my career, and father's reputation. Could you not for once have done as you were expected to?

And for a woman to be exposed to . . . to . . . *that*." His gaze went back to the burned soldier.

"You sound like Mother—and Father. Why did you do it, Edward? Did you feel sorry for me? Was it kindness?"

"Kindness? You act like I've never shown you any."

She let that go, waited for an answer.

"All my life—our life—father expected me to follow in his footsteps, to be a doctor just like him. Not once did he ever ask me what I wanted. It wasn't a life of tending a bunch of farmers and peasants and their snot-nosed brats and fat wives, pretending to be better than the rest of them. I hated him for pushing me, for insisting. I wanted to go to Cambridge, but he even insisted that it had to be Edinburgh, *his* alma mater. He held you up to me constantly as a shining example of what I could do if only I put my mind to it, because I was, after all, a boy, and therefore smarter, better, bolder than my sister. He made it a damned competition to shame me." He looked at her. "I hate the sight of blood. The idea of touching one of these poor ruined bastards makes my skin crawl. I was never meant to be a doctor."

"Why didn't you tell him?"

"I tried. He wouldn't listen to me. He thought I was just tired of being drilled on the hepatic nerves, and the muscles of the throat. He gave me a lecture about the noble sacrifice of the profession, the honor of it. I can't see any honor in being covered with puke and shit and blood. He insisted that I must go and sit that exam, that I'd feel differently once I was at school." He looked at her. "I decided I'd ace the bloody exam, score top marks, and then I'd tear up the damned letter of acceptance and throw it in Father's face, tell him I wasn't going to medical school. But then I saw you at the end of the exam. What happened, El? You were so confident going in."

She sighed. "I wanted it so much. Too much, perhaps. I knew everything on that exam, everything, and yet—I looked around that room, saw men glaring and staring. Even the proctor didn't want me there, saw my presence as a terrible affront, not only to himself and the men in the room, but to medicine itself. I was writing that exam for Father, too, I think. Perhaps I always knew he didn't expect me to succeed, didn't want it, but I wanted him to be proud of me, to see that I could do it. It overwhelmed me in the end."

"I didn't realize how badly you wanted it," he said. "I thought it was about besting me and showing off for Louis."

"Louis? It was never about him."

"You had a crush on him. And he—he looked at you as some kind of wonder."

She met his eyes, wondered if he was joking, or teasing her, even now, but she saw only cool honesty in his gaze. The distance still remained between them, an impenetrable barrier. "I had no idea," she murmured. It surprised her, even now that she knew Louis better. "He gave no sign of it."

"He gave me a lucky charm to give to you the day of the exam—a gold Louis coin from his father's collection."

"I don't remember that."

"No, I kept it." He took out his wallet and opened the pocket. He pulled out the old French coin and showed it to her, and she took it, looked at the engraved face of Louis XVI. A double meaning, then, for this was the king who'd lost his head.

"Why did you do it, Edward?" she asked again.

He regarded her for a moment. "It wasn't kindness, or brotherly affection. It shames me to say it now, of course, but then . . ." He stared at the coin in her hand. "Then it was just so bloody convenient, the perfect solution, better even than acing the exam myself. I pictured Father's face when you got top marks and I failed. He'd hate it, of course, and you— I never expected he'd allow you to go to university. I thought Mama would find you a decent husband, you'd marry, and that would be the end of it. When you did go to school, I thought you'd run home screaming the first week."

"You wagered with Louis that I would."

Edward's brows shot up. "He told you?"

"Yes. I suppose we became friends of a sort after all," she said, just to dig at him.

He sighed. "I believe I'm glad you did."

"And what will you do now?" she asked.

"You mean will I denounce you? No. It turns out you're not a fraud at all. You would have retaken that exam and passed, I assume. You did the hardest part—stuck it out at university, excelled—and you turned out to be a fine doctor." He looked around the veranda, taking in the patients and the nurses. He clenched his jaw, and he took a moment before he looked at her again, and longer still before he spoke. "I think you're far braver than I am, El. And I'm . . . proud of you. It turned out the way it was supposed to in the end." She could read the pride in his face, the admiration there at long, long last, and tears stung her eyes.

"Edward, are you happy?"

His brows shot up. "Yes, I believe so. I love the law, and I'm going to run for a seat in Commons when this is over. Who knows? Maybe I'll be prime minister someday."

"I'll be very proud of you, too, Edward."

He rose to go, picking up his cap from the table. Even after four years, his uniform still looked freshly tailored, and his boots still shone. "I must get back. You've heard about Louis's medal?"

"I have. In fact, I was there at the aid post that day. Most heroic."

"You were *there*? Did Louis know? Did *you* know it was him?"

She shook her head. "Not a clue. We were both busy."

"What will you do next, Eleanor? I suppose you'll go home."

She smiled. *I am home*, she thought, and she remembered saying those words to Fraser.

"Not until it's all over."

CHAPTER SIXTY-ONE

NOVEMBER 1918

There was a rousing celebration at the convalescent hospital when the armistice was signed and the second hand marked the moment of precisely eleven o'clock on the eleventh day of the eleventh month of the fourth terrible year of the war.

David hugged Eleanor, lifted her off her feet, and swung her around. Orderlies kissed nurses and slapped each other on the back. A chorus of "Tipperary" broke out, and everyone joined in. Afterward, a patient with a rich baritone voice sang "There's a Long, Long Trail," and everyone cried for all that had been lost.

It made Eleanor cry, and she sobbed, unable to stop, and David used his handkerchief to wipe her tears away. "I'll help you look for Fraser."

She met his eyes. "There's a chance, David. There must be, even now. I thought I'd check the CCSs and aid posts, see if anyone remembers him. If he was wounded—"

He squeezed her hand. "We'll look everywhere."

CHAPTER SIXTY-TWO

PARIS
DECEMBER 3, 1918

The harried major listened to Eleanor's query with barely disguised impatience. He shuffled through one of the stacks of paper on his desk before finally looking up. "Sergeant Fraser James MacLeod was listed missing after the first battle of Arras, on or about March the twenty-ninth. There's been no word since, and we've declared him killed in action." He stated it crisply and without emotion, looking at David instead of her.

"But someone saw him carrying wounded men during the battle," Eleanor pleaded.

"Well, we've all lost someone in this war." The major picked up a rubber stamp and brought it down on the paper in front of him, a final drumbeat, the closing of a coffin. "My condolences. Best go home if you can get on one of the boat trains. The whole army is trying to cross the Channel now the war's over."

David escorted her away. They walked down a street crowded with soldiers, smiling now, their duty done, flirting with pretty civilians or VADs. Vendors sold wine and cakes and souvenirs. Flags fluttered from every window and lamppost. Everywhere, there was an aura of celebration. The war was over, and life would go on. Eleanor walked on in sober silence, numb. It took an hour to push through the throngs and reach the crowded railway station.

She remembered the day she'd arrived in France. The platform had been packed with troops going into battle, new and shiny as painted tin soldiers. She remembered the casualties coming off the train and Fraser talking to a wounded private, working magic.

Now the train station was crowded with refugees, and the tin soldiers were grim-faced, their eyes old, their skin gray, their uniforms and boots worn out. Red Cross volunteers and nurses shepherded shuffling columns of wounded men onto trains.

Out of habit Eleanor looked for Fraser's tall figure on the platform, his dark red hair, his ragged greatcoat. She'd visited dozens of hospitals and casualty stations, questioned nurses, doctors, and officials, pushed a blurry photograph Max Chilcott had given her at them, made them look, think, try to remember one man out of thousands. She'd studied the unrecognizable wounded with bandaged faces and looked at their hands instead. "Ye can always tell a bearer by his hands," he'd told her once. The raw emotion caught her, drove the breath from her lungs.

He isn't here. He is dead. The pain bit into her, so sharp it made her stumble. The steel thread of hope that had held her up for so long, that had kept her searching, snapped under the strain of grief.

David led her to a bench as a train pulled in, loud and dirty. Steam hissed, shrouding the platform.

"I'm going to Canada," David said, scanning the crowds. "I don't want to go back to England, see it crippled by the war, see broken men, watch women mourn. My brother left me his ranch, and I want those green foothills and the mountains all around me, someplace clean and unscarred by the war. I'll be a rancher and a country doctor." He turned to look at her. "Marry me, Eleanor. Come with me."

She stared at *his* hands—surgeon's hands, clean and white. He was a fine man, a good doctor, and Fraser was dead and she was empty. She suddenly longed for a place to heal, to forget, a green place with mountains. "I want all that." She did, but the word *yes* would not come. "But—"

He was silent, and she glanced up, but he wasn't looking at her. He was staring at the platform behind her, his eyes wide, his expression stunned. Eleanor turned.

Gaunt, ragged men were climbing down from the train. People made space for them and stared. "Prisoners of war," someone muttered. "Poor buggers. Look at 'em—half-starved. God knows what the Huns did to them."

She saw the familiar armband first, the red cross brassard that was so dirty and threadbare it was barely visible. The greatcoat was even more ragged, filthy. He was turned away from her, and she couldn't see his face, but still her breath caught in her throat. His height was right, even if his shoulders were hunched, his steps tentative instead of long and sure. Surely it was grief, making her hallucinate. It couldn't be . . .

She rose to her feet, willed him to turn around so she could see his face, know for sure. She clenched her fists, and her heart leaped to her throat and lodged there, still hoping, even now. She stood still, a hundred people flowing between them, and saw only him. It was foolish to hope, but she did. She stared at him, swore she'd let go, accept at last that he was dead if this wasn't Fraser.

He turned. His face was unshaven, his eyes hidden in the shadow of the battered brim of his cap, but she recognized the shape of his jaw, the size of his nose, the way his head came up, and he scanned the platform like a man looking for someone who needed help, needed *him*.

Tears blurred her vision, and she blinked them away, looked again. She didn't take her eyes off of him as she ran forward, couldn't. She *felt* the instant when he saw her like a bolt through her chest. She watched his weary, wary gaze turn to disbelief, then hope, then surprise. He opened his arms as she reached him, and she rushed into them. She felt the terrible fragility of Fraser's body as he enveloped her, laid his chin on her head, breathed her in. "Eleanor," he said, his voice rough. "God, lass, it's really you, isn't it? Are ye real?"

She pulled back to look at him, and he cupped her face in his shaking hands and stared down at her in wonder. She didn't realize she was crying until he swiped at her tears with the pads of his thumbs, but there were too many, and he gave up. "I thought I'd never see ye again, and here ye are." He threw his head back and laughed. "Here ye are. Och, but you're thin, lass."

She laughed. He was the one who was as gaunt as a skeleton, hollow-cheeked and gray. She wanted to touch him all over, to check and make sure he was whole and healthy and real. "I looked for you. I saw Corporal Chilcott, and he—" He put his finger over her mouth. "He said he saw you killed in action."

"Not killed. Captured. They needed a medic, and they saw my armband. For a few days I carried wounded German lads off the field for them, helped their bearers. Then they sent me to the rear, to a prisoner of war camp, and I helped where I could. They had no medicine, no bandages. There was typhus, and influenza, and not much to eat. Even the Germans were starving, and we could do nothing but wait for the war to end. They threw open the gates when peace came, pointed the prisoners toward the rail station, and piled us onto trains. It took days." He stared into the distance as he spoke, his face bitter.

"Oh, Fraser," Eleanor said, and his gaze flicked back to her, his expression softening.

"It doesn't matter," he said gruffly. "Not anymore. It's all over, and somehow, we found each other again." He looked at the whirling crowds, oblivious to two people among thousands.

"A whole army couldn't keep us apart," she said. "Two armies."

He raised one brow in sardonic amusement. "I'm beginning t'think so."

He swayed on his feet, and she tightened her hold on him. "You're ill," she said.

"Aye," he said, his amusement fading. "I'm dirty, and louse-ridden, and tired. I'm not fit to touch ye."

She put her arms around him. "You look fine to me, Fraser Mac-Leod," she said, echoing what he'd said to her at the aid post, newly shorn of her hair. "Better than fine. You're beautiful."

He searched her face, and she let him read the truth of that in her eyes, and her love, and the joy that she'd found him again. Against insurmountable odds, she'd found him. It felt like a miracle, a wish granted, and she wondered if this could possibly be true, if she could be so lucky, but he was real. "I'm not letting go of you this time, Fraser," she told him fiercely, brooking no argument.

He smiled at her, and he brought their clasped hands to his lips and kissed her knuckles. "I dreamed of this, of you. Without you, I wouldn't have . . . I love ye, Eleanor Atherton. I wish I'd said it that day, told ye. I thought I'd never have the chance, that I'd regret it every day I had left on this earth. And now, somehow, you're here. I must be the luckiest bastard who ever drew breath. I intend to spend every minute telling ye so. How did ye know, how did ye chance to be here now, to-day, this minute?"

David. She'd forgotten David.

She turned back to the place she'd left him. But the bench was empty, and David was gone.

EPILOGUE

ARRAS, FRANCE
JULY 1936

Eleanor stared out the window of the train, watching the green fields go past behind the reflection of her own face. The undulating, grassy landscape was as peaceful as a rumpled bed now, adorned with new trees, though they were still spindly and tentative, as if they grew in poisoned soil. Perhaps they did—those verdant dimples and hillocks had been open wounds in the earth when she was last here, eighteen years ago, during the war.

There was another war coming now, some said. She couldn't bear to think of it happening again.

She looked at her fifteen-year-old son, Alec, sprawled on the seat across from her, his long legs taking up all the space, his nose buried in a book, as usual. He wanted to be an engineer when he grew up, not a doctor, like her. If there was another war, he'd be caught up in it, and she'd be one of the mothers who fretted and feared this time. Would it be even worse for her, since she knew more than most about the cost of war, the horrors?

She glanced at Fraser, sitting next to her, and noted his pensive expression as he, too, watched the countryside fly past. She knew he was remembering the men who'd fought here, who had endured the mud and the guns and the horror, had been wounded, or perished, the ones he still dreamed about, tried to rescue in his sleep.

She tried to think of the ones who'd survived instead, those who went home to make new lives—there was no going back to the old life one had known before the war. Time healed, perhaps, but it did not allow one to forget. How often had she wished, both for her own sake and for the beloved man seated next to her, that there was a way to forget all the things they'd seen and heard and done? She wondered again if attending this ceremony, the unveiling of the Canadian war memorial on Vimy Ridge, would lay Fraser's ghosts to rest at last—or would it just bring back terrible memories, sharpen the nightmares? She read the same painful question in the eyes of others on the train, veterans, survivors, and mourners.

Fraser's hand lay next to hers on the seat, and she touched his scarred knuckles with the tip of her little finger. He clasped her hand in his but said nothing.

"Arras!" the conductor called, moving down the train. The outskirts of the town came into view, the yellow stone buildings glowing in the summer heat. There were still bullet holes in the walls, and bullet holes in the memories of the people who lived here, and the ones who'd fought here, suffered, lost loved ones, comrades, and countrymen, and now returned in the name of honor and remembrance.

She could read the complicated emotions in her husband's eyes, but only because she knew him and he could not hide them from her the way he did with other people. He shook himself as the train pulled into the station.

"Ready?" he asked.

"Yes," she said, and she forced a smile. Alec was eager, and she let him lead the way along the crowded corridor, his steps long and colt-ish, half boy and half man. He took after his father, was handsome, clever, kind, and already taller than she was. On the platform she squeezed his shoulder, and he glanced back at her, frowning, not want-ing to be held back. She remembered recruits scarcely older than Alec getting off the train in 1918 with the same eagerness, the same longing for adventure and sense of invincibility. But that was the past. Now it was a perfect July day, fragrant with flowers and grass under the sharp grease and smoke smell of the train, and the world was at peace. At least for now.

"Dr. MacLeod?" A young woman in a neat linen suit held out her hand to Eleanor, confident and crisp despite the heat. "I'm Elizabeth Bellford—Dr. Elizabeth Bellford. My father asked me to meet you, take you to the hotel."

Elizabeth Bellford looked much like her father, with the same pale English blue eyes, snub nose, and pugnacious chin. The way she led them through the crowds with near-military precision, her spine stiff and her head high, suggested she'd make as good an officer as her fa-ther had. "How is the colonel?" Eleanor asked.

Elizabeth smiled. "Eager to see you. In fact, everyone is."

Eleanor's breath caught, and she stopped in her tracks. "Every-one?" Eleanor asked.

Elizabeth nodded, and she smiled at Fraser and Alec. "It was Fa-ther's idea. You'll see. Now, let's get you to the hotel."

Eleanor scanned the town as Elizabeth eased the car through streets filled with uniformed men, just the way it had been when she was last here in the waning months of 1918, watching the war stagger toward its end.

The soldiers were older now, unarmed, their uniforms faded and showing the creases of long and careful storage. Their wives and children tumbled along beside them, gay and colorful, excited, but the soldiers themselves were solemn, ensnared by memories long pushed aside, held back. She saw canes and crutches, limps and scars. She reached out and took Fraser's hand, felt him squeeze her hand in return.

"Where's the monument?" Alec asked. "Where's the king?"

"He'll be at the unveiling tomorrow," Elizabeth Bellford said. "And the monument is a few miles outside of town, on the highest point of Vimy Ridge." She parked in front of a small hotel. "I'm sure you'd like a chance to unpack and get freshened up. My father is hoping you'll agree to have dinner with us tonight."

"Yes, of course," Eleanor said. Fraser was watching the crowds pass, keen-eyed as always, a characteristic of a Highland Scot that had been honed doubly sharp as a stretcher bearer.

Upstairs, she took off her hat and gloves and set them on the table next to the bed. Fraser went to the window and looked out at the square below. The light reflected off the scar on the side of his jaw, a thin silver line after so many years. He had other scars as well, almost too numerous to count, most known only to her, his wife. He'd won a commendation medal for saving the lives of so many at the risk of his own, but he'd refused to wear it on this trip. She'd tucked it away in her suitcase, hoping she could convince him to put it on for the ceremony.

His beloved face was drawn, and she knew he wasn't seeing gay summer crowds, but the past. "Are you all right, *mo cridh*?" She used the Scottish endearment easily after so many years in Scotland.

He turned and gave her a brief smile that didn't quite reach his eyes. Was she wrong to bring him back here? The Canadians had invited her in thanks for her medical care of their wounded men while she'd been part of the Canadian CCS in the last months of the war, but if it hadn't been for Colonel Bellford's express invitation, she wouldn't have come at all.

There were hard memories for her as well.

Her brother was here with Maud, as part of the British delegation. Edward was a member of parliament and a cabinet minister in Stanley Baldwin's government. Alec hoped his uncle would arrange for him to meet the king. Her father had died in 1920 of a heart attack, a few months after her wedding. He'd answered the letter she'd written to him, asking if she might come for a visit with her new husband, with a crisp suggestion that they leave it until the spring, when the weather had improved. She'd been planning the trip, wondering what they'd say to each other, hoping he was proud of her at last, but news had arrived of his death, and she never saw him again or knew what he thought. He'd left no last words for her, and she had to live with that.

At the funeral, her mother had regarded Eleanor with dull grief and confusion, as if she were a stranger. Grace had aged since Eleanor had seen her last, and there were new lines around her eyes and mouth, a vagueness that hadn't been there before. She'd become a papery husk without her husband, lost. She allowed Eleanor to embrace her briefly but did not hug her in return. She'd asked no questions about her daughter's life, or the war, and made no comment when Eleanor introduced Fraser. She'd simply nodded before turning away to lean heavily on Edward's arm, letting her son lead her back to the house to lie down. Soon afterward, Edward had taken Grace to live with him and his wife on his father-in-law's estate in Devon. The Countess of Kirkswell had been on the committee to appoint a new doctor for Thorndale—Eleanor's name had not been on the list of candidates. Eleanor's relationship with her mother had remained strained over the years, and Edward's in-laws weren't about to accept the wife of a Highland estate manager into the family fold. She wondered if they even knew Edward's sister was a doctor. She sent letters to her family at

Christmas and received a card or note from Edward in return, but they did not visit.

Fraser's family hadn't exactly welcomed her with open arms, either, when she first stepped off the wagon at Glen Carraig on a crisp winter's morning, newly married and clinging to Fraser's arm, helping him walk since he was still weak after eight months as a prisoner of war. She didn't care. She loved him, and he loved her. The glen's doctor had been the first to come forward, a white-haired man who broke through the crowd of frowning clansmen with a fierce sweep of his walking stick. He'd welcomed Fraser home with a broad grin and a flask of whisky. He'd scanned Eleanor with keen interest, his faded blue eyes touching on the doctor's bag. "So you're a doctor," he said. "I'm glad ye've come, for I could use the help." He cast a sharp eye around at the clan. "Maybe now I can finally retire."

And so—in time—she'd become the doctor at Glen Carraig, accepted at last when she cured the laird's gout and eased the cough that old Angus MacLeod had suffered with for twenty years. When they got used to the idea, they were glad to see Fraser home again, even with a Sassenach doctor for a bride.

The glen had lost many sons and fathers and brothers in the war, and the ones who returned shared a bond, understood one another and the things they'd seen and done as soldiers. It took a long time for Fraser to heal, to sleep without nightmares, to stop scanning the hills and crags for wounded men and listening for signs of danger. It wasn't until Alec was born that he'd finally eased, cradling their baby son in his scarred hands, his expression soft, wondrous. He'd smiled at her, and the tension had gone out of his shoulders at long last.

It had been a good life, and a full one.

Sarah Connolly died of influenza in 1919 after nursing so many others through it. Eleanor went to her funeral in Shropshire and found Colonel Bellford there. He still walked with a cane, was frail and stooped, but he was alive. He'd been glad to see her and had promised to write. His wife had sent Christmas cards every year since, but it wasn't until the man himself wrote to ask her to attend the unveiling of the Canadian Monument at Vimy, a few miles from where 46/CCS had been, that she'd heard from the colonel directly.

So she had returned, forty-one years old now, hardly the young woman she'd been in 1918. She had gray in her hair, which she'd grown long again. She took it down now, then she crossed to slide her arms around Fraser's waist, laying her head on his shoulder. His arm circled her in return, but he kept his eyes on the crowds outside. "Another war is coming," he said.

"I know." There was no point in denying it. She knew he feared, like she did, that Alec would be part of it, be in the kind of danger they remembered all too well.

"Did you know there are over a thousand names carved on that monument, all the names of the missing, the ones who disappeared without a trace in just one battle?" he murmured. "And there are more cemeteries all around it."

She felt a shadow touch her. How easily it might have been Fraser, missing in action, dead, never found. But he'd been lucky. *They'd* been lucky. The war had given them each other. Love had kept him alive, determined to come back to her. That love had deepened, grown richer and stronger over the years. He was the other half of her soul. They could withstand anything as long as they were together.

She put her hands on his cheeks, cupped his face, reminded him of that with a kiss. "This is a celebration of peace, of hope that there won't be any more wars, and of remembering sacrifice and honor."

"It's hard, being here. I remember too much. How can it be forgotten?"

"Forgiven, perhaps? Honored?" she said. "Only that."

He stroked her hair. "Aye."

. . .

The restaurant was in a quaint French house, charming and old. According to Elizabeth, it had served as an aid post during several of the battles that raged here. Eleanor looked around, imagining the treatment areas, picturing the spot where the operating table might have stood and the place where the wounded would have sat, waiting for their turn. She looked at the cobbled floor, seeking signs of blood and mud, but there weren't any, of course. It was a perfectly ordinary room, full of tables and chairs and diners. "We've reserved a private room," Elizabeth said, and she led the way.

A young waiter swept the door open with a bow, his dark eyes scanning Eleanor and Fraser with bland curiosity. He'd probably not even been born until after the war, Eleanor thought. He'd probably grown up hearing his father and grandfather telling stories of those terrible days.

Colonel Bellford struggled to get to his feet as she entered, and Elizabeth immediately went to support her father. He patted her hand, but pulled away. "I'm not one of your patients, Lizzy," he said gently. He turned to look at Eleanor. He'd aged, was white haired and thin, his face lined, his body wracked with a slight tremor. He held out his hand. "Dr. Atherton—Dr. MacLeod, Eleanor. I'm so glad you could come. And Sergeant MacLeod." Max Chilcott crossed the room when he saw Fraser arrive, and he embraced his comrade with tears in his eyes and showed him the intricacies of his prosthetic left hand. "I can even hold a glass with it," he said, grinning. "Come and see—with your missus's permission, of course." Eleanor smiled back, and Max dragged Fraser away to the bar.

Eleanor turned back to Bellford. "It's very good to see you, sir. Shall we sit down?"

The colonel nodded, and he let his daughter settle him in his chair.

426 · LECIA CORNWALL

He began to cough, and Elizabeth held a glass of water to his lips. He looked at Eleanor. "The years have been kinder to you than to me," he said. "But if it hadn't been for you, I wouldn't be here at all."

He nodded to Elizabeth, who picked up a folder on the table and handed it to her father. "You changed everything when you arrived at 46/CCS—like a hurricane, or an artillery bombardment. No, that came out wrong. You made things better. I've not known anyone— male or female—with the kind of determination you showed, the willingness to help, to take charge simply because it had to be done and it was the right thing to do, rules or not."

He fidgeted with the string that held the file closed. "I had several letters from Sarah Connolly before she died. She wanted my support for some sort of official recognition for you. She wrote to the War Office and to the Royal Army Medical Corps. She asked me to write as well. It has taken some years. You were not military personnel, or a nurse, or part of the VAD, and female doctors were not supposed to be practicing medicine in a war zone. Some said that made you ineligible for any kind of commendation. Others wanted more proof. I was required to find witnesses to your gallantry. I needed three such witnesses. Matron Connolly was one, of course, and myself." He drew out a sheaf of papers. "These are from all the others who insisted on speaking on your behalf. Some of them you might remember—Reverend Strong wrote to me before he died, and Arthur Swiftwood, and a Captain Dalrymple, and the new Earl of Kirkswell, of course. There are many others as well, patients, and doctors, and nurses—British, Canadian, and French." He held the thick stack of pages out to her. "With so much evidence, the War Office couldn't deny you your due." He paused to catch his breath. "Tomorrow, after the unveiling ceremony, his majesty will present you with the Empire Gallantry Medal, Dr. MacLeod."

She gaped at him. "But—"

"We can't let the Canadians steal all the glory tomorrow, now, can we? They are as grateful to you as we are, of course. Many of the letters are from Canadians, both doctors and patients. Their prime minister is here and he wishes to meet you."

"I never thought, never expected . . ." Stunned, she looked for Fraser, saw him still standing at the bar with Max. She watched as they raised a solemn toast, and she suspected they were remembering Nathaniel Duncan.

"I became a doctor because of the stories my father told me about you," Elizabeth Bellford said. "And a young woman who served as a VAD at 46/CCS during the war, Miss Rose Graham, became a surgeon because she was inspired by you. Her letter is here, and she will be at the ceremony tomorrow."

Eleanor felt a touch on her shoulder. She turned to look up at David Blair. He was tanned, his face lined, his hair gray at the temples, but his gaze was still keen as he looked at her. "Will your husband mind if I kiss your cheek?"

She threw her arms around him, hugging him.

He brought a young girl forward. "May I introduce my daughter, Eleanor Blair?"

The girl dipped a curtsy, her eyes shining, her smile shy. "My Eleanor wants to be a doctor, too. She hopes to attend McGill University in Montreal. I despair that it's so far from Alberta, of course."

"It isn't for another year at least, Papa," Eleanor Blair said.

"Still too soon," David said fondly. "Now, off you go and find young company while I talk with Dr. Ather—um, MacLeod." She smiled and left them.

"You did go to Canada."

"Yes. I have a ranch close to a place called High River. In fact, the king and I are almost neighbors. He owns a ranch near mine, and breeds cattle and sheep. I raise draft horses. I'm also the local doctor, which means I see patients anywhere in a hundred-mile radius. My wife was a nurse, but she died when Eleanor was born."

"I'm sorry," she said. "She's a lovely girl, your daughter."

"The love of my life," he said with a proud smile. "There was once another, but alas . . ."

"David," she murmured.

"I still think about you, you know, imagine how it might have been if you'd come with me, if—" He shrugged the thought away and scanned her face. "You look happy—and beautiful. Fraser MacLeod is indeed a lucky man."

"I am happy," she said. "And I'm just as lucky."

He smiled. "I'm glad. If you'll excuse me, I'd best go and keep Corporal Chilcott's son from flirting with my daughter," he said. He looked at her again. "Your medal is well deserved, by the way." He kissed her cheek again. "Goodbye, Eleanor MacLeod."

She watched him walk away.

"Is everything all right?" Fraser asked, coming back to her side.

She smiled at him and took his scarred hand in hers, and she looked around at their comrades.

She stood on her toes to kiss him.

"Everything is perfect."

AUTHOR'S NOTE

When I was fifteen, I went to visit my grandfather Robert Greenwell. He noticed I was doing my history homework and asked me what I was studying. I told him it was British history, my favorite subject. He told me I should be studying more important history than kings and queens and politics, that I should learn about World War I, his history, and Canada's. My grandfather was a gruff man, the Victorian-era product of County Durham miners. He came to Canada as a boy and grew up here. When World War I began, like a lot of expats, he was keen to enlist. He was initially too young and too short, and he watched his beloved older brother go off to war without him. As soon as he was able and the rules on height relaxed, my grandfather joined up as well, and he was trained and posted as a gunner with the artillery. He rarely spoke of the war, though he considered his time in the army as the defining era of his life, but that day, at his kitchen table, he told me his brother Matthew's story.

In the spring of 1917, the battle of Vimy Ridge was part of the larger Arras offensive and was an important role for the Canadian Corps, which planned and executed the offensive to take the ridge from the Germans. Robert was with the guns, well behind the lines and firing on the German positions before the troops advanced. The Canadians were waiting in tunnels under the field in front of the ridge, and at dawn the entrance to the tunnels was blown open, and the soldiers emerged to take the ridge. My great-uncle Matthew was in one of those tunnels. Sadly, when the tunnel opened, there was a large shell crater filled with freezing water at the entrance, and Matthew's battalion was directly under the German guns. Many men, including Matthew, were killed in the earliest hours of the battle. When the fighting was over and the Canadians had taken Vimy Ridge, my grandfather came forward to find his brother so they could celebrate the victory together. He learned that Matthew was missing in action and later declared killed.

My grandfather wrote a note on the front of my history notebook. *C-21*, the number of the war cemetery where Matthew was buried. He made me solemnly promise to go to Vimy and visit his brother's grave someday.

In 2009, with my husband and my teenaged children, I finally made it. We went to the magnificent Vimy monument and asked for the location of C-21. The staff didn't know, but they suggested it might be in the local village, where the cemetery held a number of Canadian graves from World War I. Matthew wasn't there, but in the local tavern, my son asked if anyone knew where we might look next. The locals considered the problem and told us stories of their grandparents' war. One elderly lady recalled the day the English king came to unveil the monument on the ridge. "We were naughty children, and we used to climb it," she said. "But even the Nazis were in awe of that monument during the second war." Finally, one gentleman suggested that the site we sought might be the tiny war grave behind the soccer field, tucked away under green trees between farmers' fields. The track that led to it was muddy and overgrown, but there it was. Matthew's grave lay amid perhaps twenty others, all men who had died at Vimy Ridge, and very close to where they had fallen that day.

My children were so moved, and bringing my grandfather's story to life for them generated a huge interest in World War I for all of us, and that interest was a large part of the inspiration for *The Woman at the Front*.

I also have an interest in medical history. Originally I thought I'd write about a nurse, but in my initial research, I learned that while female nurses and clerks and even ambulance drivers were allowed to work close to the front lines, female *doctors* were not. The official argument was that women could not possibly be expected to perform sanitary inspections or visit men in the dangerous frontline trenches. They wouldn't be capable of enduring the horrors of war, the rough manners of wounded soldiers, or the shock of seeing and treating men with venereal diseases. Most interesting of all was the theory that while wounded men saw nurses as tender angels of mercy, they feared doctors as butchers and were terrified of hospitals and surgery, and it was believed they'd be even more frightened of female doctors.

Many of the brave medical women who applied for frontline service refused to take no for an answer and funded their own hospitals, staffed entirely by women, on both the eastern and western fronts. Their excellent work earned the admiration of patients and the medical establishment. The French Red Cross happily accepted the services of qualified medical women. Eventually, the British allowed female doctors to serve in England, and one hospital in London, the Endell Street Military Hospital, was staffed entirely by women.

In researching *The Woman at the Front*, I read many fascinating firsthand accounts and memoirs of people who supported the doctors and nurses at hospitals, aid posts, and Casualty Clearing Stations, including chaplains, nurses, volunteers, orderlies, and stretcher bearers. I fell in love with the heroic bearers who bravely went out onto the battlefield under fire and in terrible conditions to bring in wounded men who would have died without them. Originally, they were recruited from the regimental bands when it was discovered there wasn't much call for band music on the Western Front. Eventually, stretcher bearers became a more formal part of providing medical care to the wounded. They were given professional training in first aid. Both sides respected the sight of men with red cross brassards on their sleeves rescuing the wounded, but the bearers still faced terrible odds of survival in such a dangerous job. They were strong, brave, and selfless. How could I not include such a hero in my story?

Some of the people I enjoyed reading about most included medical women such as Louisa Garrett Anderson, Dr. Flora Murray, Dr. Elsie Inglis, and nurses Mairi Chisholm and Elsie Knocker, who set up and ran their own first aid post on the front lines during the war. These two brave women provided the inspiration for Eleanor's scenes at the aid post. Several other scenes are also loosely based on actual accounts.

As for the rest of the story, there are many personal touches sprinkled throughout. Charlie Nevins's brothers are named for my grandfather Robert and his brothers Matthew and Fred. Some of you who've read my Scottish romances might recognize the name MacLeod from those books. I like to think that if my doughty MacLeod heroines had had sons and grandsons after their own stories were done, they would have been every bit as brave and fine as Fraser.

And yes, there really is a town in Alberta called High River, which is near my home and very dear to my heart—especially the wonderful Museum of the Highwood, where I am a volunteer. The Prince of Wales (later Edward VIII) truly did own a ranch here, purchased after a royal visit in 1919, when the prince fell in love with Alberta. The foothills are truly every bit as beautiful as I've described them here. I hope you'll visit someday!

The rest of the story is all my own, written with the support and encouragement of my wonderful agent, Kevan Lyon, and my lovely editor at Berkley, Sarah Blumenstock. It takes a team to write a book, and to my marvelous copy editor and the production, marketing, and publicity teams at Berkley, many, many thanks. I am so proud to have you in my corner. My wonderful critique partner, the incomparable author Roxy Boroughs, read the first draft, and her advice was, as always, insightful and book-saving. And thanks to my historian (and modern feminist) daughter, Olivia, who helped me hone Eleanor into a courageous, brilliant, amazing woman who reminds me very much of her, and who overcame so much to become the incredible woman she is. My son, Griffin, has always been my sounding board for ideas and patiently listens to my rants when my stories get away from where I expected them to go, then makes suggestions to get me back to where I need to be. He's a historian by heart if not by trade. And thanks to the Military Museums of Calgary for inspirational exhibits and lectures that bring the details of the war to life. And to the Museum of the Highwood, where I volunteer and my daughter worked, and museum director Irene Kerr, for the many stories that are preserved within those walls and are so generously shared with writers like me, and so we never forget the sacrifices made in all wars.

The
WOMAN *at*
the FRONT

LECIA CORNWALL

Questions for Discussion

1. Eleanor has a difficult relationship with her father. He tries to dissuade her from practicing medicine. Is his behavior toward his daughter meant to strengthen Eleanor for the challenges of her chosen career, or is his attitude truly just Victorian scorn for smart women who don't know their place?

2. Eleanor's brother sees the war as a chance to rise in society. Is he cold and self-serving, or part of a necessary change in the social order that allowed people of talent to take higher roles?

3. Louis Chastaine strives to be a hero in his own right, taking dangerous chances to prove himself. In the end, he must bow to the strong female influences in his life to succeed, including his mother, Eleanor, and Lady Frances. Is this emasculating?

4. The book discusses various types of allies and enemies. How do these elements drive identity and create conflict in the story?

5. The colonel represents the old tradition of men as the stronger sex caring for women as the weaker. The war challenges this belief for him. What factors allow the colonel to accept the new paradigm of strong women when other men, like Eleanor's father, refuse to embrace it?

6. In this era, men had authority. How does Eleanor deal effectively with masculine authority?

7. Each class of society in this time period lived by certain expectations. Are the upper classes truly freer than the classes below them, or are the rules actually more restrictive?

8. Although some medical women practiced in war zones without the sanction of the British government, the army refused to allow women to serve as doctors on the front lines. Was it right to protect them from the horrors of war even though there was a shortage of qualified male doctors?

9. World War I saw many women taking jobs outside the home for the first time. Did the necessity for women to step up and become breadwinners and essential workers further or impede the argument for suffrage?

10. Women gained many advantages within society because of the war. Was this out of necessity or a matter of seizing opportunities previously denied to them?

11. How culpable was Eleanor in the unexpected outcome of the medical school exam? Was she truly naive, or is it likely she must have somehow known the truth?

12. Could Eleanor have returned home at the end of the war? What would she have had to sacrifice to do so?

13. Fraser finds his own way of coping with the horrors of war by refusing to consider the past or the future. How do his feelings for Eleanor challenge this strategy?

Lecia Cornwall, acclaimed author of numerous historical romance novels, lives and writes in the beautiful foothills of the Canadian Rockies with four cats and a wild and crazy ninety-pound chocolate Lab named Andy. She has two grown children and one very patient husband. When she is not writing, Lecia is a dedicated volunteer at the Museum of the Highwood in High River, Alberta. *The Woman at the Front* is her first novel of historical women's fiction.

CONNECT ONLINE

LeciaCornwall.com

🐦 LeciaCornwall

📷 LeciaCornwall

Ready to find
your next great read?

Let us help.

Visit prh.com/nextread